Cook Memorial Public Libra

3 1122 01591 3721

DEC 0 2 2020

P9-BYZ-364

Fox Crossing

Books by Melinda Metz

Talk to the Paw
The Secret Life of Mac
Mac on a Hot Tin Roof
Fox Crossing

FOX CROSSING

MELINDA METZ

COOK MEMORIAL LIBRARY
413 N. MILWAUKEE AVE.
LIBERTYVILLE, ILLINOIS 60048

KENSINGTON BOOKS
www.kensingtonbooks.com

This book is a work of fiction. Names, characters, and incidents either are products of the author's imagination or are used fictitiously. Any resemblance to actual persons living or dead, or events, is entirely coincidental.

KENSINGTON BOOKS are published by

Kensington Publishing Corp.
119 West 40th Street
New York, NY 10018

Copyright © 2020 by Melinda Metz

All rights reserved. No part of this book may be reproduced in any form or by any means without the prior written consent of the Publisher, excepting brief quotes used in reviews.

To the extent that the image or images on the cover of this book depict a person or persons, such person or persons are merely models and are not intended to portray any character or characters featured in the book.

All Kensington titles, imprints, and distributed lines are available at special quantity discounts for bulk purchases for sales promotion, premiums, fund-raising, educational, or institutional use.

Special book excerpts or customized printings can also be created to fit specific needs. For details, write or phone the office of the Kensington Sales Manager: Kensington Publishing Corp., 119 West 40th Street, New York, NY 10018. Attn. Sales Department. Phone: 1-800-221-2647.

Kensington and the K logo Reg. U.S. Pat. & TM Off.

ISBN-13: 978-1-4967-2810-4 (ebook)
ISBN-10: 1-4967-2810-6 (ebook)

ISBN-13: 978-1-4967-2809-8
ISBN-10: 1-4967-2809-2
First Kensington Trade Paperback Printing: December 2020

10 9 8 7 6 5 4 3 2 1

Printed in the United States of America

For Carolyn, Cindy, Sarah, Teena, and in memory of Allis, all as strong as Hatherley women and even more fun.

PROLOGUE

The Fox lay down in the meadow, the grass still warm from hours in the sun, and wrapped her tail around her nose, her senses taking in her world. Under the earth a few feet away, a small creature was moving through its burrow. If she wished, she could easily dig through the dirt and capture it, but she wasn't hungry, so she let it be.

She was both alone and connected to everything. She had outlived many mates and many kits and now preferred to keep herself apart from her kind. Yet, she was a part of everything that lived—or had ever lived—in these woods.

CHAPTER 1

One look was all it took. He's not gonna make it, Annie Hatherley thought. She watched the lanky man cross the street toward the store, the sun bringing out glints of auburn in his curly brown hair. He wasn't the worst noob hiker she'd ever seen. That would be the guy last year wearing jeans, flip-flops, and an aloha shirt, cotton of course, his pack filled with three more of the gaudy shirts, a carton of Clif Bars, and a large bottle of water. And nothing else.

This guy wasn't that guy, but his backpack probably weighed close to seventy pounds. Nope, he wasn't gonna make it.

Forget the pack and the boots, his calves showed her that he hadn't been doing the kind of training he needed to take on the 100-Mile Wilderness. They weren't scrawny. They were, in fact, nicely muscled, with just the right amount of hair, at least in Annie's opinion. She had a friend who liked her men to look half-bear. Took all kinds to make a world.

But this guy's calves, nice as they were, were the calves of a casual day-hiker. A serious hiker's calves usually expanded a half inch in circumference, thighs about two inches. Sadly, Annie couldn't see the man's thighs. His prAna Stretch Zion shorts hit him a couple inches above the knee. He'd made a smart choice there, the shorts stretchy and cool, with a wicking finish. And only two pockets. A lot of noobs thought they needed way more pockets than they actually did. But, despite the sensible shorts, he wasn't gonna make it. He—He was coming through the door. "Okay if I bring this in?" he asked, holding up the paper cup he carried.

"Sure." Annie watched him take in the store, her store, since her mother had gotten herself elected first selectman, basically CEO of the town, about four and a half years earlier. He took his time, looking at everything.

"These hardwood floors are amazing."

"They're juniper maple." The hardwood floors were the first change Annie had made when she took over. Her mother hadn't bothered much with aesthetics. Hatherley's Outfitters was the only game in town, the only place to buy gear in Fox Crossing, and Fox Crossing was the last town before the 100-Mile Wilderness, the wildest, and in Annie's opinion, most beautiful stretch of the Appalachian Trail. But just because the store had no competition didn't mean it shouldn't be inviting. Fox Crossing had changed over the years since her great-great-great-great-great-grandmother opened the store. An antiques store was a few doors down from Hatherley's, the Wit's Beginning Brewery was included in one of the Brew Ha-Ha Bus tours out of Bangor, and Foxy Loxy Books had just been selected as one of Maine's best used-book stores.

"Perfect with the slate." The man appreciatively ran his fingers over the smooth slate counter Annie stood behind. For a crazy second, Annie flashed on those fingers running over her skin with that same—Inappropriate thought! He was a customer. Also, a complete stranger.

"Slate from Fox Crossing is in high demand," she said, as

crisply as a new schoolteacher being observed by the principal. "There are several political graves in Arlington Cemetery made by the black slate from the local quarry. Although I preferred gray for—"

"Political graves?" he repeated, raising one eyebrow. Annie had been trying to learn to raise one eyebrow since she was about seven. Still couldn't do it.

"Don't be pedantic." Had she actually just used the word *pedantic*? People who used the word *pedantic* were pedantic. "You know I meant graves of people in politics, including Jackie and John F. Kennedy's," she continued, unable to shake the lecturing tone. At least it was keeping her brain from creating more inappropriate thoughts.

"Guilty. License to be pedantic comes with the glasses." He pushed his slightly geeky, definitely stylish tortoiseshell specs higher on his nose. "The girl—woman—who sold them to me said they gave me a 'modern intellectual look.'"

He laughed and Annie joined in. Even though he was a noob who shouldn't be within a hundred miles of the 100-Mile Wilderness, she was starting to like this guy, dammit. And not just for his perfect-amount-of-hair-and-muscles calves. And not just for his warm chestnut eyes, which she couldn't help noticing when she was looking at his glasses. He was kind of funny, and kind of smart, and had good taste in flooring and countertops.

You have to find, at the very least, a new friend-with-benefits, Annie told herself. It had been a little more than a year since Seth had decided to head west to hike the PCT, and she hadn't even started feeling lonely. Truth? Seth had been starting to get on her nerves, and she was more than kinda glad he was gone. But her zero-to-sixty attraction to this guy showed her she was getting itchy.

"So, what can I help you with?" she asked, all professional-like.

"Wait. First you have to tell me your name. I don't allow myself to be mocked by strangers."

"Annie Hatherley."

"Of Hatherley's Outfitters." She nodded. "Nick Ferrone." He held out his hand, and she shook it. His grip was also just right. Not you're-a-delicate-lady-and-I-must-not-squash-your-fingers soft, but not I-must-show-dominance-to-all hard. Also, it sent a little tingle from her fingers to low in her stomach. Dammit.

When he let go, Annie caught sight of the tattoo on his forearm, and she could feel a wide grin, the kind that gave her chipmunk cheeks, stretching across her face. The tat was of what was clearly supposed to be a fox since it had the words I'M FOXY underneath. Nick noticed the direction of her gaze and flushed. "I—"

"You had an encounter with Noah and Logan, otherwise known as Nogan," Annie finished for him. "I'm quite familiar with their hand-drawn temporary tattoos, as well as their strong-arm sales techniques. What else did you buy?"

He took a swallow of what Annie knew was Nogan's drink of the day—blackberry lemonade sweetened with local honey. She'd had one herself at lunch.

"Just a piece of the Canine Candy," he admitted.

He had a dog? Bad idea. She opened her mouth to give Nick a list of all the reasons he should absolutely not bring a dog on his hike, starting with how it would greatly lower his odds of completing the hike, and those odds were pathetic to start out with. She forced herself to take a beat. Find a way to say it nicely, she told herself. Be professional. Last hiking season she'd gotten a bunch of negative social-media reviews about her attitude. One had even called her surly. Surly! Not that it mattered. You wanted to buy gear in Fox Crossing, you bought from her.

"You're planning to hike the Wilderness?" she asked. Even though she already knew the answer.

"Yep." Those chestnut-brown eyes of his gleamed with enthusiasm.

Nick was clueless about what he was in for. Annie felt prickles of irritation run down the back of her neck. The irritation prickles were stronger than the attraction tingles. A license should be needed to hike the Wilderness, and a test—written and practical—to get one. Don't go there, she told herself. "Then I'm assuming you want to go up Katahdin when you get to the end." She managed to keep her tone pleasant. No surly to be heard.

"I couldn't say I'd hiked the whole thing if I didn't."

Couldn't *say* he'd hiked it. Was he doing it for bragging rights? Who was he trying to impress? What was he trying to prove? None of your business, she told herself. You're here to sell him stuff.

"Just so you know, dogs aren't allowed in Baxter State Park, which is where the mountain is." Yeah, that was a good approach. Nothing personal about his hiking skills. "You'll need to board your beastie before that last stretch. There are kennels in Millinocket, but that's twenty-five miles east. It's not easy. You'll only have logging tr—"

"No dog. Just me."

"Oh. Good." She let out a breath. "Then why the Canine Candy?"

"The boys convinced me it tasted just as good to humans and that there was nothing in it that would hurt me, so . . ." Nick shrugged. "Wasn't too bad."

"Wait. You actually ate a piece!"

"Well, yeah. They were watching. It tasted like an extremely healthy, very dry, mostly flavorless cookie, if you want to know."

He's nice, too, Annie realized. Dammit. He wasn't just smartish and funnyish, with excellent taste, plus the calves, and the eyes. He'd humored two nine-year-old boys by buying a dog treat when he didn't have a dog. And he'd eaten it! That was exceptionally nice.

But he's also exceptionally ill prepared, she reminded herself. He wasn't gonna make it out there. The only question was, How badly was he gonna get hurt?

Not at all, if Annie could help it. She'd try to be nice herself, but if that didn't work, well, she could deal with another "she's so surly" review. Surly sometimes saved lives. "So how long have you been training?" Annie asked nicely.

"Almost three months. Every weekend, and I usually got in a few weeknights. And I carry my pack whenever I can, like now."

"Not enough." It felt like the two words hit the ground with a thud.

"What?"

"That's just not enough time to get in shape. I can tell by looking at you you're not up for the Wilderness." Was that surly? No, Annie decided. She hadn't raised her voice. She hadn't called Nick an idiot. She'd just given him the truth, plainly spoken, and he needed to hear it.

"Just by looking at me?" His eyes weren't warm anymore.

"Yep. I've been working here since I was a kid. I can tell when a hiker's not ready, and you, my friend, are not ready."

Nick snorted. " 'My friend,' " he muttered.

The prickles of irritation were back, but they were more like ice-pick stabs now. He was already shutting down. He didn't want to hear her. Well, too bad. "Look, you could die out there. Do you get that? This slate"—Annie slapped the counter—"it's what a lot of the rock out there is made out of. And it gets slippery as shit." She managed not to say *my friend* again, but it was truth time, and she was giving him all of it. "Which makes falling and bashing your head in a definite possibility. Also, there's snow melt. We've got snow melt this time of year, and it can turn streams into white-water deathtraps. And there are swamps—"

"I read about all of this." Nick planted his hands on the counter and leaned toward her.

Annie mimicked his position, leaning in, getting right in his face, glaring at him. "Oh, you read about it. My bad. So, you know it all. Happy trails then."

"Have I interrupted something interesting?"

Annie's grandmother had come in. Of course. Why not make this situation a little worse by having her as a witness?

"Just giving a customer the rundown on what to expect out on the trail." Annie pushed herself away from her side of the counter.

Nick took a step back from his and planted a smile on his face. He turned to Annie's grandmother. "Hi. I'm Nick. The customer."

"I'm Ruth Allis. But you can call me Honey." She fluffed up her blond curls and straightened the pair of cloth fox ears attached to her hairband.

"I'm honored." The fake, being-polite smile—because, of course, he had to be polite, too—became genuine.

"Don't be too honored," Annie snapped. "Everyone calls her Honey, including me, and I'm her granddaughter. You'd think I'd call her Grandma or Grammy or Nana or the like, but, no, I'm forbidden from using any appellation that makes her sound over twenty-one." Annie knew she was taking out her frustration on the wrong person, but kept on going. "That's actually what she puts on forms, even medical ones, twenty-one-plus."

"All anybody needs to know." Honey shot Annie a reproving glance. It didn't work. Annie was way too riled to be reproved.

Nick laughed. "I agree completely. I'm going to start using that myself. Twenty-one-plus."

Honey gave Nick's arm a pat. She was such a flirt. "I hope Annie's told you how beautiful the Wilderness is."

"She was just about to tell me about the swamps," Nick answered, keeping all his attention on Honey.

"There *are* sections of trail that were blazed straight through bogs," Honey began.

Annie had to interrupt her. "Just so you know, you're not going to find much resembling an actual *trail* out there. Don't be expecting a nice dirt path."

"You'll get muddy, but you'll also see pitcher plants." Honey went on as if Annie hadn't spoken. "You're not going to get a look at those too many other places."

"I read about them!" Nick exclaimed. "Definitely going to make sure I see some of those bug eaters in the wild."

He was trail-struck. Nothing Annie was going to say would make a difference. Suddenly, she felt tired. This happened way too many times. "Was there something particular you were looking for today?" She wanted him out of there.

"I was thinking about a bug net."

"This time of year? Absolutely necessary," Annie answered. "I have several types."

"Around now, the blackflies and mosquitoes can get so thick you can't see your hand in front of your face," Honey added, finally giving Annie some backup. "The man who owns the bakery? He was found standing on a bog log shouting, 'Shoo, fly,' over and over, tears streaming down his face. And he was a marine. He got his trail name that day and has been called Shoo Fly ever since."

"Bug net it is," Nick said.

He's probably hoping for a cool trail name, like Thoreau or Seeker, Annie thought. He's one of the ones who imagines he's going to be *transformed by the journey*. She didn't bother telling him to get over it.

"Looking at your pack, I'd say you should have Annie do a shakedown for you," Honey told Nick.

"Shakedown?"

He couldn't have done that much reading about the trail if he didn't know what a shakedown was. "To let you know what's unnecessary, noob," Annie explained.

His eyes narrowed as he looked at her, and she could hear tension in his voice when he spoke. "Everything I brought is important. You're the one who said I wasn't prepared, but I have everything I'm going to need in this baby." He patted his pack.

"Take it off and open it up," Annie ordered. She wanted him out, but that didn't mean she was willing to send him into the Wilderness carrying enough weight to blow out his knees, or end up with a rolled ankle, or a stress fracture. If he managed to avoid one of the dozens of possible injuries, he could still end up so fatigued that he'd take a fall.

When Nick hesitated, Annie insisted, "Do it."

"Fine. But you'll see I have everything I need and nothing more." Nick yanked off his pack, put it on the floor, and unzipped it.

Annie crouched down and started checking out his supplies. She gave a snort of laughter when she got to a worn copy of *Walden*. Had she called it or had she called it? "Everything is necessary, huh?" She tossed it to the side.

"It's one book," Nick protested. "And it is necessary. I know a big part of the trail is mental preparation, and—"

Annie didn't bother to listen. She pulled a solar phone charger from his pack. "Don't need this. Cell service sucks out there." Annie kept on going through his stuff. She pulled out a box of Band-Aids. "Don't need this. If the injury is small enough for a Band-Aid, you don't need a Band-Aid." She pulled out a deodorant stick. "You're gonna have to stink." She pulled out three pairs of boxer briefs. "Nope."

"Come on!" Nick yelped. He probably wouldn't call it a yelp, but it definitely was.

"Bring those and you'll have to bring Boudreaux's Butt Paste for the chafing," Annie explained.

"Fine." She noticed a flush was creeping up his neck. She wasn't sure if it was caused by anger or embarrassment or both. And she didn't care. About ten minutes and fifty protests later, she had Nick's pack at a manageable weight. It took her another five to convince him to trade in the boots for trail runners.

"Is that it?" Nick asked. She noticed a little muscle in his jaw twitching. Good. Why should she be the only one who was pissed off?

"That's it." She shoved herself to her feet.

"Except that we wish you a wonderful hike," Honey said. "It's the experience of a lifetime."

"Thank you." Nick smiled at her. "Hey, we match." He held out his arm so she could see his fox tattoo.

"We're twins!" Honey smoothed down the front of her T-shirt to show off her I'M FOXY fox.

Annie took a long breath, trying to calm down. "I assume you have an extraction plan."

"I did. But the solar charger you nixed was part of the plan. I tried to tell you that."

"And I told you, you can't rely on cell service," Annie shot back. "You need a tracker."

"Yeah? And how much profit are you going to make off one of those?"

He thought this was about money? She was attempting to keep him alive, and he thought she was trying to make a profit. Not that she didn't want the store to be successful, which it was, but that didn't mean it was all she cared about. "I'll rent you one. Hell, I'll loan you one. For free. You can give it back tomorrow afternoon when you come back to town with your tail between your legs."

"Annie!" Honey exclaimed.

Nick jumped in. "I don't—"

"Shut up and take it." Annie jerked open a display case and took out one of the satellite messengers, then thrust it into Nick's hand. He stared at it, as if things were going too fast for him. "Call the number and they'll get your profile set up. If you get in real trouble, send an SOS. It will go out to a rescue coordination center. You can also send your support person a link to an app. They'll be able to watch your progress in almost real time."

Nick's forehead furrowed as he continued to look at the small device. Annie read his expression. "And you don't have a support person, do you?"

"If I needed help, I planned to call for help." He held the tracker out to her. When she folded her arms, refusing to take it, Nick set it on the counter. "I'll take the solar charger and my phone."

Annie pressed her fingers against the bridge of her nose. "Were you not listening? You might not get service and you might not always get sun for the solar. Which means"—she said the next words slowly, and deliberately—"you. Might. Not. Get. Help."

He was close to walking out. She could see that. She pressed her lips together to stop herself from saying something that would push him out the door. He needed the tracker.

"Go ahead and take it, Fox Twin," Honey told Nick. "It might come in handy." She picked up the tracker and gave it to him. He slid it into his pocket.

"I want to pay for it," he told Annie.

"Fine. How many days?"

"Ten."

"It's fifteen bucks for three days."

"Fine."

She could tell he wanted out of her place as much as she wanted him gone. She quickly rang up the bug net, the trail runners, and the rental, ran his card, and gave it back to him. "Do you need me to go over how to send the SOS?"

"I'll google it." He hefted his pack back on his shoulders. "I'll see you when I return the tracker. In ten days."

"I'll be here," Annie said to his back. He was already heading to the door. She and her grandmother watched as he crossed the street, turned the corner, and disappeared from sight.

"You can call me Grandma if you really want to," Honey said.

"I like calling you Honey."

"I know you do." Honey smiled. "That man had everything, and then some. You could have been sweeter to him. Then when he returned the tracker, he'd probably have asked you out for drinks. Or you could have asked him. Then who knows?"

Annie shook her head. "He's way too impulsive for me. He's one of those guys who thinks he's going to change his life by hitting the trail. Walking around with his copy of *Walden*. Which, fine. But you can't just *go*. You need to prep. You need to plan."

"Looked like he'd done some of both to me."

"Some. Not nearly enough. And did you see how he almost walked out of here without the tracker? Just because his pride got dinged a little? He should have thanked me for pointing out he needed the thing." Annie took her phone out of her pocket. "I have the app that will let me see how he's doing. I'm going to keep an eye on him. He clearly isn't capable of taking care of himself out there."

CHAPTER 2

She acted like I wasn't capable of taking care of myself out there, Nick thought as he spooned the last bite of cobbler into his mouth. He knew it was fantastic—the perfect combo of buttery crunch and sweet, tangy blueberries. But he might as well have been eating that Canine Candy. He'd made a dinner reservation at the Quarryman Inn as a treat before ten days of eating dehydrated meals, dehydrated fruit, jerky, protein bars, and instant oatmeal. Believe it or not, Annie Hatherley, he *had* researched, and he knew what he should be eating on the trail.

He'd also decided to splurge on a comfortable bed for his last night in civilization and promised himself he'd enjoy both again when he returned, scraggly bearded and stinking, since Annie Hatherley had taken away his deodorant. Probably, make that definitely, he should go upstairs and get into that comfy bed early, get a good night's sleep, but he was too wound up. He decided on a walk. He thought about getting his pack from the room, but one more night of carrying it wasn't going to make a difference on the trail. And he'd been training plenty, despite what Annie Hatherley thought she could tell by look-ing at him.

Annie Hatherley. Annie Hatherley. Enough with the think-ing about Annie Hatherley, he told himself as he headed out of the Inn in his new, comfortable trail runners. He got that he might not make it all the way through the Wilderness. He knew people had to give up for all kinds of reasons. He wasn't an idiot, even though Annie Hatherley clearly thought he was.

He was still doing it. He had to forget about all her negative bullshit. Haters gonna hate. Crap. Annie Hatherley had re-duced him to thinking in Taylor Swift lyrics. "Shake it off," he muttered.

You're in a new place. You're at the start of an adventure. Look around. Take it in, he thought. He slowed his pace, smil-ing as he noticed Honey in a lit store window across the street, putting a sundress with a frolicking-fox pattern on a man-nequin. The sign, all flourishes and curlicues, read VIXEN'S. That explained the fox T-shirt and the cloth ears. He wondered how much business it did. Was there a market for all fox stuff? At a glance, it looked like that's all the shop sold. Maybe people just went in to talk to Honey. She was a charmer. Unlike her granddaughter.

Nick gave a growl of annoyance. In another minute, he was going to have to take out the pocketknife he'd bought for the trip—an Opinel No 7—and excise the part of his brain that held the memory of those few minutes in the outfitter's. At least Annie Hatherley had let him keep the knife. She'd actually said it was one of the best backpacking blades.

Crap. He was doing it again. He shoved his hands through his hair. Maybe it was because before Annie Hatherley had turned into a shrew, he'd thought he felt some mutual attrac-tion between them, a *click*. He knew he'd felt it on his side. That hadn't happened in a long time. Actually, not since Lisa. It's like being happily married had switched off that part of his brain. Not that he hadn't noticed attractive women, but he hadn't noticed them in the same way. He'd have a flash of speculating what they looked like naked or what it would be like to have sex with them, your basic guy stuff. But not with any . . . intent.

But he wasn't married anymore. And he hadn't been happily married for a long time. He'd *thought* he was happily married, but how could he be if his wife was thinking divorce? How could he have been happily married if his wife—ex-wife—got married the day their divorce went through? Not even one day later. The same day.

Today, in those first few moments with Annie Hatherley, it's like an old part of himself had woken up. He usually didn't like short hair on women, but her short, dark brown hair let him focus on her face, on her clear blue eyes, her perfect creamy skin, her lips, her neck, that little dip between her collarbones.

It wasn't just the physical though. He'd liked how she busted his chops, so playful, about being pedantic. Then she did almost a Jekyll and Hyde. It was like she couldn't wait to get him out of her store and out of her sight.

Enough. He needed a drink. Something to settle him down. Get him ready for that good night's sleep. He'd seen a bar with a crazy sign on his way into town. He walked up a block, then turned left. Yep, there it was. The Wit's Beginning Brewery, with a presumably dead donkey, all four legs in the air, on the sign. He'd try one of the local microbrews, then head back to the Inn. And tomorrow the adventure started!

He could have, and probably should have, asked one of his friends to be a support person, but he wanted the Wilderness to be his thing. He didn't want to be checking in every day, didn't want even that much connection to the outside world. It felt like it would . . . like it would somehow diffuse the actual experience, suck some of the meaning out of it.

As soon as Nick stepped inside, the bartender called, "Welcome, friend." He was tall, wiry, and bald, with skin the color of a pine cone. The greeting felt so genuine that Nick headed to the bar instead of settling in at one of the tables. Most were empty, although a group of about ten was settled in at a table in the back, probably town regulars. It was early in the season for hiking the Wilderness. In a few weeks, Nick bet the place would be much more crowded.

"First time here?"

"First time in Mai—"

"Banana, is it or is it not endless-nacho night? Because we are perilously close to the end over here," someone called before Nick could finish answering.

"Big Matt, you got that?" Banana—Banana?—yelled.

"Got it," a guy called back from what Nick assumed was the kitchen.

"Let's start again. As I'm sure you heard, we have endless nachos tonight, if you're interested. Big Matt sprinkles chopped radishes on top. Sounds crazy, but . . ." Banana let out a groan that sounded almost orgasmic.

"Wish I could. But I just finished a big meal."

"What'll you have? The first drink's on me."

Nick had picked the right place. A little *pleasant* conversation would help him unwind as much as a drink. "In that case, what do you suggest?"

"My specialty. The Spirited Banana. It's a wheat beer, but in the German vein, not Belgian."

"Bring it on. But I'm gonna tell you up front that I'd have an easier time telling Coke from Pepsi, than German from Belgian beer."

"Honesty is appreciated." Banana grabbed a plain brown ceramic mug and held it under one of the taps. "Belgian is more citrusy. Esters and phenols give German wheat beer banana and clove flavors." He set the mug in front of Nick.

Nick took a long swallow, trying to pick up on all the ingredients. He got the banana and clove, but also a little apple, and, weirdly, a little bubble gum. "Smooth." He took another swallow. "I wasn't sure I'd like banana in my beer, but it works. Is that why they were calling you Banana? Because of your special brew?"

"Nope." Banana grinned at him.

"Are you going to tell me why they do?"

"Nope." Banana's grin widened.

"How about a different question. What's the story with the donkey?" Nick nodded toward the display of deep blue mugs with the legs-in-the-air donkey on the front.

"It's in honor of my first donkey. I called him Bucky." Banana pressed one fist against his heart and closed his eyes for a long moment, before he opened them and continued, "He was a feisty son of a gun. But smart. I taught him all kinds of tricks. Taught him how to count to ten. Taught him to add. Even taught him to do a kind of a hula shake. Then I decided to try something harder. I decided to train him not to eat."

"Train him not to eat," Nick repeated, his shoulders relaxing with the story and the alcohol.

"Yeah. I cut his food back a little at a time, and he was really getting the hang of it, then he died. Right when he almost had it down."

Nick laughed. It might have been the stupidest joke he'd ever heard. Which is exactly why it was so funny.

Banana laughed even harder than Nick, a low, loud *haw-haw-haw*. "That's from *Philogelos*, the world's first joke book. Or at least first surviving. It was written in Greece, fourth or fifth century CE."

Now Nick understood the name of the bar. "Hence Wit's Beginning." The bartender pointed to his nose, then pointed to Nick. "So, what's the deal with the mugs. Is it a membership thing?"

"Yep, but not the usual kind. There's no membership fee. All you've got to do is walk the two thousand, and I hand one over."

The two thousand. As in miles. The whole Appalachian Trail. "Do you have one?" This was where Nick needed to be. Banana could be Nick's Yoda. He'd send Nick on his way with everything he needed to know, the stuff you couldn't read in books or blogs.

"It's my place, so I could have as many as I want. But I'm not taking one until I finish the damn thing, and I still have a hundred miles to go."

"The Wilderness?"

Banana nodded. "Made sixteen attempts, had sixteen failures."

Nick let out a low whistle. "You never wanted to just throw in the towel?"

"Of course, I did. Sixteen times, for sure. Probably a lot more. But I'm not a quitter. I only have a hundred miles left, and I'm getting them done. This time, though, I'm waiting until I see The Fox."

"What's that?" Nick asked eagerly. "Some kind of flower that blooms at the best time to start? Or when the sunrise is a certain color? Or—"

"Why don't I just tell you?"

"That might work better."

"This is a story that takes some telling."

"Why am I not surprised?" This guy was a story himself— trail hiker, teller of ancient jokes, a beer maker, a business owner. All that, and Nick felt as if he'd barely scratched the surface.

A skinny guy carrying a plate with a mountain of nachos on top headed for the back table as Banana began. "A long time ago, before you were born, hell, before I was born, before my sweet grandmama was born, back in 1803, a fox was caught in a trap around here. Now, I don't know why, because back then there weren't a lot of animal-rights types, but a woman named Annabelle rescued that fox. She'd just lost her husband, and her baby, and was desperate to keep her little boy, not more than two, healthy and safe. The whole settlement was about to go under, and the scraggly group of settlers with it. Maybe that's why she freed that fox and took her home. Maybe she was so heartbroken that she figured any company was better than none. Or maybe death had taken so much from her that she refused to let the Reaper take another, not if she could help it."

Nick bet Banana had told this story a dozen times at least, but he looked as if he was seriously considering the reasons why this woman had saved the fox. "Some say the only reason it lived was because she nursed it. And I'm not talking with a bottle."

"You're shitting me!" Nick took a long pull on his beer.

Banana held up both hands. "All I'm telling you is what people told me. And some have said the milk, the same milk Annabelle still used to feed her little boy, saved The Fox. Some say it did more than that." He turned, took a mug, one of the plain brown ones, and poured himself a drink from one of the taps.

"I don't get you. What more could it have done?" Nick had the feeling he was walking into another bad joke. But he had to ask.

"It's just rumors and supposition. Not much worth passing on."

He's messing with me, Nick thought. He tried not to sound too eager when he said, "I like a good supposition."

"What do you think, Big Matt?" Banana asked as the skinny guy headed past on his way back to the kitchen. "Should I tell our friend the secret about The Fox?"

The man rolled his eyes. "As if I could stop you," he answered without pausing.

"I do like to tell a story," Banana admitted. "I said the settlement was close to dying out. Then a gentleman, Celyn, who had immigrated from Wales, was out riding. A fox ran right between his horse's feet—a skinny, skittish gelding named Mud. Mud dumped Celyn on the ground and took off into the woods. Celyn took off after the animal, who was not nearly as smart as my donkey, Bucky. Before he reached Mud, Celyn caught sight of something sparkling along the side of a cliff. Now, Celyn had worked at a slate mine back in the old country, and he knew what he was seeing. Mica. And where there was mica, there was usually slate."

Nick jumped in. "And that was the start of the Fox Crossing Mine Company." Banana again touched his nose and pointed at him. "I saw some slate from there today. Beautiful."

"And profitable. Turned the luck of the settlement around. Annabelle's especially. She owned the land, and she teamed up with Celyn on the mine."

"This is the part where you tell me the fox was the fox that Annabelle saved, right?" Nick loved the story, even though he knew it had to be heavy on rumors and general malarkey.

Banana gave an exaggerated shrug. "She had the same markings—one white sock, one almost-white ear, black-tipped tail, same as the one Annabelle saved. Same as the one I'm waiting to see."

"Wait. You mean same as in same?" Banana nodded. "You should take this show on the road. You're a master bullshit artist. You've almost got me believing that there's a more-than-two-hundred-year-old fox running around. And that you had an exceptionally smart donkey named Bucky." Nick was glad he'd come in. He hadn't had an Annie Hatherley thought since Banana started spinning his stories. Except that one thought he'd just had, but that one didn't count, because it was about how he wasn't thinking about her.

"Well, some people think she's a descendant of the first

one," Banana admitted. "I disagree. And you can see Bucky's gravestone out back." Banana crossed himself.

"And you're seriously not going to make another try at the Wilderness until you see this fox—or its great-great-great-et-cetera-granddaughter?"

"That's right. When I see The Fox and get me some of that luck, I'm heading straight to the trail. My backpack's packed. Big Matt is ready to take over." Banana's eyes flicked up and down Nick's frame. "Maybe you should wait for a sighting. It'd give you a little more time to condition."

"You, too?" All the good feeling Nick had going circled the drain. "You think you can tell just by looking at me that I'm not ready? Don't bother with the lecture. I heard it all and then some from Annie Hatherley."

Banana let out another of his deep *haw-haw-haw*s. "Our Annie, she's a pistol. She also has a good heart."

"In a jar on her bedside table," Nick muttered.

Banana laughed again. "It's why she's so hard on hikers. She doesn't want anyone to get hurt. I wasn't trying to say you're not ready, by the way. But anyone on the trail can use some extra luck." Banana pulled several baggies out of the pockets of his jeans. "I got chicken. I got ham. I got berries. I got a hard-boiled egg. I go out to likely spots in the woods every night and morning, scatter fox treats around me. The Fox is going to come to me. This is the year. This is the year I get my damn blue mug. Speaking of mugs, you need a refill." He got Nick a refill. "I like to talk, as you've probably already concluded. But now it's time for you to tell your story."

"My story."

"Everyone who hikes the Wilderness has a story."

"Ah." Nick took a swallow of the beer. "My thirtieth birthday is in a few days. Thought it would be a good way to mark the decade. A couple buddies and I used to talk about doing a thru-hike when we were in college. It ended up just being talk, but lately I started thinking about it again. . . ." He shrugged. "And here I am. Not a thru-hike, 'cause I don't have time, but a real challenge."

"Try again."

"What?"

"Try again."

"That's it. I'll have my birthday while I'm on the trail. Seems like a good way to close out my twenties and kick off my thirties doing the kind of thing I hope I'll be doing the next ten years."

"Sounds good. But, no." Banana nudged Nick's mug closer. "Try again when you finish that."

Another guy, short, stocky, starting to go gray, poked his head through the door. "Right back," Banana told Nick. Banana took a ceramic bottle from under the counter, filled it from one of the taps, and brought it to the guy. The guy handed him some cash.

"Shoo Fly, want to join—" a woman from the back table called. Before she could finish the sentence, the man had disappeared.

"You tried, Bev." Banana patted the woman on the shoulder before he headed back to Nick.

Shoo Fly. The name was familiar. For a few seconds, it wouldn't come to him, then the memory clicked into place. "The marine who cried because he got swarmed by blackflies, right?"

Banana nodded. "I'd still be crying if I was him. Those flies are little mofos. You got a bug net, right? This early in June, you gotta have a bug net."

"Yep." Nick finished his beer. "I should go. I want to get an early start in the morning."

"Before you go, let me ask you one more time. Why are you hiking the Wilderness?"

"Sorry. My reason hasn't changed. Unless my wife about to have a baby is a thing."

The good humor disappeared from Banana's face. "Your wife is about to have a baby and you're heading into the Wilderness? I'm going to have to ask you to leave my place. I misjudged you."

"Not my wife. My wife that was."

"And bingo."

"Bingo what?"

"Bingo was his name-o," Banana shot back. "Bingo, I think we've unearthed your reason for taking on the Wilderness."

Nick tilted his head from side to side. His neck felt stiff. Must have slept on it wrong. "I wouldn't say—"

Banana slapped the bar with both hands before Nick could finish. "Another drink on me if you want to share your sad story." Nick hesitated, giving a few more neck tilts. Banana refilled Nick's mug.

Fifteen minutes later, the mug was empty. "Oh, and did I mention that she got married the day the divorce got finalized?"

"You did not. And may I say, harsh."

"That same day." Nick stared into his empty mug. Banana refilled it. "Same day."

CHAPTER 3

"One Trail Buster." The waiter, a college-age kid, put a plate with three pancakes, three scrambled eggs, three pieces of bacon, three sausages, three pieces of toast, and a heap of hash browns in front of Nick. His stomach slowly turned over. He'd ordered it because, well, *Trail Buster*. He was an idiot. Last night he'd been more of an idiot. Starting the Wilderness with a medium-level hangover? What had he been thinking? Obviously, he hadn't been thinking.

He knew he had to eat something before he went out there, so he took a small bite of scrambled egg. "Eggs are a good choice," a familiar voice said from behind him. He looked over his shoulder and saw Annie Hatherley standing there. "They have cysteine, which makes an amino acid that's going to help your body break down all the toxins metabolizing alcohol left in your system." She signaled to his waiter. "Get this guy a banana, please, Scotty."

"I don't want a—"

"Alcohol messes up your electrolytes. You need the potassium." The waiter, Scotty, grabbed a banana from the hanger by the register and hurled it toward Annie. She caught it and handed it to Nick in one smooth move. "Did you know potassium—"

"Not interested. Because not drunk." He took a big bite of sausage and had to fight not to gag.

She raised her pointy eyebrows. "Not drunk now. But the damage has been done."

"If you're going to continue to lecture me, can you do it sitting down." Nick gestured to the seat across from him. Looking up at her was making his head hurt. Well, making it hurt worse. And that head, not doing a great job thinking. Why had he asked her to sit down? Why hadn't he told her he didn't want her lecture, period?

She walked around the table and sat down. "Potassium is vital in regulating fluid levels."

"You want to borrow my glasses?" Nick asked, mostly to get her to stop talking.

Annie stared at him. "What?"

He took them off and held them out toward her. "I've been told they look really good on pedants."

She laughed. So did he. She took the glasses out of his hand and put them on. "Well?"

He felt that *click* again, like he had in those first few minutes in her store. "I miss your eyebrows," Nick answered, not taking the time to think before speaking. Kind of like last night with Banana.

"Again, I say, what?"

"I, uh, like the way your eyebrows are kind of pointy. They don't make a peak exactly, but almost, and they give you kind of a pixieish look, I guess you could call it. A somewhat wicked pixie, possibly." Okay, he'd made it a lot worse. Since he was still holding the banana, he peeled it and took a large bite. He still didn't want it, but he needed a reason not to speak.

" 'A somewhat wicked pixie.' I have no idea what that means."

Nick shrugged. He'd said enough, way more than enough, on the eyebrow topic. She took off his glasses, leaned toward him, giving him a whiff of maybe lavender soap and warm skin, and slid them back on his face. "You're still heading out this morning?"

Nick absolutely didn't want to get into it with her again. He wasn't going to start off his hike with a head full of dire warnings. Banana may have enabled a little excess beer, but Nick had walked out of his place feeling lighter than he had in a while, almost bouncy walking back to the Inn in his new shoes. He wanted to keep the bounce.

"Yep," he told her. Then he leaned toward her and caught the pendant she wore on a thin gold chain between his fingers. "You're wearing a fox?" he asked, to keep her from saying anything more about his hike. "Miss Always-Be-Prepared believes in luck? I'm disappointed." He gave the fox a gentle twist.

"Why are you talking like you know me, when you clearly don't?" She tugged the pendant away from him. "And I don't believe in luck," she added more softly, eyes darting around the diner. "I believe that my grandmother—"

"Your Honey," he corrected. She frowned. She was cute when she frowned. He knew better than to say that. Lisa would have—No. He wasn't going there. Not today.

"My Honey makes a lot of money selling these things and all her other foxes. Let's just say I believe in that."

"I bet Honey's a true believer."

Annie picked up a piece of his toast and took a bite. "You have a lot of opinions about people you barely met."

"Says the woman who took one look at me and decided I wasn't ready for the Wilderness." And here he was, bringing up the topic he was trying to avoid.

She frowned again. It didn't look cute this time. This time, it was like her whole face was frowning, not just her mouth. Her eyes had gone cold. "That's still my opinion." She stood up.

"I've got to open my shop." A few seconds later, she was out the door.

"Okay, then," Nick muttered. He took a swig of coffee, then noticed a blond woman sitting at the counter giving him an appraising look, an appraising look with blue eyes the same shade as Annie Hatherley's. And over those eyes—pointy eyebrows.

When the woman realized she'd been caught looking, she grinned, then picked up her coffee cup and headed over to him. She sat down without being invited. "I'm not going to ask what you did to piss off my daughter."

"I didn't—"

She interrupted. "Let me finish. I'm not going to ask because I know Annie sometimes gets pissed off for absolutely no reason at all."

Nick didn't comment, trying to keep his face neutral. If Annie's mom was like his own, she could make a list of everything wrong with her daughter. But if anyone else tried it—look out for Mama Bear.

Annie's mom laughed, low and husky. That was another thing they shared. She pointed at him. "You're a smart one."

Someone gave a derisive snort, and Nick realized Annie had reappeared. "I forgot my food," she told him, then turned to her mom. "What are you doing here?"

"I was here when you came in. Not that you noticed. Looked like this guy was all you could see. And I'm the first selectman. Part of my job is making sure people feel welcome in our town." Annie's mother reached out her hand, and Nick shook it. "Belle Hatherley."

"Nick Ferrone."

Scott headed their way with a plate of blueberry pancakes in one hand, and a plate with some kind of omelet in the other. In his teeth, he held a paper bag. Annie pulled it free as he passed by. "Why'd you let me walk out of here without breakfast?"

"You walk too fast," Scott answered. "Besides, aren't you a Hatherley woman? Don't need any help from anyone."

Annie and Belle both flexed one arm and made a sound that was part cheer and part grunt: *"Harrh!"* Nobody else in the place even glanced their way. Must be something they did frequently.

"Why don't you sit down and eat that with us?" Belle asked Annie.

"Gotta work." She started for the door. "And he's gotta hit the trail," she added over her shoulder. "He's losing daylight."

Losing daylight? It wasn't even seven. He'd arranged to get shuttled to the trailhead at seven thirty. "I thought 'hike your own hike' was the motto on the trail," Nick said.

"It is. But Annie thinks her hike is the best hike, and she can't understand why anyone wouldn't want to do the best hike. When Annie hikes, she starts at daybreak."

"Of course, she does," Nick answered. "And, if you still want to know, that's why she's pissed at me. I didn't cancel my hike when she decreed that I'm not ready."

Belle's blue eyes locked on his with a familiar intensity. "Are you?"

"I guess I'm about to find out." Somehow, with her looking at him like that, he found he couldn't give an unequivocal yes. *I guess I'm about to find out* was the best he could do. But that was what he was here for. To test himself. To prove . . . what?

APPALACHIAN TRAIL
CAUTION
THERE ARE NO PLACES TO OBTAIN SUPPLIES
OR GET HELP UNTIL
ABOL BRIDGE 100 MILES NORTH.
DO NOT ATTEMPT THIS SECTION UNLESS YOU
HAVE A MINIMUM OF 10 DAYS SUPPLIES AND
ARE FULLY EQUIPPED.

THIS IS THE LONGEST WILDERNESS SECTION
OF THE ENTIRE A.T. AND ITS DIFFICULTY
SHOULD NOT BE UNDERESTIMATED.
GOOD HIKING!
M.A.T.C.

Nick had seen pictures of the sign, lots of them. It felt different seeing it in real life. He reached out and traced each of the carved letters in the words *good hiking*, his belly flipping with a mix of excitement, nerves, excess sausage, and, according to Annie Hatherley, all the toxins metabolizing alcohol left in his system.

He promised himself that was the last time he was going to think of Annie Hatherley at least until he reached the other side of the Wilderness, until he stood on top of Mount Katahdin, the great mountain, highest mountain in Maine, over 400 million years old. That should put things in perspective. Maybe that was it. Maybe it wasn't about proving something to himself, or not entirely. Maybe it was about getting himself and his life in perspective.

Glad that he was the only one who'd been on the seven-thirty shuttle, he began to recite one of his favorite passages from *Walden*. " 'I learned this, at least, by my experiment: that if one advances confidently in the direction of his dreams, and endeavors to live the life which he has imagined, he will meet with a success unexpected in common hours.' "

Nick used to believe those words in his heart, in his gut, with, looking back, a truly astonishing certainty. He wanted to get that feeling back, even if just for a little while. He had too much experience to believe it was his right to have it all the time, the way he did back when he was point guard on the varsity team, or back in college when he met Lisa, but he could use a little jolt.

He took a deep breath, savoring the Christmastime smell

of the firs. He was doing this! He was about to enter the Wilderness! He knew it wasn't as wild as it used to be. The Maine Appalachian Trail Club had a lodge with cabins and a bunkhouse. That meant warm meals and hot showers and even a freakin' sauna! But all that was about twenty-five miles away on Chairback Mountain. Nick wasn't even sure he wanted to stay there, but he was keeping it as an option. He was hiking his hike. If that meant a sauna and an actual bed to rejuvenate his body, so be it.

He took another deep breath, signed the registry with his full name, then began what he'd been calling—but only to himself—his epic adventure. He did a mental erase of the traffic sounds in the distance, so it felt like it was just the wilderness and him. His hungover head lightly pounded to the rhythm of his feet, the morning mist soft on his face. His eyes flicked back and forth as he tried to take in every detail, the ragged bark on the—What kind of tree was that? He should have brought a guide. Except Annie Hatherley would just have thrown it away.

No thinking about her until the top of Mount Katahdin, he reminded himself. He also wasn't giving any brain space to Lisa. Or her new husband. Or her very-soon-to-arrive baby. " 'I went to the woods because—' " he began to proclaim, then felt one of his feet slide out from under him. His heart lurched into his throat, and he had to pinwheel his arms until he got his balance back. That gentle mist had turned one of those granite rocks he'd been warned about as slick as goose shit.

Nick surveyed the ground in front of him as he waited for his heart rate to return to normal. That rock was only one of many, and exposed tree roots were all over the place. They reminded him of skeletal hands, with long, knobby fingers. He tried to come up with a more appealing image, but that's all that came to him. He wanted to take in everything around him, but if he didn't want to end up with a twisted ankle—or a bashed-in head—less than an hour in, he had to pay attention to where he was putting his feet. He started forward more slowly, struggling to get a smooth gait going. He'd only get two or three steps in a row, then he'd have to pause to pick his way around a group of roots or to step over a mist-slick boulder.

After about half an hour of the halting step-pause-step-step-pause, Nick had to admit to himself that he might have to adjust the amount of time it would take to get to Wilson Valley Lean-to. He'd thought because he'd be hiking over fairly flat ground, he'd get to the shelter around six thirty, cook himself up—by adding hot water—a nice chili mac and cheese, which he'd eat as the sun set. That wasn't looking likely.

Nick let out a snort of laughter. He'd decided to go on this *epic adventure* because he wanted to push himself. Test his mettle. Mettle. He realized he couldn't come up with a precise definition of *mettle*. Didn't matter. Whatever it was exactly, testing it meant more than having a night where he didn't get a hot meal with a view.

He continued to pick his way forward, eyes on the ground in front of him. Boulder. Root, root, root. Mud slick. Root, root. Boulder. Squish. He'd missed a muddy stretch. He pulled his foot free. No, not mud. He studied the grainy brown goo—with his boot print in the middle. He was pretty sure that he'd just stepped in moose poop. He'd read that early in the summer it was looser than at other times because the moose were chomping on fresh vegetation versus dry twigs and branches. He'd also read that if your boot slid over the scat, it was probably fresh, maybe only an hour or two old.

"Gotta be a pony in here somewhere," he muttered. It was the punch line to a joke his grandfather loved to tell about an optimistic boy who was happy when he was given a massive pile of manure because—gotta be a pony in there somewhere. Although in this case, there gotta be a moose somewhere around.

Nick stood still and finally raised his gaze from the ground in front of him, timeline be damned. There was a shelter before Wilson Valley Lean-to. If he didn't make Wilson tonight, so be it. Maybe he'd be hungry when he hit Katahdin, but what the hell. What was the point of this hike if all he saw was his own feet, rocks, roots, mud, and poop.

Yeah, he'd been missing out. He hadn't even realized he'd entered basically a tunnel of trees, and that the sounds of civilization had faded away. All he heard now was the sound of a breeze ruffling the trees, that and the sound of his own heartbeat. He was standing in a spot that probably looked pretty much the way it had about a hundred years ago, when the trail was blazed.

And he was alone. That's what he'd wanted. Time alone. In nature. Where he could think. Actually, where he could stop the incessant barrage of thoughts and just be. But even though he wanted it, he started getting the jimjams standing here surrounded by trees. It would be easy to get lost in them. A few wrong steps, and he could lose the path. Maybe he'd lost it already. He'd been tromping along, eyes on the ground. Had he even kept to the trail?

A blaze. He needed to see a blaze, one of those beautiful white stripes on a tree or rock. There was always one in sight. Almost always. His eyes flicked back and forth as he searched. Was that one? A really faded one? Or was that just a discolored patch of tree bark?

Nick felt panic rise up inside him. This was ridiculous. He was probably only three or so miles in. He could turn around and be back in Fox Crossing well before dark, back at a barstool in Wit's Beginning, jawing with Banana. Not that that's what he wanted. But the town was there, close. There was no reason to get all freaked-out.

Unless he was lost. Which he wasn't. That gray spot on the tree trunk up there was probably a faded blaze mark. If it wasn't, he'd be able to see a blaze mark from that tree once he got up there. The Appalachian Trail Conservancy was great about keeping the trail marked. Everything he'd read said so.

Nick kept his eyes on the probably-a-blaze and started forward. He'd only taken three steps when he hit another of those slick rocks. He pinwheeled his arms, but this time he couldn't regain his balance. He landed on his ass. Hard. He felt the jolt all the way up his spine and into his head, which was still hurting a little from the hangover.

For one wild second, he felt like giving up. Turning around and going back to Fox Crossing, assuming he could find it. Let Annie Hatherley laugh at him while, maybe, buying her a drink. No. He wasn't going to be that guy. The guy that turned around before he was one day in. He was doing this to—Well, maybe he didn't quite know why he was doing this. But it definitely wasn't to become a certified loser. Quitter? Big wuss? All of the above?

With an exaggerated groan that somehow made him feel better, Nick shoved himself to his feet. He looked behind him. Saw a blaze. Okay, he was definitely still on the trail. He lowered his eyes to the ground. He was only going to end up on his ass again if he didn't scan for rocks, roots, and mud slicks. And moose poop. But he would definitely stop and look around periodically because a moose was somewhere around and he wanted to see it. He was in Maine, for chrissakes. He had to see a moose. He also had to get his eyes up often enough to make sure he stayed on the trail.

About—He wasn't even sure how far. His pace was so uneven, matching the uneven terrain, that he had no idea how far he'd gone. Not good. He'd been out for just under three hours. However many miles he'd gone, he'd reached his first bog crossing. Nice. Something about crossing a bridge appealed to him. It made no actual sense, but crossing a bridge made him feel like he was really going somewhere. And he'd have a lot of these puppies to maneuver before he reached Katahdin.

He put one foot on the plank and pressed down, testing the stability. The wood felt a little spongy, but not bad. It would hold him. He started across. At least keeping his eyes down would make it easier to spot pitcher plants. As a kid, he'd been fascinated by carnivorous plants, and some of that fascination still held. A plant that ate meat. Cool.

Before he was even a quarter of the way across the bog, Nick started regretting that he hadn't put on the head net Annie Hath—The head net he'd bought in Fox Crossing. The blackflies were liking this section of the trail, and they were liking him. He'd gotten a few mosquito bites earlier in the day, but suddenly he was under attack. He didn't want to try to get into his pack. He could see himself going plop into the muck as he tried maneuvering the net out. Instead, he picked up his pace, just a little. When one of the flies kamikazed into his eyeball, he picked up his pace a little more.

Hey. It looked like maybe there was a pitcher plant over there. He turned, just a little, to get a better look. Bad choice. A second later it was Nick overboard. At least he'd managed to keep his feet under him, which meant he was only covered in the ooze up to about his knees.

This time he didn't fantasize about turning around and getting back to a barstool at Wit's Beginning. This time he laughed, really laughed, from the gut. He was hiking the freaking 100-Mile Wilderness!

The Fox studied the man. She had watched humans almost since birth, and still they puzzled her. She understood the behavior of the other creatures who shared her world because they shared the same needs. They needed food and water and shelter. They needed mates and kits.

Humans though, even after so many years, she found unpredictable. She knew they had the same needs as the creatures of the forest, but when those needs were satisfied, the humans often didn't seem content.

This human carried food. She could smell it. And she had seen him near a place of shelter that many other humans had found satisfactory. This was not the place for him to seek a mate. Still, he stumbled on through the woods, searching, searching. He didn't realize, as she did, that when he was still, when he was observant the way her kind were, he stopped searching, momentarily.

CHAPTER 4

"How's our boy doing?" Honey asked as she waltzed into Hatherley's Outfitters, decked out in a full fifties-style poodle skirt, complete with fluffy petticoat. Except that instead of a poodle, Honey's skirt featured a sassy-looking fox.

"Our boy?" Annie felt her cheeks getting warm, like she was guilty of something. Which she wasn't.

"Don't pretend you haven't pulled up that app that shows you exactly where that tracker—meaning our boy—is." Honey spread out three napkins—fox print of course—on the slate counter next to the register. She always brought lunch over on Thursdays. Not that she wasn't over here at least twice daily the rest of the week. Which usually Annie loved, but today— Why did she have to be here asking questions Annie didn't want to answer?

"A-nn-nn-nn-ie." Honey drew out the name into a ridiculous number of syllables, making the *nn*'s go high and low, almost like she was singing.

Annie sighed. She might as well just admit it. "Okay, I

checked on him. He's doing okay. Not beating any speed records, but moving in the right direction."

Honey smiled as she put three wax-paper-wrapped sandwiches on the napkins. "Sometimes slow is nice." The way she said it made it clear she wasn't talking about hiking.

"Am I going to have to put in earplugs?" Annie demanded. She kept them stocked at the store. Nothing worse than sharing a shelter with a snorer. She should have thrown a pair in Nick's backpack. On second thought, nope. He was responsible for himself. Her fingers drifted to the phone in the pocket of her shorts. She curled those fingers into a fist. She wasn't going to check him. Again. She shouldn't have checked on him at all. He knew how to send out an SOS if he needed help.

"I don't know why you have such trouble acknowledging that your grandfather and I have a wonderful sex—"

Annie whipped a pair of earplugs off a nearby display. "I'll do it if you don't stop."

Honey smirked as she began setting out fruit cups—with a fox design, of course—but she didn't say anything else about the s-e-x.

"I'm not sure Mom is coming today." Annie got a bottle of root beer and a bottle of sarsaparilla out of the cooler. She sold the whole line of Maine Root drinks. "There's that vote coming up later this month about whether or not to widen Main Street. You know she's going to talk to every citizen of voting age before the meeting to make sure it goes her way."

"She'll be here. She knows I'll vote against her if she crosses me."

"Big talker," Annie said, but she took out a bottle of Maple Syrup Lemonade, her mom's favorite, then got the three stools she kept in the back for the weekly lunches. As if all she'd been waiting for was a seat, her mother strode through the door as soon as Annie had her stool in place.

"Your husband is a stubborn old coot," Belle told Honey. She grabbed the nearest sandwich and unwrapped it.

"My husband, as in your father?" Honey asked.

"Yes. But I'm thinking of disowning him. He thinks widening the street is a great idea. He doesn't understand that a big part of Fox Crossing's charm is *small-town* charm. And that means cute little streets."

"Even if the cute little streets get clogged with traffic?" Annie asked, just because sometimes it was fun to wind her mother up.

"Yes! And if this town had passed the bike-share program, traffic wouldn't be a problem. A bike share—"

"Stop!" Honey pointed her finger at Belle. "No lectures during lunch."

"No lectures. Okay. How about if Annie tells us more about the guy she was having breakfast with this morning."

Annie groaned, feeling an interrogation coming. "I wasn't having breakfast with him. I was merely sitting at his table while I waited for my breakfast order."

"She was staring at him so hard that she didn't even notice her own mother sitting at the counter," Belle told Honey.

"We're talking about Nick?" Honey popped a strawberry in her mouth, then rooted around in her fruit cup for another one.

"How do you know about him?" Belle demanded.

"Just because you're the town Grand Pooh-Bah, that doesn't mean the rest of us don't know things." Honey ate another strawberry. "I met him yesterday. Nice manners. Nice butt." Annie groaned again. "I told this one here that she should have been sweeter to him. It was clear they had a spark."

"There was no spark."

"Oh, yes, there was. Why else wouldn't you realize your own dear mother was sitting mere feet away from you this morning?" Belle grinned at Annie.

"Why else would he even talk to you this morning after you

were so rude to him yesterday?" Honey added. "She told him he wasn't ready to take on the Wilderness."

"Which he isn't," Annie told them both. "This morning only proved it. He was obviously hungover. You don't go off into the woods with a hangover."

" 'I don't drink and I don't chew, and I don't go with boys that do,' " Honey said in a singsong. "My daddy used to say that to me when he thought I was being prissy. In case you didn't make the connection, I think you're being prissy. I'm sure it wasn't as if he were falling-down drunk." Honey pulled out her cell and hit a speed-dial number.

"Who is she calling?" Annie asked her mom.

"The Prissy Police?" Belle suggested. "Nick seemed clear-headed enough to me," she added when Annie rolled her eyes.

"Not clearheaded enough to have a support team," Annie muttered, then her attention snapped to her grandmother.

"How many drinks did you serve him?" Honey asked. She listened for a moment, then turned to Annie and Belle. "Banana says Nick drank enough to feel good last night, but not too bad this morning. Banana says possibly he woke up with a little headache this morning, but no big whoop."

"You actually called—"

"Hush. I'm talking," Honey interrupted Annie. "So, what did he tell you, 'cause I know everybody always tells you everything," she said into her cell.

"She actually called Banana," Annie whispered to Belle.

"Of course, she did." Belle didn't bother to lower her voice and ignored Honey's glare. "If she doesn't know something herself, odds are Banana will. People talk to bartenders."

"Why does she even care?" Annie heard a whine in her voice. Sometimes being around her mom and grandmom turned her back into a teenager. "A billion hikers go through here."

"And your grandmother can give you the dirt on at least half of them," Belle countered. "And she cares because of the spark."

"There was no spark!" Annie realized she sounded even more like a surly teenager, but she didn't care. They weren't listening to her.

"Thanks, Banana. Charlie and I will be in for trivia tomorrow night. The Smarty Pints aren't going to be able to take back the trophy from the Brewsual Suspects without us." Honey put her phone down, then took a bite of her sandwich, dabbed her mouth with a fox napkin, then took another bite.

"She's not going to tell us unless we beg," Belle told Annie. "Please, please, please, tell us what Banana told you." Belle's tone wasn't in the slightest bit pleading.

"I don't want to know, period," Annie muttered.

"I told you. He said Nick drank enough to feel good, but not enough to feel too bad this morning."

"And?" Belle prompted.

"And he's divorced, and his wife—she got married on the day the papers were signed. That same day." Honey took a sip of her sarsaparilla, looking from Annie to Belle, waiting for a reaction.

"How long ago?" Belle asked.

"More than a year. The ex is about to have a baby with her new hubby. She could be giving birth as we speak."

"That is no reason to come out here and hike the trail with basically no preparation," Annie stated.

"How did I raise a daughter who is so judgmental?" Belle asked. "Me. The ultimate flower child."

Annie gave a derisive snort, and Honey laughed. "You are the first selectman of the town, baby. That's not a position held by a flower child," Honey said.

"And you always think you're right. Which is almost the definition of judgmental," Annie added.

"What about when I'm right that people shouldn't be judgmental?" Belle countered.

Annie opened her mouth, then shut it. She wasn't going to

get into some argument with her mother over basically nothing. It could last all day.

"He's not the first to try to fix a broken heart by spending some time with nature," Honey said. "You know getting out there puts things in perspective, Annie. Don't tell me you don't."

Annie sighed. "Okay, fine. But he should have prepared more. We all know when someone gets hurt out there due to their own stupidity, they aren't the only ones who pay."

There was a long pause, and Annie knew they were all thinking about Luke Caron. His senior year of high school, Annie's sophomore year, he'd gone into the Wilderness as part of a team searching for a couple who hadn't shown up in Fox Crossing when they were due. The couple made it back to town. Luke didn't. And he would have if that couple had had a tracker or basic compass skills or the basic sense to watch for blaze marks.

Luke had parents, grandparents, friends, and all had been left devastated. The whole town of Fox Crossing had felt the blow. Annie hadn't had any special claim on him, but her heart had broken a little back then. She'd never admitted it to anyone, but she'd had a huge crush on him. Stupid huge. She'd even made a list of his likes and dislikes. She'd basically been a little stalker. Somebody like Luke shouldn't have had to die because hikers went skipping off into the Wilderness as if it were Disneyland, which had paid attendants everywhere to make sure nothing bad happened.

"Anyone can get injured out there," Belle said gently. "Even with all the preparation in the world. Look at Banana. He came out of the Wilderness on a stretcher that one time."

"But most of the other times he turned back? He was helping some noob who got in over their head. On one of the rescues he broke his wrist, remember?" Annie answered, surprised that her eyes were stinging with unshed tears. She blinked them away, covering the action with a fake sneeze. She must be about to get her period. There was no reason to get so emotional just thinking about a boy who had died a pointless death so many years ago.

"I believe you've helped a few people back to civilization. I believe that's even a service you offer," Belle said.

"When I think it's safe. When I can get to them by one of the logging roads." Annie took a swig of her root beer.

"Oh, right. When was the last time you had to turn back because you were in danger?" Her mother had this irritating thing she did, where she acted like she was trying to remember things she actually knew everything about.

"I've done all two thousand two hundred miles three times. And only one of those times was in sections." The first time Annie had done more than an overnight hike was with Luke Caron—well, Luke Caron and the rest of his family and her mother, but a lot of the time the two of them had hiked a little stretch ahead. She'd been thirteen. He'd been fifteen. And spending all that time with him made her love him even more. Yes, love. *Crush* was too weak of a word. It might have been puppy love, but to her it was the real deal. "I know what I'm doing. I'm first-aid certified. I've successfully brought in twenty-seven hikers—" Even though Annie knew all her mother's little tricks, she'd let herself get caught. "All those times I knew I was safe," she added, but her voice sounded weak, even to her.

"Anyway, your noob is doing fine." Honey was playing peacemaker, the way she had so many times. Annie wasn't sure having a mother who was only seventeen years older led to more arguments, but it felt like she and her mom had had a million of them.

"Your noob?" Belle asked.

"She means Nick. I set him up with a tracker, and, yes, I checked on him. I would check on anyone I thought needed it." That was absolutely true. But she had to admit—not to

Belle and Honey, but to herself—that she'd checked on Nick more often than she would check on anyone else. And her fingers still wanted to get ahold of her phone and check on him again. "So, Mom, you think you have the votes you need? Even if Grandpa votes the other way?" Annie was interested. She thought her mom was right about keeping Fox Crossing's small-town charm. But, mostly, she just wanted a subject change.

"Probably. I'd like to get Shoo Fly to the meeting. He's the only business owner on the street that hasn't promised me a no vote, other than Dad."

"Good luck with that." Annie tried to think of any occasion where Shoo Fly had been a part of a group of more than three people. Three people including him. She couldn't come up with any.

Honey took one of Annie's strawberries. "Maybe Shoo Fly should get himself back on the trail, even just for a few days, especially if he joins up with the bubble." The bubble, as in the group of hikers who set off from Springer Mountain around April 1. Most of them came through Fox Crossing in August and September. It was the most lucrative—and annoying—time of year. "A lot more women are hiking the trail after that book," Honey added.

Annie had heard it called the Wild Effect, after that book by Cheryl what's her name. "And most of them are unprepared."

Honey flicked her hand, dismissing Annie's comment. "That's not what we're talking about. We're talking about how Shoo Fly needs a woman."

"How would you even know that? Have you ever gotten more than three words out of the man?" Belle demanded. "Because if you have, you go right over to the bakery and tell him to vote no at the town meeting when the article about the street comes up."

"He doesn't talk to me more than anybody else," Honey answered. "But nobody wants to be alone like that."

"Um. I live alone. So does she." Annie jerked her chin toward her mother.

"And both of you would be happier if you found someone to love, someone to love you," Honey answered.

"Mom—" Belle began.

"Honey—" Annie said at the same time.

Honey held up her hands in surrender. "Forget I said it. You're the two happiest women I've ever met. But I have the feeling Shoo Fly would be happier if he had a girlfriend."

"How do you know he even likes girls? Nobody knows anything about him," Annie said. "I bet even Banana only knows his usual drink order, and everybody talks to Banana."

"*Pfft.*" Honey gave another hand flip. "Woman, man, whatever. He'd be happier with someone. I've seen his eyes, and his eyes talk even if he doesn't. He's lonely."

"What he is, is a victim of PTSD," Belle told her.

"You don't know that," Annie protested. "You can't assume everybody who served in Iraq has PTSD."

"Can I assume everyone who served in Iraq and keeps almost completely to himself has PTSD?" Belle asked.

"Maybe he believed our governor when she said people from Maine value privacy," Annie suggested. "Maybe that's why he decided to live in Fox Crossing. Maybe we should all mind our own business."

"Excuse us for caring about our fellow citizens," her mother said.

"Is that what was happening?" Annie asked. "I thought we were gossiping."

Honey again attempted to smooth things over. "Well, I was gossiping *because* I care about my fellow citizens," she told them both. "But I'm certainly not going to start knocking on Shoo Fly's door with eligible women—or men—in tow." She sighed. "I'd just like everyone to be as happy as your grandfather and me. I don't understand why neither of you is married. You've had the perfect example of a happy marriage right in front of you your whole lives."

"There are lots of ways to be happy," Belle answered. She looked over at Annie. "And we're Hatherley women. We can handle whatever comes at us, man or no man." Belle bent her arm, making her biceps pop. Annie did the same.

"*Harrh,*" they growled.

Honey curled her own arm up. "*Harrh!*"

"Mom, we've told you and told you. That's a Hatherley woman thing. And you are not a Hatherley woman."

Honey didn't lower her arm. "I most certainly am. *Harrh!*"

"Let's not have this argument again," Annie said. "You know to my mom a Hatherley woman has Annabelle Hatherley's blood in her veins. Which you don't, because you were formerly an Ouellette."

"Both of you have as much Ouellette blood as Hatherley, and you're the better for it. Besides, Annabelle Hatherley was married," Honey told them.

"But her husband was dead when she was twenty-three. And she never bothered to get herself another one," Belle reminded her.

Annie realized they were all still standing like the "We Can Do It!" woman. She let her arm fall to her side and picked up her sandwich. "I'm too hungry to have this conversation. We've had it a few times before, like once or twice a year."

Honey and Belle both lowered their own arms. "If being a Hatherley woman means being too proud to admit you need another person, then I'm happy I'm not one."

"And that is part of the conversation I was just talking about," Annie answered. "And now I'll say what I always say— I'm not opposed to having a guy in my life. I actually have had a guy in my life. Case in point, Seth and I lived together for almost two years."

"To save on rent, maybe. To have a bed warmer. Didn't stop him from running off to California." Honey ate the last strawberry from Belle's cup.

"You act like he left me."

"Because he did."

"No, he left. And it was fine with me." This whole lunch was made up of conversations they'd already had. But Annie kept going, hoping that if she explained again, Honey might finally get it. "Seth had something he wanted to do. It wasn't something I wanted to do. So, he went to California to hike the PCT. More power to him. Maybe he'll even come back this way at some point, and if we're both interested, maybe we'll spend some more time together."

Honey took a strawberry out of Annie's cup. Why didn't Honey make herself a cup of all strawberries? That's all she wanted to eat. But that was yet another conversation they'd already had. Honey always insisted she liked all the fruit, even though it obviously wasn't true because she always left most of the non-strawberries uneaten. She was so stubborn that she might as well be a Hatherley woman. *Harrh!*

"Well, my money's on Nick, because of the spark, which you didn't have with Seth." Honey scanned the fruit cups for strawberries she'd overlooked. When she didn't find one, she picked up her sandwich.

"There's no spark." Suddenly, the urge to check on Nick was too strong to resist. Annie jerked her phone out of her pocket and pulled up the tracker app, careful not to let her mother or grandmother see the screen.

"She's checking on him," Belle said.

Honey smiled. "Of course she is."

CHAPTER 5

"Could be worse. Could be raining," Nick muttered to himself, as he pulled his Frogg Toggs on over his clothes. It felt like at least a couple days since he'd stood knee-high in mud, laughing with the joy of being out on the Appalachian Trail.

"No rain, no pain, no Maine." Nick turned and saw a man, probably early fiftysomething, zipping up one side of a double-wide sleeping bag. A lump in the bag showed there was still an occupant. "That's what they say."

Nick hadn't known he had company in the shelter until he woke up that morning. Last night he'd conked out as soon as he'd dry-swallowed a few Advil for his split lip. Somehow, he'd managed to smack himself in the face with a rock. He'd stepped on the rope when attempting to fling said rock over a tree branch as a counterbalance to his bag of food, the bag of food he'd been attempting to keep away from bears and assorted woodland creatures.

"What's with the lip?" the man asked.

"Turns out flinging a rock over a branch not only takes a lot of practice"—Nick had made multiple attempts. He'd stopped counting once he got into the double digits—"it can also be hazardous. It might have been better to take my chances with the bear."

"Had almost the same experience back in Georgia. Wham! Right in the forehead."

"Oh, no, Mr. Bill!" a high voice called from the depths of the double-wide.

"And there it is. That's how I got my trail name. I was hoping for something . . . more, something more fitting to the endeavor."

"I don't—"

"Mr. Bill? *Saturday Night Live*?" the man prompted.

"Oh, yeah." Now Nick remembered. "Claymation guy. Got squashed a lot." He'd lived with his uncle for about a year after he graduated from college, and Uncle Vince had given him a course in what he considered the Essentials of Comedy, including old *SNL* clips.

"For two weeks, he tried to get people to call him Tamanend." The bag was unzipped, and a chubby woman around the same age as the man wriggled out. "For two weeks, I tried to explain the concept of cultural appropriation."

"I don't think it's cultural appropriation when it's from a book written by a—"

The woman—Mrs. Bill?—made a beak out of her fingers, then opened and closed it several times. "Quack, quack, quack."

"That's code for shut up," Mr. Bill explained. "After thirty years of marriage, we have a code for pretty much everything."

"He tried not to answer to Mr. Bill." She stretched, then walked over to her husband and gave him a friendly hip bump. "But—"

"But she tricked me into it," Mr. Bill interrupted.

"And everyone knows that once you answer to a trail name, that's it. It's yours." She smiled at Nick. "So, what's yours?"

"Haven't got one. I just started in Fox Crossing. Someday I

want to do the whole thing, but I'm just starting with the Wilderness."

She rubbed her hands together. "I love giving trail names."

"She loved it so much she gave herself one before we set foot on the trail, which I think is the cowardly way to go."

"It's not like I named myself Princess Leia, although that would have been extremely cool." She smoothed her faded purple T-shirt down. Across the front was the word LOON in curly script. "That's me. As in 'crazy as a.' Because I'm walking more than two thousand miles, peeing outside almost all the way, out of loooove." Loon batted her eyes and gazed up at her husband with exaggerated adoration. "It's his life dream to walk the whole trail, and since I'm his life partner, here I am. Do you know how long it's been since I've had a Mint Milano? And I love—"

"Less than a day," Mr. Bill cut in.

"Because we just made a stop in civilization. Now back to the name." Loon studied Nick.

"Will it help if I tell you I have long passages from *Walden* memorized?" Nick asked hopefully.

" 'I went to the woods because I wished to live deliberately,' " Mr. Bill proclaimed, beaming.

He'd gotten the quote exactly right. A lot of people said *wanted* instead of *wished*. Not that people walked around quoting Thoreau all the time. But online Nick had seen *wanted* a bunch of times.

"Maybe he should be called Deliberately," Mr. Bill suggested.

"Nope," Loon said without even thinking about it. "A man who whacks himself in the face putting up a bear bag does not get to be called Deliberately. Not when pretty much everyone has decided hanging bear bags never works, and when you can easily buy an Ursack, which also keeps out mice."

Mr. Bill finger-quacked at her. She kept talking. "Mr. Bill is taken, thanks to you," she told her husband. "I'm thinking Igor." She pronounced it *Eye-gore*.

Nick laughed, then winced, as pain shot through his lip. He needed more Advil. "I can't really argue with that."

"Not after giving Igor's most famous line," Loon agreed. "With props to you for knowing *Young Frankenstein* at your tender age." That was also thanks to Nick's uncle Vin. Nick had watched that movie at least fifteen times since that first viewing.

"And he knows Mr. Bill. He's an old soul," her husband agreed.

"Old Soul sounds like a trail name," Nick hinted.

"What did you say, Igor?" Loon asked.

"That Old—"

Loon and Mr. Bill both laughed. "You answered to it, Igor. Now it's yours," Mr. Bill said.

"Could be worse," Loon told Nick.

"Could be raining," they all completed the movie line together. Then Nick's stomach growled loudly, as if it wanted to join in the conversation.

"I forgot to take food out before I hung the bag, and the idea of taking it down last night . . ." Nick shook his head.

"I'm making you breakfast," Loon declared.

"By make, she means she'll give you one of her Pop-Tarts," Mr. Bill said.

"No, I like this one. I'm going to give him two of my Pop-Tarts," Loon answered.

When they set out about a half an hour later, a light rain coming down, Nick felt reenergized, and not just from the sugar rush. Mr. Bill and Loon made him feel like he was part of something bigger, part of the trail community. It didn't matter to them that they were thru-hikers and he was only going to be out here for about ten days. They'd welcomed him, shared their food, and given him his trail name.

"We're going to have to pick up the pace if we want to make Chairback Gap while the sun's still up," Mr. Bill said when they paused for a water break. "I couldn't get that one"—he jerked his head toward Loon—"out of bed until almost ten yesterday or we would have made it to the Long Pond Lean-to last night."

"I begged for a zero day," Loon admitted. "I offered him every sexual favor I could think of to keep him under the covers, but no."

Nick hoped he kept his expression neutral. That was way too close to hearing his mom talking about doing it. "I don't think I could have made it one more step when I got to the shelter," Nick admitted. "I knew I had to cross Wilson Stream, but I wasn't expecting—" He shook his head. "If there wasn't that rope going across, I think I'd have turned around right there."

"Only in Maine would that be called a stream," Loon agreed. "*River* doesn't even adequately describe it. What's bigger than *river*?"

"*River* is by definition larger than all other waterways," Mr. Bill answered.

Loon snorted and told Nick, "The man has no imagination. I say *river* doesn't do it. Let's make up a word."

"*Wirariver*," Nick suggested. "To indicate both its width and the rapidity of the water?"

"Nice." Loon smiled at him. "If there was any doubt you deserved two Pop-Tarts, it's completely gone."

"Then there was that climb to get up to the shelter." Nick's whole body was hurting, even more than when he climbed into his sack the night before.

"Less talking, more walking," Mr. Bill told them.

"I don't want to say it, but I gotta say it. I'm not going to make the Chairback Lean-to in a day. That's almost twice as many miles as I made yesterday."

"Don't worry about it. You're just getting your hiking legs," Loon told Nick.

"Yeah. You should have seen us our first couple weeks on the trail." Mr. Bill slapped Nick on the shoulder. "Good spending time with you."

"Bye, Igor," Loon added, and they strode off.

Nick took another swig of water. At least he didn't have to worry about running out. The Wilderness was practically made of the stuff, and he had a UV pen to deal with sterilization. "Okay, onward." He'd realized yesterday that when he was alone on the trail, he talked to himself. A lot.

As he started back down the trail, he felt his spirits flag a little. Less than two days on the AT and he was not only talking to himself, he was cycling through emotions like a teenage girl pumped full of hormones. He'd thought that story of a marine crying over some blackflies was an exaggeration, but not anymore.

Mr. Bill and Loon had got him thinking about Lisa. His marriage hadn't gotten close to the thirty-year mark. He and Lisa had only gone four and a few months. She said it was because he was stuck in the "rebellion" stage. He couldn't remember what the other stages were, even though she'd made him read an article that outlined them all.

She thought his quitting his job and doing contract work as a small-business coach was irresponsible. She thought at their age getting some stability was the goal, stability that would let them start a family. He thought their age was the perfect time to take risks, especially since his parents had turned the family house over to him when they moved to a senior-living community. And it wasn't like he didn't have experience getting a small business going. His dad and his uncle Vin had started a home-inspection business together, and Nick had been their unofficial intern from age thirteen on. He'd seen everything firsthand, and he knew he could help anybody who dreamed of owning their own business get started. So the risk? Yeah, it was a risk, but not as much as Lisa acted like it was.

He didn't see why he—and she—couldn't take a couple more years to rebel before they settled down completely. If Lisa had had some "selfish" thing she wanted, he would have supported her.

Anyway, he didn't think the security thing or the rebellion thing was the real reason they split. It was just a reason that sounded good. She'd fallen in love with somebody else. Who knew how many months she'd been going through the motions when she was in love with this other guy? She wouldn't tell him, said it wasn't the point. But she married him the same day she and Nick got divorced, so it seemed like it pretty much *was* the point.

And the guy—Nick preferred not to use his name—with him, Lisa could quit her job and have a baby and then stay home with said baby. Which wasn't something Nick even thought she wanted. When she talked about having a family, he thought it was part of that five-year plan she was always going on about during the last couple years they were together. So a baby a couple years, maybe three, out. Clearly not. She got pregnant less than six months after signing the divorce/marriage papers.

He wondered if Annie Hatherley had a five-year plan. Probably did. She seemed the type. He wondered if she'd ever been married. "Stop thinking about her," he ordered himself. And he was talking to himself again.

He was going to be out here less than two weeks. He wasn't going to waste it thinking about the past or Annie Hatherley. He wanted to get out of his head and pay attention to what was around him. That was the whole point.

And what was around him? He stopped and focused. A brook. Who knew what they called it in Maine, but to him it was a brook. And the trail was running right beside it. It was

like a view from a nature calendar, and he'd been completely ignoring it. He pulled in a deep breath, then began to walk again,
realizing the ground here was a little spongier than it had been
on yesterday's stretch of the trail. The rain was still coming
down, maybe a little harder, but the sound of it hitting his rain
gear was soothing, now that he was bothering to notice it. He
took in one more deep breath, then continued on.

The Fox paused, pain moving from her foot to her leg to her
core. She knew the pain was only a memory from long, long ago.
Yet, every time she passed through this section of the woods, she
felt it all again, the ground giving under her, the snap, the metal
teeth, the agony. Then the hunger, the thirst, the cold, the des-
peration.
Until The Woman came.

Annie ate an apple as she walked to work. Usually she
stopped by Flappy Jacks for breakfast, and if not that, then for
coffee. But her mother was almost always there for breakfast,
too, "getting the temperature of the town," and Annie didn't
feel like dealing with her mother this morning. When Annie
was in a certain mood, everything her mother did felt annoying. And that certain mood? Annie was in it today. She felt
twitchy and irritable. She pulled out her phone and checked it,
even though she told herself she would only check it every few
hours, and she had just checked it about twenty minutes ago.

Her noob was fine. *The* noob. That's what she meant. *The*
noob. He'd gotten going at a reasonable hour, and while he
wasn't moving fast, he was moving. She'd been relieved—No,
not relieved. She'd merely noted that he'd crossed Wilson
Stream without a problem yesterday. At least not a problem
that had made him turn around. Today, he'd probably find the
trek over Barren Mountain grueling, with those scrawny calves
of his. She found herself picturing his calves, not really all that

scrawny, and the rest of his lanky form, that curly reddish-brown hair, the chestnut-brown eyes.

"Oh, good god," she muttered. "Please just stop it." Yeah, he had her talking to herself. She really did need to find a nice guy, somebody who she could have some good sex with, while not getting all relationship-y. Because she'd been a little relieved when Seth had decided to go hike the PCT, and a part of her, a decent-size part, was glad to have her little cabin back to herself, with all the decisions hers alone. Which meant if she wanted to have cereal for dinner, she had cereal for dinner. Seth loved to cook, and that meant deciding what to eat way too many hours before Annie even knew if she'd be hungry.

Which was no big thing. The big thing was that she never quite felt like she loved him all the way. And vice versa. It was way too easy for them to go their own ways. He didn't even ask if she wanted to come to California with him. She didn't even consider going.

She turned the corner onto Main Street. Relationships were—

"Annie!"

The excited cry jerked Annie out of her thoughts. "Chloe!" She rushed toward her old friend. "Why didn't you tell me you were coming?"

Her friend shrugged. "You know me, I like surprises."

"And you know me, I don't. And I'm the one being surprised, not you." Annie gave her friend a tight one-armed hug, holding her apple core in her free hand.

"You're very easy to surprise, too, since you have all those routines. Half an hour before opening, and here you are. I'd try to coax you to breakfast at Flappy's, but I know you've already been there."

"You're wrong. See, you don't know everything about me." Annie held up the apple core. "I ate as I walked."

"Yeah! I get pancakes!" Chloe exclaimed. She was the kind

of person who exclaimed a lot. "Unless you are really, really trying to avoid someone. Are you? You must be! Because otherwise, you'd have been to Flappy's to eat or to get a to-go order."

"I was sorta, kinda avoiding my mother," Annie admitted, because Chloe always got everything out of her anyway. "But she won't bother criticizing me if we're together. She'll have a billion questions for you. She loves your butt."

"Well, I *am* extremely lovable. So is my butt." They turned around and headed for the diner. "And I have a billion questions, too. Mostly for you, but some for Belle, and, of course, Honey and Charlie. And Banana. And, well, pretty much all the year-rounders."

"Is the rest of your family going to be rolling in soon?" Annie asked as they walked. Chloe and her family had spent a few weeks in Fox Crossing almost every summer when Chloe was growing up. They still met up in town every few years.

"I'm flying solo this time. I'm trying to finish my thesis. Which means I'm basically trying to start it. I have about three pages done. Pages I don't like. I figured I'd hole up in one of the cabins by the lake and have a writers' retreat for one."

"What's the topic?"

"Don't laugh. No, forget that. It's impossible. Go ahead and laugh. It's about romantic love, reciprocal romantic love, and the effects on self-esteem." Annie gave a snort-laugh, and Chloe smacked her on the arm. "See? I knew it. I knew you'd laugh."

"It's just that I should have known, without even asking, that it would be something connected to love. The first day we met, at the playground, you had me playing bridesmaid to your bride. Remember?"

"And? Is that a bad thing?"

"I just think being in love is one way to be happy, not the only way," Annie said.

"Which is because you've never really been in love."

"Unfair!" Annie protested. "Just because my experiences don't fit your idea of love, you're saying I haven't experienced it?" Except, deep down, she thought maybe Chloe was right. Luke Caron couldn't count, not as real adult love. And if she'd really loved Seth, why hadn't it hurt more to be without him? "You should be writing your paper on the effect of watching way too many rom-coms at an impressionable age."

"Not a bad topic. But I already have one." They reached Flappy Jacks, and Chloe held the door open for Annie. "Let's table the love convo. I can't handle a fight with you until after pancakes, blueberry pancakes, a stack so high it almost topples."

"Conversations aren't fights." Annie led the way to an empty booth and they both slid into seats. "But I'm happy to change topics." She did a quick scan for her mother. Yeah, there she was, busy talking to Summer Martin, probably locking down her vote.

"Chloe-bobloe!"

"Banana-boana!" Chloe jumped back to her feet and met Banana as he headed toward her from his usual stool at the counter. Annie stayed where she was, smiling as she watched their reunion. Playing the Name Game with Banana had always cracked her and Chloe up, since *banana* was already part of the chant. One of those things that didn't seem quite as hilarious once you were in your double digits.

"The Banana is sitting with us," Chloe announced as she towed him over to their booth. "I'll go get your food." She practically skipped over to the counter. Somehow, even at almost thirty, Chloe could make the move look happy and cute instead of dorky.

"Have you checked on Nick?" Banana asked.

Annie didn't bother to ask how he knew she had access to Nick's tracker. Once one person knew something in Fox Crossing, everybody knew. They knew even faster when one of the somebodies was Banana or her grandmother.

"I checked on him last night." True. Also true that she'd already checked on him a few times that morning. Which wasn't something she wanted on the Fox Crossing gossip network. "He made it to the Wilson Valley Lean-to."

"He probably ran into Loon and Mr. Bill. They were at my place night before last, getting ready for that last push to the end. Loon had pretty much convinced her husband to let her sleep in if she couldn't have a zero day."

"They stopped by the store yesterday morning about ten, did a little restocking. They weren't planning to do a lot of miles, so they probably did cross paths with Nick." She was glad that he'd get the company of two experienced hikers. Less likely he'd get into trouble. Maybe she'd turn out to be wrong. Maybe he'd make it all the way to Katahdin. A lot of hiking the trail was mental. It wasn't all calves. But if he did make it, it would be because he got lucky. He hadn't trained nearly enough.

"Did you get their story?" Banana asked. Annie shook her head. Banana always got more out of people than she did. Maybe because she spent more time checking gear and giving trail advice than gossiping. "Mr. Bill had hiking the trail on his bucket list, and Loon decided to support him by going with, even though, according to her, the best way to celebrate their thirtieth anniversary would involve a lot of chocolate and a soft mattress. Now that's what I call love."

"Did someone say my favorite word?" Chloe asked as she returned to her seat in the booth and handed Banana his plate and coffee mug.

"Chloe is here to write her thesis on romantic love," Annie told Banana. "Big surprise."

"It's a big part of life, which means it's a big part of psychology. So, who were we talking about? Who's in love?"

"Nobody you know. A couple hiking the trail," Annie told her.

"Amazing couple," Banana added. "The wife committed to thru-hiking the AT, just because it was her husband's dream."

"Wow. That makes me a little teary."

Annie wasn't surprised to see that Chloe's eyes *were* a little wet. Her emotions had always been close to the surface. She was sure if they watched *13 Going on 30* right now, Chloe would cry. Even though she'd seen it a billion times. She also cried over most life insurance commercials, a lot of diaper commercials, and every birthday card. Annie had once even witnessed her crying because "the moon looked so beautiful."

Scott came over with a mountain of blueberry pancakes and the two-egg special. "I ordered for us when I was at the counter. Also, I paid."

Annie batted her eyes at Chloe. "I love you."

"I love you, too."

Banana looked back and forth between the two of them. "It's good to see you two together. Brings up all kinds of memories. I hope Miranda remembers all the good times you three had when she was still living here."

When Miranda was about eleven, she had moved to Oregon with her mom. She'd come back a few times, but never for long.

"What's Miranda up to?" Chloe asked.

"Just got promoted to master sergeant." Banana didn't elaborate, and Banana pretty much always elaborated.

"That's so great," Chloe said. "I'd love to see her again."

Banana only nodded in response.

Annie picked up a piece of bacon, then paused with it partway to her mouth. She gave a sniff.

"What's wrong?" Chloe lifted one of her pancakes so she could spread butter between it and the next one down.

"I thought it was rancid." Annie took another sniff, then put the bacon back on her plate. "It's not the bacon, but something smells off."

"It might be me." Banana patted his pockets. "I'm carrying bait for The Fox. Maybe some of it has been in my pockets too long." He pulled out a baggie. Something inside it was slimy. "I didn't realize the bag had a little tear in it. This isn't going to attract anything but a vulture." He waved at Scott. "Mind throwing this away for me?" Scott's nose wrinkled when he took the baggie, but he didn't comment.

"I think we're going to need some explanation." Annie took a bite of her toast.

"Most definitely," Chloe agreed.

"I've decided this is the year I finish my section hike of the AT. I'm hiking the Wilderness. But I'm not going until I see The Fox," Banana told them.

"Maybe I should get some fox treats, too!" Chloe finished distributing butter to every layer of her pancake stack. "I've been coming here my whole life, and I've never seen The Fox."

"Well, I've lived here my whole life, and I haven't either. It might be that The Fox has . . ." Annie decided to be tactful. "Crossed over the rainbow bridge." Chloe looked distressed. But reality was reality. Even if some DNA had been passed along that gave foxes unusual splotches of pure white fur, that didn't mean that there was *always* a fox with unusual markings around. Maybe whatever genes controlled the fluky color patterns skipped a generation sometimes. "It's been a few years since there was a sighting, right?" Annie looked at Banana for confirmation, but he ignored the question.

"You're talking about The Fox like it's just a fox," he told her. "It's lived for more than two hundred years. There's no reason to think it's not still right out in our woods."

"Banana, come on," Annie said. "I know you love a good story. But we both know a two-hundred-year-old fox is about as real as your brilliant donkey, Bucky."

"You can see Bucky's headstone right out behind the bar," Banana reminded her.

"You're right." Annie had seen the stone many times. On Halloween and Banana's birthday it tended to migrate, a few times with an assist from Annie, to the village square, and Banana would have to retrieve it. "I shouldn't have questioned Bucky's existence when there is such hard proof."

"I completely believe in Bucky. And I absolutely believe in The Fox. The Fox has been seen at least every few years going back to Annabelle Hatherley's days. I looked them up in old issues of the *Maine Courant*."

"Yeah, I remember. I missed out on a trip to Lily Bay, sitting with you by the microfilm machine," Annie answered. "But come on, we all know stories about The Fox are part of the town charm. That's why the paper still prints them. It's not as if they're fact-checked."

Banana looked over at Chloe. "We know the truth."

Chloe nodded. "My parents, too." Annie knew what was coming, and that there was no stopping it. "That's how they met. They both saw The Fox at the same moment, right in the middle of Main Street. They started talking, and by the end of the summer, they were engaged. That story was in the paper. And it was true. I have no reason to doubt the other stories."

Annie let out a slow breath. She should just drop the subject. She knew that. But they were being ridiculous. "Banana, you're an experienced hiker. Okay, you've had some bad luck—"

"You said it. Luck! You believe in luck!" Chloe exclaimed.

"Let me rephrase. You've had some bad weather. You had the norovirus. You had a fall. You turned back to help out another hiker—three times. Those things could happen again. There are things that are out of your control. But your experience and your fitness level up your odds of successfully hiking all the way to Katahdin and back. It doesn't make any sense to wait until you see an animal that probably doesn't even exist."

Banana seemed unfazed. "Better watch out, or I'll tell your grandma on you."

"You better watch out, or I'll tell her you called her my grandma," Annie shot back.

"Speaking of Honeypie." Chloe always used the pet name. "You think she and Charlie could use help at Vixen's this summer? I'll go crazy if I try to write all day long. Also, I need money."

Annie laughed. "I'm sure they'll hire you. Everybody loves your ass."

Chloe grinned. "Got that right." Her grin faded to a smile, then disappeared entirely.

Annie leaned toward her. "What, Chloe?"

"Nothing. Only that I've had more than the average number of breakups for a woman my age, and I was always the one being broken up with. So, everybody doesn't really love my ass, at least not for long. It doesn't take a psychology grad student to figure out why I chose the connection between romantic love and self-esteem as my topic." Chloe laughed. Even someone who hadn't known her forever like Annie and Banana had would be able to tell it was fake.

"Chloe, you're acting like—"

Chloe interrupted, "Don't. Don't, Annie. I don't want to hear how you're single and happy, or how your mom never got married and is great. *I* want to get married. I do. I always have, you know that. And I'm almost thirty, and I was sure it would have happened by now. And I know there are all kinds of fulfilling, worthy things I can be doing with myself, instead of thinking about all this, and I actually do a lot of those things, but I want to share my life with someone. Like that hiker couple Banana was just talking about."

She was talking so fast now, it would have been hard for Annie to get a word in. She decided letting Chloe vent was probably better than anything Annie'd come up with to comfort her.

"That's why I'm really here. Not to write, even though I need to write. A ton. And I love this place, and all the great people here. But that's not why I came either. I came because I wanted to see The Fox." Chloe looked Annie in the eye. "Go ahead and laugh. Call me ignorant or superstitious or whatever."

Annie shook her head. "That's not what I'm thinking." What she was thinking was that out of all the millions of times she'd seen Chloe get emotional, this time felt different. Chloe was in real pain.

"The Fox brought my mom and dad together. You've seen them. They're this perfect couple. I want what they have." She turned to Banana. "So, I'll carry around anything you think will help. I need to see The Fox. This summer. I need to see her."

CHAPTER 6

There it was. Long Pond Stream. And on the other side, the shelter where he'd be spending the night. He'd only made about eight miles, but they'd been good miles. Wet, squelchy, squishy miles. But definitely good, partly because some of that wet was a waterfall, the second he'd seen since he left Fox Crossing. It wasn't as spectacular as the first, Little Wilson Falls, which looked like a stone staircase hewn by a giant. But this one was just so damned pretty, with the light filtering through the trees that grew thick all around it.

Nick had been tempted to take a soak in the pond where the falls splashed down. Even though it was raining, he'd still been hot and sweaty. But it seemed like the blackflies thought the spot was as nice as he did, and he'd decided not to linger. They'd still managed to find some exposed skin to feast on, even though the netting he wore protected his face, and his rain gear covered most of his body.

Another part of the wet was several ponds, and at the edge of one of them—a moose! He'd heard it before he'd seen it, and the sound had panicked him. He'd heard moose sounds described as low grunting, but his had made what sounded like a moan, a long, vibrating moan. He'd lurched toward the sound, sure he'd see an injured animal or hiker. Instead he'd spotted a moose, a female. Maybe it was just the males who grunted. Nick had stood there, frozen, staring. She'd stared back. Then she'd given another moan and plodded off. Amazing. Just amazing.

And at another patch of the wet stuff, he'd seen a beaver dam, no beaver, but still. Amazing. That's the word that kept coming into his head whenever he stopped walking, allowed his gaze to move up from the rocky, root-choked, muddy path, and looked around. He'd been right to come here. Yeah, his knees were aching from a long stretch where the trail made a steep descent. His lip still hurt. His feet felt like they were growing moss between his toes. His backpack seemed to be digging grooves into his shoulders. But being out here was worth it. He'd managed to achieve long stretches without thought. He'd tried meditation a few times and sucked at it, thoughts pounding at him the whole time. But today, at times he'd slipped into that meditative state without effort.

Now he just had to cross that stream, do a little more walking, and he could take off his shoes and put on dry socks. That would be bliss. Something else two days of hiking had given him—a deep appreciation of things he usually took for granted, like dry socks. He promised himself when he was back home, he'd remember to be grateful for dry socks. And warm food. Probably by the time he got to the top of Katahdin, he'd have dozens of things on his gratitude list. That was enough of a reason to be out here. He'd spent way too much time lately walking around feeling like his life sucked, when he had so much.

Nick scanned the trees on the opposite side of the *stream* and saw a white blaze on one of them. Something else he was grateful for? All the people who kept this trail marked. And the person who had strung a rope from that tree to one on his side.

He'd managed to rock-hop across several smaller streams that day, but the current was faster here, and he appreciated having the rope to keep him steady.

"Okay, let's go." Every mile he was out here, it seemed like he talked to himself more. But who cared? Nobody. Because nobody was around to hear him. He walked over to the rope and grabbed it with both hands. The first rock was one easy step away. It was flat, which Nick had learned meant it could be slick with algae, but with the rope to help him keep his balance, it should be no problem. He took the step, slid just a little because, yeah, it was slimy, then, after he made sure he was steady, he took another.

"Lather, rinse, and repeat," he muttered as he kept moving. About a third of the way across he hit a spot where the next rock he needed would definitely take more than a step. More than a hop. More like a leap. And the top was smooth, which meant it would probably be slippery.

Nick decided to wade the rest of the way. If he tried jumping it and fell, he could lose his grip on the rope. Wading, with the rope to help keep him on his feet, seemed less risky. He loosened the shoulder straps on his backpack and undid the hip belt. He should have done that back onshore. If he did land in the water, the pack could drag him under and hold him there until he drowned.

"And on that cheery note . . ." Nick tightened his grip on the rope and stepped into the stream. The cold water only came up to midcalf. He could feel the current tugging on him, but with the rope, he didn't have a problem staying upright. He locked his eyes on the blaze painted on the tree on the opposite shoulder and slowly moved toward it, now even more grateful to the person who had tied the line around the trunk.

After about ten steps, he realized he was humming "500 Miles" and laughed. He hated that song, but somehow, he'd managed to hear it at least five hundred times in his life. Hadn't even the Chipmunks covered it? He began to sing it, doing his best Alvin.

He took another step, and his foot plunged into a hole. The current hit his knees instead of his calves, and he went down, unable to keep his fingers on the rope. His head went under.

He gasped, inhaling a lungful of water. Thrashing his arms and legs, he struggled to reach the surface. Don't, he told himself. Don't. He shoved away his instincts to fight against the water, forcing his body to remain still. Then moving deliberately, he shrugged out of the pack. Without its weight, he popped back to the surface and managed to suck in some air. He wanted to swim as hard as he could for shore, but overrode his instincts again. He knew what he was supposed to do. He'd read the articles. He'd watched the videos. He got himself onto his back, feet up, and lifted his head to survey what was downstream.

Boulder coming up. He angled his feet and managed to push himself off when he hit it. Okay, what now? He kept scanning the water ahead of him. Eddy! An eddy up ahead, over to his left. The water would be slower. If he could get himself to it, he might have a chance. He began to backstroke, angling against the current.

Crazily, inside his head, "500 Miles" started up again, Alvin squeak-singing. Nick began matching his strokes to the beat.

Annie got a fire going in the living room. She didn't need it, but it was gray and drizzly out, and she wanted the light and color of the flames at least as much as their warmth. She was just feeling . . . off. Which was weird, because Chloe was in town and was going to be here for the whole summer. That should have been more than enough to boost Annie's mood, but instead she felt itchy and restless.

She considered flopping down on the couch, but decided to stretch out on the rug instead, so she'd be in the optimal position for flame gazing. Almost immediately, she stood back up.

Lying on the rug brought up memories of having sex with Seth in the same spot. And thinking of Seth made her think of what Chloe had said—that Annie had never really been in love.

Was that true? Or did Annie just expect love to feel different from what she'd felt with Seth? Had she really loved him? she wondered as she wandered into the kitchen, twisting and wriggling out of her bra as she went. She always got her bra off pretty much as soon as she got home. Rings, too. And shoes. They made her feel encumbered, and when she got home, she wanted to be comfy.

Deciding she wasn't hungry or thirsty, she headed back into the living room, settling in her favorite armchair. Her thoughts returned to the whole love thing. Okay, so she hadn't minded much when Seth left. But what about before him? There'd been Gray. And those months with him had been scorching. But they'd burned out fast, both of them realizing that even though their bodies were a perfect match, their personalities weren't. There was Tomas. But they'd had almost the opposite problem. Good conversation, liked the same movies, the same music, the same books. But not much spark, forget about enough fire to scorch.

Spark. That made her think of Honey, and her insistence that Annie and Nick had a spark between them. Maybe they had. But her time with Gray had shown her spark wasn't everything. Although the spark with Nick, and she'd admit, at least to herself, that there'd been a spark, hadn't been only physical. He was quick-witted and funny and she liked that sparring-teasing that they'd gotten into. But he was also careless. It was careless to go off onto the trail without being as prepared as possible. And Annie hated careless.

Thinking about Nick, her fingers got that twitchy feeling. She wanted her phone. She wanted to check on him. But she'd checked on him as soon as she got home, and he was doing fine.

He'd get to the Long Pond Lean-to early, but not so early that he'd decide to press on. She figured after two days, even short-ish days, on the trail, he'd be looking forward to getting into some dry clothes, especially dry socks, and getting some food and some sleep. The mice would probably be ready and waiting for him. Careless hikers would have trained them to associate people with food. But she thought Nick could deal with the mice, especially since his mummy bag would cover the top of his head.

Maybe she should text Chloe, make sure she was settled in okay. But Chloe had said she wanted to get some writing time in that night. She'd spent the day learning the ropes at Vixen's, because of course Honey and Charlie had hired her. They al-ways needed help during hiking season, and they both adored Chloe.

And Honey would be completely behind Chloe's desire to see The Fox. Honey thought love was everything, just the way Chloe did. Honey was probably mentally matchmaking al-ready, considering every eligible male in Fox Crossing. Not that she would stop there. She'd have her feelers out with friends from Portland to Frenchville, asking about sons and grandsons and nephews.

Which, fine. But Annie wished so much of the way Chloe felt about herself wasn't tied to how some guy felt about her. Annie hadn't quite realized that was true for Chloe, until Chloe'd had that little outburst in Flappy Jacks that morning. Maybe doing research for her thesis would help her work her way through connecting her self-esteem to anyone but herself.

It was possible. Annie didn't have a guy around to make her feel good about herself. But she did feel good. Mostly. Except tonight. When she felt moody and restless, twitchy and itchy.

She got up and walked out onto the porch, the setting sun obscured by clouds. A high-pitched cry sent a shiver through her. She knew it was just a fox, even though it sounded almost like a woman screaming. That song would never have gone viral if it had real fox sounds in it. The real deal was no "ring-ding-ding-ding-dingeringeding!"

The Fox could see things now that she couldn't in her early years, the years before the cold, the hunger, and the thirst almost took her life as she lay trapped and bleeding, before The Woman saved her. She'd always known, deep inside, that everything in her world was connected, but now she could actually see the connections, those between predator and prey, between mate and mate, mother and kit, root and earth, star and river. The connection that formed between her and The Woman had opened her eyes, opened her heart. The Fox lifted her head and let out a cry over the beauty and pain of all those connections.

The woman was close. The woman who was blood of The Woman, the younger of the two now living. The Fox focused on her, letting everything else fade. This woman's connections to the mountains, trees, earth, river, were stronger than most. She also had powerful connections to other humans nearby. The Fox saw the connections as shimmering cords of light, some so bright they dazzled her eyes. A new cord had recently formed, thin, very thin, but there was shine there. As she watched, that cord began to vibrate, then tremble and twang. The Fox had seen this before. The connection was close to snapping. Watching it, an involuntary scream of warning escaped her throat.

The cry came again, closer, and Annie turned toward the sound. In the half-light of the cloudy evening, she could still see that the fox had unusual markings. One almost-white ear. One white sock. Black-tipped tail. The little hairs on the back of her neck prickled. It was The Fox. It was real.

She had to get a picture. Honey would kill her if she didn't.

And she owed it to Chloe and Banana after she'd pretty much tried to convince them The Fox was dead. She rushed back into the house, grabbed her purse off the kitchen counter, and pulled out her phone. The Fox was still there, sitting as if posing for Annie, her one white paw placed slightly in front of her body.

Annie took as many pics as she could before The Fox turned and trotted toward the woods that ringed the lake. A moment later, it disappeared. "Holy cannoli," Annie muttered, using one of her grandfather's favorite expressions. Then, since the phone was in her hand and all, she pulled up the tracker app. Nick was moving fast.

Way too fast. Her gut clenched when she realized he wasn't on the trail.

He was in the river!

Nick knew he had to find a way to get warm. But he needed to rest first. Just a little. It had taken everything he had to get himself over to shore and haul himself out. His rain gear had a tear in one leg, but was still giving some protection from the wet, muddy ground and the rain that was pattering down on him.

He allowed his eyes to close. He'd rest for a few minutes. Just one or two. Then what? He had no dry clothes, no food, no tracker. Everything had been swept down the stream—no, the river—with his backpack.

Hopelessness swamped him. He was going to die out here. This is how it happened. A misstep, leading to catastrophe, leading to death. Another life claimed by the Appalachian Trail. Another unprepared hiker meets his doom. "Guess Annie Hatherley was right about me," he muttered.

Speaking her name sent a jolt through him. Annie Hatherley wouldn't be lying here in the mud, not even for two minutes. She'd be fighting for her life with everything she had.

Had he used up everything he had? No. He grabbed on to

the exposed roots of a nearby tree and used them to haul himself to his feet. Immediately his right ankle rolled, and he went back down, with a hiss of pain. He'd turned the ankle when he stepped into that hole, turned it or broken it.

So, options. He could crawl. It would keep him moving at least. Or he could look for something to use as a crutch. . . . He scanned the area around him. Over there, a downed branch that might work. He dug his fingers into the mud and hauled himself toward it. The squelching, sucking sound he made sounded like a long fart, and he laughed like a nine-year-old boy would. Better than whimpering. He felt like whimpering. Instead, he planted his fingers in the mud again and pulled himself forward again.

The shelter. He needed to get to the shelter. It wasn't far. Probably not much more than a mile. He started to laugh again and realized he was borderline hysterical. Minus the borderline. Focus on the shelter, he ordered himself. It would at least give him three walls and a roof. It would get him off the cold ground. It might not be enough to save him. But it was the only shot he had.

When he reached the branch, he didn't allow himself to rest. Rest and you wake up dead. Ha. He was cracking himself up. He used both hands to lift the branch and jam one end into the mud, then used it for support as he got his good foot under him and got himself upright.

He took one step with his good foot, then managed a step with the bad one, letting the branch take some of his weight. All he had to do was lather, rinse, and repeat about—How many steps in a mile? Didn't matter. He had no choice but to go until he got there. There was no Plan B. He'd just pretend he was Annie Hatherley. A stupid Annie Hatherley. The real Annie Hatherley wouldn't have put her foot down without testing the bottom.

He stopped abruptly. The real Annie Hatherley also wouldn't go walking off into the woods without looking for a trail blaze. He'd almost walked into the freaking Maine woods with no map, no compass, no nothing.

Annie pulled her SUV to a stop. This was the closest she could get on the logging road. She leaped out, strapped on her headlamp, and hoisted her emergency kit over one shoulder. Don't be dead, don't be dead, don't be dead, she thought as she walked. Yes, walked. She wanted to run, but running over the boulders and roots, in the rain, in the dark, not smart. She'd only end up needing to be rescued herself.

The headlamp she wore let her see a few feet in front of her. *Don't be dead, don't be dead, damn you, Nick Ferrone, don't you dare be dead.* Except he was. The tracker showed him in the water. Maybe he'd been slammed into a rock or gotten caught under a downed tree. Maybe he'd drowned before she even checked on him tonight. Maybe the tracker was on his corpse.

But she had to make sure. He had to be dead, but she had to make sure. Don't be dead, said the tiny piece of her that had hope. The tiny ridiculous part of herself. He was dead. All she was going to do was, maybe, bring his body back.

She reached the edge of the river. The tracker said he should be here. She pulled her LED flashlight out of her pack and flicked it on, then pointed it at the water. The beam trembled. Because her hand was trembling. She tightened her grip. She didn't see him, but the tracker said he was here. She scanned the water more slowly, then she saw it, his backpack snagged by a rock.

Maybe he'd known enough to loosen his pack before he tried to ford the river. Maybe it had gone down the river without him, and he'd managed to get himself to shore. She was finding him, alive or not. She pulled out her phone and opened the tracker. It only took seconds to confirm that before Nick, or Nick's backpack, had started the fast movement downriver, he'd been on the trail. She decided to backtrack to the spot where she knew there was a rope strung to help with the crossing. Which didn't mean that spot was always the best place to cross. Nick probably hadn't known that. He should have if he'd fully prepped. But he probably hadn't. So, she'd go to the place with the rope and slowly walk down the river until she found him. Maybe, probably not, but maybe he'd still be alive.

Annie walked at a reasonable pace back to her SUV and drove as close as she could to the crossing. It only took about nine minutes. Then at a horribly slow, reasonable pace, she hiked to the edge of the stream. The rope was intact, but she didn't see Nick. She began picking her way downstream, stopping frequently to study the bank and the water. About half a mile down, she spotted a section of mud that looked as if something had been dragged across it. She headed across it. Her heart felt like it rolled in her chest when she saw tracks. Human. The person who'd made them had clearly been injured and was using a branch as a makeshift cane. Nick. It had to be Nick. And he was alive.

She didn't know that. All she knew was that he'd made it out of the river. The urge to run was almost overpowering. But that would be a stupid choice, and Annie didn't make stupid choices, at least not out here in the woods.

Even when she saw Nick lying on the ground, she wouldn't let herself rush to him. She maintained her careful pace, then, when she finally—finally, finally, finally—reached him, she dropped to her knees. "Nick. I'm here. You're going to be okay."

"Amnie?" he mumbled, blinking up at her.

"Yeah, it's Annie. Annie to the rescue."

Okay, he was conscious. She did a quick evaluation. Pale

skin. Dilated pupils. And way too still. He should be shivering violently, but he wasn't. That meant his body was shutting down to conserve on glucose.

"Do you . . . like chickmups?"

"Chipmunks? Sure. Why not. They're cute." She had to work against her instincts. She wanted to rub warmth back into his skin, but that could cause him to go into cardiac arrest. She opened her pack and pulled out a tarp and an EnsoLite pad. She put the tarp down first, then laid the pad on it. He needed insulation between his body and the ground. Next, she unzipped a sleeping bag and spread it on top of the pad, then smoothed a plastic sheet on top of the bag. "I'm going to move you over onto this." Slow and gentle, she coached herself. Keep it slow and gentle.

Nick struggled to sit up. "No." Annie put her hands on his shoulders to stop him. "Let me do it. You stay still."

"You're not . . . bosh of me." His words, especially *boss*, came out slurred.

"Yeah, you're right. You're the boss of you and look where it got you. Now stay still." She managed to ease him on top of the pile she'd made, then carefully began stripping off his clothes.

"Hey." He clumsily batted at her hands. She ignored him and kept working. He batted at her again. "Hey. Dorn't. Um-uh."

Slow and gentle, she thought again, as she got the last of his clothes off, using her knife to slice the cloth when she had to. As she began maneuvering him into dry clothes, he protested, "Toosh hut. No."

Hot. He'd said he was hot. That meant the cold was paralyzing the nerves in the walls of his blood vessels, and they were dilating. That's why he felt hot. Annie felt fear and panic slice through her. He was in the last stages of hypothermia. He needed to be in a hospital—now. But she couldn't do that until she got him warmed up enough to walk to the SUV.

She shoved her emotions down. She had to focus. She began activating warmer packets and placing them on his cold skin— under his armpits, on his chest, on his groin, and on both sides of his neck.

"No. Hut. Hut," Nick insisted, continuing to struggle weakly.

"Shhh. Shhh," Annie crooned. She folded the bottom of the plastic sheet up over his legs, then folded over each side, picturing the instructions for the hypothermia "burrito" wrap as she worked. Next, she zipped him into the mummy bag, then used the same steps she had with the plastic sheet to wrap him in the tarp. He rocked back and forth, trying to free himself. She straddled him to keep him still.

She reached over and pulled a thermos out of her pack. She'd taken the time to mix hot water and Jell-O packets before she left the house, even though everything in her had been urging her to go, just go, and get to Nick as fast as possible. She'd known he'd need the sugar and warmth.

"Open your mouth." As Annie used one hand to help him lift his head, she repeated more sharply, "Open your mouth." This time he obeyed, and she poured a little of the warm sugary water down his throat.

Nick sputtered and coughed. Annie waited until he'd swallowed, then gave him another mouthful. The liquid went down more easily.

He mumbled something. Her name was the only word she heard.

"Shhh. Don't talk. We're going to get you warmed up. You're going to be fine. You're going to be just fine."

Please, please, please. Please be okay. The thought was more of a prayer.

All Annie could do now was watch him and be ready to start

CPR. As he warmed up, his heart could start beating erratically or stop.

"I wersh going to shtop thinking about yoush. Alwaysh thinking yoush," he told Annie. Always thinking about her? What did that mean? It meant he was out of his head. Proof? He began to sing that five-hundred-miles song in a shaky falsetto. About ten minutes later, she felt a violent shudder go through his body. His teeth clacked together, and he stopped singing.

"You're shivering. That's good. That's so good." His body's heat-regulating system had kicked in.

His eyebrows came together. "Anniesh?"

"Yep. I'm here. I'm right here with you. As soon as you get warmed up enough to walk, I'll get you to a hospital."

"Whsssh." He cleared his throat and tried again. "What hashened?"

"What happened is that you fell into the stream. Probably because you chose the wrong place to cross." Anger started mixing with her fear now.

"Why are yoush sishing on me?"

"To keep you still. I wrapped you up to keep you warm, and you kept trying to get free." He looked confused. His body bucked as he tried to sit up. She leaned forward and put her hands on his shoulders. "Don't try to move." Her face was so close to his, she could see that his chestnut-colored eyes were ringed in a darker brown.

"Why are you alwaysh telling me whasht to do?"

She let go of his shoulders and pulled a Snickers out of her jacket pocket. She opened it, bit off a piece, and held it to his lips. "Eat this." She didn't bother replying to his question. Obviously, he still wasn't thinking clearly, or he'd know she was always telling him what to do because he was too stupid to decide for himself.

Nick let her put the piece of Snickers in his mouth. He finished it, and she gave him another. When he'd finished the whole bar, Annie studied him. "Do you know where you are?"

"Wooshds." He corrected himself: "Woods. Got ankle shtuck croshing river."

He was still slurring, but was not as confused as he had been. "I think we should try to get you on your feet." She climbed off him and began unwrapping the layers that covered him. "I don't know if you remember, but you sprained your ankle. Lean on me as much as you can." She moved to his side and helped him get one arm around her shoulder. "Okay, on three. One, two, and three."

Nick let out a yelp of pain as he lurched to his feet, Annie taking as much of his weight as she could. "Now we're going to walk, and we're not going to stop walking until we get to the logging road and my SUV. Deal?"

"Deal."

They started forward slowly. Annie could hear his breathing grow ragged after only a few steps. Cardiac arrest was still a possibility, but she had to risk it. The temperature had dropped to about forty, and it would probably start to rain again. She had to get him off the trail and indoors.

"Got to rest," Nick told her when they were only about halfway to the road. He started to lower himself to the ground.

"No!" Annie grabbed his wrist to keep his arm around her. "It's not much farther. I know you can do it. Come on." If he went down, she might not be able to get him up again. "Come on." She started to sing the five-hundred-miles song. A moment later Nick joined in, in his quivery falsetto. They sang the song again and again until Annie's SUV came into view. "We're almost there. See, there's the road."

Annie had to help Nick into the seat. Then she had to buckle the seat belt for him. He didn't have his coordination completely back. When she got herself behind the wheel, she looked over and saw his head lolling. "Nick!" It took a long moment for him to look over at her. Was he starting to slip into unconsciousness? "What's my name?" she asked. He just stared at her. "Who am I?"

"Annie Hatherley," he finally said. He wasn't slurring. That was something. "To the rescue."

"Damn right." Annie turned the key in the ignition and started for the hospital. "I'm saving your ass."

CHAPTER 7

Nick heard soft snoring. Had he ended up going home with someone? He'd gotten kind of drunk at the bar. But after that— Everything rushed back into his brain. Hiking. Rock, roots, mud. Mr. Bill and Loon. The stream/river. Annie. The hospital.

He opened his eyes. He was in a hospital bed. IV in his arm. He turned his head without lifting it from the pillow and saw her. Annie. Sprawled out on a recliner, snoring lightly. As if she sensed him looking at her, she opened her eyes. They stared at each other, and Nick could almost see the memory of the night before returning to her.

"You stayed."

Annie sat up. "I need coffee." She stood and started for the door.

"Wait." She paused and looked at him over her shoulder. "Thank you for saving my life."

She gave a dismissive hand flip. "It's what I do." And with that, she was gone.

It's what she *did*? What the hell? She rescues him, she stays all night with him in the hospital, then she acts like—Like what? Like he was a stranger? Well, he practically was. Nick let out a long breath and did an inventory on his body. He felt banged up pretty much everywhere, his right ankle was throbbing dully, and his arms and legs felt heavy, as if he'd run a marathon. Not that he'd ever run a marathon, but it's what he imagined they'd feel like if he had.

He tried to bring up more details from the time after he got knocked into the river by the current. He remembered leaning on Annie, leaning hard, as she led him to her SUV, but he didn't remember her finding him. He thought she'd been sitting on him. . . . But that didn't make sense. Had he been singing like Alvin the Chipmunk? That really didn't make sense. He must have been seriously out of it for a while. Had he said anything crazy?

"Was I singing like a chipmunk?" he asked when she walked back in with a large coffee.

"Was that what you were doing? I hadn't thought of it as a chipmunk, but, yeah." Annie took a swig of her coffee. Before he could ask her another question, she said, "You were pretty out of it yesterday. I figure you probably need a recap."

"Yeah."

"Stage three hypothermia, when I found you. By the time I got you here, the ER doc pegged you at stage two."

"Is that better or worse?"

"Better. You get worse than stage three, you're dead." Annie's tone was brisk and matter-of-fact. "They gave you an IV of warm fluids just to be on the safe side, and now, you're basically recovered. No more signs of hypothermia. They want to watch you the rest of the day to make sure you don't have any complications."

"What kind of complications?" He wished she'd come all the way in and sit down, instead of hovering just inside the doorway.

"Mostly irregular heart rhythms. But you're hooked up to a

monitor, and it's not going off, so you're probably good. Also, you sprained your ankle. Partial ligament tear. You won't need a cast or splint or anything. They'll give you some exercises," Annie rattled off. "I have to get to my store, but I'll come pick you up tonight. You're in Greenville. You probably didn't know that."

"I didn't." That's all he could come up with. He was still trying to process everything she'd said.

"No hospital in Fox Crossing, and you needed a hospital." She took another swig of coffee. "So, I'll be back later."

"Annie, just a sec." But she was already gone. Again. He had more questions, and he wanted to really thank her for coming after him. How had she even known he needed help? He'd lost the beeper along with his backpack.

Well, at least she'd said she'd be back. He closed his eyes, and once he did, he realized how exhausted he was. He let the darkness pull him down.

Annie knew her store was fine. Her mother was pinch-hitting, and she'd run the place longer than Annie had. Her mother would probably have Cody, one of two new seasonal employees Annie had hired, completely trained by the time Annie got there.

But first a shower, long and hot, she decided as she pulled the SUV up in front of her cabin. She texted her mom as she headed inside, telling her that she'd be in, in about an hour. Before she reached the bathroom, she received an answer, her mother ordering her not to come in at all.

She could ignore the text. She ignored her mother at least half of the times she gave one of her orders, but ignoring her would involve a face-to-face argument, since her mother was already at the store, and Annie didn't feel up to that today. She'd been awake most of the night, her gaze moving from Nick to the monitor over his head, where she checked his heart rate and temperature.

Maybe she'd split the difference—have a shower, have a nap, then go in. But after the shower, her body felt warm and heavy, almost liquid, and she knew if she got into bed, she'd sleep the whole day away. Her mother could handle anything that came up. Annie knew that for certain. Maybe, just this once, she'd let her. Annie climbed into bed and started to lie down, then sat back up.

She needed to set her alarm or she might sleep right through going to the hospital to pick up Nick. He was supposed to be good to go around six. She reached for her cell, then hesitated. What was she doing? She wasn't responsible for the noob, not anymore. She'd gotten him safely off the trail, and he was going to be fine. The doc had just wanted to keep an eye on him to make sure he wasn't going to get pneumonia or, don't even think it, a heart attack.

Annie had been in the room when they'd done an EKG, and she hadn't seen anything but a nice, even pattern, no clusters of irregular spikes. Once, around 4:00 a.m., Nick's monitor had started doing a fast, loud *beep-beep-beep*, lights on the screen flashing. She'd lunged to her feet and over to his side, her heart pounding so hard it felt like she was the one who should be hooked up to a monitor. But it was a false alarm. Nick's finger had slipped out of the sensor.

Later that morning, when she'd gone for coffee, Annie had been able to finagle a look at his blood and urine test results. No sign of kidney or liver damage. Which meant Annie had managed to bring him in, in time. She'd done her duty, and then some, by staying the night. She wasn't responsible for him, not anymore.

She lay back down, setting the cell on her nightstand, then

sat right back up again. She wasn't responsible for him, but she'd told him she'd give him a ride home. Annie suddenly realized she was nibbling at the cuticle of her thumbnail. She whipped her hand away from her mouth. She hadn't done that for years. Years!

Okay, she wasn't responsible for Nick, but she'd promised him a ride. He was in Greenville, and it's not like he could call an Uber to get back to town. She was the closest thing he had to a friend in town. Except Banana! He'd gotten drunk at Banana's place. Banana could go get him.

Annie made a quick call, and, of course, Banana said he'd go get Nick. Banana was like that. Annie was usually like that, too. But today, she was exhausted. Yeah. She was just too tired to drive back to Greenville.

She put the phone back on the nightstand and snuggled under the covers. Somehow, even though she'd arranged for Nick to get back to town and had completely done her duty, she found herself thinking of him. About what he'd said when she found him. About how he was thinking about her too much. What did that mean? What had he been thinking? Was he thinking about how right she was about his chances on the trail? Or something else?

There was no reason to try to interpret his words. He was delirious when he'd said them. Around the same time, he was singing like Alvin the Chipmunk. That proved he wasn't in his right mind. She flipped over onto her left side, then switched back to her right. She couldn't get comfortable. Sitting up all night in that recliner had probably messed up her back. She rolled onto her stomach. What was she doing? She was never able to sleep on her stomach. Annie returned to her right side. That's how she always slept. That was normal. And that's what she wanted—normal.

When the phone woke her, Annie wasn't sure if she'd been

asleep one hour or ten. She felt groggy. "Hello?" Nobody answered. Annie realized she was holding the phone upside down and flipped it. "Hello?"

"Time to get up." It was her mother. She could be so annoying. She was the one who thought Annie needed rest, and now she was giving Annie a wake-up call. "Come meet your grandmother, Chloe, and me at the BBQ."

"I hardly got any sleep last night," Annie complained, but she climbed out of bed as she spoke. Her mother was going to win this one. Annie was only half-awake, and she needed to be fully charged to go head-to-head with her mom.

"You won't sleep at all tonight if you don't get up for a little while. And you need to eat dinner, so you might as well eat with us. Besides, Chloe just got into town. You've hardly seen her."

"Fine." Annie hung up without saying goodbye. She grabbed her gray maxi dress off the rocking chair in the corner of the room. A little wrinkled, but it always got a little wrinkled a few minutes after she put it on anyway, so she yanked it over her head, added her pointy-tocd fake-snakeskin ankle boots and a jean jacket. She stopped by the bathroom for a hair check. A little fluffing with her fingers and it was good to go. She loved short hair.

The walk into town woke her up completely. Banana should have picked Nick up by now. She checked her texts in case Banana had given her an update on how he was doing. Nope. Nothing from Nick either. Why would there be? He'd already told her thank-you. What else was there to say?

When she reached the BBQ, she paused for a moment before she went inside, giving Nogan the chance to pounce. "Annie! Don't eat dessert in there," Noah exclaimed. "It's four bucks for a brownie. We're selling them for three."

"Ours are a lot better, too," Logan added.

"What are you two trying to buy this time?" Last year

they'd saved up for a trampoline, which now sat in Logan's backyard.

"Seats on the first SpaceX flight to Mars," the two boys said together.

"Okay, I'll take one." Annie opened her purse, but before she could take out her wallet, Piper, who'd been waitressing at the BBQ as long as Annie could remember, opened the door.

"What did I tell you two?" Piper demanded. "No badgering customers."

"She's not a customer yet," Logan protested.

"And we're not badgering. We're offering a service," Noah chimed in.

"Well, move along and offer your service somewhere else." Piper flapped her hands at them, and they retreated around the corner. She shook her head and held the door open for Annie. Annie wished her mother hadn't called her. She wasn't feeling social. She was feeling . . . she didn't know what she was feeling, but she did know that she didn't want to be here. But here she was, so she stepped inside.

Chloe gave her a wave from Annie's mother's favorite table— dead center, so she could see everyone. Actually, it was Annie's grandmother's favorite table, too, and for the same reason. But her mother wanted to see people to take the temperature of the town, get votes, things like that. Her grandmother just liked to people watch. It gave her more to gossip about.

"I ordered you your usual," her mother said when Annie sat down.

"Thanks." Annie hated it when her mother ordered for her. What if she wanted something different? She didn't, but what if? Man, she was feeling irritable. She had to get over it. She turned to Chloe. "How was the first day at Fox 'R' Us?"

"Vixen's," Honey corrected, even though obviously Annie knew what the shop was called. "And why aren't you advertising for me?"

Dang it. Annie usually wore something from Vixen's, even if it was something little. Honey was always giving her fox things. "Sorry, Honey. I forgot. But I think Chloe's got the advertising covered in this area of the restaurant." Annie's friend was completely foxed out—fox hair clips, fox earrings, fox necklace, fox decals on her nails, VIXEN'S T-shirt over a skirt covered with foxes wearing skirts covered with foxes.

"Are you wearing the underwear, too?" Annie asked, then realized she already knew the answer. "What I meant was, which pair did you choose?" The shop sold several styles, including one with a big fox face over the butt, complete with ears that extended up a few inches above the waistband.

Chloe laughed. "The high-cut briefs with the foxes all over."

"You're shameless, Honey," Belle said. "I hope you're paying Chloe for being a walking, talking billboard."

"She has to be familiar with the merchandise so she can sell it," Honey told them.

"And now that I'm wearing the undies, I can say they are comfy as well as cute."

"See? That's what the customers want to know." Honey patted Chloe's arm. "This one is a natural salesman."

"Salesperson," Belle corrected, and Honey rolled her eyes.

Piper arrived and set a pulled-pork sandwich and double coleslaw in front of Annie. "Nogan just asked me if I'd buy their brownies and sell them here, since I won't let them sell on the sidewalk. They offered me seven and a half percent."

"Maybe I should have a talk with them about cottage-food licenses, and licenses to sell food from the sidewalk." Belle started to type a note into her phone.

"Don't be silly," Honey scolded. "The boys are part of the town charm. People love them. Check out hashtag Nogan if you want proof."

"They've grown up so much since last time I was here. They

were just out of first grade. Now they're entrepreneurs," Chloe said.

"I buy something from them pretty much every day," Annie admitted. "I have a hard time resisting them."

"You've always had a soft heart. Remember that summer when you had me and Miranda help you decorate boxes for recycling batteries and fluorescent light bulbs?" Chloe asked. "We talked businesses all over town into putting them out."

"You should show your customers some of your heart," Honey commented. "It would improve your Yelp ratings, for one thing."

"Since I turned the business over to Annie, the ratings for Hatherley's Outfitters have gone down everywhere," Belle told Chloe. "They don't like her attitude."

"What attitude? I've known her forever. She's delightful." Chloe grinned at Annie. Annie forced herself to smile back. She didn't care if people didn't like her, but she did care if her mother thought she was hurting the family business. Sales were still good. That's what mattered. You wanted supplies before or after the Wilderness, you went to Hatherley's. Only place in town.

"She *is* delightful," Honey agreed. "She just doesn't want anyone to get hurt on the trail, so she is a little *discouraging* to people she doesn't think are ready for the Wilderness."

"A little discouraging?" Belle repeated. "She practically escorts them out the door, like a bouncer with an ugly drunk."

"That's what I should have done with Nick Ferrone. I knew he wasn't ready, and he nearly died out there." Annie took a bite of slaw, but swallowed without tasting it, the memory of Nick's gray skin and glazed eyes filling her mind.

"Anyone can get hurt while—" Honey began.

"True," Annie interrupted. "But some things, a lot of them, are preventable. He had to know that fording streams was part of hiking the Wilderness. Did he bother to learn any techniques for finding the best place to cross? I don't think so. I think he saw the rope and was like, 'D'okay, that's where I go.'"

"You made him take the tracker," Belle reminded her. "Then you went out there and saved his life."

"Have you been saving lives again?" Chloe kicked her foot against Annie's. "How many is that?"

Annie shrugged.

"She's done twenty-seven—no, now it's twenty-eight—rescues, starting when she was seventeen," Belle answered for Annie, who was surprised her mother remembered the exact number.

Chloe leaned toward Annie. "Was this one really close to dying?"

"Yeah. Yeah." Annie flashed on Nick lying on the ground, motionless. "He'd almost gotten to the paradoxical undressing stage. I've never seen that before, heard about it, read about it, but not seen it. His body temperature couldn't have been much more than eighty. It was only eighty-three point one when I got him to the hospital. And there he was, telling me he was too hot."

"You really did save him. Wow. Is he still in the hospital?" Chloe asked.

"They wanted to watch him the rest of the day. Banana's probably got him back to town by now." Annie took a bite of her sandwich and again swallowed without registering how it tasted. And it was her favorite.

Honey raised her eyebrows. "Banana didn't tell me that."

Annie gave a mock gasp. "Oh, no. I wonder how long the Fox Crossing Gossip Network was down. Or"—she widened her eyes—"maybe it's still down." She hoped her theatrics would get them off the subject of Nick. Her responsibility to him was done, and she didn't want to keep talking about him.

"I can't believe I've been in town almost two days without going to Banana's. We're going to the Wit's Beginning right after dinner," Chloe told Annie.

Annie wasn't in the mood for Banana's place. She hadn't felt social enough for dinner, so she definitely wasn't up for a bar. "I'm still kinda tired."

"No." Chloe shook her head. "I'm not accepting that. I'm the visitor, and that means you have to do what I want."

Annie could refuse. It's not as if Chloe could physically drag her there. Annie was a lot stronger. But if she refused, it would become this whole big thing. And why make it a whole big thing? "Okay, fine."

"Okay, perfect." Chloe speared a bite of chicken salad. "Is everything the same between Miranda and Banana?" Her tone lost its playfulness. "When I asked him about her, he didn't say much."

"Afraid so," Belle answered.

"I was hoping they'd have fixed things somehow."

"She does the same thing her mom used to," Honey explained. "Banana calls and says he wants to come for a visit, and Miranda almost always has a reason it's not a good time. I think it's been almost seven years since they've seen each other face-to-face."

"I can't imagine going that long without seeing my dad." Chloe shot a look at Annie. "I'm sorry. I shouldn't have said that."

"It's fine. I never had a dad, not one that I knew anyway, so it's not like there's somebody to miss." Honey made a little tsking sound, but didn't comment. "This one's enough of a parent for me." Annie jerked her chin toward her mother. "I don't think I could handle another one."

"Thanks, baby." Her mother leaned over and gave Annie a one-armed hug. "Hatherley women. We don't need men." Together they did the biceps curl and *harrh*. Honey shook her head, but a smile tugged at her lips.

"That just gave me a great idea. I was telling Annie how

I'm going to write my thesis on self-esteem and romantic love."
This time Chloe didn't start to get emotional as she spoke. "I
could use the perspective of some Hatherley women." Chloe
gave a quick biceps curl and a soft *harrh*.

"Sure. Hit me," Belle answered.

"Okay, so I haven't had time to formulate the actual questions I want to use. I guess I'm kind of making you guinea
pigs." Chloe thought for a moment. "When you're in a relationship, do you think your self-esteem goes up, down, or stays
the same. And the other way around. When you're not in a relationship, do you experience a change in your self-esteem."

"Definitely no change," Belle answered with zero hesitation. "Self-esteem comes from within."

"But it's not inherent. You're not born with or without self-
esteem. You're not even born with a sense of self. It comes from
your experiences. Gradually, you form an image of yourself,"
Chloe said. "What I'm interested in, for my paper, is how much
romantic relationships affect self-esteem. If any," she quickly
added. Trying to be fair, because Annie knew Chloe felt a huge
effect. Annie hated that her friend couldn't see all the awesome
things about herself because she hadn't gotten married. Maybe
it was because her parents were so freakishly happy, one of
those couples who never stopped holding hands or kissing behind the menu when they went out to eat.

"I can say for certain that Charlie makes me feel good about
myself," Honey declared. "Sometimes when I wake up, I look
in the mirror, and I ask myself, 'Who is that old woman?' And
something shrivels up inside. But then Charlie calls me 'gorgeous,' and I feel gorgeous."

"Okay, but does that just happen with Dad?" Belle asked.
"What if I tell you, you look nice?"

"I appreciate it. But it's not the same."

"Does it have to be Grandpa? What if it's another man? Because we all know you love to flirt." Annie realized she'd taken another bite of her sandwich without tasting it. Dang it. She loved the BBQ's pulled pork.

"Hmmm." Honey gave a mischievous smile. "It depends on the man. Say, for example, Annie's hiker told me I'm gorgeous. That would make me feel pretty nice."

"Not my hiker." Annie felt like she had to keep making the point, even though no one paid any attention.

"Does Charlie ever get jealous?" Chloe picked up a red crayon and began drawing hearts on the butcher paper that covered their table.

"He knows he's my one and only." Honey grabbed a crayon and started putting pink arrows through Chloe's hearts.

"Tell me your fox story again." Chloe drew an extra-big heart.

The last thing Chloe needed was to hear another retelling of how The Fox brought together Annie's grandparents. Chloe's parents' own fox story is what had started her crazy quest. "Wait. I forgot to tell you!" Annie exclaimed. "I had a sighting! I saw The Fox!"

"How could you not tell us right away?"

"It happened last night. Going after Nick pushed it out of my head."

Chloe stopped doodling. "Tell me ev-er-y thing."

"There's not that much to tell. I heard that screaming sound foxes make sometimes, and I went out on my deck. The Fox was out there. Almost right in front of me. I took a few pictures because I knew I'd never be forgiven if I didn't. Before I sent them, I checked Nick's tracker, since my phone was already out. That's when I realized he was in trouble."

"Wow!" Chloe breathed. "The Fox is incredible."

"It didn't really do anything. It was just passing by. Although it did stick around long enough for me to take the pics."

"She doesn't get it," Chloe said to Honey, then turned back to Annie. "You don't get it. The Fox saved Nick's life!"

"Annie saved Nick's life," Belle protested.

"The Fox got Annie to check her phone at the right time," Chloe insisted.

"A little earlier would actually have been better." Annie wasn't going to give The Fox credit for psychic powers or whatever Chloe thought it had.

"But a little later and he would probably have died," Honey said.

"Okay, true. But seeing The Fox didn't change my luck. Not really. It changed Nick's, and he's not the one who saw it. You can't really count this as one for The Fox."

"Oooh. Maybe this is how The Fox is getting you two together." Chloe drew a big, fat heart in front of Annie. "I think you're going to end up marrying him."

Annie sighed. "I think I'm ready for that drink."

CHAPTER 8

"Sorry. They told me I'd be ready to be released at six." Nick sat on the edge of his hospital bed, wearing the clothes Annie had dressed him in the night before.

"It's the demon paperwork to blame," Banana answered, flipping through the channels on the TV, even though he hadn't found anything he wanted to watch during the other flip-throughs. "No worries. Big Matt is holding down the fort." Banana tossed the remote down when his phone chirped. As Nick watched, Banana's expression went from disbelief to astonishment to something like joy.

"What?" Nick asked. "Not that it's any of my business, but your face. You look like you got some incredible news."

"Annie saw The Fox! She even got a picture. Honey, her grandmother, sent it on." Banana held up the phone so Nick could look. The Fox was smaller than he expected, small and slender and—he searched for the right word—elegant, definitely. Self-possessed, maybe? Bold? The way it was looking right into the camera wasn't bold exactly, but The Fox somehow gave the impression that it was an equal to the person holding the camera. To Annie.

"I knew it existed. I knew it hadn't gone over the rainbow bridge. It was right outside her cabin. It's close. This is my year. I'm going to finally get those last miles." Banana punched the air, and for a moment he looked like a teenage boy instead of a sixtysomething man.

Nick slapped him a high five. After the air punch, it seemed appropriate. "What's the game plan? Surround Annie's place with chicken and bacon and all that odiferous stuff and hide in the bushes?"

"I'll have to think about it." Banana's brow crinkled. "I wonder if I've been going about it wrong, trying to use bait. The Fox just came to Annie. Maybe I have to let The Fox choose the time and place. Maybe trying to force it is even stopping it from happening."

Now that they were talking about Annie, maybe it would seem normal for Nick to ask some questions about her. He'd been wanting to since Banana walked in and said Annie hadn't been able to come. Maybe Nick could bring her up casually. "Why do you think The Fox picked Annie?" Nick wasn't sure The Fox actually picked anybody, but Banana believed, and Nick decided just to go with it.

"I'm asking Honey for details." Banana thumbed a text. "Maybe The Fox knew Annie wasn't a believer. She was just saying the other day that maybe The Fox had died, if it even existed." He held the phone up to Nick again. "Now, she has to know it absolutely exists. The markings are just the way they're always described. One mostly white ear. One paw that's white instead of the usual black. I have to ask if Annie got a look at the tail. The Fox's tail is supposed to have a black tip, instead of the usual white." Banana kept texting.

"Yeah, Annie told me that she didn't believe in The Fox. Maybe it—"

"She."

"Maybe, kind of like you were saying, *she* wanted to show Annie she was wrong." Nick definitely didn't think The Fox could somehow know what was said about it when it wasn't around. Or that it would understand if it was around. But he wanted to keep the conversation on Annie.

"Annie's hardheaded. Now she'll probably say that a fox with the special markings does exist, but it's just a descendant of the first fox, and no fox has the power to bring good luck. But just wait. Something lucky is coming Annie Hatherley's way."

Banana's cell chirped. "Another text from Honey." He read it, then looked at Nick. "This is so freaky. But freaky isn't freaky when it comes to The Fox. Honey says that Annie said she had her phone out to take a picture of The Fox, and since Annie had the phone out, that made Annie check the tracker. That's how she knew you were in trouble."

"Holy shit."

"Preach."

"The doctor said if Annie'd been even ten minutes later getting to me, I probably would have died."

"You got lucky." Banana clapped Nick on the shoulder. "Fox lucky."

"I hope Annie didn't get sick, being out in the cold looking for me." Nick was hoping that would prompt Banana to tell him why Annie'd decided not to pick him up herself.

"She just said she was tired." Banana didn't look up from the phone, as if he thought The Fox might leap out of it.

"Yeah. I bet she was. She stayed here all night."

That got Banana looking up. "She did?"

"They wanted to make sure I didn't have any organ damage, check out my heart, and liver, and kidneys. Maybe she didn't want to leave until they'd done all the tests."

"Makes sense. Annie takes her responsibilities seriously, and she was thinking of you as her responsibility." Banana shrugged. "I don't think she's done that for anyone else she rescued though." Nick was glad to hear it, even though he probably shouldn't have been. "Maybe they all had family or friends to stay with them, so she didn't feel like she needed to."

"I want to do something for her. To thank her. What do you think about me taking her to dinner? As a thank-you." And because Nick didn't want to leave before he saw her again.

"She might say there are no thanks necessary. She'd probably see it as doing what needed to be done. You'll have to be prepared to be persuasive."

Nick rubbed his jaw, feeling the stubble that had grown in. "Truth? I have no idea how to be persuasive with Annie Hatherley. She seems like someone who is dead certain about everything."

"You got that right. It runs in the family. Her mother, Belle, same way. She thinks she should make all the decisions about the town, no voting necessary. The annoying thing is, she's usually right."

"Annie was right when she said I wasn't ready to hike the Wilderness."

"Maybe so, maybe not. I have years of experience, and I haven't made it through the Wilderness. We're talking about nature, here. Humans can't control nature, much as we try."

"I was being so careful!" Nick burst out, frustration about how badly the hike had ended suddenly rushing through him. "I studied every patch of ground before I took a step! I was going to stop at the Long Pond shelter because I knew I needed rest before I went farther. And I crossed right where I was supposed to cross. Right where the rope line was strung. I could see a blaze on the tree right across the river from me. And, yes, I said *river*, because it is a river, no matter what you lobster eaters call it—"

Banana laughed. "Lobster eaters. I like that. And I'm from Virginia originally, so I'm with you on the river/stream thing. But, just so you know, a rope line isn't a guarantee it's a safe spot to cross."

"Someone went to the trouble of putting it there. I figured they must have chosen a good spot. And like I said, it was right in the trail line."

"Water flow isn't predictable like that. When the trail was blazed, the spot where you crossed was probably the best. But the weather, the temperature, even a new beaver dam, can change things."

Nick's burst of frustration about wiping out when he'd been doing everything right turned into shame. "I should have known that. I think I even read that somewhere. I read a ton of hiking advice. Not that I should have needed to read it. It's basic common sense. I just saw the rope, saw the blaze, and didn't bother to actually think."

"I've never met a hiker who hasn't made a stupid mistake. At least yours came with a relatively small price."

"Yeah." Nick ran his fingers over the plastic brace supporting his sprained ankle. "I could have slammed my head into a rock. At least I remembered to put my feet facing downstream."

"And you got yourself out."

"But I still would have died if Annie hadn't showed up." Nick suddenly felt cold again, cold as he had out in the woods. He really would have died if Annie hadn't shown up.

"A brush with death now and then helps keep things in perspective. I got a little shock myself the other day. A friend of mine has been telling me and telling me that this psychic she goes to is always right. She's been nagging me to go, so I finally told her okay."

Nick smiled. Banana had gone into storytelling mode, probably to distract Nick from thinking about how close he'd gotten to ending it.

"So, I get there, and the first thing this so-called psychic told me was that my father was going to be governor someday. I told her my dad's dead, and you know what she said?"

"No idea."

"She said, 'You have no clue who your real father is.'" Banana laughed and repeated the punch line. "That's another one from *Philogelos*."

"Seriously? You didn't really go to a psychic?" Nick tried to keep a straight face, but couldn't.

"Want another one? I—"

Banana was interrupted by a nurse rolling a wheelchair into the room. "You're good to go after I get one more signature." The nurse handed Nick a small electronic pad. "This is just to confirm that you've been given your discharge summary, which I am giving you now." He handed Nick a folder.

Nick signed. "I forgot to ask about driving."

"No driving while your ankle is in the brace. When you follow up with your GP in a week or so, they can give you an idea how long that will be."

"I guess I can take the train back home. Or maybe someone would come pick me up." Nick got a better idea. "Or I can just stay in Fox Crossing until I'm healed up. I was planning to be away two weeks anyway." Yeah, he'd stay. He'd see how that dinner with Annie went, once he managed to persuade her to go. That *click* didn't happen that often. He wanted to see where it led.

"At least tell me what he looks like," Chloe begged as she and Annie strolled toward Wit's Beginning, after a stop at the Hen House for ice cream cones.

"I'm not going to indulge your crazy. I wouldn't be a good

friend if I did." That was the truth. Fixating on The Fox bringing her the perfect guy wasn't doing Chloe any favors.

Chloe took a lick of her cinnamon ice cream. "I'm eating this every day I'm here. I've gone to tons of ice cream places, with all kinds of bizarre flavors—pickled mango, if you can believe that, at a place in Hawaii—but here is the only place I've had cinnamon. Just tell me what color hair he has."

Annie laughed. "Brown. Okay? He has brown hair. Brown hair with reddish highlights."

"Oooh. You took a good look, didn't you? Noticing the highlights."

"I'm observant in general." Was her face getting warm? She'd better not be blushing. There was nothing to be blushing about. At least it was dark, so Chloe couldn't see. If Chloe saw, she'd never shut up about it. "And he was in the store for a while. I did a shakedown for him. Now that's it. That's all you're getting. Tell me about Jules."

"She's engaged. And she's my little sister. It's so wrong. I'm going to have to be a bridesmaid, and I know she's going to make me wear mint green, because it's her favorite color, and we both know I look like not-so-fresh death in mint green." Chloe stopped licking her ice cream and took a big bite. "I love cinnamon. I'm still eating it every day. But now I'm upset and I must have chocolate. Trade me."

Annie took the cinnamon cone and handed Chloe her chocolate/chocolate chip. Chloe was dramatic. She'd always been dramatic. Like she wasn't really going to actually eat cinnamon ice cream every day. But underneath the hyperbole about her sister's engagement was a streak of real pain. Annie wished she knew what to say. She could tell Chloe that there were lots of great things about being single—*harrh*. But that wouldn't help. Maybe it was because Chloe's parents always made marriage look so wonderful, almost in a "Valentine's Day every day" kind of way. "Actually, mint green only makes you look a little washed-out."

Chloe gave a snort-laugh. "Nobody will be looking at me anyway. Everybody only looks at the bride," she muttered. "You know I know I'm being a baby and that I'm really very happy for Jules."

"I know."

"I'm keeping this." She waved the chocolate cone at Annie. "And I want another lick of that."

Annie handed over the cinnamon cone. "Have both. Some situations require two-fisted licking."

"You may have one of the cones when I'm done," Chloe pronounced with exaggerated magnanimity.

Annie smiled. Chloe knew that Annie liked the cone at least as much as the ice cream. That was the great thing about old friends. They knew so much. The little stuff, and the big stuff. Like Chloe also knew that Annie had followed Luke Caron around for almost one entire summer, making notes about, for example, what flavor of ice cream he ordered the most. Chloe knew because she was there.

Orange sherbet. Annie hadn't realized she still remembered Luke's favorite, but she had. Orange sherbet. Thinking about him still hurt. He was way too young to die.

Annie forced her thoughts back to Chloe. The other great thing? They could pick up where they left off whenever they got together, even if it had been years, even though they both sucked at keeping in touch. If they'd been better at it, Annie would have realized how desperate Chloe was feeling about still being single.

Chloe started walking faster when they turned the corner and Wit's Beginning came into view. "You won't tell me about your future husband, but Banana will." She burst into a run.

Annie chased after her. "Don't! He's not my future any-thing!"

They reached the brewery at the same time.

"My cinnamon ice cream fell off down the block." Chloe handed the empty cone to Annie. As soon as Annie started to take a bite, Chloe ducked inside. Still clutching the cone, Annie followed her, but Chloe reached the bar two seconds before Annie did.

"Banana! I want to know everything about the hiker Annie rescued. Everything!"

Banana looked from Chloe to Annie. "He seems like a decent guy. Good sense of humor."

"Translation—he laughs at your jokes," Annie said.

"What else? How old is he? What does he do? What does he look like?" Chloe leaned across the bar. "I need to know everything. It's Annie's future husband we're talking about." She spun to face Annie. "And when I'm your bridesmaid, you absolutely can't make me wear mint green."

"I'll do a nice, pale yellow instead." Annie had gone shopping with Chloe a bunch of times. Pale yellow really did make her look like not-so-fresh death.

Chloe slapped her on the arm, then returned her attention to Banana. "Why aren't you talking?"

"I'm scared of Annie. First drinks on the house for both of you."

Annie wanted to get off, way off, the subject of Nick, but she had to ask, "How's he doing?"

"See, you love him," Chloe teased.

Annie ignored her. Sometimes you just had to ignore Chloe.

"Good. Has to be on crutches for a few days and keep wearing the ankle support until a doc gives him the okay not to." Banana put beers in front of Annie and Chloe. Annie got hers in one of the special blue mugs for hikers who'd done the whole AT. "You can go see for yourself. He's in my guest room. I didn't want him to go back to the Inn until he can get around a little better."

Annie hesitated. She'd done her duty. But, still, he was over there by himself. He might need something. He had to be pretty weak, and he was on crutches. She looked over at Chloe. "You are not allowed to make a big deal of this, but, yeah, I'll go check on him."

Chloe made a clapping motion, but didn't let her palms touch, so there wasn't any sound. "That's me not making a big deal."

"Go through the kitchen and get him a plate of something," Banana told Annie. "Big Matt will hook you up."

Annie nodded. She thought about telling Chloe to come with her if she was so curious, but decided Chloe's energy level might be a little high for someone in a weakened state. "Back in a few."

"Take your time. Banana and I need to talk about The Fox, and where she's most likely to turn up next," Chloe answered.

About ten minutes later, Annie was carrying a foil-covered plate of Big Matt's special fully loaded cheeseburger and fries up the front steps of Banana's place. She knocked on the door, then opened it. "Don't try to get up," she called. "It's just me. Annie."

Nick didn't reply. Annie walked inside and found him asleep on Banana's beat-up leather sofa, one foot propped on a pile of pillows. She took the opportunity to study him. He was still so pale, the stubble on his face looking almost black in contrast. But he was fine. Banana had him all set up with his ankle elevated. She'd just leave the plate on the coffee table and go.

Soundlessly, she crossed the room. The plate made a soft clink as she set it down, and he opened his eyes.

"Annie. It's you."

It's you. Like he'd just been thinking about her. She still wondered what he'd meant out in the woods when he said he was thinking about her too much.

"Banana sent me over with food." Annie pointed to the plate and backed up a few steps. "Do you need anything? Something to drink or anything?" Before he could answer, she said, "Silverware. You need silverware." She hurried to the kitchen, then took her time with the cutlery. Seeing him, it felt . . . strange.

No, that wasn't the word. But she couldn't think of a better one. A lot of times people she'd rescued stopped by the store to say thanks. But it was after they were already up and around. Nick still looked so . . . vulnerable. It's like her brain had slid into low gear. Her thinking wasn't as fast as usual.

Maybe she was feeling . . . different with Nick because there was an intimacy to the hypothermia rescue. It was the first she'd done. Or maybe it was staying with him all those hours in the hospital. She'd never done that for a rescue, only for her grandfather when he had that angioplasty.

"Can't find it?" Nick called.

Annie held the knife and fork in one hand. "No, I got it." She put them back in the drawer. "But I just remembered it's a burger and fries. I'll get you some napkins instead. Did you want ketchup or anything? Something to drink?"

"Just some water."

Annie took her time getting a glass and filling it and taking napkins out of the drawer by the sink, but then there was no other reason to keep her in the kitchen. And no reason to want to stay in the kitchen. If anyone should feel . . . awkward, it should be him. He's the one who had gone off into the woods after she told him he wasn't ready.

She pulled in a deep breath and returned to the living room. She put the water and the napkins on the table, then clapped her hands. "Need anything else before I go?"

"You're going? Now?" Nick sounded alarmed.

"If you don't need anything else. Banana thought you'd want food, so I brought food." Honey would have had a fit if she'd heard that. Annie had sounded borderline rude. She hadn't meant to, but she had. "How are you feeling?" she added, hoping to make up for her brusqueness.

"Considering everything, good. Tired, but good. Thanks to you." He struggled to push himself higher up on the pillows behind his back. Should she help him? No, he had it now. "Thank you, Annie. I can't remember if I said it before, but even if I did, I owe you at least a hundred more."

"You don't owe me anything. It's what I do. Extraction. I know all those old logging roads. Before I could drive, I was riding on them with my mom."

"It might be routine to you, but it's not to me." Nick reached for the glass, and Annie picked it up and pressed it into his hand. "Can you sit down for a minute? My neck's starting to hurt looking up at you."

"Sure. Okay. Why not." Annie dragged one of the armchairs up close to the couch. She watched as Nick tried to get the foil off the plate one-handed.

"I'll do it." Annie removed the foil. How had she forgotten it was a burger and fries when she'd watched Big Matt dish them up himself. Nick had gotten her all . . . flustered. She picked up the plate and held it out.

"I didn't think I was hungry, but now that there's food in front of me, I'm starving." He took a bite of the burger. "Thanks for bringing this over."

"You're welcome," she answered, as if she had, as Honey would say, been raised among humans.

"*That* you let me thank you for." Nick shook his head, took another bite, then tried to stretch his arm out far enough to put the burger down.

"You're going to fall off the edge." Annie plucked the burger out of his hand, set it on the plate, then put the plate down on his lap. "That should work."

"Thanks."

"Would you please stop thanking me?" she demanded. He couldn't expect a *you're welcome* every time if he was going to say *thank you* every two seconds. She realized she was biting her cuticle and made herself stop.

"Okay, let me have it." He made a gimme motion with his fingers, like he was inviting her to come at him. "Here's the part where you say, 'I told you so.' "

"I told you so," Annie shot back. "I told you, you weren't ready. I told you, you were going to get hurt. And look what happened."

"Feel better now?"

"Actually, yes." She reached over and took one of his french fries.

"Me, too." When Annie reached for another fry, he caught her hand lightly in his, tightening his grip slightly when she started to pull away. "You saved my life. Can we both take one minute to acknowledge that? You saved my life, Annie."

She met his gaze directly for a long moment. Her chest tightened, and she realized she'd started holding her breath. She sucked in some air. "I'm glad I saved your life. I wasn't sure I was going to make it in time." Her voice was suddenly trembling. Her hands, too. It was like she was back on the logging road, almost sure she'd be too late. Almost sure the best she'd be able to do was retrieve his body. "I almost didn't." Her eyes were stinging now, and she blinked fast. She was not going to cry. She hated to cry, especially in front of someone. She wriggled her hand free and grabbed a french fry, breaking her gaze from his.

"In the Talmud it says something like if you save a single life, you save the whole world. That means you've saved the whole world more than once."

"Are you Jewish?" That should be a safe topic. She didn't want to say—or hear—anything that would make her feel like crying again.

"On my mom's side, which means yes. But on my dad's side, I'm Catholic."

"Take away the sides, and what are you?"

He thought for a moment. "I'm open. Open to all possibilities."

"A transcendentalist like Thoreau?"

"Close to that as anything. Speaking of, did you by any chance save my copy of *Walden*? Or did it end up in the trash?"

"I might have kept it with the dozen or so I've pulled out of other backpacks during shakedowns." Although his was the only copy she actually had. She'd eventually have donated it to the town's Little Free Library. Eventually.

"How about you give it back when I take you out to dinner?"

"Did I miss you asking me out to dinner?" Annie was finally easing back into what felt like her usual self. Now that they were past the intense part of the conversation. The way he'd looked at her while holding her hand . . . intense and . . . Again, she was struggling for the words. *Inquiring* . . . No. *Soul-searching* . . . Didn't matter. It was over. They'd moved on. They were back to where they'd been at the store—before she knew for sure how unprepared he was. Back to where they'd been at Flappy's—before she remembered how unprepared he was. Had that only been three days ago?

Nick was saying something. She pulled herself away from her thoughts and tuned back in to him. ". . . if I had asked you, what would you have said?"

"That shows a lack of—I can't even think what. I can't think straight tonight. I keep losing my words. Basically, it shows that you're a chickenshit. You don't get to know what I'm going to say before you ask. Ask if you want to find out."

"Would you like to go out to dinner with me? Let me do that much to thank you."

"I have to get back to the brewery." Now that she'd made

him ask, she wasn't sure what she wanted to say. "One of my friends is waiting over there for me."

"Now who's being chickenshit? I asked, and you didn't answer."

"Fine. Yes. Monday night. Seven o'clock." Annie stood up and started for the door, then paused and looked at Nick over her shoulder. "I'll drive. Since you obviously can't."

CHAPTER 9

Some nights, like this one, The Fox was pulled to the town, to the humans. Her connection to The Woman called her there to seek out the two females who shared The Woman's blood. She'd followed the youngest, enjoying the bright shine of the cord connecting her to the human female who walked alongside her, a cord that had been formed many years ago.

Her need fulfilled, she was ready to return to her woods, until she scented another human, familiar, connected to both her women. She decided to move closer. He shimmered with the light of hundreds of connection cords, and when she was near him, she felt all that light warming her deep into her bones.

The front door slammed, and Nick jerked awake, pain slamming through his ankle. It took him a few seconds to orient himself. He was on Banana's sofa. It was Banana who'd slammed the door.

"I got the go sign!" Banana announced, dropping into the armchair Annie had pulled up next to the sofa. "I saw her. I saw The Fox. It's almost like she was waiting for me. I was locking up at my place, and there she was. The moon's so bright to-night. I could see every detail, the black tip of her tail, the one white paw, that one ear that's mostly white. Most gorgeous thing I've ever seen. So tomorrow, I go. This time, I make it through the Wilderness." He laughed, running one hand over his bald head. "I forgot to say—how are you? How's the ankle feeling?"

"Good. I'm good. Thanks for sending over the food with Annie."

"Are you thanking me for the food part, or the Annie part?"

"Both. Hey, I got her to agree to go out to dinner with me."

"A lucky night for both of us, then." Banana's cell rang. He pulled it out of his pocket and answered it. The expression on his face immediately changed, going from happy and excited to wary and guarded. Nick wondered if he should try to hobble to the guest room. This was obviously a call that should have privacy. Before he could decide if it would be more disruptive to get up and gather up his crutches, Banana walked out of the room and into the kitchen. He didn't come back for about twenty minutes, and when he did, he looked shell-shocked.

Nick didn't want to get in Banana's business, but pretending nothing had changed didn't seem right either. "Everything okay?"

"That was my daughter." Nick nodded. Banana slumped down into the chair by the couch and ran his hands over his face. "That was my daughter, and it isn't a major holiday or my birthday."

"Is everything okay?" It was all Nick could think to say.

"Fine."

Nick waited for Banana to go on, but he just sat there, staring at the floor. "We don't know each other very well. But here I am, recuperating in your home, after you picked me up at the hospital, and after I told you my whole sad story about my messed-up divorce the first night we met." Nick struggled to sit up. "Based on all that, can I say that you don't look like everything's fine?"

"My daughter, Miranda, needs Jordan, my granddaughter, to come stay with me. Which is huge. Miranda and I aren't estranged, or at least we pretend that we're not. I get those phone calls on holidays and my birthday, presents, too. Nice, thoughtful presents. Expensive cookies, a knitted blanket, that kind of thing. Presents you give a stranger. And I call and send nice, don't-really-know-you presents back. I visit, too, not often, but when Miranda runs out of excuses, I go out to Oregon for a few days." Banana shook his head. "All of which means, Jordan barely knows me. Last time she saw me, she was a little more than five. I'm sure she's not thrilled to be coming here."

Nick wanted to say he was sure that wasn't true. But that kind of false comfort wasn't going to help Banana. "How old is she?" he asked instead.

"Ten. Just turned ten in April. I knew Miranda included me as part of her family-care plan. She's in the army. Her husband, too. His mom has early-onset dementia, and his dad can't deal with that and Jordan. So that left me."

"Her mom?"

"Died four years ago. Stomach cancer. I thought maybe after that Miranda and I might get closer. I thought maybe she felt as if she were being disloyal to her mother by being close to me. Our divorce wasn't a—What do pretentious celebrities call it?"

"Conscious uncoupling." Nick knew that one off the top of his head. Lisa liked to toss around that phrase. She also liked to tell everyone how they were still friends. He didn't deny it, but it didn't feel true.

"Right. Ours was not that. Ours was ugly, with a lot of yelling, a lot of name-calling, a lot of blaming. And we let Miranda see way too much of it. She was about the same age Jordan is, almost ten. She ended up living with her mom, and when her mom got a job all the way across the country, which wasn't long after the divorce—" Banana shook his head. "I let her go. I didn't fight it. While she was growing up, I saw her more than I do now. But it wasn't enough."

"Enough that she trusts you with her daughter."

"I wasn't her first choice. That was her husband Sean's sister. But she's pregnant, and it's high risk. She's confined to bed for the next couple months. So it took a couple bad situations for Miranda to consider me. She just put my name on the forms because she had to put someone. She didn't think she and Sean would be deployed at the same time, at least not before his sister was back in commission."

"An unexpected opportunity then." That was something Nick could say with total sincerity.

"You're right. An opportunity to form a bond with my granddaughter and, if I manage that, even get closer to my daughter. If I don't screw it up."

The dog was starving. The Fox could see prey everywhere, but the dog seemed blind to it. The Fox could also see death closing in.

Life and death commingled everywhere in her world. Yet, somehow, this dog pulled at her. Once she had been taken from death when she was caught in its jaws. She felt called to do the same for this dog. She could see the ragged stumps of the cords attached to him, all dark. And there was a human she had observed in the town. He had one strong cord that was dazzlingly bright. He had room for more, and he had the capacity for powerful connections. These two, the dog, the man, could be brought together. She could do that much.

Annie heard the door of the shop open, and she forced a smile onto her face. The smile turned genuine when she turned from the socks she was stocking—she could never keep enough of the ones with the Katahdin logo—and saw Chloe and Honey heading toward her, instead of probably woefully underprepared hikers.

"Why didn't you tell us you have a dinner date with your hiker?" Honey demanded.

"First, he's not my hiker. Second, did you close down your store to come over here? Third, how did you even know that—" Annie shook her head. "Scratch that last one. You know because Nick is staying with Banana, and Banana's ears and mouth pretty much function as a unit. He hears it, he says it."

"Your grandfather is completely capable of handling the store. Except when a woman buys fox underwear. You know how he blushes. You get that from him, along with that fair skin." Honey clapped her hands twice. "Now, do you think I enjoy having Banana tell me things I should already know, things about my own grandchild?" Her tone was stern, but her blue eyes were twinkling.

"What about me? We've been friends for years!" Chloe added, all mock outrage.

Annie sighed. "I'm not even going to attempt to convince either of you that I have a right to privacy."

"Good." Honey gave an emphatic nod that sent her fox ears pitching forward.

"It would be pointless." Chloe adjusted Honey's ears for her.

"I will say it's been less than twenty-four hours since he asked me. More importantly, he asked me to dinner as a thank-you for saving his life. Don't turn this into a thing."

"Banana said Nick was pretty excited about getting you to agree . . . to get thanked," Honey said.

"He doesn't even live in the state," Annie reminded them. "As soon as his ankle's good to drive, he'll be going back home."

Honey shook her head. "Banana said—"

Annie interrupted, "I'm starting to intensely dislike the words *Banana said.*"

Honey went right on. "Banana said that Nick is going to stay for the time he was planning to be on the trail."

"And Banana thinks it's because of you," Chloe chimed in.

"What does it matter if he leaves in a couple days or a couple weeks?" Annie shot back. "He's leaving soon. I'm letting him take me to dinner to thank me. That's where it stops."

Honey and Chloe exchanged a look. "Honey told me there was a spark between you. And how often does that happen?"

Annie realized Chloe was expecting an answer. "Sorry. I thought that was rhetorical. Since you and Honey already have all the answers for me."

"No, seriously. How often?" Chloe asked.

"I've already told my *grandmother* that there wasn't a spark." Annie moved on to the rack of topo maps, checking how many were left, hoping that would signal she was done with the topic.

"She is *so* stubborn," Honey told Chloe.

"How often does she think a truly great guy comes along?" Chloe asked Honey.

Annie had been intending to just ignore the two of them until they changed topics, but she couldn't. "Chloe, you've never even met him. And, Honey, you were around him for about five minutes. You don't know anything about him, except that he's cute."

"She thinks he's cuuute." Chloe made her voice nasal and high for the *cuuute*, doing a Rudolph the Red-Nosed Reindeer impression from that part where he finds out a girl reindeer likes him.

"He's thoughtful, too, asking you out to dinner to thank you," Honey added.

"I saved his life. Most people do something nice for you if you save their life."

"He's sweet, too, letting Nogan put that tattoo on him. And

Banana's letting him recuperate at his place. That says a lot. Banana is an excellent judge of character."

"Fine. Just fine. I give up. He seems like he probably is a great guy. But—"

Chloe put her hand up in a stop-right-there gesture. "No buts. Give him a chance, that's all. Don't decide now that there's no possible way there could be anything between you two."

"Fine," Annie said again. "But if I fall in love with him and move away from Fox Crossing to be with him, it's on both of you."

"If it made you happy, I'd be happy." Honey cupped Annie's cheek with her hand. "Truly. I'd be overjoyed. And I'd come visit. A lot. I worry that . . ." Honey let her words trail off, letting her hand drop.

"Worry that what?" Chloe coaxed.

"Oh, go ahead and say it," Annie told her grandmother. Annie didn't think she'd want to hear it, but whatever it was, was clearly important to Honey.

Honey pulled in a deep breath. "I just worry that you look at your mother as your example. That you think being a strong woman—*harrh*—means being alone, never needing anybody. But being with a man you love can make you stronger. I'd fight dragons for your grandfather, and I'd win."

Annie felt her eyes prickling with tears. She didn't even need to look at Chloe to know that her friend had gotten teary, too. What was Annie supposed to say? That she didn't want a relationship like her grandparents'? Of course, she did. Who wouldn't? But it's not like that happened for most people. Just because you got married, that didn't mean it worked.

"My parents are like that, too. They always say they are best friends, and they really are. I'm not saying they never argue or anything like that. But they . . . they turn to each other. Always." Chloe circled her hands in a helpless gesture. "I can't say it better than that. It's just something you feel when you're around them. And I want that."

"Of course you do." Honey patted Chloe's shoulder. "Who wouldn't?" Honey looked at Annie. "Even your mother, although she's pretended for so long she doesn't need anybody, it might feel like truth at this point."

"Are you sure you're talking about my mother? The one who got herself pregnant at seventeen because she decided she wanted a baby?"

"She didn't exactly get herself pregnant," Honey said.

"You know what I mean. She wanted a baby. She picked out a guy she thought had good genetic material and made sure she got pregnant. She didn't tell him because she didn't want anything permanent with him."

"She got something permanent though. And despite what she might have told you, it wasn't always easy," Honey shot back. "I think she'd have been happier if she found a man who wanted a family as much as she did and then had a baby."

"So, you're saying you have to be in a relationship to be happy?" Annie asked. "I don't buy it. I think you should be able to be happy on your own, and if someone comes along you want to be with, that's gravy."

"It's not gravy," Chloe protested. "It's the whole turkey."

"Think about the paper you're working on. Do you think it's good to get your self-esteem from another person?" Annie challenged.

"No, but—"

"You have to have it inside. Happiness is like that, too. You have to be able to find it in yourself. I wouldn't want to be happy only when some guy decided he wants to be with me," Annie told Chloe. "And I don't think you want that either."

No one spoke for a long moment, and the air felt charged

with emotion. Honey finally broke the silence. "Banana gave me some other interesting news. Miranda asked him to take care of Jordan. She and her husband will both be deployed at the same time."

"That's huge!" Annie exclaimed, happy that she was no longer the topic of conversation.

"I'm hoping this will bring him and Miranda close again. Remember how they used to be when you girls were little?" Honey asked.

"I remember Banana and Miranda would have lunch dates, just the two of them. And remember how he got an appointment at Vulpini so Sherri could teach him how to do Miranda's hair like Scary Spice?"

"Right." Annie smiled, remembering. "Buns in the front, party in the back! He did them for us, too."

"Banana was such a wonderful dad. I was a little jealous. The downside of having two lovebirds as parents is they don't always notice other people, even their kids."

"How old is his granddaughter now?" Annie asked.

"Jordan's ten," Honey answered.

"Ten," Chloe repeated. She looked at Annie. "Miranda isn't that much older than we are. We could have ten-year-old kids by now."

"I'm not ready for that." Annie gave a mock shudder. "And I definitely wasn't ready for a baby when I was twenty-three. Forget about seventeen, like my mother."

"Good point," Chloe said. "We should try to see Miranda when she's here, assuming she'll be here to drop Jordan off. It's been so long, but I still remember the three of us hanging out on my summer vacations. Until she moved to Oregon with her mom after the divorce."

"I think Lea had a lot to do with what ended up happening between Banana and Miranda," Honey said. "There were so many times that he'd suggest a trip to see Miranda, and there'd be some excuse, vacation plans or stomach flu or something else, especially after Lea remarried. It's like she wanted to forget that she ever had another family." A small line appeared between Honey's eyebrows. "Now Miranda does the same thing. I know Banana wants to see her and Jordan and Sean. But there's always some supposedly good reason why it's not a good time."

The door to the shop opened, and Logan and Noah rushed inside. "Can we put this sign in your window?" they asked together.

"If you take down the sign you already have up," Annie told them. Nogan had so many businesses that they'd end up completely covering her windows with flyers if she'd let them.

"What are you two selling this time?" Honey asked. Logan handed her one of the flyers. Her lips twitched as she read it:

Nogan's Walk & Wag
After a walk with us,
your dog will be wagging!
Little poops $5.00
Big turds $10.00
We'll be your dog's best friend!

"You're charging by the size of the, uh, output?" Chloe asked, reading over Honey's shoulder.

"Yeah. Cleaning up the poop is gross," Logan said.

"You can feel it through the plastic bag, all warm." Noah gave the unnecessary elaboration.

"But five bucks extra? I think that will lose you some customers."

"Shoo Fly was going to pay it. But we couldn't get the dog to go with us," Noah answered.

"Shoo Fly got a dog?" Honey protested.

"Yeah. It's really big, and really skinny, and really ugly," Logan told her.

"It's not really his," Noah added. "He's just keeping it for now."

"How'd Shoo Fly end up with it in the first place?" Honey asked.

"It chased The Fox into his yard," Noah said.

"The Fox?" Chloe yelped. "Not just *a* fox?"

"That's what he said."

"When did he see it? How close did he get? The dog didn't hurt The Fox, did it?" Chloe asked, breathless.

Both boys shrugged. "We gotta get the rest of these flyers up." Logan started for the door. Noah followed, pausing to tear off the flyer for the man candles they'd been selling.

"A third Fox sighting!" Chloe gave a little bounce on her toes. "I'm going to be next. I can feel it."

"I need to talk to Violet about getting a story in the *Around Town*," Honey said. "A bunch of hikers have signed up, now that she has it online. They're going to love hearing that The Fox is out giving her luck. And they're going to show their love by buying lots of foxy merchandise."

"I'm not sure having to take care of a stray dog is exactly lucky," Annie pointed out.

"Give it time. Trust The Fox." Honey turned to Chloe. "We should get going. There's a shipment of fox-body pillows we need to unpack. They're super soft and fuzzy. I'll give you one at cost, if you want one, Annie. Although your hiker would be more fun to cuddle." Annie stuck her tongue out at her grandmother. Honey laughed, then linked arms with Chloe and started for the door.

Chloe turned back and grinned at Annie. "Want to do a shopping trip to Bangor?"

Annie shrugged. She wasn't much of a shopper, but with Chloe it would be fun. "Sure."

"Good. We can find something for you to wear on your date!" Chloe hurried out of the shop before Annie could tell her it was a thank-you dinner, not a date.

Even though her nerves were twanging with anticipation.

CHAPTER 10

"I have no idea what a ten-year-old girl would want in her room," Banana admitted. He stood in the doorway of his guest room.

Nick studied the room from his seat on the bed. It felt kind of like a motel room, fine, but stripped down. Nothing on the walls, nothing on top of the dresser, plain blue bedspread. "Posters, maybe?"

"But of what?"

"I have absolutely no idea." Nick tried to remember his sister's room when she was that age. All he could think of was the sign on the door in pink and purple marker that said TRESS-PASSERS WILL BE EVISSERATED. The word *evisserated* was underlined with shiny black nail polish. Her spelling wasn't great, and he didn't know the word *evisserated* and wouldn't have even if it had been spelled correctly. When he asked his mom for a definition, she just said not to go in his sister's room without knocking. Not helpful for Banana. "Let's ask Google."

Nick took out his phone and did a search for *tween girl bedroom ideas*. Banana sat down next to him and they studied the images together. "They look so sophisticated," Banana said. "Not a stuffed animal in sight."

"Lots of throw pillows, though. Maybe some of those and a new bedspread? Something more colorful."

"I like how this one has quotes and doodles on the wall. Maybe I should get her some of those Sharpie paints and let her go at it."

Nick flashed on the sign on his sister's door. "Or you could paint a wall with chalkboard paint. Then she could change up what she had on the wall whenever she wanted to."

"Good idea." Banana ran his hand over his scalp. "The real question isn't what to do with the room, it's what do I even talk to her about. She's not going to even remember meeting me. We've spoken on the phone, but only for a few minutes at a time. She's never even been to Fox Crossing. When I could actually get Miranda to agree to a visit, I always went to them."

"I've seen you in action. Talking is your strong point. You can tell her about Bucky, for starters."

"I don't think that's exactly ten-year-old humor. She'd probably think I was senile." Banana rubbed his head. "I wonder what her mother has told her about me."

"That way lies madness."

"Yeah. Paint and pillows. I can at least do that."

"I need to give you your guest room back. You up for giving me a ride to the Inn?"

"You're still planning to be here another ten days or so?"

Nick nodded. That would give him time to see how his dinner with Annie went. He'd felt that *click* of mutual attraction after being around her for less than five minutes; then when she rescued him, something deeper started up. At least it had for him.

"Stay here a couple more days. Miranda isn't going to drop Jordan off until Thursday. Then I'll give you a ride to Violet's Boardinghouse for Trail Widows. Great prices, great view, breakfast included. And Violet is a good cook. Nothing against the Inn, but Vi's is the way to go for a longer stay."

"Trail widows?" Nick rubbed his chin. His scruff was getting truly scruffy.

"The women whose husbands are hiking the trail. Occasionally there are even a few widowers. More women are hiking the trail. It's a lot closer to a fifty-fifty split than it used to be. Still about ninety-five percent white, though."

"You're kidding."

"Nope. And of that five percent, less than one percent are black."

"Why?"

Banana thought for a moment. "That feeling that if you're black and you go into the woods, you might not come out."

Nick was staggered. To him, that seemed like something from the Jim Crow era. "You're talking even now?" He did a quick calculation. Banana was probably early sixties. That meant he was born in the late fifties. Johnson had abolished the Jim Crow laws in . . . Nick couldn't remember. He couldn't even remember. He felt a burst of shame.

"Hell, yeah, now. Some of that's old fears, picked up from my parents and that generation. I'm not actually scared I won't make it out alive. But I've been standing on the side of the road with hiking buddies of the white persuasion. There are times they get rides, and I don't. I've hiked through towns with the Confederate flag flying in way too many places, and I've gotten the you-don't-belong-here looks."

"I don't even know what to say. Can I apologize for all white people?" Nick felt stupid saying it, but it seemed better than saying nothing.

Banana laughed. "You definitely can't." He stood. "I'm going to the paint store, see if they have that chalk paint. Want to hobble along?"

"Sure."

Banana handed Nick his crutches, and he slowly made his way to the door and out to the bright yellow Jeep Renegade. Fortunately, his good foot was the one he needed to use to step in. "How'd you end up getting into hiking?" he asked once Banana backed out of the driveway.

"It wasn't my love of the great outdoors. Show me a door I'm not supposed to go through, and that makes me want to kick it down. Then I got hooked. I started doing section hiking of the AT and basically never stopped. Changed my life."

"How so?" That's what Nick had wanted. He'd wanted hiking even a section of the trail to somehow change his life. Pretty stupid, but true.

"You know what a bar blazer is?" Banana asked as he eased his truck into a parking space a few blocks down from the Outfitters. It would have been an easy walk if Nick weren't out of commission.

"Never heard of it."

"It's basically a pub crawl, a long one. You hike the trail, stopping at every town and hitting a bar. When craft beer started getting big, amber blazers started up. Pretty much the same as bar blazers, but stopping at whatever town has a microbrewery. It's gotten to be a big thing. A guy I met on the trail and I started talking about Fox Crossing and how it really needed a brewery. We pretty much talked ourselves into opening one. He was from here, had some land. And here I am."

"Your wife was okay with that?" Lisa would never have been okay with that. She couldn't deal with Nick's becoming a consultant, even though he had the ins and outs of starting a new business down cold. He'd watched his dad and his uncle do it, then he'd majored in business administration.

"Yeah. She was a city girl, but the idea of raising our daughter in a small town appealed to her. Miranda was about five when we moved here." Banana let out a long breath. "Lea worked with me and my buddy to get Wit's going. We were the entire staff at first—bartender, bottle washer, floor sweeper, cook, we did it all. But at some point, and I've never figured out exactly when, Lea decided that she'd spent way too much of her life following my dream. I would have done anything. Left the bar. Moved wherever. But it was too late. She'd already decided I wasn't what she wanted."

"I know the feeling. I thought my wife and I were on the same page, but obviously not. Although maybe we were until she met the guy who is now her husband."

Banana slapped his palms down on the steering wheel. "Let's get in there and get that paint. We have a room to girlify."

Nick was happy to have the subject change. He didn't want to think about Lisa and how right this minute she might be having some other guy's baby.

"I forgot to call Big Matt!" Banana exclaimed as he helped Nick out of the truck and onto the sidewalk. "Before I left the brewery yesterday, I told him I'd seen The Fox, and that meant I was hitting the trail and he was in charge."

"Is Big Matt the guy you opened the bar with?"

"Nope. I bought my partner out. He and his wife decided to retire to Florida. No more shoveling snow." They slowly started toward the paint store.

"How long is Fox luck supposed to last? Will you still be covered once your granddaughter's back home and you can give the Wilderness another shot?"

"You know what? I got the call from my daughter the same night as I saw The Fox. And now I have the chance to get to know Jordan. I think I might have already gotten my luck."

"And we have a winner. That dress is perfect," Chloe decreed.

"It better be. I've tried on every other dress in the mall." But

Annie had to admit the dress, cream with black flowers scattered here and there, looked good. It was more sophisticated than what she usually wore, sleeveless, with a hem that was shorter on one side.

"Do you need shoes? That dress requires strappy little sandals."

The only answer Annie could give was a groan. She could hike all day, but shopping? A few hours and she was exhausted, exhausted and cranky.

"I'll take that as a no."

"Wait! I just remembered. I do have sandals. We can go home."

"Are they strappy?"

"They have more than one strap."

Chloe narrowed her eyes. "Are they Tevas or anything else that might be found in, say, your store?" she asked sternly.

Annie groaned again. But Chloe was right. Annie's hiking sandals were fine with the casual maxi dresses she liked to throw on, but not with this dress. "Fine. New shoes." She pushed Chloe out of the dressing room and shut the door. She took another look in the mirror, then shimmied out of the dress. It did look good. Nick would like it. Not that it mattered. She was buying it for herself, not Nick. But thinking about him made her nerves go twangy again. Because it had been a while, that's all.

She pulled on her clothes. "I forgot to ask. How are you set for underwear?" Chloe asked as soon as Annie came back out.

"I have plenty of underwear."

"Underwear that can't be purchased at, say, your store?"

"I give myself a good discount," Annie snapped. "And just because panties are moisture wicking, that doesn't make them unattractive."

"Okay, clearly we need to hit the food court before anything else. You're getting hangry."

"I'm not hangry. I just have underwear already."

"We'll talk again after giant pretzels."

After a giant pretzel and about half a vat of Coke, Annie felt her shoulders loosen. She hadn't realized how tensed up she'd gotten trying on all those dresses.

"Feeling better?" Chloe asked.

"Yes. But I'm still not ready to stand up."

"I'm in no rush." Chloe started tearing her napkin into little pieces and depositing them in her empty soda cup. "I wonder if I'd had your mom, if I'd still feel like love was more important than anything."

"Where'd that come from?"

"Just thinking about that conversation we had with your grandmother yesterday. She was saying maybe you didn't think you needed a relationship because you didn't see your mom in one. She didn't ever have a live-in boyfriend or anything while you were growing up, right?"

"Right. She'd go out, but she never even had the guy pick her up at the house. She kept that part of her life separate from me."

"What about holidays? Did she ever bring anyone to Thanksgiving or Christmas?"

"Nope. Honey and Grandpa always had holidays at their place. They always invited anyone who didn't have other plans." Annie thought about it. "I guess one of them could have been someone my mom was involved with, but if so, I never got that vibe."

"And after you moved out? Nothing?"

"Nothing serious. No one at all for—" Annie had to think about it. "Not even anything casual for at least six years. She still doesn't ever bring anyone to Thanksgiving or Christmas. I brought Seth while we were together."

"Your mom's not even fifty, right?"

"Almost, but not quite."

"You think she ever thinks about getting married or living with someone or any of that?"

"We don't really talk about that stuff. I guess if the right person appeared, and they would have to appear, because she's definitely not going to go looking for them, it's possible she—" Annie stopped. "Even as I'm saying that, I'm not sure it's true. I can't imagine someone else living in my mom's house. She has everything exactly how she wants it, and I mean *exactly*. And she'd never leave her place to move in with someone."

"I read that Mia Farrow and Woody Allen lived on opposite sides of Central Park when they were together. Maybe that kind of deal would work for Belle. She and whoever could live on opposite sides of the lake and kayak over for visits."

Annie laughed. "Now that might work."

"And you really, seriously don't care if you don't ever get married?"

"I really, seriously don't."

"But what about kids?"

Annie thought about that once in a while. She was thirty-two, and unlike a guy, she had a limited amount of time to have a baby. "I don't know," she admitted. "I don't know. Maybe if I don't meet someone in the next five years or so, I'll think adoption. You were talking about how our parents—or parent—influence us. I had a great role model for a single mom."

"Truth." Chloe bent her straw and added it to the cup on top of the pieces of napkin. "If I were Belle's kid, maybe I'd feel the way you do. Maybe I'd be more okay with being single."

"Maybe. Your parents definitely made marriage look fun. I can see how that would make you want what they have."

"They were, and are, so into each other that sometimes I felt like an intruder. I know my sister felt that way, too. I bet when one of them dies, the other one will go within six months."

Annie stood up. "I think I want to hit Victoria's Secret. Not for Nick, who is not seeing anything but the dress, because we're going on a thank-you dinner, not a date. But because I could use at least one set of underwear that matches."

Chloe smiled.

"Don't gloat," Annie warned her.

"Wouldn't think of it."

Probably that extremely large Coke was a bad idea, Annie thought. It was after one, and she still felt wide-awake. She climbed out of bed, put her favorite baggy sweats on over her pj's, and tied on her trail runners. She needed a walk.

She took the trail that led from her cabin to the path around the lake. When she reached her favorite boulder, she took a seat and stared out at the water. Her thoughts returned to her mom and moved on to her father. Which was Chloe's fault, with all her talk about parents and love and all that.

Annie didn't even know her father's real name, just his trail name—Doppler. Her mother claimed that was all she knew herself. And that made sense. On the trail, almost no one went by their actual name, and Annie was the product of a casual trail hookup. Her father wouldn't even know he had a kid.

When she was a kid, Annie kept thinking maybe he'd show up in Fox Crossing. Not because of her, because he didn't know she existed, but to hike the trail again. Or maybe even because he wanted to see her mother. It never happened.

Annie pulled in a long breath, then let it out slowly. She'd had enough thinking for today. She closed her eyes, listening to the sound of the water gently lapping against the shore, the sound that could almost always bring her to a calm place.

In the distance, a loon wailed. It sounded almost like the howl of a wolf, beautiful and somehow lonely. It was nothing like the undulating sound people called the loon laugh. That was the one the birds used when they were alarmed. The wail was used when the loon had become separated from a chick or a mate. It was used when the loon wanted to regain contact.

The Fox scented one of the women, the younger one, who was blood of The Woman. Something inside The Fox always responded to that scent, a reminder of the deepest connection in The Fox's long life. She moved closer until the woman came into view. Cords of light connected her to the water, to the trees, to the loon across the lake, to The Fox herself, to dozens of humans, forming a shimmering web.

The Fox sought out the cord that had almost snapped the last time she had seen the woman. It was whole, still thin, but stronger than it had been before. The Fox couldn't see the future, at least not yet, but she thought the connection would hold.

CHAPTER 11

Hearing Annie pull up in front of Banana's house, Nick felt a surge of anticipation. It had only been two days since he'd seen her, but it felt longer. He'd tried to come up with a reason to stop by the Outfitters, but everything he'd thought of seemed like a transparent excuse to see her. A lot of women would like that, but Annie could be prickly, and he didn't want to risk it.

He got himself out to the porch just as she was starting up the walkway. The faint breeze ruffled her short hair and the hem of the flowered dress she wore fluttered around her knees. "You look beautiful," he said after he'd maneuvered the porch steps.

Annie ran her fingers through her hair. "My friend Chloe wanted to go shopping in Bangor. I found this dress on the sale rack."

"Good find." When he reached her, he wanted to give her a hello hug, but the crutches made him awkward, and she didn't stand still for long. She hurried back to the SUV, opened the passenger door, and held his crutches while he eased himself inside.

"I thought we'd go to the local barbecue place," Annie said as she turned on the ignition. "It has a big menu, so if you're not in the mood for barbecue, there are lots of other options."

"Nope. I made reservations at 380 Grill." Banana had told him it had great food, and great atmosphere. Banana also knew a woman who worked there and had made the reservation for Nick so he and Annie would get a great table.

"There's a good steak place right in town, if you want steak."

Nick hadn't wanted to take her to a place in town, where absolutely everyone knew her and would be stopping by to say hello. He wanted at least a little privacy. "I was thinking lobster. Banana said the chef does one with a sherry cream sauce that's amazing. You ever had it?"

"I usually eat local. And the Grill is on the pricey side. I only went there once, for my twenty-first birthday. Did you even check the menu online?"

She sounded a little annoyed. Maybe he should have consulted her about where they should go. Too late now. "This is a thank-you dinner, remember? I put a high value on my life. I was hoping they'd serve one of those desserts with truffles and caviar, sprinkled with flakes of gold, so I could really show you how much I appreciate what you did for me."

"Gold is toxic."

Nick laughed. "That would be ironic—feeding you a deadly dessert to show you my gratitude for saving my life. But I think if gold is close to pure, it doesn't do any damage."

"How crazy is it that people will pay crazy money to eat something that has no taste and at best 'doesn't do any damage'?"

"But it's sparkly."

Annie smiled. "It is sparkly," she conceded, then pulled out onto the street. "How's the ankle feeling?"

"Good." Actually, it was aching, but he didn't want to waste the time he had with Annie talking about that. "Banana told me you've hiked the AT three times. I gotta know—what's your trail name?"

"Oh, no. That's in the vault."

"Now I'm intrigued. I'm not going to be able to enjoy my dinner if you don't tell me."

"That's too bad. I know you were really looking forward to that lobster."

"Come on. I'll tell you mine," he wheedled as they passed a wooden THANK YOU FOR VISITING FOX CROSSING sign and turned onto a two-lane highway, the woods on either side.

"You know it's not fair to choose your own."

"I didn't. I met a couple at a shelter. The woman, Loon, gave me the name."

"I met them. They stopped in to get a few supplies. I was hoping you'd run into them." So she'd been thinking about him. "They're experienced hikers. I knew they'd bail you out if you'd gotten in trouble." So she'd been thinking about him—and how he was going to get himself hurt since he'd ignored her advice and headed into the Wilderness.

"How'd you find me, anyway? The tracker was in my pack. It got swept down the river."

Annie flushed. Her skin was so fair it was easy to see the color climbing up her neck and into her cheeks. "I, um, had my phone out, and since I did, I decided to check on you. The tracker showed you going way too fast. I thought it was you who'd gotten swept away by the current. Your backpack had gotten snagged by the time I got there. I realized it had gotten away from you, so I backtracked. I was afraid I was only going to find your body."

"You would have if you'd gotten to me much later." Neither spoke for a moment. "Glad you checked the tracker," Nick finally said.

She glanced over at him. When her eyes met his, there it was, the *click*. "Me, too," Annie answered, then returned her gaze to the road.

Silence began to build up between them. It wasn't exactly uncomfortable, but it was heading that way. He waited another minute, then blurted out, "I looked at a list of first-date conversation starters." Why had he said that? The whole point of looking up the questions was to avoid awkwardness, not create it.

"This isn't a first date. It's a thank-you dinner," Annie corrected him.

"Right. I know that. I just wanted to have some ideas for talking to someone I don't know that well. Obviously, I should have asked one of the questions from the article, not announce that I read it."

Annie laughed. "We've had conversations already."

"About me being unprepared for the hike."

"Also, hangover advice."

"And that."

"Really though. Why'd you think you needed ideas? You seem like the kind of guy who can talk to anyone."

"I'm no Banana, but I do okay." Since she didn't consider this a date, Nick didn't want to tell her that it had been a long time since he'd been on a date and was feeling out of practice. He and Lisa had gotten together at the beginning of college, and he'd only gone on two dates in high school, possibly because until he was a senior—a senior in his second semester—he'd been shorter than almost every girl there. "I've had a lot of downtime the last few days. I was fooling around on my phone. Google was there. So I asked."

"Well, since you did the research, let's hear one of the questions."

"They were in general categories—work, hobbies, growing up, entertainment, food, dating history, and hopes and dreams." He tried to do an Alex Trebek. "The questions range in value from fifty dollars to two hundred and fifty dollars. If you're ready, let's play."

"Let's go with hobbies, Alex."

Nick smiled. At least she knew what he was going for. "Do you have any hobbies, Annie?"

"All the outdoor stuff—swimming, kayaking, hiking, cross-country skiing."

"Hiking you say. I've heard some hikers have trail names. Do you?"

"Nice try."

"Okay, okay. Choose another category."

"Work."

"Did you ever think of doing anything besides going into the family business?"

"I pretty much grew up in the store. My mom ran it before me, and so on all the way back to the first Hatherley woman."

"*Harrh,*" Nick growled.

Annie shot him a smile. "Exactly. Annabelle Hatherley. I have half her name, my mom has the other half. And we have her store. My store now. My mom handed it over to me when she got so involved in the town politics. Or maybe she just gave that as an excuse. The store was a little small for the two of us. We got on each other's nerves."

He barely knew either of them, but he wasn't surprised. "Do you—"

"I think it's my turn to ask a question, but I'll wait until we get there." Annie turned off the highway, drove through a town that wasn't much bigger than Fox Crossing, then pulled into 380 Grill's gravel lot.

Once Nick had extricated himself from the SUV and was on his crutches, he had to take a moment just to take in the view. The restaurant sat at the end of a peninsula. The lake around it was huge. It had to be Moosehead. Nick couldn't get a glimpse of the opposite shore, just little islands here and there that made it look like trees were growing out of the water. "Does this ever get routine, a view like this?"

"Yeah," Annie admitted. "It can just become background. You have to make yourself notice it." She seemed to be doing just that, staring out at the water. Nick realized what he was staring at was Annie, and he forced himself to return his gaze to the lake. The sun was just beginning to set, turning the smooth surface golden in spots.

This time, the silence that grew between them didn't feel at all awkward. He felt connected to her as they both took in the same view. *Click*. That one was more than attraction. It came from that feeling of being in sync.

They didn't move until another car pulled into the lot, breaking the spell. As they started toward the restaurant, Nick was extra-careful to make sure his crutches were firmly set each time he took a step. The last thing he wanted to do was land on his butt, putting Annie in the position of taking care of him again.

The hostess's friendly smile widened when Nick gave her his name. She led them over to a high-backed booth that wrapped around him and Annie, keeping them out of the view of the rest of the diners. Perfect. He had to remember to thank Banana for hooking him up.

Annie rubbed her hands together. "Now I get to ask a question."

"The answer is both. Or neither."

"I didn't ask anything."

"But I knew what you were going to ask—boxers or briefs, right?" Maybe he could turn this thank-you dinner into an actual date with a little flirting. "I'm a boxer-briefs guy. So the answer is neither or both, depending on how you look at it."

"You're forgetting I pretty much stripped you down in the woods."

She'd seen him naked? He felt the back of his neck get hot. Of course she'd seen him naked. He didn't remember her getting him out of his clothes, but obviously she had. "I was forgetting that. I don't have clear memories of a lot of what happened after I fell in the river."

"*Stream*," she corrected. "You said something about thinking about me too much." Oh, great. What else had he puked up? "I wasn't sure what that meant. And now that's going to be my question. What did that mean?"

Nick raked his fingers through his hair. He wasn't going to tell her he kept having pissed-off thoughts about how wrong she was about him. That might just irritate her. He wasn't going to tell her about the *click*. That would be rushing things.

But there was something true that he wanted her to know. "From the time I fell in the water, my memories are pretty fragmented and hazy, but at one point I remember deciding to just pretend I was you. A stupid version of you who ended up falling into a stream, which the actual you wouldn't have done. Thinking that, it helped keep me moving. I was trying to get to the shelter. At that point I was still coherent enough to have a plan. You were kind of saving my life before you actually saved my life."

Their waiter came over before Annie could answer. "I want to order champagne," Nick told the man, then turned to Annie. "But only if you like champagne."

"I like champagne."

"We'll have champagne," Nick told the waiter.

"We have several choices," the man replied.

Problem was, Nick knew nothing about champagne. Well, he knew it had bubbles. He could grab the drinks menu and fake it, but he'd rather have some guidance. "I have a problem. I'm pretty much a beer guy, and I just realized I don't know what to actually order." He looked at Annie.

"I got nothing. I drink what they hand me on New Year's and weddings."

"Here's the thing, she saved my life," Nick told the man. "I want to toast her with a great champagne. What would you suggest?"

"Without breaking the bank," Annie added.

"That doesn't matter. Not tonight."

"Do you have a preference on sweetness?" the waiter asked.

Nick looked at Annie again. She gave a helpless shrug. Nick turned back to the waiter. "Uh, no preference."

The waiter picked up the drinks menu. "Since you're drinking it before dinner, I'd recommend a *blanc de blancs*, like one of these." He indicated three of varying price ranges.

"Let's go with this one." Nick pointed to the most expensive. He knew most expensive didn't always mean best, but he assumed it had to be pretty good. The waiter nodded and headed off.

"There are still times when I feel like I'm not an actual adult, and that was one of them," Nick admitted to Annie. "I'm two days away from thirty, and I have no idea how to order wine, other than saying red or white."

"Most guys would have faked it."

"Wouldn't risk it with you. I have a feeling you'd be really good at identifying bullshit."

Annie laughed. "You're right. I like that you just admitted it up front. Now I get to ask you another question. You asked me two in the car." She studied him for a moment. *Click.* Just her eyes on him gave Nick that jolt of raw attraction. "What's most important to you?"

"No category? Just most important, period?"

"Yep."

"Of course, you'd ask something like that."

"What's that supposed to mean?" Annie demanded.

"It means you're direct. You say what's on your mind."

"Damn right. So? What's the answer?"

"I need to think for a minute. It's not like you asked my favorite color." The answer came to him slowly, in pieces. "I guess I'd say my connections to other people. My family. My friends. Even little connections, like the guy at Starbucks who knows my order and will commiserate with me every time the Pirates lose, which is a lot."

Annie nodded. "I don't have a big family, and I'm not someone who has tons of friends, but the ones I have, I treasure."

Click.

The more he was around her, the more he wanted to be around her. He didn't care it was almost a nine-hour drive from Bensalem to Fox Crossing. He'd make it every weekend if she'd let him. That was the problem. Convincing her to give him a chance.

"I'm inviting myself for breakfast. Cereal is fine," Chloe said when Annie opened the door. "I have to know the details of the date with the hiker, and I can't get them at Flappy's with half the town sitting there."

"It wasn't a date. But come on in." Annie led the way to the kitchen, opened a cabinet, and pointed. "There are your choices." She took a carton of milk out of the fridge, grabbed two bowls, and sat down at the kitchen table.

"Are you sure the thank-you dinner didn't turn into a date at some point?" Chloe sat down and dumped Raisin Bran into both bowls.

Had it? If she was truthful, that spark that she'd always felt between them almost started a fire. The way he'd looked at her when she walked up to Banana's to pick him up? The way she had to keep telling herself to stop staring at him? Definitely date-like. "Chloe, we're talking about a guy who lives in Pennsylvania. There's no point in starting something up with him."

"There are trains and cars and planes. Take the distance thing out, and would you want to start something up with him?"

Annie hesitated. Last night had been pretty much perfect. Great place. Great food. Great drinks. And great company. All combined with that about-to-burst-into-flames attraction.

"Don't bother answering. I can see from your face that you would."

"Okay. Yes. I would. But distance is a factor, and we barely know each other." Even though she felt as if she'd known him much longer than she had.

"So, get to know him. Honey said Banana said he was going to be here for another week and a half." Chloe spooned some cereal into her mouth.

"He told me. But that's not much time."

"Why are you being like this? When's the last time you met somebody you liked, and don't say you don't like him, because I can tell you do. And Honey said you two have a spark."

"I don't know if I even want to get involved with anybody right now. It's been nice being on my own."

"You have to catch me up. What was the deal with what's his face who you were living with?"

"Seth. And the deal was we were together for about two years, then he wanted to go to California to hike the Pacific Crest Trail, and I didn't want to go with him."

"Well, did he say he was coming back? It's not like it takes decades to do the hike."

"Five months on average. I couldn't leave the shop for that long." Not that he'd asked. "Also, he thought maybe he'd stay in California for a while, which he ended up doing. He wasn't exactly a fan of our winters."

"Did he take his stuff?"

"He didn't have that much, but, yeah. We basically left it at that we weren't making any commitments, and that if he came back sometime, and if I were free, maybe we'd start something up again."

"How romantic," Chloe snarked.

"It wasn't that kind of thing. We weren't serious." Annie struggled to come up with a way to describe their relationship. "We just liked each other's company, and we liked having sex."

"Have you heard from him since he left?"

"He sent me some pics of the trail, let me know how many miles he was getting in. We both let communication peter out."

"And you're fine with that?"

"And I'm fine with it."

Chloe gave her a long look. "Sometimes I just don't understand you."

"Right back at ya."

"All right, let's back this up." Chloe waved her spoon in a circle, sending a few droplets of milk flying. "He didn't break your heart. You aren't waiting around, hoping that maybe, possibly, he'll come back. Right?"

"Right."

"And he's been gone exactly how long?"

"A little more than a year already."

"But even after that long, you're not sure if you want to get involved again." Chloe shook her head. "You do know that cute, smart, funny guys don't come along every day. Especially cute, smart, funny guys who are also nice."

"You haven't even met him."

Chloe waved her spoon hand in a dismissive gesture, sending more milk droplets flying. "I already told you, I don't have to have met him. I got the scoop from Honey, and Banana."

"Did Banana or Honey happen to tell you he's only been divorced for about a year?"

"Is that the real reason why you're not sure if you want to get involved with him?"

Annie sighed. "With the divorce and the distance, I don't think the odds of things working out are very good."

"I'm about to go all psychologist on you."

"And tell me this is all coming from my mother, and how I didn't have a model of a happy relationship?"

"No. Well, maybe. But that's not what I was thinking. I was thinking about you and Luke Caron."

"What?" Annie suddenly felt nauseous and short of breath, like that time she'd gotten altitude sickness hiking Longs Peak. "What even made you think of him?" She thought she sounded okay, at least.

"His mom came into the shop to chat with Honey. And it got me remembering things. The other day when I said you'd never been in love, I was wrong. I was forgetting about Luke."

"Come on, Chloe. Luke thought of me as a kid sister, when he thought of me at all. His parents and my mom were friends."

"He might have thought of you as a kid sister, but you were gaga over him. There was one summer when you dragged me every place you thought you might have a Luke sighting."

"It wasn't real. It was a crush. I was fourteen that summer. I hadn't even started high school. He was sixteen. He'd been in high school two years. He had his own group of friends. I didn't even know him that well."

"You knew everything from his favorite ice cream to his favorite band. I think you even knew what kind of deodorant he wore. Am I remembering it right? Didn't we follow him into Martin's Mercantile and pretend to be reading greeting cards whenever he looked our way?"

"I think so." Annie tried to sound like she was having trouble remembering, but even the details were still clear. She'd bought a nail polish so she could stand behind him in line. "But like I said, it was a crush. A crush isn't love."

True. But what she didn't say was that the next summer, Luke's last summer, they'd hiked from Old Rag Mountain to

Katahdin. They'd been on the trail for almost three months, and she and Luke had walked most of it together, a mile or two ahead of her mom and his parents, talking about everything. That's when the crush turned into love, at least for her.

"It was more than a crush. You were devastated when he died. I was here the summer after, remember? Almost a year had gone by, but you were still mourning him."

"Everyone in town was devastated."

"Why is it so hard for you to say how much it hurt?"

"Chloe, it was a long time ago. No matter how much it hurt, and I admit it, I was shattered. For a while. But that was, what? Seventeen years ago?" she asked, even though, even now, she knew exactly how long it had been, down to the day.

"If he'd lived, you'd probably have ended up getting a crush on someone else. But he died before that could happen. When he died, you had all these huge feelings for him, reciprocated or not. That kind of hurt can stay with you." Chloe's expression was serious. "Here comes the psychologist part. I think you have an avoidant attachment style. You're afraid to get hurt the way you did when Luke died, so you push men away."

Impatience surged through Annie. "I told you Seth and I lived together for about two years. That's not pushing him away."

"It is if you didn't really love him," Chloe insisted.

"Don't try to stuff me in a box and put a label on it. We don't even really know each other. We see each other, what, every few years? And it's not like we talk or text or anything much when you're not around."

Chloe lowered her head and focused way too hard on scooping some cereal onto her spoon. She was hurt, but Annie didn't care. Chloe pushed too hard.

After eating a couple bites, she looked at Annie and said, "But when we see each other, we can always go right back to being besties. Or don't you think so?"

"It's like that for me, too." Annie was already feeling bad for being so snappy. "But that doesn't mean you know everything about me."

"Sorry. I said I was going all psychologist. I shouldn't have."

"Doesn't matter." Annie knew Chloe would never intentionally hurt her.

"Spoon toast?" Spoon toast was something they'd come up with when they were kids.

"Spoon toast." Annie clicked spoons with her friend.

"Just give things a chance with your hiker. Just a teeny-weeny chance."

"Fine." They clicked spoons again. "Actually, I'm going out with him again."

Chloe let out a whoop. "Why didn't you tell me that as soon as I showed up?"

"I knew you'd make a big thing of it, and it's no big thing. It's just that it's his birthday. His thirtieth. I didn't want him to spend it alone. It sucks to be alone on your birthday. See, no big."

Chloe nodded, but a smile was tugging at her lips and her hazel eyes were bright. Annie knew her friend hadn't believed a single word. "It really is no big."

Chloe nodded again, breaking into a wide smile.

Whatever. Annie knew what she knew. She didn't want Nick to spend his birthday solo, so she was going to hang out with him. There was nothing more to it.

CHAPTER 12

"Here it is, Violet's Boardinghouse for Trail Widows," Banana announced as he pulled up in front of a white clapboard building that had almost as many massive columns as the Parthenon, seven of them rising up three stories. And those were just the ones Nick could see from the car.

"Wow." Nick eased himself out of Banana's Jeep. "Wow. How many rooms?"

"Five. With five full baths." Banana joined Nick on the sidewalk. "The original owner was Celyn Hanmer."

"The guy with the horse who realized there was slate here?"

"The same. He came a long way, baby. Violet told me she—" Banana broke off, staring down the block. "Would you take a look at that." Nick followed Banana's gaze and saw a stocky middle-aged man heading toward them, leading a big—big but bony—dog, its coat a mottled mix of browns, blacks, and grays. "Shoo Fly, that may be the ugliest creature I've ever seen, and, yes, that includes the proboscis monkey and the monkfish," Banana called.

The dog stopped, head and tail drooping. "You scared him." Shoo Fly bent low and said something into the dog's ear. Reluctantly, it began to walk again, slowly, Shoo Fly walking beside it in a half crouch, continuing to talk to it.

"Low voice," he said when he and the dog were a few feet away.

"I heard you'd taken in a dog. But are you sure that's what it is?" Banana asked softly, then seemed to realize Shoo Fly didn't find the comment funny. "Poor guy. It looks like he's been on his own for a while."

Nick agreed. The dog's hip bones were jutting out, and Nick would have been able to easily count each rib if he'd wanted to.

"He wouldn't eat, even though look at him," Shoo Fly answered. "I tried different foods, but the only way I could get him to take a bit is if I fed him by hand."

"I'm now picturing you in a toga holding a bunch of grapes, and I'm not sure I'll ever be able to get it out of my head." Banana gave his *haw-haw-haw*, and the dog dropped to the ground and rolled onto his back, exposing his belly.

"Sorry, boy, sorry," Banana whispered to the dog. He started to put out a hand to pet the animal, then pulled it back when the dog whimpered. "Sorry," he said to Shoo Fly.

"He does that a lot." Shoo Fly leaned down and managed to coax the dog back to his feet. "The day I found him, I heard all this barking and went to check it out. I saw this guy chasing The Fox across my backyard. When he saw me, he stopped running and practically crawled over to me. Then he did what he just did to you, rolled over and showed me his belly. I thought about taking him to the shelter, but..." Shoo Fly shrugged.

"You did the right thing. He needs personal attention," Banana said, keeping his voice low.

"Yeah. I'm going to get him back to a good weight and try to get him used to being around people other than me. Then I can find someone to take him." The dog leaned against Shoo Fly, and he put a hand on his head. "I think he's had enough socialization for today." Shoo Fly turned, giving a wave as he and the dog started slowly back down the street.

"The Fox has never been seen so many times in such a short time, not since I can remember." Banana ran his hand over his head as he watched Shoo Fly crouch-walking beside the dog, whispering encouragement into his ear.

"I was surprised Shoo Fly talked so much. I saw him that first night at the bar, and he didn't come all the way inside. Somebody asked him to join that group at the back table, and he didn't even answer."

"I always bring his growler to the door when he stops by," Banana answered. "You're right about him talking more than usual. He doesn't have much use for small talk, which means he doesn't have much use for a lot of people. Clearly he found that dog worth talking about."

"Honey told me about him. He was a marine, and now he owns the bakery, is that right?"

"You have to try his special Shoo Fly pie." Banana put one hand on his stomach and rolled his eyes heavenward. "It has butterscotch and whiskey and who knows what other magical ingredients. It's on the menu as praline cream, but nobody calls it that."

"Are you two planning to come in or should I bring out a couple chairs?"

Nick turned and saw a woman, maybe late fifties, dressed in shades of purple from head scarf to high heels.

"We're coming, we're coming," Banana answered. "Violet, meet Nick. Nick, Violet," he said when they reached her.

She gave Nick's hand a hard shake. Everything about her seemed to be big and bold. Huge house, loud voice, and a personal style that screamed, "Hey, look at me." "Are you going to be okay hauling yourself up the stairs? All the bedrooms are on the second floor. The sofa in the reading room is very comfy. I can make it up for you, if you'd rather. I could hang some kind of drape to give you some privacy."

"Thanks, but I can make it."

"Let me look at you a minute." Violet took Nick's chin in her hand and turned his head from side to side.

"I told you, he's just in town for vacation. You can't use him in one of your plays," Banana told her. "Casting is more like conscription with Violet," he added to Nick.

To Nick's relief, Violet released him with a long, loud sigh. "Well, you would have been perfect for the part of the killer with a heart of gold who has disguised himself as a clergyman."

" 'Killer with a heart of gold'?" Nick repeated.

"Maybe the killer should be a con man. And maybe he should be undercover as a kindergarten teacher. I need to do a rewrite." She turned and started across the foyer with long strides. Then she whirled—*whirled* was the only word for it— back to face them. "Banana, get Nick settled, would you? I have him in the first room on the left." She reached into her pocket, pulled out a key, and tossed it to Nick, who managed to catch it and stay upright on his crutches.

"Will do," Banana said to Violet's back as she swept—yes, *swept*—out of the room.

"She takes a little getting used to, but she's one of my favorites," Banana said as he led the way over to the freestanding staircase that spiraled up three floors.

"Can you get the crutches? I think I'll have an easier time just using the railing for support." Nick handed them over.

"You want to hang at the bar tonight?" Banana asked as they started up the stairs. "Violet usually has some kind of entertainment, a movie or cards or board games, downstairs, but you might rather go to the Wit's Beginning. I can pick you up. My daughter and granddaughter won't be here until the morning."

Nick carefully took another step. "Actually, I got Annie to agree to go out with me again."

"I heard."

Nick grabbed the stair rail with both hands and turned to look at Banana. "No offense meant, but you talk a lot. I didn't tell you because I wasn't sure Annie would want everyone in town knowing she was going out with me. And not for a thank-you this time. Although, I'm not sure she thinks of it as an actual date. It's possibly more of a friendly hanging out with a guy on his birthday. Possibly pity is involved. Did you hear anything from your source?"

Banana gave his *haw-haw-haw* laugh, the one loud enough to terrify Shoo Fly's dog. It was clear to Nick that the dog was always going to be Shoo Fly's. The guy just hadn't realized it yet.

"I may have heard something or other," Banana admitted.

"Do you know where Annie's taking me? She said since it was my birthday, she'd do the organizing. Also, that I should dress casual. That's all she'd give me."

"I'm not saying a thing, except that Annie has something special planned for you."

"I borrowed my grandfather's rowboat," Annie told Nick as she helped him maneuver the little wooden pier. "Usually, I'd take you out in my kayak, but I didn't want to take the chance, even though it would be just a small chance, of flipping."

"Not ready to save my life again?"

Annie answered by reaching down and snagging one of the two life jackets waiting in the boat and waving it at him. She held on to first one crutch, then the other, as he put it on. She checked that it was tight enough, then put on her own.

It had only been two nights since they went to dinner, and she'd been feeling so comfortable with him. But now she felt tongue-tied and awkward. The most words she'd gotten out in a row since she picked him up at the boardinghouse were the ones about her kayak versus the rowboat. She blamed Chloe. Chloe had made tonight such a *thing*, telling Annie to give him a chance and not be, what was it? Conflict avoidant? No, *attachment* avoidant. Annie was the opposite of conflict avoidant. Anyway, no matter what Chloe thought, it didn't make sense to start up something with Nick. Annie loved Fox Crossing and couldn't imagine leaving it, not for anyone. And it's not like Nick would want to move to a town whose population dropped to 713 off-season. Not many people would.

"What are you thinking about?" Nick asked, pulling her out of her crazy inner monologue.

"Nothing. Safety. Lake safety." She reached out her hand to help him into the boat, and when her skin met his, she felt that spark, an electric tingle that ran all the way up her arm. That hadn't changed since the other night.

"Safety," Nick repeated as she sat down on the bench seat across from his. "Very important."

"I thought I'd just take you around the lake, since it's so early. Or are you hungry now?" What was wrong with her? Why couldn't she get into that conversational groove they'd had going last time? It was definitely Chloe's fault. She'd gotten Annie all self-conscious. "The perimeter of Lake Hebron is about nine miles. It has two basins. One that's shallow, so warmer water, and one that's cool with good oxygenation, which make it good for game fish. Do you fish? I could have brought poles."

"Your lung capacity is impressive." Nick smiled at her.

"What?"

"You gave all those lake stats without taking a breath."

Annie closed her eyes for a moment, pulled in a deep breath, then let it out. "For some reason I'm a little nervous tonight." He'd been honest with her when he admitted he didn't know how to order champagne. She figured maybe she should give him a little honesty in return. She still felt embarrassed that she'd lied to him about her new dress being from the sale rack. It was silly, but she hadn't wanted him to think she cared enough to buy a new dress for their date. Their thank-you dinner, she meant.

"I'm sort of nervous, too. It feels like the stakes are a little higher. Last time it was just a thank-you dinner."

"Right. Last time, there was an objective. You wanting to thank me, which wasn't necessary."

"I hold a high value on my life. It was hugely necessary."

"I just realized we have an objective tonight, too." Annie began to row, the long, smooth strokes bringing her at least a little calm.

"How so?" Nick's gaze was so warm, it was almost like he was touching her.

"It's a birthday outing. All that needs to happen is for you to have a good birthday."

"Going out on the lake with you—objective met."

"I thought you might want to get out and see at least some of what you would on the trail, even though it's from a different perspective."

"You were right. Do you think we should come up with a new objective for the night, since you already nailed the first one? Or should we just wing it?"

"I'm not the wing-it type."

Nick laughed. "Yeah, I've noticed. Do you have an objective to propose?"

Annie's brain began formulating possibilities. Keep getting to know him better. Figuring out if there were any big deal breakers looming—like his divorce. What was the situation there? Finding out if kissing him would be as amazing as those sparks she kept getting suggested it would be.

That last one got her belly doing a fast loop. Just thinking about kissing him was turning that spark to fire. Chloe had said to give him a chance. Kissing him would definitely qualify. "I do have one idea." Annie stopped rowing, letting them drift. "How about if our objective is to see if we . . ." How to phrase it? "If we are compatible. Physically." Because if they weren't, then that would decide things.

Nick raised his eyebrows. "What are you suggesting?" He sounded way too intrigued.

"Kissing," she answered. A kiss, she quickly amended. She needed to find out if he tasted good to her, if that fire got brighter or ended up going out all together when he really touched her.

Nick leaned forward, his eyes flicking down to her lips. Her heart gave a hard kick in her chest, the anticipation almost painful, then he paused. "You meant now, didn't you?"

Annie answered by cupping his face with her hands, urging him forward. She wasn't sure she'd survive if she had to wait. She felt Nick's warm mouth curve into a smile as her lips met his, and she couldn't help smiling back. Their teeth connected with an audible click, and they both pulled back, just a fraction, laughing.

"We can do this. We have the technology," Nick said without raising his head, his lips brushing against hers as he spoke. And they were kissing. And Annie didn't think she'd ever be able to get enough. She parted her lips and Nick instantly responded, deepening the kiss.

Annie forgot where they were, forgot everything but the feel of him. She moved closer, and their knees knocked. The rowboat began to rock, and she forced herself to pull away.

"We're going to need these life jackets if we aren't careful." She looked down and adjusted one of her jacket's fasteners, even though it didn't need adjusting, somehow unwilling to look at him until she'd managed to slow her breathing and ... and *compose* herself.

Nick used his fingers to tilt her chin up. He waited until she met his gaze, and her breath hitched, what little composure she'd managed to achieve disappearing. "I'd say compatible." Nick's voice was a little husky.

At least she wasn't the only one who'd been affected by that one kiss, that one little, completely explosive kiss. "I agree." Her voice was a little breathless. "Good to know. If we weren't, that would put us on the friend track."

"What track are we on now?"

She took a minute to consider the question. "The let's-see-what-happens track." She took up the oars again.

Nick gave a slow smile that made her want to kiss him again. Immediately. Although it absolutely wasn't necessary to meet the physical-compatibility objective. "I like that track," he said.

"Me, too." It was true, but the wait-and-see track made her feel a little off-balance. Honey always told Annie that she made things too black-and-white, but she liked knowing where she stood.

They fell silent, the sound of the oars moving through the water and the breeze moving through the pines enough for her, and it seemed to be enough for him. That was good to know, too. It would be hard to be with someone that didn't feel at least some of the connection to the wild world that she did. If she didn't get herself away from the town regularly, she started feeling tense and unhappy.

She took them to a small island, so small it could only hold a cluster of trees—and them. "Want to get out for a while?" She hadn't been planning to take him here. It was one of the places she came when she wanted to get away from everything human. But it felt right.

"Yes."

She tied up the rowboat, then helped Nick out of the boat. The warmth of his fingers made her want his hands on her. But the plan was to keep it slow. She had to remember that there were obstacles. He lived hundreds of miles away, five hundred and something. She'd looked it up, but she couldn't remember. And he was divorced. Just a little more than a year ago, he'd been married. Which is why the plan was to keep it slow.

"How about if we eat here?" she asked. Eating would give them something to do that didn't involve touching.

"Great."

Annie snagged the picnic basket and cooler she'd stowed in the rowboat, then found a good spot to spread out the blanket she'd brought. Nick sat down. "The other night you said you were a beer guy." She took out the growler Banana had filled for her, poured a cup for both of them, then sat down across from Nick.

He raised his cup in a toast. "To our new objective."

Annie touched her cup to his. "We don't have a new objective yet, though."

"I thought we were still working on determining physical compatibility." Nick ran the back of his hand down the side of her cheek.

Damn. "No, we've met that objective already." She took a sip of her beer.

Nick put his cup down. "We might not have collected quite enough data to make a definitive determination."

Annie laughed and put down her own cup. She had the feeling she was going to need her hands. They'd only kissed once. Doing a little more kissing still qualified as slow. Sort of.

"Okay, scale of one to ten, ten being the most . . . physically compatible, how's this?"

Annie expected him to kiss her again; instead he took her hand and turned it palm up. Annie watched as he began lightly tracing each finger, then increasing the pressure as he rubbed circles into her palm.

This shouldn't feel so good. All he was doing now was massaging that dip between her thumb and forefinger, and her whole body was responding, flooding with heat. Why was this happening? She was fully clothed. He was only touching her hand, just her hand. Hand touching definitely qualified as slow.

She looked up at him, and he met her gaze. "One to ten?" he asked after a long moment, continuing to caress her hand. *Caress*, that was the only way to describe it. He seemed in no hurry to move on. "One to ten?" he said again.

"Ten." It made her feel vulnerable to say it, to admit how his touch was affecting her. He gave a slow smile, then slid his hand up her arm until he reached the soft, tender skin on the inside of her elbow.

Annie felt overpowered. She hadn't been expecting this. It was too, too—It was too intimate. The way he was looking at her, the care he was taking as he touched her. She moved her arm away by reaching up and taking his glasses off. She folded them neatly and set them aside. She moved closer to him and heard his breaths coming faster. That gave her a burst of satisfaction. She had power over him, too.

She kissed the side of his neck, the scent of soap and warm skin filling her. She was glad he didn't wear cologne. She moved her lips down to his throat, kissing him there, then his cheek, his brow, before moving to his mouth. And they were kissing. Again.

Annie wanted to get even closer, feel his body against her, and this time she didn't have to worry about capsizing. She slid toward him, and something cold and wet splashed onto her leg. She jerked away. "I spilled your beer."

"Who cares?" He put his hands on her waist, urging her toward him, but Annie broke away. She scrambled back, then picked up the growler and refilled his cup.

"We were going to eat, right?" She began to unpack the food, hands trembling. Another few minutes and they'd have been stripping each other down. It was too fast. Too much. At least that's what her brain was telling her. Her body and her emotions had other ideas. But she barely knew him. And there was the distance and the divorce.

Nick put his glasses back on. He looked a little dazed.

"I brought sandwiches. We have chicken with pesto and sun-dried tomatoes or roast beef with blue cheese and horseradish."

"Can you repeat that? I just realized I somehow wasn't paying attention."

Annie put one of each sandwich and some chips on a plate and handed it to him. "Why not try both. And I have cake, of course. It's your birthday, you have to have cake."

He stared down at it for a moment, as if he'd forgotten what food was, then took a bite of the chicken sandwich. "Good."

"I think it's time for a new objective." Annie fixed a plate for herself.

He nodded, then nodded again. "Okay. Any ideas?"

Annie's pulse was almost back to normal—almost. What was she trying to do here? She struggled to organize her thoughts. Tonight was supposed to be for giving him a chance, for deciding if there was any point in starting something up. "I guess just getting to know each other better." That was squishy for an objective, but it's what they needed. Physical compatibility only went so far. "What about your divorce? What happened there?"

Nick rubbed the back of his neck. "What happened there? A

lot of things. Even I probably don't know all of them. A couple years ago, I decided to leave my job and try consulting. She wasn't crazy about the idea, but I pushed, and she ended up agreeing. Looking back, really thinking about it, I realize I used the fact that my parents had given us the house as part of the pushing. I kind of felt entitled to take the risk when I'd already contributed so much to our financial security. It's not exactly fair to call it my contribution when it was a gift, but—" He shook his head. "I didn't even start thinking about how it might have felt to her when I used the house as part of my rationale for leaving my nine-to-five job."

Annie waited, sensing he wasn't finished. He took a long swallow of his beer, then went on. "She brought up having kids as a reason for me to stay at my job. I didn't even think we were planning to have kids for three or four more years, so it didn't seem like a good enough reason to me."

Nick paused, brow furrowing. "Somehow we got out of sync. I don't know how else to say it. All this, this badness started building up between us. We didn't talk about it, not really. We talked about what to have for dinner or whether we should paint the house. But I was resentful because she wasn't being supportive of what I wanted to do. And I guess she felt the same way about me. We were each thinking about what we wanted, not what we wanted as a couple." He gave a helpless shrug, then picked up his sandwich again, although he didn't take a bite.

Her question had tanked the mood. She should have known it would. Maybe she had. Maybe that's what she'd wanted. It had been getting too intense between them. And this was part of getting to know him better.

"And she already got married again?"

"This really is a small town. You've already heard everything about me."

"Not everything."

"Yes, she got married again. Right away. So fast there was no question that she'd had something going with the guy while we were still together."

He suddenly sounded exhausted. She was supposed to be helping him celebrate his birthday. This wasn't the time to interrogate him about his failed marriage.

"What's your favorite color?" It was a stupid question, but it was the least personal question she could think of.

"I feel like I'm getting whiplash."

"I just realized I was asking questions that were way too personal."

"No. That's okay. I just—just wasn't expecting to go there, at least not right now. But it's okay."

"Did you end up switching to consulting like you wanted to?"

"Yeah. It's actually going great. I help small businesses get started. My dad and my uncle started a home-inspection business when I was a teenager. I got to see everything that went into it, and how much having their own company meant to them."

He had a passion for his work. She could tell that even from the little he'd just said. On a scale of one to ten, that was a ten for her. The divorce though . . . It was still fresh. Was he even ready to start something new? She didn't want to get in a rebound situation.

"Do you have anybody working with you? Or is it just you?"

"For now, it's just me. Sometimes I'm crazy busy, but I don't want to take on the expense of even a part-time employee. Not yet."

He was being sensible there. And he clearly didn't mind working hard. Annie appreciated that. "How did you get clients? Must be hard at first. I'm lucky there. Hatherley's is the only outfitter in town. That alone drives the business."

"I managed to use my degree and the experience I had with

my dad and my uncle's company to get a teaching gig at an extended-education program. People that took my class were at least thinking of starting a business. The class was a chance to show what I had to offer. I also started vlogging, giving lots of advice for free and doing free webinars for a site that targeted entrepreneurs. That gave me more ways to demonstrate what I could bring to the table. I took a lot of webinars, too, and went to seminars. I wanted to make connections with tech people, marketing people, anyone future clients might need."

"Who might also throw business your way."

"Exactly." Nick finally took a second bite of his sandwich. Annie realized she hadn't even started eating and popped a potato chip into her mouth. "Once I got a few people to give me a chance, I started getting a little good word of mouth going."

"I'm impressed. Didn't your wife see . . . She must have seen the effort you were putting in."

Nick raked one hand through his hair. "Maybe. At that point things were pretty messed up between us. I was working a ton. Most of it was necessary, maybe all of it, but it also gave me a way to absent myself. Instead of getting in there and trying to work through our problems, I avoided them. I avoided her."

"How long were you married?"

"Just over four years, but we were together since our first year at college."

Wow. Longer than Annie had expected.

"She was almost my first girlfriend. Definitely my first serious one. Junior year she had an apartment with a friend. Her roommate moved out at the end of the first semester, and I moved in. It wasn't even a big decision. It was just, like, she needed a roommate, and why not me, since we were together all the time anyway. I don't think either of us was thinking long term, not back then."

"Did you—"

"My turn. You said the objective was getting to know each other. That goes two ways. I'm supposed to be getting to know you better, too." Annie expected him to ask a question about her past relationships, but he said, "What's your trail name?"

She had to tell him. He'd answered her question about the divorce, and he hadn't held back about his part in the breakup. "Mooncalf," she admitted. He wiggled his fingers in a gimme motion. She was going to have to go there. "I did a section of the trail the summer between ninth and tenth grade. I went with my mom and a couple she was friends with. They had a son, Luke, who was two years ahead of me in school. I had a huge crush on him. I guess it was obvious. I tried to act normal. But his dad saw it. One day he called me Mooncalf, and it stuck."

"That's adorable. Why didn't you want to tell me?"

She'd hoped he'd let it go with her quick explanation. "It's kind of embarrassing."

"Everybody has crushes at that age. But I can see how it'd be embarrassing having the boy's dad tease you. Or was the boy a jerk about it?"

"No. He didn't make a thing about it."

Nick smiled. "What was he like? I'm curious what made young Annie's heart go pitter-pat."

This was the last thing she wanted to be talking about, especially with Nick. "Oh, you know, the usual for a teenage girl. He was cute, athletic, smart." There. That should do it. Her answer had been too boring to prolong the conversation. And it was the truth, at least part of it. "What about you? Any big crushes in high school?"

"Of course. Dozens of them. But I never actually did anything about them. Okay, I did things like figuring out where they lived and walking my dog by their house a gazillion times. Also, I'd walk casually past their locker a lot. But if they happened to be at their locker, I'd just duck my head and walk by really fast," Nick admitted. "You may not believe it, but I was not always the confident, well-adjusted, smokin'-hot guy you now see before you."

"You? Nah."

"Just so you know, I haven't stalked anyone for more than a decade."

"Me either."

"What were you like in high school?"

"Confident, well-adjusted, smokin' hot," Annie immediately answered, then laughed. "I'd known practically everybody I went to high school with practically since birth. They all knew that I laughed so hard I peed my pants in the fourth grade. Fourth. They all knew I broke my sixth-grade teacher's nose. We were playing softball, and he was catching, and even though he always told us not to throw the bat after we hit, I forgot and threw the bat. They all knew I'd never even met my dad."

"Did kids give you a hard time about your dad?"

"Not really. This one kid. But everyone thought he was a jerk." Annie took a bite of her sandwich, then added, "There was this book I loved when I was a kid, about a girl who moved to a new town and changed everything about herself. But there was no way to do that in Fox Crossing. We all knew each other too well."

Although that whole year after Luke died, she felt like she was just pretending to be the normal Annie everyone knew, when inside, she felt decimated. She didn't care about grades or friends or boys. She didn't care about Christmas or her birthday, and she skipped her junior prom. Food tasted bland in her mouth, and even the beauty of the woods couldn't reach her.

Time eventually did what time does. Her memories of Luke grew fuzzy around the edges, and that brought a different kind of pain, the pain of realizing she was losing him in a different way than she had when he died. She forced her attention back to the present and found Nick looking at her.

"What were you thinking about just then?"

She didn't have to tell the truth. She barely knew him. She didn't owe him her most painful memories, even though he'd told her about his marriage falling apart. She could tell him that she was thinking about what she needed to order for the store. Or about an argument with her mom.

"I was thinking about Luke." It was like the words had slipped out without her permission.

"The crush. Does he still live in Fox Crossing?"

"No." Annie hesitated. "He died. That summer. Almost as soon as we got back from the hike."

Nick lightly rested his hand on her wrist. "I'm sorry."

"It was a long time ago." Annie picked up her beer, the motion causing Nick's hand to fall away. "Are you ready for cake? I brought cake. I didn't make it. I got it at Shoo Fly's. He's an amazing baker. I got chocolate because pretty much everybody likes chocolate. I hope you like chocolate." Damn. She was doing it again, that nervous overtalking. She forced herself to stop, then looked at Nick, hoping he'd just let the subject of Luke go.

"I love chocolate." Nick took the last bite of his sandwich and wiped his hands on a napkin. "But you're not finished yet."

Annie realized she had more than half of her sandwich still on her plate. "Now that I'm thinking of cake, all I want is cake." She opened the box and set the cake between them. She'd already put candles in, and now she lit them. "Do you mind if I skip the singing? I suck at singing. And 'Happy Birthday' is actually a hard song."

Nick laughed. "It's fine." He pulled in a deep breath and blew out the candles.

"You got them all. That means you get your wish."

"That's actually up to you. Will you go out with me again? Even though we don't have a good reason, like a thank-you or a birthday?"

There were so many reasons to say no.

She looked into his eyes. "Yes."

Even with the lake water separating them, The Fox could feel the woman's raw joy. Even from a distance, she could see the dazzling brightness of her newest connection cord. The Fox gazed at it, the way she gazed at the moon and stars, soaking in the beauty.

CHAPTER 13

Nick walked back out to the doctor's waiting room, holding his crutches under one arm. Banana stood and put his phone in his pocket. "Looks like it went well."

"I've been cleared to walk, unless it starts getting painful, and she gave me a few basic exercises. But she doesn't want me to drive until all the tenderness is gone. I'm thinking I'll stay at least another week. I can do most of my work remotely, and I'd like to get out in the woods at least a little. Not the Wilderness, of course," Nick added quickly. "I know I'm not ready for that."

Banana's phone buzzed as they walked toward the front door. "Probably Honey again. She wants to know how it went last night. I guess Annie's not giving enough details." He opened the door for Nick.

"If Annie's not saying, I don't think I should either. But if you guarantee it'll just stay between you and me . . ."

"Not a problem. Did I ask you how it went when I picked you up? No. Because I figured if you wanted me to know, you'd tell me," Banana said. "Although I thought you'd want to tell me right away, considering I took you in when you needed help, found you a place to stay, fed you, drove you to the doctor, got you the best table at—"

"Okay, okay. You're right." Nick climbed into the Jeep, then waited for Banana to get behind the wheel. "I couldn't have asked for a better birthday. All because of Annie. She brought me the best chocolate cake I've ever had."

"And?"

"And it had chocolate buttercream frosting with chocolate ganache on top of that. Like I said, amazing." Nick tried to keep a straight face, but cracked up about two seconds later. "It really was a great night."

"Good. I know Annie wanted you to have a good birthday." Banana pulled out onto the street.

"I couldn't even wait until the night was over before I asked her out again. I had to know. If she hadn't agreed . . ." Nick shook his head. "Let me ask you something. Annie said you'd done a bunch of trail rescues. Did you ever save anyone's life?"

"I don't know, not for sure. But there's one time I can think of where it's likely I did."

"Did you feel a connection between the two of you?"

"Definitely." Banana thought for a moment. "But I felt that with a lot of the people I spent time with on the trail. Maybe it's having a common goal. Maybe it's that everyone who decides to spend months on the trail is a little crazy, and crazy recognizes crazy? I don't know."

Nick used his fingers to comb his hair off his forehead. "I feel this pull toward Annie. It's so strong, even though I've only known her a few days. Like I was saying, I felt like I needed to know for sure that I was going to see her again. Not just wanted, *needed*. It's a little freaky, really. I've never felt so much for someone so fast. I started wondering if it was partly because she saved me." He'd been pretty out of it that night, but he remembered a feeling of intimacy. He'd turned himself completely over to her. He'd had to.

"If it was just that, I think it would start wearing off at some point."

"That makes sense." It definitely hadn't started wearing off. It had gotten stronger. When she'd touched him, that first short kiss, it had been incendiary.

Banana pulled up in front of the bar. He hauled a sack of party decorations out of the back seat. "I hope Jordan will like this little party. I wanted to be able to introduce her to a bunch of the town kids all at once, so she'd know she'd have friends here this summer. But now I'm wondering if she'll feel overwhelmed."

Nick could see it going either way, depending on the kid, but he wasn't going to say that to Banana. The party was already a done deal. "I think it's going to show her that you're really happy to have her here."

"I hope it shows her mom that, too." Banana grabbed the door handle, but hesitated. "Once, on Jordan's fifth birthday, I sent her one of those American Girl Addy dolls, actually a whole gift trunk with books and accessories and all that."

"I only vaguely know what you're talking about, but sounds like a great present."

"Miranda was really into those books and dolls when she was little. I was thinking about her when I picked it out. But it pissed her off. She accused me of trying to buy Jordan's love. I wasn't. I don't think I was, at least. Miranda and her family were always booked when I wanted to visit, and sending stuff was something I could do. To try and be in Jordan's life, even if just a little." Banana seemed to realize that he was still holding the door handle and quickly got out of the car.

Nick eased himself onto the sidewalk. He'd gotten so used to the crutches that it felt weird not to have their support.

"It's too late now, but I started thinking what if Miranda thinks I'm still trying to buy Jordan's affection? It's not like I spent a ton on the party. Shoo Fly insisted on giving me the cake, Honey loaned me some fairy lights, and I already had soda and stuff for nachos at the bar. I really only bought a few extras. But I don't know my daughter well enough to know how she'll react." Banana gave a wry smile. "My own daughter."

"Maybe having Jordan here will change that. You'll have time to get to know her, and that might build a kind of bridge back to your daughter."

"Miranda should be happy to see Annie and some of the other kids, kids who are now adults, that she knew from when she was a girl." Banana led the way into the bar, then dumped the party supplies on the nearest table.

"How old was she when she left?"

"Eleven and a bit. But she came back a few times. Not often, and not for long, but still."

"Where do we start?"

"I rented a helium tank. You can be on balloon duty. Big Matt and I will start getting the streamers up. I don't want you getting on a ladder, not on your first hour off crutches." Banana started for the double doors leading to the kitchen. "Maybe helium was a mistake. Maybe I should have gone for regular," Nick heard him mutter.

Banana was really nervous. Nick wasn't sure what he could do to make a party for a ten-year-old turn out great, but he'd give it his best. He hoped Banana's daughter would have to see the party as a sign of love. It seemed obvious to Nick, but he'd learned that it wasn't always easy to decode someone else's feelings, learned that the hard way.

"I'm trying to remember how old we were the last time we saw Miranda," Chloe said as she and Annie started walking to Banana's bar for the welcome party.

"It was before Luke died." That was one big marker on Annie's personal time line, before and after Luke. "I think just the summer before. So, when we were about to go into ninth grade." And he was about to go into eleventh.

She thought about telling Chloe that she'd talked a little bit about him, Luke, with Nick. That should prove to Chloe she was wrong about Annie's emotional scars, or whatever Chloe would call them. How bad could they be if she had been willing to talk about Luke with a guy she barely knew?

The thing was, though, that it didn't feel like she and Nick barely knew each other. She'd never felt comfortable with a guy so fast. And her attraction to him was off the charts. When he'd kissed her palm, she'd felt it down to the bone. She hadn't told Chloe any of that. It felt too special. Too intimate. It felt like talking about it would take away the magic. She'd just given Chloe a few tidbits—they'd rowed around the lake, she'd brought him a birthday cake—and left it at that. She hadn't even said that she'd agreed to go out with him again. She didn't want to analyze the way she felt, and Chloe loved to analyze.

"I wonder if we'll have that thing the two of us have with Miranda," Chloe said. "You know, the way we can pick our friendship right back up whenever we see each other."

"I don't know. We've never gone more than a few years without getting together. That might make a difference."

"Holy guacamole," Chloe breathed as they passed through a curtain of gold fringe and into Wit's Beginning. The place was almost unrecognizable, shining with garlands of white fairy lights. Miniature golden trees draped with more of the lights served as centerpieces. Huge bouquets of gold and silver helium balloons bloomed in every corner. A banner reading WELCOME HOME, MIRANDA AND JORDAN! ran the length of one wall, and on top of the bar sat an enormous cake in the shape of a fox. No, not a fox. The Fox. Its tail was tipped with black, and it—she—had that white ear and the white sock on one front leg.

"Everything looks beautiful," Annie told Banana when he hurried over to greet them.

"I hope it's okay for a ten-year-old. I thought maybe I should do a *Frozen* theme or something. But Nick and I googled decorations for a tween party, and a lot of them seemed to go more fancy."

"It's perfect," Chloe assured him. "My ten-year-old self is squealing with delight."

Banana ran his hand over his bald head, which was lightly sheened with sweat. "It's been five years since I saw Miranda and Jordan. Jordan wouldn't even be able to pick me out of a crowd."

"Well, that's about to change. When are they supposed to get here?"

"They should already be here. I told Miranda I'd come pick them up in Bangor, but she wanted to rent a car. Maybe they decided to stop for lunch."

Violet and one of her trail widows pushed their way through the gold fringe curtain, and Banana hurried over to greet them. "I don't think I've ever seen Banana all nervous and agitated before." Chloe's brows drew together. "I wonder if he told Miranda about the party? If it's a surprise, it might be a little overwhelming, especially for Jordan. She won't know anybody."

It was a little overwhelming for Annie, and she knew everyone. She liked her people in small groups or one-on-one, and the bar was filling up. She wasn't surprised. Everybody loved Banana.

"Can I get you two something to drink?" Annie felt heat rush through her body, just hearing that voice. She turned, and the feeling intensified when she saw Nick smiling at her.

"Chloe, this is Nick." Annie briefly rested her hand on his arm. "And Nick, this is Chloe, one of my oldest friends. She's in town for the summer, staying in one of the cabins by the lake."

"Great to meet you," Nick said. "I want to hear every story you have about Annie, especially the embarrassing ones. But first, drinks. What will you have? Banana's put me to work as backup bartender for the party."

"I'll have a beer," Chloe told him. "And don't ask what kind. Just a regular beer beer. The other night, Banana was trying to teach me, but he started going all Charlie Brown teacher, *mmwah*, *mmwah*, haziness, *mmwah*, whirlpooling, *mmmwah*, *mmmwah*, fruitiness."

Nick laughed. "I feel you. I'm the same way. Annie knows." He winked at her and she felt another rush of heat.

"Oh, wait, no. I'll have a Moxie. I haven't had one since I got here. I could order it online at home, but it's not the same," Chloe said.

"It's soda. Banana has it on tap," Annie explained, seeing Nick's blank look. "I'll have one, too."

"On it." Nick headed for the bar.

"Wow, Annie, he's so cute!" Chloe exclaimed. "I love those glasses. And that curly hair. Just makes you want to run your fingers through it. Except, of course, if he's infatuated with your friend. Which he is."

Annie shook her head. "You can't know that. He was only over here for about ten seconds."

"I only needed to see how he looks at you. He—"

"They're here!" Banana yelled. He signaled to Big Matt, who was set up as DJ, and the music cut off. Banana pulled back the gold fringe curtain and Miranda and her daughter walked in.

"Miranda looks so sophisticated," Chloe murmured to Annie. "I'm not sure I would have recognized her."

"Eighteen years is a long time." Annie took in Miranda's tailored pantsuit and the way twists of her hair wrapped together to form a kind of crown bun. She definitely looked more big city than little bitty town.

Banana, beaming, led Miranda and Jordan to the dance floor he'd cleared in the center of the room. "A lot of you know my daughter, Miranda, but this is my granddaughter Jordan's first visit to Fox Crossing." He put his hand on Jordan's shoulder. She didn't jerk away, but she moved enough to make his hand fall off her. "I can't wait to introduce her to all of you."

Annie applauded with the rest of the group. Miranda gave a friendly wave, but Jordan stared at the ground, shoulders a little hunched. "She doesn't look happy to be here," Annie said when the music started back up.

"Can you blame her? Her mom and dad are both going to be out of the country, and she's staying with someone she only knows from phone calls a few times a year," Chloe answered. "Banana will win her over. He's great with kids. Remember how much fun we had when we'd do sleepovers? Remember when he made us a whole miniature golf course out of cardboard?"

"I'd almost forgotten about that! There was a windmill, and he used a blow-dryer on it to make it turn when we got to that hole." Annie smiled at the memory. "I was actually a little jealous of Miranda and Banana's relationship. I didn't spend a lot of time thinking about not having a dad, but sometimes those two, together, they made me feel like I was really missing out."

"I even felt that way sometimes," Chloe admitted.

"But your dad's great."

"I know. He is. And I never doubted he and my mom loved us. But I never felt like I had all their attention, not the way Banana was with Miranda. Maybe it's just that Miranda was an only child."

"Or maybe he's just one of those adults who still likes to play. Honey's like that. She was always up for being the supervillain when I wanted to play superheroes. She even made this crazy costume out of one of those Mylar emergency blankets and cheetah-print duct tape. She'd probably do that today if I asked her to."

"Definitely. Yesterday at work, she spent almost half an hour talking to a little boy in a fox language they were making up together."

Annie laughed. "I would—"

She was interrupted by Nick returning with the drinks. "I decided to get one for myself. Got to try the local favorite." Nick handed cups to Annie and Chloe. He took a swallow of his drink, and Annie could tell the moment the aftertaste hit. He grimaced; she and Chloe exchanged an amused look.

"At first it was like a combo of root beer and Coke, but better than either of them. Then—" He grimaced again. "I can't even describe it."

"Like licorice?" Annie suggested.

"No. I know licorice. I like licorice."

"Like a mentholated cough drop exploded in your throat?" Chloe asked.

"More like died there."

"It's one of those things you either love or hate." Chloe tapped her cup to Annie's, then took a long drink. "Love it!"

"Some people say it's an acquired taste," Annie told Nick. "Maybe you . . ." Her words trailed off. A nearby couple had started toward the dance floor, giving Annie a look at Banana, Miranda, and Jordan. They were sitting at a table at the edge of the dance floor, just sitting. The Fox made out of cake stared down at them from the place of honor on the bar. "It doesn't look like they're even talking." Annie tilted her chin toward Banana and his family.

"Uh-oh." Chloe's brows drew together. "Do you think we should go over there?"

"It might make it even more awkward," Annie answered.

"I have an idea." Nick thrust his cup into Annie's free hand.

"You drink that." He crossed the room and took the microphone from Big Matt. A few seconds later, the music cut off.

"It's that time," Nick called out. "Time to see who has it and who doesn't. It's time for Minute to Win It. Logan, Noah, get up here. Violet, Honey, you, too. Who else wants to play?" He looked over at Banana's table. Annie looked over, too. Miranda was shaking her head, and Banana and Jordan were clearly taking their cues from her.

"I want to play!" Annie declared. She wasn't much into games, but Nick was trying to help Banana, and she wanted to have his back. Chloe nodded, and they joined Nick and the others on the dance floor. Bob and Yvette Martin from the mercantile came up too. And the Pelletier twins, who were about Jordan's age.

Nick took a tray of cookies off the bar. "Okay, everybody, tilt your head back."

Annie let her head fall back, looking up at the ceiling. She heard Honey giggle, and Logan ask, "Is there going to be a prize?"

"Of course there is going to be a prize," Nick answered. Annie felt him step up beside her. She had to be imagining it, but she could have sworn she could feel the heat of his body through his clothes and hers. He brushed her hair away from her face, then put something light on her forehead.

"What's that?" Annie asked. Nick didn't answer, just touched the fox pendant she wore at her throat before he stepped away.

"I've put a cookie on each of your foreheads," Nick announced a few moments later. "When I say go, you're going to try to get the cookie from your forehead to your mouth, without using your hands."

"I dropped mine already," someone called. Annie thought it was Oliver Kusugak, from the post office.

"I'll get you another one," Nick answered. "I'm also going

to need judges. You three!" Annie was sure he'd just picked Banana, Miranda, and Jordan. "Come on over here. I need you to make sure no one cheats. No hands allowed. All right. Ready, set, go!"

Annie began raising and lowering her eyebrows, trying to get the cookie moving. It slid down onto her right eye. She gave her head a little shake.

"Mine got stuck to my mustache," a man called. Annie was sure it was Dale Simpson, the owner of Foxy Loxy's. He did have a truly impressive mustache, inspired by that of his favorite author, Herman Melville. Dale wanted the matching beard, but his wife said she'd move out if he went there.

"No, you can't touch it!" a girl called out. Had to be Jordan. She sounded like she was already getting into the game. Annie smiled. Nick was so fun. And kind. And—And she found herself thinking about him so often. How had she gotten such strong feelings for him so fast? She felt as if she'd climbed onto a rocket and had no idea where it was taking her. It was a little scary. But she liked it. Annie's smile widened, and the cookie tumbled off her eyelid. With a quick twist of her head, she managed to catch it between her teeth.

"We have a winner!" Nick yelled.

CHAPTER 14

"You're steaming up my glasses," Nick murmured into Annie's ear.

She plucked them off, then leaned across him so she could stow the glasses in the pouch that hung on his side of the double hammock. After Banana's party, they'd decided on grilling at her place instead of going out. And after they ate, well, the hammock was right there in Annie's backyard.

Annie started to return to her side of the hammock, but Nick wrapped one arm around her waist, capturing her against his chest. "Yes? There was something you needed?" she asked.

"I can think of a few things." He ran his hand lower, to the curve of her hip. Then his cell vibrated.

"Is that your phone, or are you just happy to see me?" Annie gave a little wiggle that put more of her body flush against his.

"I'm delighted to see you, but that was the phone. And I should answer. It's already gone off three times. I just need to make sure there's not some emergency."

"Sure." Annie rolled off him, then climbed out of the hammock. "I'm going to go get more beer." She headed for the house.

Nick managed to sit up and pull his phone out of his pocket. No calls, but a bunch of texts. The subject line of the first one told him everything: *Our wonderful new baby!* He felt like he'd been sucker punched in the gut. Which was crazy, because this wasn't a surprise. He'd known this was coming. Lisa had called him herself to tell him she was pregnant. Part of that staying-friends thing. He'd even given her a shower present, for chrissakes. He hadn't actually gone, but he'd sent something. He couldn't remember what right now. His brain felt scrambled.

He didn't click open the text. He didn't want to see a picture of the *wonderful new baby.* Maybe if Lisa had talked to him about how soon she wanted kids before she started screwing some other—

What was going on with him? He felt as furious as he had when he found out Lisa wanted a divorce, and, PS, already had a new husband lined up. But that was old stuff. He'd gotten past it. Way past it. But somehow his body hadn't gotten the message. His fingers were clenched around the phone, his heart giving heavy thuds against his ribs, and his scalp was prickling.

"Get a grip, get a grip, get a grip," he muttered to himself. He forced himself to look at the next text. It was from Marcus, first friend he'd made when his family moved to Bensalem when Nick was fifteen. All it said was *Thought you'd want to know that Lisa had the baby. Call if you want.* Nick was sure the other new texts would be variations of the same. Why did Marcus think Nick would need to talk? This wasn't about him. It had nothing to do with him.

"Is everything okay?" Annie asked when she came back out, holding another Wit's Beginning growler.

"Yeah. Yeah." He struggled to decide what to say to her. He was having trouble forming a coherent thought. "It's a minor work thing," he finally managed to say. "I need to take care of it." He scrambled off the hammock and started for Annie's driveway, then realized he didn't have his car because he still wasn't supposed to be driving.

"Let me just get my keys. Are you sure everything's all right?"

"Yep." It should be. It should be, but it wasn't.

The Fox didn't understand what had happened. She'd stopped to take in the dazzle of the connection cord between the two humans. Then the light dimmed, and she could smell the panic coming off the male. There was no threat to him that she could see, but the tang of his sweat and the heat rising in his body showed her he felt danger close by. She felt his agitation in her own body and retreated deeper into the woods to escape it.

She'd been called to help the dog, and she had helped. But even if she desired to help the man who had formed such a bright connection to the female with the blood of The Woman, The Fox couldn't. She'd seen hunger and thirst in the dog. She'd seen the need for new connections. But the man . . . She didn't understand what the man needed. He seemed to have everything he needed right there with the woman.

"Will you two keep an eye on Jordan?" Miranda asked. "I'm worried about her. Her dad and I have never been deployed at the same time. She's always had one of us with her."

"Absolutely," Annie promised. She took a bite of her orange-cranberry muffin. Her mom was keeping an eye on the store so Annie could meet up with Miranda and Chloe for a late-morning coffee. They had Flappy's pretty much to themselves.

Annie had thought maybe she'd see Nick when she'd come to Flappy's for early-morning coffee. She'd mentioned to him that she pretty much always made a Flappy's stop, and he'd said something about getting addicted to the pancakes. They hadn't had plans or anything, but she'd thought he might stop in, and she couldn't help feeling a little disappointed that he hadn't. He'd seemed so strange last night when she'd driven him home. He hadn't even kissed her when she dropped him off.

"Of course," Chloe said. "And you know Banana is going to do everything he can to make sure she has a good time while she's here."

Annie forced her mind away from Nick. Reassuring Miranda was important. "We were just talking the other day about all the fun stuff he came up with for us when we were kids, like that cardboard minigolf course."

Miranda frowned a little. "How old were we?"

Annie looked to Chloe. "I think I was around nine, which makes Chloe seven and a halfish, so you would have been ten."

Miranda shook her head. "I sort of remember. Was there a castle?"

"Yes!" Chloe exclaimed. "A castle made of LEGOs with a drawbridge!"

"So many of my memories of back then are so vague. You're the psychology student, Chloe. Isn't there something about why memories from before a certain age fade?" Miranda asked.

"There's something called childhood amnesia." Chloe began tearing her napkin into little bits. "Kids who are eight or nine remember about twenty percent less than kids who are around seven. It's just part of the way our brains form."

"I feel like I remember tons of things that happened before I was eight," Annie protested.

"Well, adults play a big part in what we remember," Chloe explained. "When they turn what's happened to us into a story, give it a setting, give it context, it's easier to remember."

"Honey and Charlie still love telling stories about me when I was little," Annie said.

"I guess that means my mom didn't tell a lot of stories about little me," Miranda said. "Not surprising. Her time in Fox Crossing wasn't the best."

"You remember doing some stuff with us though, right?" Chloe asked.

"Of course." Miranda smiled. "Didn't we spend a lot of one summer following around a boy one of you had a crush on?"

"That was me." Annie didn't tell Miranda what had happened to that boy and was glad Chloe didn't either. There was no need, especially when Miranda was already stressed, not that she'd said so, but it was easy to see in her tense posture.

"I'm sure I'd remember more if I still lived here. I'd have kept on seeing the same people and places. Everything would have been connected."

"True," Annie said. "I see most of my teachers from kindergarten to high school all the time. That keeps the memories fresh. It's not just from hearing stories."

"Once my mom and I moved, I hardly ever saw my father. Now he's acting like . . ." Miranda hesitated. "He's acting like we're close. Like he knows me."

Chloe shot a fast glance at Annie. "I think he's probably acting that way because that's what he wants your relationship to be like."

"I think he wanted to see you more," Annie added. "I'm not sure your mother—"

Miranda didn't let her finish. "Don't put that on my mother. My dad knew where I was if he wanted to see me."

Annie wasn't going to argue. It wasn't her place to tell Miranda that maybe her mother had kept Banana away. Annie and Miranda weren't close. They hadn't been for years. And you needed to be close to have such an intense conversation. Although, weirdly, she'd already started having those kinds of conversations with Nick.

"I needed a father back then," Miranda continued. "I don't now."

Except that she did need Banana to take care of her daughter, his granddaughter. Annie kept that thought to herself, too. Miranda picked up her coffee cup, then set it back down. "It's empty. I forgot I drank it all. See, my memory isn't great, even about things that just happened."

Annie raised her hand to signal Scotty for a refill. "I don't need more," Miranda said, and Annie put her hand down. "Too much caffeine makes me jittery, and I'm jittery enough. I know Jordan will be safe here." Annie was glad to hear that Miranda trusted Banana in that way. That was big. "I'm just afraid she's going to be miserable."

"What's Jordan into? What do you think she'd like to do while she's here?" Annie asked.

Miranda sighed. "She's an inward-focused child. She likes to draw and read. Half the time, she's off in a daydream. I've been trying to correct that."

"Daydreaming isn't necessarily a bad thing," Chloe said. "If it prevents her from making connections with people or from getting her homework done, that could be a problem. But daydreaming actually makes people more empathetic. It can also motivate people to meet their goals. It's the power of positive visualization."

"Isn't it great to have a psychologist for a friend?" Annie said. "Chloe's actually here working on her thesis. She decided to rent one of the lakeside cabins to get some writing done."

"You really think daydreaming isn't harmful for Jordan?" Miranda asked. "She's pretty much of a loner, although when I see her with other kids, she doesn't seem to have trouble engaging."

"I daydreamed all the time as a kid," Chloe admitted. "Once in a while, it was a problem. Like I'd always forget where I put my backpack, and sometimes I'd completely tune out the teacher." She smiled. "This one time, I found a fuzzy caterpillar on the playground. I took it inside with me and put it in my desk. The whole rest of the day, I was imagining all these adventures the two of us would have. I think that might have been the day we learned the sevens times tables, because I still have to start from the fives and then add if I need to multiply."

Annie stared at Chloe. "You're kidding."

"I'm not," Chloe insisted. "But I don't actually need the times tables that often. My phone does the math for me."

Miranda glanced at the clock. "I have to go. My flight leaves tonight, and I want to get Jordan as settled as I can. I'm hoping if I spend time with her and my dad together, then she'll do better when I'm gone."

"We have your number. We'll text you updates on how she's doing," Chloe promised.

"Thank you. That's going to make it a little easier." Miranda stood. "It was great reconnecting with you two." She gave Annie and Chloe quick hugs, then left.

"It's sad that she doesn't even have the stories of all the fun stuff she and her dad did together," Chloe said as soon as the door shut behind Miranda.

"I didn't think I should get into it with her, but I know for sure Banana wanted to see her after she and her mom moved to Oregon. What I always got from my mom and Honey was that Lea always had some reason why it wasn't a good time for Banana to visit. He went out a few times, but he wanted to go a lot more." Annie ran one finger around the rim of her coffee cup. "I know firsthand that Banana wanted to go visit Miranda after she was an adult. He wanted to spend time with her and Jordan, but Miranda did the same thing her mom did. She almost always came up with reasons why it wasn't a good time for Banana to go out there. She never completely cut off contact, but almost."

"Families. They're complicated," Chloe offered. "How great

was your boyfriend yesterday though? Things were looking extremely awkward between Banana, Miranda, and Jordan until he started those games."

"He's not my boyfriend," Annie protested.

Chloe gave a dismissive flip of her hand. "Just a technicality. A few more dates, and you'll be a couple. And I know you'll go on more dates. You liiiike him."

Annie felt a smile breaking across her face. She tried to hide it, but she couldn't. "I do like him. And we're actually going out tonight." They hadn't made firm plans for breakfast, but seeing Nick tonight was definite.

"You said you were going out to dinner after the party."

"We actually ended up cooking burgers on the grill at my place." Annie didn't mention how Nick had gotten kind of weird before he left. Chloe would want to pick it to pieces, and Annie didn't want to make a big deal over something that was probably no big deal.

"So tonight will be"—Chloe did an exaggerated finger count, mouthing the numbers as she went—"four times you've gotten together. Plus, the whole thing where you saved his life. I'm revising my opinion. He *is* your boyfriend. It's all in the math."

"Says the woman who just admitted she doesn't know the sevens times tables," Annie joked.

"Says the woman who will shortly have a master's in psychology." Chloe countered. "Whether you admit it or not, you and cutie-pie Nick are a couple."

CHAPTER 15

Nick felt like his veins were pumping pure adrenaline instead of blood, energy coursing through him. He wanted to run to Annie's store, but he knew his ankle couldn't take more than a walk. He couldn't wait to tell her his idea. It was brilliant, if he did say so himself.

"Nick." The shout-whisper came from behind him just as he reached Hatherley's. He turned and saw Shoo Fly and the hound slowly approaching, Shoo Fly still having to coax each step out of the beast. "I'm trying to get him socialized. Can you slowly, really slowly, give him a pat."

"Sure." When they got close enough, Nick reached out to pet the dog.

Shoo Fly caught his wrist. "Not on his head. Go for under his chin or his chest. And crouch down. And don't look him in the eye."

"O-kay." Wondering what he was getting himself into, Nick slowly hunkered down in front of the dog, eyes on his front paws. When the dog didn't growl, Nick gave him a light scratch on the chest.

"Good boy, good boy," Shoo Fly murmured.

"Is it okay if I stand back up?"

"Yes. But slow." Nick inched his way back to a standing position. "Thank you. I need him to learn to trust people if I'm going to find him a home. He deserves a good one."

"He's clearly been through a lot. Poor guy."

Shoo Fly nodded. "Thanks for stopping."

"Anytime. What's his name anyway?"

"I'm not giving him one. That's for his new people to decide. I'm just getting him presentable enough that someone will adopt him."

"He already looks better." The dog's ribs were still visible, but they didn't look about to poke through his skin.

"Come on, dog." Shoo Fly took a small step. "Here we go. Good, good dog."

When they'd inched past him, Nick walked into Annie's. "I can't believe you were talking to Shoo Fly. Shoo Fly doesn't talk to anyone unless it's necessary, especially to people he doesn't know."

"He knows me a little. I met him the other day with Banana. He stopped me so I could interact with the dog. Shoo Fly's trying to get him used to people so he'll have a better chance of getting adopted." Nick grinned at Annie. "The Fox brought the dog almost to Shoo Fly's door. Are you still so sure there's no such thing as luck?"

She came around the counter, looped her arms around his neck, and looked up at him. "I have to admit, I'm feeling pretty lucky right now." She kissed him soft and sweet. "I thought maybe I'd see you at Flappy's this morning, but wasn't expecting you to come by the store. Did you miss me?"

"Horribly." Nick thought about apologizing for leaving so abruptly the night before, but he didn't want to talk to her about Lisa and the baby. Not when he had much more important things to say. "I missed you, and, also, I couldn't wait to tell you about this genius plan I came up with."

"Genius? Well, let's hear it." She kept her arms around him.

How could he have freaked out about Lisa having a baby when he had started up something so amazing with Annie?

"Okay, remember how I thought I was prepared to hike the Wilderness because I'd done some practice hikes at home?"

"Which weren't nearly enough." She gave him a quick hug before she released him.

"Exactly. And there are lots of people like me who decide to hike the AT, right?"

"Right."

She was going to love this. It was going to make things between them so much easier. "So, I'm going to start a boot camp, a place where wannabe Appalachian Trail hikers can get trained right. I'm thinking I can get Banana to be one of the instructors. Maybe even Shoo Fly, since the dog's got him a little more willing to talk to people. What do you think?"

"You're going to start this here?"

"Of course, here. The trail's here. You're here. And if I start a business here, then I'm here, too. It's win-win-win-win."

"That's crazy." Annie backed up a step. "You can't just start a business like that. You have to research. You have to have a business plan. You have to—"

Nick didn't let her finish. "I'm a consultant for people who want to start a business. I know all the steps. I started researching last night. There's nothing like what I have in mind anywhere. I'm not talking anywhere in Maine. I'm talking anywhere. It'll be a place where people can learn everything— how to pitch a tent, what equipment is necessary and what is just useless weight, trail first aid, how to read a topogr—"

"You're not doing this for me, are you? We barely know each other, Nick. It's seriously crazy to start a business so we can be in the same town."

Why wasn't she excited? Couldn't she see how perfect this was? "Of course, you're a factor. Honestly, a big factor. But I know how to recognize a good business opportunity, and this is one. I can't believe no one's done it before."

Annie took another step away from him. "Have you thought about how short the hiking season is? No one can even start the southbound hike until Baxter State Park announces that the Hunt Trail is open. That could be mid-May. It could also be well into June. And the northbound hikers don't really start arriving until a few weeks into June."

"But I can have the boot camp running before that. There's a lot of training for hikers to do before they're ready for the trail. You know that more than anyone."

"Fox Crossing can get snow into April, and it can start up again in October. That means you're talking about a business that can only operate less than half the year. Less than half!"

"I'm aware of that."

"Then you have to be aware that your idea is ridiculous. It will never work."

"I can make it work, same as you do," Nick insisted. She was already shaking her head, not even giving him the chance to explain. He rushed on. He'd make her understand. "You do enough business during the season to make your place a success. Honey, too, I'm assuming. But anyway, I have other ideas. This place is ripe for a festival, like Trail Days in Virginia. Damascus, where they have it, is almost exactly the same size as Fox Crossing."

"The Trail Days festival is in May, Nick. May!" Annie cried, her face flushing with anger. "Have you forgotten who you're talking to? There's nothing that happens along the trail that I don't already know about."

Nick held up both hands. "Please, just listen to me. I was thinking about a winter festival, with ice sculptures, cross-country skiing, sled-dog races." She'd started shaking her head again, and he talked faster. She needed to hear him out. "People could come in costumes, like they do at Mammoth in California. There would be arts and crafts. Honey would sell a ton of fox stuff. There'd be food. I bet your mother would help me get the town selectmen on board."

"You've spoken with my mother for less than ten minutes total. You can't possibly know what she'd do," Annie protested.

"She wants what's good for the town, and a festival would be great. I have tons of ideas. And they wouldn't all have to be for a festival. Some could go all winter long. Snowmobile adventures, snowshoe tours." His brain was firing so fast he could hardly keep track of his thoughts. He knew what it felt like when he heard a business idea that would work, and this one was going to work. Big-time.

"You're clearly just making this up as you go along."

Nick laughed. "Some of it, yes. But in a good way. I just keep thinking of more and more possibilities. Don't worry. I'll come up with a solid business plan. I'm just brainstorming."

She crossed her arms. She looked more disapproving than she had when she'd found out he was planning to hike the Wilderness, and that was saying something. "To be clear, you're not planning on doing this right now?" she asked, her words clipped.

"I'm planning to do the hiking boot camp this year. The season has barely started, and there's not a lot of start-up stuff I'd need to do. When we were heading out of town to go to the 380 Grill, I saw a FOR RENT sign on a big barn. I'm thinking I could use it as office space and also a place for indoor classes. I looked it up, and there are fifteen acres on the property. That's perfect for training. Also, we can go out and do short sections on the actual trail."

"You know you're talking about a lot of money."

She wasn't getting it. He had to make her see what an opportunity this was. "I had to sell the house, the house my parents gave me and Lisa. I told you about it, remember? I had to sell so I could give her half. I still have mine. I have the start-up money to get up and running."

"Nick, listen to me. Listen!" There was so much more he wanted to tell her, but he forced himself to stop and pay attention. "You have to be very sure that this doesn't have anything to do with being in the same town as me."

"Of course, it—"

"It can't. Because this"—she gestured back and forth between the two of them—"this isn't going to work. I should have known that. The first day we met, I saw how impulsive you are, how reckless. I can't be with somebody like that."

"You're breaking up with me?"

"No. I'm not breaking up with you because we aren't together. We've gone out a few times. It was nice. It was fun. But it's nothing that can last. We're way too different."

Nice? Fun? It was more than that, and she knew it. "What does that matter? The times we've been together—amazing. You can't tell me they weren't."

"They were just a few hours here and there. They weren't real life. In real life, being with somebody like you would never work."

Nick raked his hair away from his face. " 'Somebody like that.' 'Somebody like you.' What do you even mean?"

"I mean, somebody irresponsible, somebody reckless, somebody who never thinks of the consequences." Annie didn't yell, but her voice was tight with anger. "Have you even thought for one second what could have happened to me when I had to go after you? People die trying to rescue other people."

"But you're trained. You know the woods. You—"

"So was Luke. And he died going after somebody bumbled off into the woods, just like you did."

Luke? It took him a moment to remember who that was. Luke, her crush. Who died.

"Annie, I'm sorry about—"

"I can't talk to you anymore. You have to leave, Nick. Right now."

"You can't—"

"I said right now. Go!"

He could see there was no point in trying to talk to her right then. She clearly wasn't able to listen. He'd give her a little time. He'd let her cool off. Then he'd find a way to make her understand. Understand that he knew what made a business work as well as she knew her woods. But more than that, he'd get her to admit that what they had between them didn't come around often. He'd get her to admit that she didn't want to walk away from it any more than he did.

Annie realized she was trembling, actually trembling. "Nothing is wrong. You're fine. You're absolutely fine," she told herself. She managed to walk behind the counter. She picked up the sweater she kept back there and pulled it on, wrapped her arms around herself, and sank down on the stool behind the cash register. She was still shaking. "You're fine," she said again. Her body was reacting as if she'd narrowly escaped death. All that had happened was that she'd broken up—no, not broken up. All that had happened was she had decided that Nick Ferrone wasn't anyone she wanted to keep going out with. She hardly knew him. She'd met him less than two weeks ago. This was no big thing.

Maybe he wouldn't go through with his insane idea, now that she'd told him there was no possibility of anything happening between them. Maybe he'd actually use his brain. She didn't understand how he could make a living advising other people on how to get their businesses going. Not if she'd just gotten a look at him in action.

Annie closed her eyes and pulled in a deep breath. There. There now. She wasn't trembling anymore. She stood. Her legs felt wobbly, but they held her. She had things to do. She always had things to do. What? What, what, what? Inventory! She'd done inventory a week ago, but inventory was important. She'd do it again.

Before she could start, the door chimed and a couple, both probably in their thirties, came in. "We just got engaged, and we decided to celebrate by hiking to Mount Katahdin!" the guy announced, all pleased with himself.

"Actually, we won't be engaged until we get there. That's where he's going to give me the ring," the woman added, wrapping her arm around her fiancé-to-be's waist. "We need everything. We didn't even bring backpacks."

"We were planning to go to a bed-and-breakfast on the lake in Greenville, but on the way, we decided this would be much cooler."

"Do you mean that you left your gear at home, or that you don't have any gear because you've never done this kind of hike?" Annie thought she'd managed to keep her tone pleasant.

"We've gone on some day hikes," the woman answered.

Stupid, but not your business, Annie told herself. Dangerously stupid, but not your business. "Well, first you're gonna need a map." She slapped one on the counter. "Then you're gonna need a compass." She put one next to the map. "And you're gonna have to know how to use both of them."

The woman began, "We have GPS on our ph—"

"You're not always gonna have service." Annie came around the counter and grabbed a UV pen. She slammed it down on top of the map. "You're gonna need this to purify water. No drinking fountains on the AT." She added two fly nets on the pile. "There are a lot of blackflies. Mosquitoes, too. And ticks. You're gonna need repellent with twenty percent deet, minimum." She added a bottle on the growing pile. "Lyme disease isn't a joke. Use it. Oh, there are leeches, too. Nothing I can give you to deal with those."

The man began, "Your attitude—"

Annie pointed at him. "Don't. You're going out there, you're going to need this stuff." She glanced around the shelves. "You'll need rain gear. No rain, no pain, no Maine. You have to be ready for thunderstorms. Don't try to cross an open ridge during one. Unless you want to get struck by lightning." She put two sets of Frogg Toggs on the pile. "Obviously, you'll need a first-aid kit. You get hurt out there, you're gonna be hurting for a long time. There are people you can hire to extract you." Annie didn't mention that she was one of those people. She was not going after two people who had made zero preparations for the hike. "But those people might not be able to get to you quickly."

The man began again. "I don't think—"

Annie interrupted him, not even bothering to look in his direction. "Keep clean." She slapped down some hand sanitizer. "You pick up the norovirus out there, and you'll absolutely be an unhappy camper. Diarrhea and hiking, not a good combination. Also, not romantic."

"Uh." The man looked at the woman. "Uh, we just need to—We'll be back."

That was bull. They weren't coming back. They'd made her get all this crap out, and they weren't going to buy any of it. Thoughtless. Annie began returning the items to the shelves. Before she'd finished, the door chimed again. She jerked her head up and saw Chloe coming in.

"What are you doing here? . . . That came out wrong. I meant, hi. Hi, Chloe."

"Hi." Chloe walked over to her. "Are you okay?"

"Fine." Annie stuck the bug nets back in place.

194 / Melinda Metz

"You realize you're crying, right?"

"No, I'm not." But when Annie ran her hand across her face, her fingers came away wet. "Allergies," she told Chloe. "Does Honey need change or something?"

"No. It's just that a couple came into Vixen's and said you— the person working at Hatherley's was acting erratically. I wanted to make sure you're okay."

"Acting erratically? Those two were the ones acting erratically. They decided to head off into the Wilderness on a whim. A whim. They didn't have one piece of equipment. They said they'd been on some day hikes, but I'm pretty sure that meant they'd walked a few miles on a greenway once."

"Annie, do you hear how loud you're getting? Why are you so upset?"

"Why?" Yeah, she was talking loud. "Why?" she repeated more softly. "Because odds are, someone is going to have to go in after them. So, they aren't just putting themselves at risk."

Chloe went to the cooler and got Annie a bottle of water. "Drink some of this."

Annie obediently took a few swallows. She could tell Chloe would harangue her until she did. "See, I'm fine. Talking normal volume. Drinking water. You should go back to Vixen's and tell my grandparents that a couple unprepared hikers pissed me off."

"Is that really all that's going on? Did something else happen?"

"Did Banana call Honey?" Annie heard the sharp edge in her voice. She had to get a grip.

"I don't think so. She didn't say anything. What would Banana be calling Honey about?" Chloe picked up the hand sanitizer and returned it to its shelf.

"I thought Nick might have told Banana I broke up with him." Annie grabbed the UV pen and put it back in the display.

"You broke up with Nick! Why? What happened?"

Annie was going to have to answer the question eventually. Might as well be now. Then Chloe could pass the info on to Honey, who could tell Banana, and in a couple hours the whole town would be up-to-date.

"He's lost it. He decided he's going to start a business in town. He's not just thinking about it, exploring the possibility, he's decided." Her pulse was thundering in her ears. She had to calm down. It didn't matter what Nick did or didn't do. Had nothing to do with her.

"What kind of business?"

"What does that matter? It's an incredibly risky thing to do."

"Is it that he wants to be able to spend time with you?"

"Yes! At least partly!" Annie realized she was getting loud again. She couldn't help it. It was all so irresponsible. "Why ridiculous is that? I mean how. How ridiculous is that?" She could hardly think straight. She pointed at Chloe. "Don't you dare say it's romantic or anything like that. It's reckless and stupid. By the end of the summer he'll probably have lost all the money he got from selling his house. I don't want any part of that."

Chloe opened her mouth to answer, but Annie cut her off. "I can't talk about Nick and his craziness right now. I'm at work. I have things to do." She snatched a map, but couldn't remember where it went. Her pulse was hammering harder, and she felt a little dizzy. "Do you mind just going? The place is a mess. I need to get it organized."

"All right. But, Annie, call me if you need anything. We don't have to talk. We can just go see a movie or sit and stare at the lake. We could even go right now. I'm sure your mom would watch the store the rest of the day. Or your assistant. You let him stay while we were at Banana's party."

"I don't want to do anything until I get this place back in order. Please just go. . . ."

Chloe nodded and started for the door. "Wait." She turned back. "I forgot about Jordan. Can you do something with her? I want to. I just can't right—"

"I've got it covered," Chloe promised. "Call me if you think of anything else I can do."

It felt like it took a solid hour for Chloe to turn back around and leave. When the door finally shut behind her, Annie put her face in her hands for a moment, then jerked her head back up. She didn't have time to wallow. She had to put the rest of the mess away. Then she was doing inventory. And then she was washing the windows. She had much more important things to focus on than Nick Ferrone's recklessness and stupidity.

CHAPTER 16

"I know you have the bar to run, but what do you think?" Nick asked Banana. "You think you could put in some hours at the boot camp?" Nick had spent the last two and a half hours giving Banana all the details, or as many of the details as Nick knew himself. He'd only been hit with the idea the night before. He'd been so sure Annie would love it. He still couldn't believe she'd freaked out on him. Now wasn't the time to think about it. He had to focus.

"You're thinking you can really get it running this summer?" Banana shot a glance at Jordan. She sat in the armchair farthest from the couch, reading. She'd looked up long enough to give Nick a fast hello when he showed up, but that was it.

"Absolutely. I'm planning to launch July fifteenth. That gives me more than a month."

"Do your months have the same number of days as my months? Because if they do, I don't see how you can pull it off."

"There's not much prep to do. I've just got to find the right instructors and get the word out. There are tons of groups online for hikers. I'm going to start putting out the word right away. I need a better name for it. Boot Camp is the wrong vibe."

"Boots Camp. Like hiking boots," Jordan suggested, without looking up from her book.

"That's brilliant," Nick told her. "It gives me all kinds of ideas for a logo."

"I love it!" Banana cried. "You're really creative, Jordan."

Jordan didn't respond to their praise, but Nick spotted the beginnings of a smile tugging at her lips.

"You're my top pick, Banana, but whether or not you come on board, I'll need more instructors. I'd like at least one of them to be a woman," Nick continued.

"Annie's the best choice. She's thru-hiked the AT two times, once leading a group, and she's section-hiked the whole thing, too. Have you talked about all this with her?"

Nick didn't want to talk about it. He was still trying not to think about it. There was no point thinking about it until she had time to calm down. "She . . ." Nick hesitated. "She . . ."

"She doesn't think it's a good idea."

Nick let out his breath in a whoosh. "Yeah. Those weren't the words she used, but she definitely doesn't think it's a good idea."

"Hmm. Annie has strong opinions about hikers who don't prep enough."

"I know! That's why I thought she'd love the idea. It's all about making sure that hikers are better prepared than I was. But she hardly let me get more than a couple words out before she was shooting the whole idea down." Nick decided to tell Banana the rest. He'd hear soon enough anyway. "She broke up with me. Well, she said she wasn't breaking up with me because we weren't really together. But breaking up is what it feels like to me."

Nick realized Jordan was staring at him. As soon as she saw him looking back, she lowered her gaze to her book.

"What was her problem with the venture?" Banana asked.

"She thinks I'm being reckless, trying to start up a business so fast."

Banana raised his eyebrows. "You've got to admit, she has a point."

"But she's not taking into consideration that this is what I do." Nick got up and started pacing around the room. Thinking about Annie and how she'd shot him down got him too agitated to sit still. "I help people start businesses. And that's because I saw my dad and my uncle start a business. Not just saw. I helped them. I know how much getting their own company going meant to them."

"Why not wait?" Banana asked. "Why not keep doing the consulting you've been doing and plan on starting up next season?"

"I go with my gut. My gut says this is the right time." Nick hit his shin on the edge of the coffee table and bit back a curse, since he knew Jordan was listening.

"Maybe you should sit back down," Banana suggested. "You're not completely healed from your last injury. You don't want another one."

"Okay, okay." Nick sat. "Okay."

"You realize that, while you aren't ranting yet, you're heading that way, don't you?"

Nick realized that he was bouncing the heel of his good foot up and down, making his whole leg jounce. He had to put one hand on his knee to stop the motion. "Sorry. Annie's reaction did make me a little crazy. I was blindsided."

"You haven't known her long, but you've probably known her long enough to know she's cautious. I didn't actually think you'd get her to go out with you after that thank-you dinner. I figured she'd think since there was no future in a relationship with you, it didn't make sense."

"See, that's why I thought she'd be for the Boots Camp. It

means me moving to Fox Crossing. It means that the two of us could have a real shot."

"How big a factor was Annie in this whole proposal?"

Nick's heel started bouncing again. He made it stop before he answered. "I really like her. That first day I met her, I definitely felt—" He glanced over at Jordan. Her attention appeared to be back on her book, but he suspected she was still listening to every word. "I definitely felt attracted to her. And even though she reamed me out about my lack of preparation for taking on the Wilderness, I couldn't stop thinking about her. Then when she saved me, I felt like something real formed between us, and every time I've been with her, I feel it more strongly. Except for today, when she broke up with me."

Banana studied him for a moment, and his steady gaze made Nick's heel start bouncing yet again. "Now that Annie's out of the equation, are you sure this is what you want? And if you are sure, why here? There are towns up and down the trail that you could do your camp."

Banana had a good point. Nick hadn't even thought of starting the business in a different town. The barn and the land were for rent here, and the price was good, but he could probably find something in several other spots that would work as well. It would take time though.

"I can jump right in here. There's the perfect setup. And I'm not going to let Annie Hatherley run me out of town. She can disapprove, but she can't forbid me to move here and start a business," Nick answered. "And I already have some ideas for the off-season, ideas that might bring more business to the town. Annie Hatherley might not like my ideas, but I think Belle Hatherley might."

"Call it barkeep's instinct, but I feel like there's a missing piece here. Like when you tried to tell me the reason you were hiking the Wilderness was because your thirtieth birthday was coming up."

"That *was* part of the reason."

"But your ex-wife was about to have a baby." Banana clapped his hands. "And, bingo. I don't know why I didn't see it before. She had the baby, didn't she?"

"What does that have to do with anything?"

"Just answer the question."

"Yes. Lisa had her baby."

"When?"

"Last night."

"Hella bingo," Banana said, and Jordan gave a snort of laughter, while pretending to read. "You actually think it's a co-incidence that you came up with the idea to move and start a new business on the night your ex had her baby?"

"Lisa and I have been divorced more than a year. I'm not still making decisions based on anything she does."

Banana just looked at him. And looked at him. And looked at him.

"Are you going to break up with me, too?" Nick finally asked.

"No. But I think you should go into this with your eyes open."

"Maybe the whole Lisa thing is a factor. But is it wrong to want a fresh start? Bensalem isn't nearly as small as Fox Crossing, but I still run into Lisa once in a while at the grocery store or the movies. I'd rather live in a place where that doesn't happen."

"A fresh start can be a good thing. Self-awareness, also a good thing."

Nick nodded. Some of the juiced-up energy that had been shooting through him began to fade. "Does this mean you don't want to be part of the Boots Camp?"

"This summer is pretty busy for me." Banana nodded toward Jordan.

"I don't need a babysitter," she said, still staring at her book.

"That's not what I meant. I want us to have time to do stuff together. Get to know each other."

"I don't need a babysitter."

Nick saw pain flash across Banana's face. "I wish he'd been my babysitter when I was out hiking last week," Nick told Jordan. "Somebody had to come out and rescue me because I didn't know the right way to cross a stream. I fell in and almost died." That got her looking up from her book, although she didn't say anything. "I managed to get myself out, but I had hypothermia. My body temperature had gone down to around eighty-two degrees."

"Hiking's stupid," she muttered.

"Your grandfather told me he started hiking because he doesn't let anyone tell him what to do," Nick said.

Jordan looked at Banana. "Who was telling you not to hike?"

"It wasn't as much of what people said. It was just that when I saw pictures of people outdoors, hiking, or camping, none of those people were black."

"Huh." Jordan returned her attention to her book, but Nick thought she'd been impressed, at least a little, by her grandfather's going out on the trail, just to prove he could.

"If you can't do it, I'd still like to have an African American instructor at the Boots Camp. That stereotype about black people not being outdoorsy is still pretty strong."

"You can do it. I told you," Jordan said. This time she looked at Banana as she spoke.

"I guess I could do a little teaching," Banana said.

Nick knew that Banana wanted to spend every second with his granddaughter, but Nick thought Banana was smart to back off a little. Coming on too strong would just push her away.

"I'm also going to need an assistant," Nick answered. "You want a job, Jordan? I was only a couple years older than you when I helped my dad and my uncle start a business. Maybe you could help me figure out what kind of classes kids your age might be interested in. I'll also need help with all the social media. I'll need someone taking pictures for Instagram, helping me with tweeting and vlogging."

"I helped my friend Gina do a makeup vlog." Jordan closed the book, using one finger to hold her place. "Is this a paying job?"

"Absolutely."

"I'm in."

"Me, too," Banana said.

At least something was going right. Nick just needed to give Annie a little time. When she saw he knew what he was doing, she'd come around. She had to be feeling some of the same things he was. It couldn't all be one-sided. It would be impossible for him to feel so connected to her if she felt nothing.

The Fox paced back and forth in the stand of trees. The young female with The Woman's blood wasn't right. She didn't smell of illness, or of the panic The Fox had scented on the man the last time she saw him. But something wasn't right. Her newest connection cord, the one that stretched between her and the man, it was withering, darkening. And it seemed to be making the other cords go dim.

The Fox let out a series of high barks, signaling other foxes that something was wrong. Although she spent most of her time alone, it comforted her to know that others of her kind would understand her distress.

"Annie, we're taking you to lunch." Honey stood in front of the counter, Chloe on one side, Annie's mother on the other. "You've been hiding out for three solid weeks."

"I haven't been hiding. I'm right here. In my store. Which is on Main Street." A queasy feeling started up in Annie's gut.

"You know very well what I meant. You haven't been to Flappy's, even for a to-go order, and you've gone to Flappy's at least five times a week for years."

"You haven't been to the BBQ or Banana's," Chloe chimed in. "You've had me meet up with Jordan by myself, except that time we went to Bangor."

"She likes to read. I thought she'd like to see Stephen King's house," Annie protested. "Everyone who gets close to Bangor wants to go by there."

All three women ignored her explanation. Which even Annie had to admit, at least to herself, was pretty weak.

"You didn't go to Shoo Fly's the last two Tuesdays. And you never miss junk-drawer cookie day." Honey reached across the counter and squeezed Annie's arm. The tenderness she saw in her grandmother's eyes made her want to cry. And she hated crying.

"You haven't been anywhere but right here and home. Oh, and Stephen King's house," Belle added. "That's stopping. Now."

Annie didn't like her mother's tone. "I'm well past the age where you can tell me what to do." She realized she was gripping the counter with both hands and forced her fingers to relax.

Honey slapped Belle's arm. "Don't you know your own daughter well enough to know she hates being told what to do? Now it's going to be twice as hard prying her out of here."

"I'm not telling, I'm coaxing," Chloe said. "Come out with us. Pleeease."

"You're being a coward," Belle said flatly.

Honey whacked Belle in the arm again. "Not helping. At all."

Annie's chin went up. "I'm not being a coward. The bubble is approaching. Any day we're going to be overrun with hikers. I need to be ready. That's what I've been doing these past two weeks, getting ready."

"Oh." Belle slapped the side of her head. "I'm sorry. I didn't understand. I thought you were too cowardly to face Nick Ferrone after the two of you broke up."

Honey shook her head. "You're hopeless," she told Belle.

Belle acted as if she hadn't heard.

"We didn't break up," Annie protested. "We went out four times. And one of those times was a thank-you. And one was because I didn't want him to be alone on his birthday. Hence, we weren't a couple. Hence, we couldn't possibly break up."

"Baby, it looks like Nick is here to stay," Honey said gently. "He bought the Allens' barn and the land around it."

"He bought it? He said he was going to rent it." Nick was even more crazy reckless than she'd thought.

"They gave him a good deal," Belle said. "It made sense to buy."

"He's already started advertising his Boots Camp," Honey continued. "It's starting up next week."

"I know. There are flyers in every window on the street. Including yours," Annie told her grandmother.

"Which means you can't just wait until he leaves town to go all the places you love to go," Honey told her.

"I'm not waiting for—" Annie stopped when she saw Honey, Chloe, and Belle all looking at her with the same determined expression. She was never going to get them out of here, not without her. "It'll have to be a quick lunch. I have a lot to do." She called Cody out of the back room. "You're in charge." Cody blinked in surprise, then nodded.

"BBQ?" Chloe asked.

"I've been thinking about a pulled-pork sandwich all morning," Honey answered, and they all started down the sidewalk. Annie balked as they started past the restaurant's big front window. Nick and Banana were sitting at a table near the back.

Annie quickly turned and took a few steps until she was out of view. "You set me up."

"I didn't," Honey promised. "I know it seems like something I would do, but I didn't."

"Me either," Chloe added.

"I might have told Banana that the four of us might be coming to lunch somewhere around this time," Belle said, without a hint of apology in her tone.

"Mom!" Annie exploded.

"It was for your own good. Now let's go in there. Rip off the Band-Aid." Belle gave Annie a little nudge.

"If I go in there, I'm not talking to him."

"Fine. Don't ever talk to him again," Belle answered. "All I want is for you to go wherever you want to go, no matter who else happens to be there." Annie opened her mouth to say she'd been too busy to go anywhere, but Belle steamrollered over her. "And don't bother trying to convince me you haven't wanted to go get your breakfast at Flappy's or have a drink at Banana's or buy one of those disgusting junk-drawer cookies."

"Sacrilege," Honey murmured. "Those cookies are manna from heaven." No two batches were exactly alike. The cookies were made from the odds and ends Shoo Fly had around the kitchen, from blueberries to pretzel sticks to gummy bears.

"Are we going in or not?" Belle asked.

Annie answered by marching over to the door and leading the way in. She pointed to a table by the window, and Piper nodded. She came over almost as soon as they'd seated themselves, serving up their usual drinks, then getting their orders.

"I heard that you got the votes you needed to stop Main Street from widening," Annie said to her mother. Annie was struggling to act naturally, even while she could feel Nick's gaze on her. "Did Shoo Fly come through with his vote?"

"He did. He actually stayed for the whole meeting. Not only that, he proposed a change to one of the town ordinances. He wants dogs to be allowed in outdoor eating areas," Belle answered. "His plan is to put an outdoor patio off one side of the bakery and add dog treats to the menu."

"I was proud of him," Honey added. "He stood right up in front of everybody and made his case. He didn't look in the least bit nervous."

"I was proud of him, too," Belle said.

"This must mean he's decided to keep the beast." The dog was filling out and seemed less skittish, possibly because Shoo Fly went out in advance of the walks and gave dog treats to people the dog might encounter. Annie always went out to the sidewalk when they headed past her store to hand out the biscuits. The dog had started associating people with yumminess.

"The beast now has a name, as of yesterday," Honey said. "It's Clarence, after the angel in *It's a Wonderful Life*. I'm the one who named him. I'm going to make him a little angel charm for his collar."

"That's a little bit of a stretch, don't you think?" Annie asked.

"I don't think so," Chloe said. "He's changing Shoo Fly's life, just like the angel changed Jimmy Stewart's."

"Clarence got Shoo Fly to go to a town council meeting, something I've never been able to accomplish," Belle added.

"Actually, it was The Fox," Honey said.

"Right!" Chloe exclaimed. "The Fox brought Clarence to Shoo Fly!" She looked over at Annie. "And she brought—"

"Don't say it," Annie interrupted. "That fox didn't bring anyone to me. I happened to see it around the time I checked my cell and realized Nick was in trouble." His name felt strange on her lips. She'd managed to avoid saying it almost since he walked out of her store.

"Okay, I won't say it," Chloe answered. "Should I also not say that he's heading over here right now?"

Annie had a moment to slap a neutral expression on her face, and he was there, at her side. "Hi, everyone. Hi, Annie. I don't want to interrupt your lunch. But before your food comes, could I talk to you for a minute?"

She didn't want to talk to him. She'd said everything she had to say. But she also didn't want to have him trying to say whatever it was he thought he needed to say in front of everyone. "Sure." She stood up. "Let's go outside." She strode out, then down the sidewalk far enough to be out of the sight line of anyone in the BBQ. "What?" she demanded.

Nick held up both hands, as if in surrender. "I wanted to see if, since I'm going to be living in town, and it's a really small town, if we could be friends. Or if that's impossible, if there's anything I can do to make you tolerate the sight of me if we happen to cross paths," he added quickly.

Annie started to get that dizzy, pulse-pounding-in-her-ears reaction. He was standing too close. She could smell that soap-and-skin scent of him. She needed to go back to the Outfitters. She backed away one step, then made herself stop. This was her town, dammit. Her mother was right. She needed to be able to go anyplace she wanted, and she wasn't going to be able to do that if she didn't resolve things with Nick.

She struggled to put her emotions aside, and her pulse began to slow, the dizziness fading. She was going to run into Nick now and then. It would be impossible not to. And she could handle it. It wouldn't be for long. Only until his crazy business failed. "I'm not avoiding you, if that's what you think. I've just been busy. I have no problem if we end up at Flappy's or Banana's at the same time."

"Good to know." Nick seemed to want to say more, but he just repeated, "Good to know."

"So."

"So," Nick said.

"So, I guess I'll go back in."

"I guess I will, too."

When Annie sat back down at her table, she knew she was going to have to give the three women some kind of update. "Everything's okay with us."

Honey looked across the room at Nick, then back at Annie. "You don't mean you're going out again." It wasn't a question.

"No, but now that we've spoken, it won't be awkward if I run into him someplace."

Her mother nodded. "Good job."

It's only until his business goes under, Annie reminded herself.

CHAPTER 17

The scent of Violet's cinnamon rolls hit Nick's nose as he headed downstairs. He needed to find a permanent place to live, but wasn't in a hurry. He'd enjoyed the company of Violet and the trail widows these past weeks. He'd also enjoyed Violet's cooking. But this morning, he was going to Flappy's. And if Annie was back to her usual schedule, she'd be there, too.

"The cinnamon rolls are hot," Violet warbled in a tremulous—tremulous but loud—soprano. Cooking brought out the diva in her. Nick decided he could eat one roll and still put away breakfast at Flappy's. It was probably a good idea to let Annie get there first. Last week, she'd said she had no problem seeing him around town, but he still wasn't sure she wouldn't turn around if she spotted him at the diner before she stepped inside.

"On my way," Nick called back. He hurried into the kitchen and sat down at the big table where Violet served up breakfast. He took a seat between Hannah de Lugo and Courtney Borst. Both their husbands were out on the trail. Hannah's husband had started at Katahdin, and this would be the first town on his route. Courtney's husband had started at Springer Mountain. He was almost done with the hike.

"What's everybody have planned for the day?" Nick asked as he slid one of Violet's enormous cinnamon rolls onto his plate.

"I'm doing the final rewrites on the play. Auditions are this weekend," Violet answered, singing the words *auditions* and *weekend* as she began scrambling a skillet full of eggs. "Since you're going to be a permanent resident, I hope I'll see you there, Nick." His name got the musical treatment, too.

"Getting the business going is taking all my time right now, otherwise I would."

Violet beamed at him. "That means I can count on you for the December production. Things will have slowed down by then." She continued her blend of singing and speaking.

"Actually, I have some ideas for the winter." Violet narrowed her eyes at him. "But, of course, you can count on me to audition." He wanted to be part of the community, and from what Banana had told him, Violet's theater company was big in Fox Crossing. "I can't guarantee you'll want to cast me after what you see."

"Don't worry about that." Violet stretched out one hand and managed to pat his head while still scrambling the eggs. "I am an excellent director. I could coax a solid performance out of a rock."

"Hannah and I are going to the day spa in Greenville," Courtney said. "I made a deal with Santi when he decided he was going to do the thru-hike. I get to spend the same amount of money on things I want. And hiking the Appalachian Trail ain't cheap."

"You must have the fresh-lemon-and-thyme salt scrub," Violet told them. "The thyme is grown right there in the garden."

She stopped stirring and her expression turned dreamy. "I think Sarah is really more of a lemon yellow, rather than a butterscotch." Violet had given Nick a lengthy explanation of the way she assigned a color to each of her characters, but he hadn't quite followed it. "I must rewrite the scene where she meets Bradley." She let the fork fall and wandered out of the kitchen.

Nick jumped up, picked up the fork, rinsed it, then finished scrambling the eggs. He spooned some onto plates for Hannah and Courtney and left some in the pan for Violet, although she might not reemerge for hours.

"Aren't you having any?" Courtney asked.

"I have a breakfast meeting." Well, he hoped it would be a meeting of sorts. "But I couldn't pass up Violet's cinnamon rolls."

"Me either. I might even have a second," Courtney answered. "I didn't tell this to Santi, but I decided for every pound he loses on his hike, I get to gain one."

Nick picked up his pastry and took another big bite. "I'll eat the rest on the way. Enjoy the spa." On the short walk to Flappy's, he tried to strategize. Maybe he'd have the most success if he really did approach his conversation with Annie as a business meeting. He did have an idea on how they could do some business together. It would give them a safe topic.

When he walked into Flappy's, his eyes went immediately to Annie. He didn't even have to look around. Just bam! It's like her body sent out a signal to his. He walked over. Keep it business, he told himself. "Would you mind if I join you? There's something I wanted to talk to you about. It's about Hatherley's, actually."

"All right." She didn't smile, but that didn't matter. She'd agreed to let him talk to her.

"I started my first session of hiking boot camp—Boots Camp we're calling it—this week." She nodded, and it seemed like all the response he was going to get. "A couple people asked if we were going to sell equipment, too."

"I save your life, and you're going to put me out of business?" Annie demanded.

Shit. How'd it go so wrong so fast? "No. No, no. I wanted to ask you if you wanted to sell some basics over at the barn. We'd handle the sales and split the profits."

"Hatherley's is less than three miles from the barn." Annie stabbed a bite of omelet with her fork, but didn't bring it to her mouth. "If anyone wants to buy supplies from me, I think they'll manage to get from the barn to my place without a problem."

Nick hesitated. He wasn't sure if he should say this next part. But she needed to know, and he was probably the only one who would tell her. "Uh, so a few of the hikers stopped by your place, and they said . . . They said they didn't feel welcome because—"

Annie interrupted, "Welcome?"

"Maybe that's the wrong word," Nick said quickly. "They didn't feel like you had time to answer all their questions." That was sugarcoating it, with heaps of sugar.

"That's ridiculous. Helping people choose equipment is my job. If there's a crowd, Cody or Mimi are there. That's why I hired summer help."

He was going to have to be more direct. "What people are saying to me is that you're rude. That's why they were asking if I would sell—"

Again, she didn't let him finish. "Go ahead and sell." She finally ate the bite of food on her fork.

"Really? Great! Your equipment would definitely help bring people to the Boots Camp, so I think we should do a forty-sixty split. That's me getting the forty." Usually the retailer would get the sixty, or at least do a fifty-fifty split, but he wasn't trying to make a profit, not from Annie's supplies.

"That's not what I meant. I meant that you should sell equipment directly."

"But, like you said, the barn and Hatherley's are really close together. I don't want to pull business away from you."

"Hatherley's has been in Fox Crossing almost since the town was founded. I'm not worried about losing a few customers."

"It was just an idea." It was just an idea that Nick had hoped would give him a reason to have more contact with Annie. "It's not something I want to do on my own."

"If you think you can make sales, you should. You're *trying* to run a business."

She'd emphasized the word *trying*. She clearly expected him to fail. No wonder the prospect of losing some sales didn't bother her.

"I will, then." He stood. "Okay, so, good talk. I'll see you." Nick walked to the counter and took a seat. He wasn't hungry, not after the wagon wheel of a cinnamon roll, but he wanted it to look like he'd come in for breakfast and just happened to run into her.

When she saw that he was making good money selling supplies, which he would, he'd offer her another chance to team up. And he wouldn't even say "told you so." That would get them to business associates. From there, they'd move on to friends, and then back to where they should be.

Annie checked the numbers again and felt her stomach clench. They hadn't changed. She was down nineteen percent from this time last year. Nineteen percent. Nine-teen per-cent.

She'd checked trail stats. The number of hikers that set out from Springer Mountain in April was up a few hundred from last year, which meant she should have had more customers. Which meant she should be up a little, not down a lot.

A soft tap on her door pulled her attention away from her

laptop. She couldn't help smiling—even though, nineteen per-cent!—when she saw Clarence sitting there politely, Shoo Fly at his side. She picked up a couple of the molasses peanut-butter treats Shoo Fly had started baking and headed outside.

"He's got a new one," Shoo Fly told her. "Clarence, sit pretty." Clarence raised his front legs in the air, balancing on his haunches.

"Look at him! Look at that good boy! Can I give him . . ." Annie showed Shoo Fly the treat, and he nodded. "Here you go, superstar." Annie flipped it to the dog.

"Okay," Shoo Fly said. Clarence immediately let his paws drop back to the ground, and Shoo Fly gave him an affectionate head rub. Annie thought that meant as much or more to the dog than the treat had.

"How long did it take to teach him that?"

"Couple weeks. I read that it will strengthen his core mus-cles. He's gotten really into playing Frisbee, and having a strong core will keep his back from being injured with all that jumping."

"He's looking great." The dog was lean now, gaining some muscle, instead of emaciated, and his short, multicolored coat shone. Clarence wagged his stumpy tail as if he'd understood the compliment, then knocked his head into her knee, his way of asking for some petting. Annie crouched down in front of him and started scratching his chest. Clarence gave a contented grunt.

"Shoo Fly, I was wondering. . . . Can I ask . . . ?"

"Whatever it is, it's okay."

She knew she could trust Shoo Fly. He was talking to a lot more people than he used to, thanks to Clarence's insistence on greeting anyone who would allow it, but that didn't make Shoo Fly a gossip. "How are your sales so far this month? Mine are down a little." She kept scratching Clarence.

"Up a little. But a lot of people, and a lot of dogs, stopped in this week to see the new patio. I sold a lot of treats. I even started stocking dog ice cream. I didn't have either of those last year, so that gave me a bump. I don't know if it will last. Novelty is a factor."

Clarence had done more than encourage Shoo Fly to interact with more people. He'd inspired a whole new revenue stream. Annie needed to brainstorm. Maybe she could add something to her inventory.

"We've got to keep going. Clarence has a playdate at the park."

Annie stood. "A playdate?"

"He's gotten really good with people, but he's still a little skittish around other dogs. Yvette Martin's going to introduce him to Teddy."

"Good choice." Annie had once seen Teddy, a golden retriever mix who weighed in at least a hundred pounds, cower when a kitten, weighing in at not more than three, hissed at him. "See you two tomorrow."

Shoo Fly waved, and Clarence's tail continued to wag, as they headed off. Annie returned to her laptop, open on the store's counter. The numbers hadn't magically changed while she was out on the sidewalk. Still nineteen percent down from last year. It didn't take a business genius to figure out why. Nick Ferrone and his Boots Camp. He'd started selling equipment two weeks ago. No, two weeks and three days. He'd moved fast once she'd told him he should go ahead and sell hiking supplies. If she'd agreed to team up with him, she might even be up a few percent.

But teaming up with him would have meant a lot more contact between them, and she didn't want that. Every time she saw him, she felt pissed off. His Boots Camp shouldn't be working. He hadn't planned. He hadn't prepared. He'd been completely reckless. And it had paid off, at least going by the Boots Camp T-shirts she saw around town. She hadn't been able to bring herself to actually ask Banana or anybody else how it was going.

Annie decided to go back to earlier summers and check the numbers. They were pretty consistent, except for a big drop the year after Annie took over. Her first summer was in line with the summers her mother had been running the place, but then there'd been a big dip before the sales evened off again, evened off at the new low. Annie couldn't believe she hadn't realized that. And now she was nineteen percent lower.

Nick's business explained this year's drop, but Annie had actually improved the store after her mother handed it over. The place was much more attractive and welcoming, and Annie had added some popular items, like those socks with the Katahdin pattern. Those sold like crazy. Except the last few weeks. Nick must be selling them, too. Or else hikers who bought from Nick didn't even bother to check out what she had.

"What am I going to do?" she whispered. There had to be something. Shoo Fly had improved his business. There had to be a way she could do the same. She typed "How to improve retail sales?" into Google and started skimming the articles that came up. Over and over, she read that customers were looking for an experience when they came into a shop, something that made it worth shopping in person instead of online. Several articles mentioned sales staff that could educate the customer and help them choose the right products. Which Annie so did. She'd tried out everything that she stocked in the store, and she knew what worked. She—

Her door chimed as her mother walked in. Annie had completely forgotten it was Thursday. That meant lunch with her mom, Honey, and now Chloe, too. Annie went to the cooler and started pulling out the sodas. Should she tell her mother about the drop in sales? Annie ran the place, but her mother and grandparents each owned part of it, along with Annie. At some point she was going to have to tell them, and she would. Once she'd found a way to turn things around, she'd tell them both that she'd needed to course correct after the store started getting competition from Nick.

"Hi, Mom." Annie handed her her usual Maple Syrup Lemonade, then popped the top of a root beer and took a long, long swallow, stalling. Her mother had the gift of getting Annie to say things she had absolutely no intention of saying.

"What's new, pussycat?" her mom asked as she headed to the back room for stools. Annie had forgotten the stools!

"Not much." She hurried after her mother and grabbed the other stools they'd need. "Shoo Fly was by with his beastie. Clarence has a new trick. And he looks so good. He doesn't look like he's starving anymore, just like he's a very weight-conscious supermodel. And his coat is so shiny." She was almost babbling. That's what she did when she got nervous, and her mother knew it. Annie set the stools in front of the counter, then plucked a few hairs off her mother's crisp white shirt. "I guess you saw Clarence today, too." Then she stopped talking so her mother could have a turn. That's what normal, not nervous, people did.

"That dog's so smart. And sweet." Belle took a seat on one of the stools. Annie stayed standing. She felt too jittery to sit right that second. "I don't know how anyone could abandon him. If that's what happened. That's how most dogs end up on their own in the woods."

"He ended up with the right person." There. She was doing better. She'd slowed down.

"He sure did. Shoo Fly cooks him two meals a day, plus snacks and those treats he bakes. No store-bought dog food for Clarence."

The door chimed again. Annie rushed to open it for Honey and Chloe, even though, of course, the door was unlocked, and she wasn't fast enough to reach it before they came in. "Hi. Welcome. Hello." She was about to start another jabber-fest.

She could feel it. She pulled in a deep breath. "What's for lunch?" A question was a good way to get someone besides herself talking.

"Antipasto sandwiches. Honey outdid herself," Chloe answered. "Mozzarella, spicy salami and prosciutto, marinated artichoke hearts. All kinds of yum." She laid the sandwiches out on the counter while Honey put out the napkins.

"We were just talking about Shoo Fly and Clarence," Annie said, hoping they could talk about the pair for most of the meal. That way she wouldn't end up blurting something out about the nineteen percent drop.

"Did you hear that Shoo Fly's teaching a course over at the Boots Camp?" Honey asked.

"He already has a business to run. And he just added the patio and everything," Annie protested. Banana had a business, too. Why was he one of the instructors? Was everyone in the town going to end up working for Nick?

"It's only a couple hours a few times a week," Honey said. "He goes over the equipment you need to bring if you're backpacking with your dog, gives tips for getting dogs in condition, and he and Clarence do demos of the most important commands—stop, leave it, that kind of thing."

"It's been good for Shoo Fly and Nick. Pretty much all Shoo Fly's students end up stopping by the bakery patio and buying treats for their pooches and themselves," Belle added. "And Shoo Fly sends hikers with dogs to Nick to sign up for classes and get supplies."

Her mother sounded approving, which made sense. As first selectman, she was all about what was good for the town. But had she thought about how the more people who went to Nick's, the fewer people who came to Hatherley's?

"Shoo Fly could send people here," Annie muttered. She couldn't believe Shoo Fly would choose Nick over her. Nick was practically a stranger.

"But you don't stock dog backpacks or foldable water bowls or any of that stuff," her mother reminded her.

Because dogs only made it more likely that hikers wouldn't successfully navigate the trail. A dog could get injured. A dog could drink untreated water and get sick. A dog could bolt after any number of creatures that lived out there in the wild.

"You're right," she admitted. She unwrapped her sandwich. It had sounded amazing when Chloe described it, but when she got a whiff of it, the smell didn't appeal to her. She took a small bite, then put the sandwich down.

"Eat, Annie," her mother urged. "You've gotten way too thin. You must have lost ten pounds since—" Annie caught Honey sending Belle a warning look, and Belle stopped mid-sentence. "In the last month," she finished.

Annie knew her mother had been about to connect Annie's weight loss to Annie's breaking things off with Nick. Not that there was much to break off. They'd only gone out a few times, including his birthday and her thank-you. She'd told all three of them that multiple times. There was no point in saying any of it again. She took another little bite of her sandwich so her mother—and Chloe, and Honey—wouldn't nag.

"Vixen's has had a little bump in sales, too," Honey said. "Usually hikers come to town for a meal and a night in a real bed, and they might do a little shopping. The Boots Camp gives people a reason to stay in town for days at a stretch."

Annie's business was the only one taking a hit. She couldn't even stand to look at her sandwich. She casually covered it with a napkin, hoping no one would notice. Nick's business wasn't going to fail. He was going to be in Fox Crossing permanently.

CHAPTER 18

Nick lay on the sofa in the corner of the barn he'd designated as his office, attempting to write each letter of the alphabet with his foot. His ankle was feeling good. He'd even been cleared to hike. But his doc thought continuing to do the ankle-strengthening exercises was a good idea, because once you had a sprain, it was more likely you'd get another. Also, because sprained and rolled ankles were incredibly common in hiking, and Nick wasn't going to give up hiking. Once Banana thought Nick was ready, he was going to try the 100-Mile Wilderness again, and he planned to section-hike the whole two thousand.

"I've scheduled a week's worth of tweets," Jordan announced. She reclined on a beanbag with his laptop open on her belly. Nick had bought the beanbag because she'd insisted it was necessary for optimal work performance.

A few weeks ago, his friend Marcus had driven up with Nick's laptop and a bunch of clothes. He'd put the rest of Nick's stuff in storage. Nick had told Marcus he was busy with the Boots Camp start-up and didn't want to make the drive, which was true. Also true? Nick was being a weenie. He wasn't ready to go back to Bensalem, even though the possibility of running into Lisa and her new family was slim. Marcus hadn't called him on it. Not Marcus's style.

"Instagram?" Nick asked.

"Did a week's worth yesterday," Jordan answered.

"I want us to get a planthehike.com account going, too. Same kind of things we're posting on Instagram. Mention Boots Camp, but don't try to sell anything. Make sure to put on some pictures of Clarence. People—"

"Love that dog," Jordan said along with him. "I actually started an Instagram account for him. I just added video of him doing his new commando-crawl trick."

Nick sat up. "I should have thought of that. Clarence could be the next Winston the White Corgi. He has a great rescue story. People love rescue stories. We should run it by Shoo Fly, though."

"Did it." Jordan kept tapping away. "I'm going to put up some vids of Clarence with his dog pals on the bakery patio."

"Are you double-dipping?"

Jordan grinned at him. "Maybe."

Nick laughed. "Good for you."

"Shoo Fly pays me in cookies. Those junk-drawer ones are insane."

"Your granddaughter has true business savvy," Nick told Banana when he came into the barn. "Do you have her doing social media for the Wit's Beginning?"

"He isn't even on Facebook." Jordan adjusted her position so the laptop screen was blocking most of her face.

Banana took a seat on the sofa. "I've never done a lot of advertising. You come to Fox Crossing and you want craft beer, you end up at Wit's. A few years ago, we got added to a bus tour, and that got more people coming in. What do you think, Jordan? Should I have a Facebook page for the bar?"

"Uh, yeah."

"You want the job?"

Her fingers stilled. "Maybe."

"Shoo Fly's paying her in cookies, but I don't think Miranda would be too happy if you paid her in beer," Nick said.

Jordan laughed. Nick had only heard her laugh a few times since she arrived. She was loosening up, at least around him and, clearly, Shoo Fly. Not so much with Banana.

"You already did the party, and you did that whole bedroom for me." Jordan lowered the screen a little.

"That's because I was so happy you were coming to visit. Nick knows. He helped me google what kind of room a girl your age would like."

"I like it." Jordan started typing again. "But if you wanted to buy me something, for helping you with the bar's social media, buy me one of those Instax Mini cameras. I saw one at the Mercantile when I was there with Chloe and Annie. Mint green. It develops pictures right away."

"The camera I had when I was your age did that, too." Jordan raised her eyebrows; her expression, on the part of her face that was visible above the screen, was dubious. "It did!" Banana insisted. "You know. Alright, alright, alright, alright." He shook one hand as she spoke. Jordan's eyebrows went even higher. "It's a Polaroid. I'm shaking it like a—"

"Before her time," Nick said. "I was about twelve when that song came out."

Banana turned and stared at him. "Impossible." Nick nodded. Banana pressed his hands to the sides of his head and groaned. And Jordan laughed again. "I think I still have my old Polaroid. If you want proof, I can drag it out when we get home."

"Okay. That would be . . . okay." Nick heard wheels on the gravel driveway. "Clarence is here!" Jordan put the laptop aside and raced out of the barn. Through the window, Nick watched her open the passenger door of Shoo Fly's pickup to let the dog out. Clarence jumped up, put his paws on her shoulders, and started licking her face as if it were covered with peanut butter.

"Until just now, I had no idea she liked the room," Banana said. "Do you think it could be possible that she actually likes me, too? I know she likes you and Shoo Fly. Annie and Chloe, too."

"Yeah, but there are no stakes with any of us," Nick told him. "You're her grandfather. It's probably harder to figure out how she's supposed to feel about you."

"You're right." Banana let out a deep breath. "Who knows what her mother has said about me. Even if she hasn't said anything much, Jordan's a smart, observant girl. She has to have drawn conclusions about why there've been barely any visits."

"Probably. But now she's making new observations. She's getting to know you firsthand."

"That's a stretch," Banana protested. "It's not as if we have long heart-to-hearts."

"She's listening to you, though. Even when you're not talking directly to her. And she's seeing how you are with your friends, and how you are when you're teaching. And it's only July. You have more time together."

"Maybe before Miranda comes back, Jordan will actually call me Grandpa. Have you noticed she doesn't call me anything?"

"It'll come." Nick stood up and grabbed the laptop, deciding Banana could use a little distraction. "Take a look at this." Nick pulled up the Excel sheet he'd been working on before Jordan commandeered the laptop. "Haven't been in business two whole months and we're showing a profit."

"Nice chunk from the supply sales."

Nick closed the laptop and put it on the coffee table. "I know."

"Shouldn't that be 'I know' exclamation point, smiley face?" Banana asked, putting an excited, happy spin on the words.

"It's just that—How much of that business do you think would have gone to Hatherley's if there wasn't another option in town?"

Banana's expression turned serious. "Most. But you said you talked to her about it before you decided to start selling equipment."

"I did. And she said I should go ahead. But I still feel like crap." Nick flopped back down on the couch. "There are already a couple things I should reorder, but I'm thinking maybe I should just sell all the inventory and leave it at that. It would lower the profits for sure, but Boots would still be okay."

"And Annie Hatherley would be wicked pissed."

"She wouldn't even have to know. Unless you told her."

"I'm not the only source of gossip in this town, just the best. She'd find out. Count on it," Banana answered. "She'd find it condescending and patronizing, and you'd feel the full Hatherley woman wrath coming down on you. And don't think you already have, because you haven't."

"The woman saved my life." And made Nick laugh and made him think and turned him inside out with wanting her. "The last thing I want to do is hurt her business." He shoved his hair off his forehead. "I have no idea what to do. You?"

"I got nothing. All I can do is buy you a beer later."

Nick dropped his head back and stared at the ceiling. "The woman saved my life."

Annie left the Inn feeling better than she had in days. She'd gotten the manager, Steven Seavey, to agree to put her coupons in the welcome materials he left in each room. The coupons gave visitors to the Inn a fifteen percent discount at Hatherley's.

She'd come up with the plan after a few days of wallowing in self-pity and hopelessness over how much her profits were down. She was a Hatherley woman. That meant she figured out what needed to be done and did it.

She also had a special promo planned. She'd gotten in a rush order of sun hats with the Hatherley's logo on them. Each customer who spent more than twenty dollars in the shop would get one, and they were the good ones with capes, sunglass locks, wicking headband, and crown ventilation. They usually went for forty-three bucks, retail. She'd be taking a real hit giving them away, but if it got more traffic into Hatherley's, it would be worth it. She'd hired Nogan to help get out the word and had promised them an extra buck for every customer who mentioned them while taking advantage of the promo. She knew firsthand how persuasive those two could be.

For the first time in weeks she felt hungry. She walked into Flappy's with springy steps, feeling like she'd been wearing a heavy pack and had finally taken it off. Sure, the Boots Camp had taken a bite of her business. But that didn't mean she couldn't get it back.

Her gut tightened a little when she saw Nick at one of the tables by the window, but she'd actually been hoping to see him. He was in Fox Crossing to stay. It was time to make peace with him. Real peace. That was part of her action plan. She was through feeling like a victim. She had control over her own life.

She headed right over to him. "Want company?"

His eyes widened in surprise. "Absolutely."

"Scotty!" she called as she sat down. "I'm not doing the usual. I'll have the Trail Buster."

"You got it," he called back.

"How's the ankle?" she asked Nick.

"It's feeling good. The doc's given me the go-ahead to go back on the trail. Not that I'm going to try the Wilderness again any time soon," he added quickly. "Not until I pass all the tests Banana put in place at the Boots Camp."

"Sounds good." Annie wasn't ready to talk hiking or the Boots Camp. Too painful, at least for right now. "You know how that day at the BBQ you said you wanted us to be friends?" She didn't wait for him to answer. "Well, I want that, too. First, I owe you an apology."

"Annie, you have nothing to—"

"Just let me say this. Please." Nick nodded, and Annie got on with it. "I hugely overreacted when you told me you were going to start a business here. There was no reason for me to go off on you like that. I thought it was reckless, but, obviously, it was none of my business. I'm sorry I treated you like that." Wow. That was like taking off another backpack, one filled with rocks. She let out a breath and smiled at him. "So, what's new?"

"Wait. Back up a little. Are you saying that we can get back to where we left off?"

He sounded so eager, so hopeful, and for one insane moment Annie wanted to say yes. Yes, she wanted to go back to steaming up his glasses! Yes, she wanted to go back to his kissing her palm and everywhere else! But it wouldn't work.

"Back to being friends," she clarified. "For the other, I don't think we're a good match. We're too different."

"But, different is—"

"Nick, please don't. Okay? Just don't."

He nodded. "So, you wanted to know what's new. I'm thinking of staying at Violet's through the winter. I've been too busy to look for a place, and I get a kick out of her."

They could do this. It was going to work. "You have to know that you will absolutely get cast in her holiday play."

"So she informed me. Have you ended up in many of her productions?"

"I'm pretty sure Violet gave up on me the year I was cast as a hailstorm."

"A hailstorm?"

"Her plays tend to be extremely dramatic with lots of special effects that could only be pulled off with a professional Broadway crew, which Fox Crossing obviously doesn't have. As the hailstorm, I wore a gray leotard and tights and I was supposed to run around and around a house that was part of the set, throwing cotton balls."

"Cotton balls?"

"Yes. She wanted golf balls, but she was vetoed by, well, pretty much everyone. So, there I was, racing around and around, flinging cotton balls, and I ran so fast in so many circles that I got so dizzy I fell off the stage and into the orchestra pit. I forgot to mention this was a musical." Nick laughed, and Annie remembered how much she liked his laugh. "It's been about twenty years, but Violet has never cast me again. Which, fine by me."

"If I don't want to be in Violet's plays year after year, all I have to do is fall off the stage, is that what you're telling me?"

"You might also need to dent a tuba and bruise a tuba player."

Scotty brought over her food, and Annie's stomach growled in response to the amazing smells. She put hot sauce all over her eggs and hash browns. "For several minutes, I'm going to be too busy eating to converse," she warned Nick, then dug into her food.

"I'll just soliloquize, pedantically." Nick took off his glasses, polished them on his shirt, then replaced them. "My topic? The wrongness of putting hot sauce on breakfast foods. The worthy egg is simply too mild to—"

Annie covered her mouth, afraid she was about to laugh out a bite of worthy egg.

"Are you okay? Do I need to Heimlich you?"

"I'm fine." Annie took a long swallow of water. "But clearly I need to do my part in this conversation."

"I was hoping you would. Not that watching you inhale your breakfast isn't a bewitching sight."

His words were light, but the way he looked at her . . . He'd agreed to be friends, and everything he was saying could be said by a friend. But the way he looked at her. "Uh . . . now I can't think of anything to say." His gaze had gotten her all flustered, and she didn't get flustered. Usually.

"Well, we're friends. What would you and your friend Chloe be talking about if she were here instead of me?"

Probably you, Annie thought. She and Chloe had done a lot of talking about Nick this summer, but she couldn't say that. "We might talk about her thesis."

"What's the topic?"

Annie hadn't thought this through. She didn't want to sit here talking to Nick about love. "Self-esteem. How self-esteem is affected by romantic love, which, unfortunately it seems to be."

"Why is that a bad thing, though? When someone loves you, they see all these good qualities in you. Wouldn't that boost self-esteem?"

"But should how you feel about yourself come from another person?"

"Well, ideally, no. But we're talking about human beings. My self-esteem definitely took a hit when my wife told me she wanted a divorce."

Wow. This conversation had taken a fast turn toward the serious. Annie took a bite of her hash browns while she tried to figure out a response.

"If I'm honest with myself, that's part of the reason I wanted to hike the Wilderness. I was looking for something, a test, a way to prove to myself that I could cope," Nick added. "That must sound ridiculous to you."

"No, it doesn't. The trail does test you, and not just physically. It comes down to being tired, and bored, and hurting, and hot or cold, but digging down and finding a way to keep going. Which is why I shouldn't have told you that you wouldn't make it that first day you came into my store. I could draw some conclusion based on how heavy your pack was, and the circumference of your calves."

"You were checking out my calves?" Nick looked way too pleased with the idea.

"Not checking out, evaluating." Annie tried to will away the warmth she could feel spreading across her cheeks. Why was she blushing at the mere mention of his calves? She wasn't some Victorian maiden. "And what I was saying is that I really couldn't know if you'd make it or not. You need mental stamina for the hike, and filling you with doubt, the way I did, that was wrong. I was wrong. And I'm just realizing I need to apologize for that, too."

"Don't. You were right. I wasn't prepared. If you hadn't badgered me into taking that tracker, I'd be dead right now." Nick briefly rested his hand on her wrist, and even that quick touch started her body humming. "And you have reasons, big reasons, for wanting to make sure people are prepared for the hike. Your friend . . ."

"My friend." She met Nick's eyes for a long moment, seeing the compassion there. "And now you've started this training program, so hikers will be more prepared. It was a good idea. It's a good thing you're doing."

That was what a friend would say. And she'd found the words easy to speak, probably because they were true.

"I know we haven't even finished this breakfast, but how about breakfast tomorrow?" Nick asked.

Happiness blossomed in Annie's chest. A friend asking her to meet for breakfast shouldn't make her so happy, but it did. Obviously, she was still carrying around some nonfriend emotions. Maybe she shouldn't spend too much time with Nick until they died out. But she found herself saying, "Okay. Breakfast tomorrow."

CHAPTER 19

"Do you want to go get a drink?" Chloe asked when she came into the Outfitters a few minutes before closing. Her step didn't have its usual bounce, and her tone was flat.

"Desperately," Annie answered.

"Oh, no. What's wrong!"

"You first. You've had to deal with way too much of my drama this summer."

"It's nothing." Violet would have her work cut out for her if she decided to cast Chloe in a play. She was a horrible actress.

"Tell me on the way to Banana's." Annie walked over to the door. "Mimi will close up, right, Mimi?"

Mimi gave a start and dropped the carton of Clif Bars she'd been about to price. "Right!"

"The girl always acts like she's terrified of you," Chloe said once she and Annie were outside.

"I know! And I'm not the boss from hell. I never yell or anything. I think she's seen me have too many *disagreements* with customers. She's afraid I'm going to turn on her. Cody's a little better, but not much." Annie would have to work on that. "Now tell me what's going on with you."

"I hate my paper! I want to trash it. Every time I work on it, I feel more depressed and hopeless. You know that questionnaire I did as a pilot study?"

"The one I took?"

"Yeah. I had twelve other friends take it, too, just so I'd know if I needed to tweak it before I use it for real. And the results, so horrible." Chloe's pace slowed. "The self-esteem of almost all of them depends so heavily on whether or not they're in a romantic relationship."

"Nick thinks that it's normal to have higher self-esteem in a relationship because it's confirmation that you have all these great qualities that the other person has fallen in love with."

"But what if you only feel like you have those qualities while you're with the person? What if when that person doesn't want to be with you, it feels like it's because they discovered you really suck?"

"Good point."

"Wait. You said, 'Nick thinks.' Are you and Nick talking?"

"We've been talking since that day you and my mom and Honey dragged me to the BBQ."

Chloe flicked her hands, like she was sweeping away Annie's words. "You know what I mean. After you saw him at the BBQ, you decided to be civil, which meant speaking to him if it couldn't be avoided. That's not real talking. So, are you two *talking* talking?"

"Yes. I even apologized to him for overreacting when he told me he was going to start a business. And you know I hate to apologize."

"I do know." Chloe picked up her speed, getting a little bounce back in her step. "In fact, I believe you still owe me an apology for what happened to Toh-Loo. I found it when I was visiting my parents, and when you touch it, it still only says, 'Me sleep again,' and goes back to sleep."

"I told you before, someone at school told me if you shook a Furby, it would say something demonic. I was curious. And, of course, I wanted to protect you, my friend, from a possible demon toy," Annie protested. "I thought I told you I was sorry, but if I didn't, I'm truly sorry about the Toh-Loo incident."

"Buy me a drink, and it's forgotten. . . . Wait. Thinking of my beloved Furby completely pushed the important part out of my mind. You and Nick are *talking* talking."

Annie paused outside Wit's. It would be packed in there, too noisy to have a real conversation. "We are. And it felt really good. I think we're actually going to be able to be friends. Now back to you. You're really having trouble with the thesis, huh?"

"I've written about three sentences. No, actually, I've written three thousand sentences and deleted all but three. I hate writing about my low self-esteem."

"Not specifically your self-esteem. You're clearly not the only one whose self-esteem is linked to whether they're in a relationship." Annie wished she could somehow make her friend see how awesome she was—funny, smart, cute, caring. "Maybe writing about it will help you break out of the pattern."

"I hope so. But I can't stand to think about it anymore, at least not tonight. Which is why we're getting drinks. What's going on with you?"

"I have spent the entire day trying to be nice. No, not trying. I succeeded. I was pleasant to every single customer."

"Good job." Chloe backed up to let a couple hikers get through the door.

"But there was this one woman. I really don't think she's ready, and I just sold her stuff, whatever she wanted. I didn't try to stop her. I made sure she had an evacuation plan, and then I let her go." Remembering it, Annie felt a mix of guilt and anger. The stupid, stupid woman could get hurt out there.

"Annie, you're not responsible for every hiker that comes through Hatherley's."

"I feel like I am though. Because I know what they're facing, and so many of them have no clue. Not all. I'm getting people who started at Springer. They know. If all my customers were like them . . . But that's not going to happen. I have to find a way to deal."

"Do you though? Because there are other jobs. You always assumed you'd end up working at Hatherley's, but you don't have to."

But she did. At least until she got the store's profits back up. Even if she was able to manage that—She stopped herself. Even *when* she did, she didn't know if she could leave Hatherley's. "I need to—"

"Chloe! Annie! Hi!"

Annie turned and smiled at Jordan. She and Nick were coming down the sidewalk—slowly. They each had a triple scoop of ice cream to keep balanced on a cone.

"Help!" Jordan called. "Mine is about to fall! One of you take some."

Chloe hurried over and took a bite off the topmost scoop on Jordan's cone, stabilizing the tower.

"Aren't you going to save mine, Annie?" Nick asked.

"Sure." She walked over to him. With his eyes on her, she suddenly felt extremely aware of her mouth and her tongue as she leaned forward and took a lick of the chocolate/chocolate chip.

"You have a little . . ." Nick touched the side of his mouth.

"Oh." Annie wiped the spot she thought he'd indicated.

"Other side." Before she could react, he reached out and swiped the drop of ice cream away with his thumb. And she felt his touch all the way down to her belly. Friends, she reminded herself. You're friends.

The top two scoops on Nick's cone plopped onto the sidewalk, and they both laughed. Like friends would. 'Cause that's what they were. Just friends.

Nick watched the tail on the fox clock, Flappy's version of the old Kit-Cat Klock, swing back and forth. If Annie was true to her schedule, she'd be here within the next five minutes. They'd had breakfast together four times since she surprised him by joining him last week. They'd fallen back into an easy back-and-forth. But Annie hadn't done anything to make him think she'd let him out of the friend zone. And he wanted out. Badly.

A quick double knock on Flappy's front window pulled him out of his thoughts. He knew he'd see Annie coming through the door in about two seconds. And there she was, coming toward their usual table with her long, athletic stride. He liked watching her walk. It gave him a strong *click*, which he ignored. He wasn't supposed to be thinking about her like that anymore. She'd made that clear.

"How's tricks?" she asked as she dropped into the seat across from him.

"Silly rabbit, Trix are for kids."

"I actually started a petition for the rabbit to get some Trix when I was in the third grade."

"Why am I not surprised? How many signatures did you get?"

Annie grinned. "All of them."

"Usual?" Scotty called before Nick could comment.

"Usual," Annie called back.

"By 'all of them,' you mean everybody in your class?"

"Nope."

"The whole school?"

"Nope. The whole town. All seven hundred and . . . I can't remember the exact number from back then," Annie answered. "I got help. I organized teams to go door-to-door."

"I was more of a Franken Berry guy. I still eat it once in a while. Tragically, it's now only available around Halloween."

"I didn't eat Trix until I moved out of my mom's house. She was strict about healthy food. I couldn't even score a box at one of my friends' houses. Their parents all knew my mom's rules." Annie shook her head. "Growing up in a small town has its downside."

"My dad got Franken Berry Stool back in the seventies when he was a kid, and I still got to eat it." Annie raised her eyebrows, her beautiful pointy eyebrows. *Click.* "It was this thing where Franken Berry turned kids' poop pink. It had some kind of indigestible dye in it."

"Are you close with your parents?"

"Yeah. I talk to them at least once a week. My dad likes to . . ." Nick didn't finish. He'd been about to say his dad liked to hear about how the business was going and offer advice, but Nick didn't want to mention the business. It was going strong, but there was always going to be a connection in his brain between the business and things going so wrong between him and Annie. "He likes to ask me for help with crossword puzzles. He's amazing with all the obscure words, but every once in a while, there will be a pop culture reference he needs an assist with."

"My mom loves crosswords. She does them in pen, red pen, and she gives herself a grade based on how many squares she missed out of all the squares in the puzzle. Now when I do them, I feel like it doesn't count unless I use a red pen, too."

Scotty hurried over, two plates balanced on his right forearm, coffee pot in his left hand. He quickly served them, then rushed off. The place was jammed. Every table, and every stool at the counter, was taken. The bubble had arrived, and the pungent odor of hiker mixed with the scent of bacon and coffee.

"Do you grade—" Nick started to ask, but was interrupted by Nogan's arrival at their table.

"We came for our money," Logan told Annie, sticking out his hand.

"Sorry. Nothing new since I paid you last time."

Logan and Noah exchanged a frustrated look. "We'll keep working on it," Noah said. He stuck out his wrist. "We just started making these paracord bracelets."

"They come with a tag that says HANDMADE BY NOGAN, FOX CROSSING, 2020," Logan added. "'Cause people love us. We could work out a bulk deal if either of you want to sell them in your stores."

Annie fingered Noah's bracelet. "Nice work. I'll take some. You should, too, Nick. You know about these?"

"Beyond making a fashion statement, no."

"They have an inner core of two-ply nylon yarn. It's what they make parachutes out of. You can pull it apart if you need cord," Logan explained. "You can use it for fishing, or as part of a splint or tourniquet."

"You can use the cord to sew up a hole in a tent or hang game to dry. It can hold five hundred and fifty pounds," Noah added.

"Sold. How many do you have?" Nick asked.

"Twenty so far, but we can make more," Noah answered.

"Lots more and superfast," Logan agreed. "We can get my little brother and his sister on it."

"I'll take fifty. How much?"

Noah and Logan held a brief, whispered consultation. "For fifty, we can do a buck apiece."

"Done."

"You want fifty, too, Annie?"

She shook her head. "Ten to start."

The boys did another consultation. "One fifty-three a pop," Logan told her.

"Seriously? Fifty-three cents more than for Nick? I used to babysit both of you."

"We can only do a buck for bulk orders," Logan said.

"Ten isn't bulk," Noah added.

Annie shook her head at them. "Fine. Now let us eat."

"Maybe we can hire Jordan to make some, and my mom," Logan said as the two headed for the door.

"I'm going to be working for them in a few years," Annie told Nick.

"We'll all be working for them in a few years. What else are you selling for them? Whatever it is, they're holding out on me."

Annie got busy putting cream and sugar into her coffee, even though he knew she usually took it black. "I hired them to get the word out about a special I'm running at the Outfitters. Free sun hat if you spend twenty bucks."

"Nice. How's it working?"

Annie blew on her coffee. *Click.* He liked watching her blow on her coffee, even though it should have been cool enough since Scotty had poured it before the boys came over. "Not too well," she finally answered. "I still have more than half the hats I ordered. I'm usually better at the numbers."

Crap. This was his fault. He shouldn't be selling merch. When she'd told him she didn't want him to sell merchandise from the Outfitters, he should have dropped the idea of selling supplies. Yeah, she'd told him to go ahead and sell, but he shouldn't have done it.

"Annie . . ." He thought about what Banana had said, about how Nick would bring Hatherley-woman wrath down on him if he stopped selling supplies. But he couldn't just let his business damage hers. "Me selling supplies is clearly—" She held up one hand, signaling him to stop, but he kept on. "It's clearly hurting you. I mean hurting Hatherley's Outfitters. That's not—"

"Nick," she interrupted, "I've always been the only game in town. It kept me from realizing how unhappy my customers were. Now that they have a choice, that's completely clear. And good for you that you saw a need and filled it."

"I never wanted to—"

She interrupted again. "To what? To have a successful business? That's crazy, Nick. Don't make this personal. It's not about you and me, it's about which of us is giving customers what they want. If Hatherley's had been doing that on my watch, they'd have stayed with us."

"How bad is it?"

"Bad enough."

"What if we revisit the idea of having the Boots barn be a kind of outpost of Hatherley's?"

"That's just charity. That's just giving me part of your profits for nothing. I bring nothing to the table." Annie sighed. "I'm just going to have to tell my mother what's going on. And my grandparents. We all own part. It's more than a business. It's been in my family since the beginning. I grew up in that place. Literally. I had a bouncy chair in the doorway leading to the back room."

"Is there anything I can do?"

"Nope. It's not about you or the Boots Camp. It's about me. I looked, really looked, at all the comments on every site I could find. The negative comments, and there are a lot of them, so many, and they're about me. Not the selection of merchandise. Not the prices. Me. And how rude, and condescending, and bitchy I am."

Her tone was matter-of-fact, but he could see pain in her

eyes. He realized that every single time they'd had breakfast, six counting today, she'd been dealing with all this stress and worry. He hadn't had a clue. "You'll figure something out. You're the one who got every single person in this town to support a cartoon rabbit." It was the best he could come up with, and it wasn't nearly enough.

CHAPTER 20

Now that she'd decided to tell her mother the truth about the business, all Annie wanted to do was get it over with. After she opened up the Outfitters, she shot her mother a text asking if they could talk after work. About ten minutes later, her mother showed up.

"What's wrong?" she demanded, loudly enough to get Cody's head turning in her direction.

"I asked if you could talk tonight," Annie protested.

"And you never do that. What's wrong?"

"Cody, you're in charge for an hour or so," Annie called to him. "Let's go in the back," she said to her mother, and led the way to the storeroom.

"You're freaking me out, Annie. What's going on?"

"The store is tanking. Business is twenty-three percent down from where it was this time last year. And all you have to do is look at social media to know why. It's me."

Her mother sat down on a case of backpacks. Annie sat on the unopened case of Hatherley's promo sun hats across from her. "Slow down and take me through it."

"I've never really had to try to attract customers. If hikers wanted supplies, they came to Hatherley's. It's the only game in town. Then Nick started selling the same stuff at the Boots Camp."

"Is he underselling us?"

"No. I checked his prices on his website, a website that's much better than mine."

"You shouldn't be taking all the blame here. The Hatherley's Outfitters site is the one I put into place."

"True. And when you did it, it was good. I've done little tweaks, but it needs a major overhaul. Anyway, the site isn't the real problem. It's that people find me condescending and abrasive. And they love Nick. They're always saying how friendly he is, and helpful."

"Nick doesn't know half of what you do about choosing the right gear," Belle protested.

"I'm sure he's done a lot of research. And he has Banana and Shoo Fly to give him advice," Annie said. "I've been working on it. I tried doing a promo."

"With the hats. And?"

"Here they are." Annie slapped the box she was sitting on. "And there's another box that's still more than halfway full. I expected a lot more people to show up and spend their twenty dollars. Those hats are the best out there."

"Steven mentioned to me that he'd agreed to include coupons for the store in his guest packets. That was a good idea."

"Well, it didn't work. The coupons and the hats brought in a few people, but not enough to keep business even at the same level as last year. I'm so sorry, Mom. I know how much the store means to you, and Grandpa, and Honey. And when you let me take it over, it meant so much to me, and now I've completely screwed it up. And I don't know if there's a way to fix it. If there is, I haven't been able to think of it."

Her mother leaned forward and gripped Annie by both wrists. "There's nothing for you to apologize for, Annie. Having a competitor open up a few miles away would hurt any business."

Annie broke away. "If you were still running the Outfitters, it wouldn't have happened. Maybe the store would have taken some kind of hit, but not a devastating one."

"You don't know that, Annie."

"Yes, I do. You're good with people, and you always handle everything perfectly. Even having me. You wanted a kid, so you found someone whose genes you liked and got pregnant. Then you raised me all by yourself. You're a true Hatherley woman." Annie's *harrh* was more like a moan. "I'm not."

"That story, about how I had you? About how even as a teenager I was this strong, self-assured Hatherley woman who knew what I wanted and went out there and got it?" Her mother waited until Annie met her gaze. "It's not true."

"What!"

"I didn't want a baby. I was only seventeen. A baby wasn't on my mind at all. Which doesn't mean that I didn't want you, once I knew you were on the way!" Belle exclaimed. "But the pregnancy was an accident. And I did tell your father, whom I was crazy in love with. And in response, he took off. Because he was a seventeen-year-old boy heading off to college in a few weeks. I didn't want to tell anyone the truth, so I didn't, and everyone, even your grandparents, thought I was just going after what I wanted without thinking it through, the way I always did."

Annie felt like her brain was stammering. She couldn't completely take in what her mother had said. Her mother had lied? Her father knew about Annie and hadn't wanted her? Annie had been an accident?

Belle scooted her box closer to Annie's. "I shouldn't have blurted it out like that. I wasn't planning to tell you, ever. I didn't think you needed to know. Better to think you had a father who didn't know about your existence rather than one who bolted when he found out about you. At least that's what I thought."

"I . . . I . . . don't know what to say." Annie managed to stand up, even though it felt like the floor was rolling beneath her.

Her mother stood, too, and gave Annie a long, hard hug, one of the ones that made her ribs ache, but in a good way. "Why don't you take the rest of the day off. I'll stay here in case it gets too busy for Cody."

Annie gave a snort of laughter. "Our place? Not likely."

The Fox knew the woman, the younger of the two who were blood of The Woman, was near. She was agitated. She smelled the way the creatures of the forest did before a storm, or when they sensed the ground would soon begin to shake. But there was no storm to come, no trembling. The tang of burning wood was in the air, but the fire was small and distant. The Fox trotted through the trees, only her tiptoes touching the earth, until she could see the lake and the path that ran beside it. One ear rotated toward the sound of the woman's footsteps, and shortly she came into view.

The source of her agitation was unclear. She wasn't injured. No predator was nearby. Another human was moving toward her, but she did not seem to sense its presence, even though the fox could see the cord of connection between them. There was much the woman's kind missed.

The Fox was unable to predict what their encounter would bring, although she had observed the two together several times. She knew when moose would shove at each other to prove their strength. She knew how long it took a bobcat to squeeze all breath out of a deer. She knew the scent of a female porcupine's urine changed when it was ready to mate, and how the males would respond. But, as long as The Fox had lived, she had not mastered predicting human behavior.

The Fox turned away from the path. It was time to feed. There was no need to hunt. She knew a bush heavy with berries, more than enough to satisfy.

Nick walked slowly down the path around the lake. His speed had nothing to do with his ankle injury. The ankle was feeling good. It was that the trees on the other side of the path kept getting his attention. He'd just been reading a book about the way they communicated, and it was as if he'd been transported to an alien planet where almost everything was sentient. He didn't know how he'd gotten to be thirty years old without ever being taught that trees basically talked with one another, but it had happened. That tree right there, which he now knew, thanks to Banana and a lot of time with a tree guide, was a northern red pine, that tree might actually know that Nick was there.

If some of a tree's leaves were being eaten by insects, a pulse of electricity went out, and the tree sent chemical messages to other trees about the insects. The trees responded by producing chemicals that would make them less appealing to insects. If trees really did know when humans were around, shouldn't trees be firing chemicals to keep humans away? Humans had done a lot more damage to trees than bugs ever could. "I'm sorry," Nick said. Not that he thought that the trees could understand English, even though he'd learned that they could hear. A scientist had had the idea of playing a recording of a caterpillar eating leaves to a tree, and the tree had reacted as if the caterpillar was really there. It had heard the sound, heard it and understood. He wondered if—

Annie. He'd just come around a bend in the path, and there was Annie. He'd been thinking about her off and on all day, her and the trees. There had to be something he could do to fix the way his business was decimating hers, but he couldn't figure out what. At least not yet. "Wait up!" he called.

She turned and came down the path to meet him. "Hi. How's it going? Just out for a walk?"

She was talking fast, without quite meeting his gaze. He'd thought they were doing better, a lot better, but maybe now that she'd realized how much her business was suffering because of him, she wasn't going to be able to stand being in his presence. If she were a tree, maybe she'd be sending out a chemical attack right now.

"Yep. Out for a walk, partly to condition the ankle, but mostly just to take in the sights. "Also, I'm trying to learn the names of trees." He pulled his little identification guide out of his pocket for her to see.

"Great. Sounds great." She took a swig from her water bottle, and he saw that the cuticle around her thumb was all torn to hell. She'd obviously been chewing on it, probably stressing about the business losses.

"Wanna walk together?" Nick wasn't sure what else to say. At breakfast that morning, he'd tried to get her to reconsider teaming up to sell Hatherley's merchandise at the Boots barn, but she'd given him a hard no.

"Sure. I was just heading up to Buck Hill. But we don't have to go that far, if you don't want. I've already gone up there three times." She took another pull on her water bottle.

"You mean today?"

Annie nodded. "It's only about four miles from there to town and back. The slope's gradual. It's a good conditioning workout. Although there's a long stretch with a lot of roots and rocks. Is your ankle going to be up to it?"

"With these it will." Nick pulled out two collapsible hiking sticks from his day pack, and Annie smiled her approval. "Also, just so you know, I informed Banana of where I would be hiking and when he could expect me to return."

"Well done." They started walking.

"Do you do this hike a lot?"

"Yeah. Although not usually so many times in one day. I just—" She shrugged.

"You just what?"

"Just had a lot on my mind. Walking helps me think."

"Is this about Hatherley's, what we were talking about this morning?"

She gave a short bark of laughter. "You'd think, but no."

"You know what helps me think? Talking." Nick waited. In a lot of ways, he was still getting to know Annie, but he definitely knew she didn't like to be pushed.

"It's not something that even really matters," Annie answered, after about a quarter of a mile. "It changes nothing in my life. Really, nothing is different."

"But it's got you hiking up the same hill for the fourth time today." She didn't reply, so Nick waited again. "Lot of woodpeckers around here, huh?" he commented after about another quarter mile of silence. The trunks of the trees—he needed to look them up—were covered with holes.

"Yep. Fun fact. Woodpeckers' tongues can be almost as long as their bodies."

"How is that even possible? How can they fit it back in their mouths?"

The trail narrowed, and they could no longer walk side by side. Annie took the lead, and Nick got out his hiking sticks to help him maneuver over the roots and rocks that were starting to crowd the trail.

"You're not going to believe the answer. Their tongues go up over their brains, then around the side, then under the lower jaw and into their mouths." As she talked about the woodpeckers, Nick could see the tension easing out of her body, her shoulders lowering, and her stride loosening. "But their tongues aren't just muscles, like ours. They're bone and cartilage. When the tongue is retracted, it helps stabilize the woodpecker's skull."

"I never thought about how their bodies would absorb all that stress." Every day Nick learned there was something else he hadn't ever thought about. He was loving it. He'd always enjoyed the learning curve.

"Their entire bodies are designed for all that drilling and rapping. They have exceptionally strong necks. And they have plates of spongy bone under their skulls that help protect their brains. They also have little feathers over their nostrils that keep them from breathing in wood particles, and they have extra protection for their eyes. They have upper and lower eyelids, and then a third eyelid that they can see through. That's what keeps their eyeballs from popping out."

Her tone held a touch of the wonder he was feeling as he learned all that for the first time.

"Did you study biology or—"

"Nope. Self-taught. Which actually means taught by so many people, almost everybody I've hiked with since I was a kid. My mom wanted me to go to college, but I was learning everything I wanted to know already."

"You should be working at Boots." The words were out before Nick could think them through. Well, it was the truth, whether she wanted to hear it or not.

She didn't respond. Nick didn't want to wait for another quarter mile to find out her answer, if she decided to give one. "Let's stop for a minute." This wasn't a conversation he wanted to have with her back.

She turned toward him. "You okay? Is your ankle acting up?"

"No. It feels good. I just wanted you to know I'm serious. I would hire you in a second. You would be a huge asset at Boots

Camp. Teaching, for sure. But next year I want to do some section hikes led by our instructors. And this winter I want to do some snowmobile tours, maybe snowshoe, too."

"I have to find a way to get Hatherley's back on—"

Nick didn't let her finish. "Forget Hatherley's for a min—"

"I can't forget Hatherley's. It's been in my family pretty much since Fox Crossing was founded. It—"

"Pretend it hasn't. Just pretend working there is just a job. Do you like your job, Annie?"

"I can't do this right now. I've just had—It's too much, Nick."

His timing sucked. Her business was losing money. She was under stress from whatever it was she hadn't told him. And he'd chosen this moment to try to make her reevaluate what she should be doing with her life. "Sorry. Why don't we just . . . walk. Or if you'd rather be alone—"

"I don't."

Well, that was something. "Got any more cool woodpecker facts?" he asked as she again took the lead down the trail.

She laughed. "When they peck a tree, the force on their brains is ten times what would give you or me a concussion."

Okay, made her laugh. And the tension hadn't returned to her body. He hadn't screwed up too badly. He tried to follow his own advice and just walk, appreciating what was around him right now, which absolutely included Annie.

CHAPTER 21

When Annie started down the path that led back to her cabin, she was feeling much better. What did it matter if a seventeen-year-old kid hadn't wanted her? It's not like it was the actual her, it was just the idea of a baby, any baby. It had just been a shock finding out that her mother had been lying to her all these years.

It had been good running into Nick. Her brain had been in overdrive, veering back and forth between what her mother had told her and how much business Hatherley's had lost, and somehow, just having his company had calmed her down. He was a good guy. All those breakfasts had reminded her of that.

Her stomach growled, and as she climbed up the steps to her front porch, she tried to remember what she had in the house for dinner. She let herself inside. She'd been planning on grocery shopping after work, but that—She realized she was breathing in the scent of her mother's apple-and-pork stew. "Mom?" she called.

Her mother walked out of the kitchen. "I figured you'd go out hiking and that you'd come home hungry."

"I am. Thanks." Annie and Belle looked at each other from across the room.

"Are you doing okay?"

"I'm fine. Really."

"Well, come get food." Belle returned to the kitchen, and Annie followed her. Annie got down a couple bowls from the cabinet and brought them over to the stove for her mom to fill.

"Thanks for doing this," Annie said, when they sat down at the table together. She took a big bite of stew. Delicious.

"I had to do something. I couldn't stop thinking about you. I don't think I told you about . . . everything the right way. I should have led up to it more. I should have told you a long time ago. Or maybe I should never have told you."

Annie couldn't remember her mother ever sounding tentative before. Maybe she felt uncertain more than she showed it. On the outside she was all confidence. "I'm glad you told me, Mom. I don't think there should be such a huge secret between us."

"I actually told your Honey and your grandfather the truth after I told you. And you know what? They already knew. Turns out that neither of them believed their seventeen-year-old daughter had decided to go get herself pregnant because she was so eager to have a baby." Belle gave a snort of laughter.

Annie smiled. "I never even considered trying to put anything over on Honey and Grandpa when I was a kid. They seemed to know everything. You, too."

"Me? I was making up pretty much everything as I went along when you were growing up. I could have, and should have, asked your grandparents for advice, but I was determined to show them I had everything under control." Belle shook her head. "I probably didn't convince them of that either."

"Did you talk to them about what I told you, about the store?" The thought of her grandparents finding out how badly she'd run the family business made Annie feel nauseous with guilt and shame.

"I did."

"What did they say? Are they upset? Are they mad at me?" Suddenly she felt like a kid again, wondering how all the adults were going to react about some bad thing she'd done.

"Of course, they're not mad at you. Neither am I."

"But I told you. It's my fault. It's the way I treat customers. If I—"

"Stop it," Belle interrupted. "What we all realized was that we should have had a conversation about whether or not you even wanted to run the store instead of assuming that you would take over."

"I did want to run it. Did and do," Annie insisted. She put down her spoon. She couldn't eat while they were talking about this.

"Well, maybe you shouldn't." Her mother's words were gentle, but Annie knew what they meant. She'd screwed up so badly that she shouldn't even be working at the business that had been in the family since Annabelle Hatherley started it. "Tell me honestly. Do you enjoy your job?" Annie opened her mouth to insist she did, but her mother didn't let her speak. "Don't just say yes. Think about it," Belle ordered. She was back to her usual bossy self, all tentativeness gone.

Annie forced herself to take a moment to consider the question. Did she enjoy working at Hatherley's? Sometimes she did. Sometimes a customer would come in who loved hiking as much as she did, and they'd get into a great conversation about the trail, and what new equipment was out, and whether that equipment was an improvement. That was great. She liked doing the ordering. She didn't mind doing the bookkeeping. "I enjoy it sometimes. But nobody enjoys their job every minute of the day."

254 / *Melinda Metz*

"Can you give me a percentage? How much is sometimes?"

Annie struggled to turn her feelings into a number. "Maybe thirty percent?"

"Oh, sweetie. That isn't nearly enough. And we should have discussed this a long time ago." Her mother put her spoon down. "The store was a godsend to me when I got pregnant with you. It was a great place to work, where, more importantly, I could have you with me. When I started getting involved with town politics, I just assumed you'd want to take over, and my parents were all for it."

"Of course, I wanted it. It meant so much to me that you and Honey and Grandpa had faith in me."

"But what about now? You just said you only enjoy it thirty percent of the time."

And that was true. She hadn't been expecting that when she took over. She'd just been thinking of it as a place for hikers, hikers just like her and the friends she'd made out on the trail. She'd worked in the store when her mom was in charge, but she'd never noticed how many of the customers were dangerously inexperienced, probably because her mother ran interference for her without Annie even realizing it. "It's ours." That was true and would be even if she hated every second she was at work, which she didn't.

"It will still be ours if we let someone else manage it. We can do as much or as little as we want. Right now, I don't want to spend a lot of time on it. I'm too involved with the town council. But if we find a good manager, I wouldn't mind doing the rest."

"I can't even imagine my life without Hatherley's. It was always what I was going to do."

"And that's my fault. I assumed because it made me happy, it would make you happy, too."

"I honestly have no idea what I would do instead." But the possibility of not having to be at the Outfitters every day made

Annie feel almost giddy. Her appetite surged back and she took a big bite of her stew.

"Maybe you'd like to rethink college. We have the money."

"Definitely not that." Sitting in classrooms all day held no appeal. She had to do something though. She'd have to do the Buck Hill hike as many times as it took to figure it out.

"The stew is great, Mom. Thanks for making it." Annie took another bite, then those feelings of guilt and shame came rushing back, and she put her spoon down. "There's something else I should tell you. Nick offered me the chance to sell our merchandise out of his place, with him taking a cut. It was a good deal, but I didn't even consider it. I didn't even talk to you and Grandpa about it. I could have prevented all those lost profits if I had. I was so sure people would keep coming to Hatherley's. I didn't take into consideration how unpleasant I am. Rude, bitchy, condesc—"

"Stop it, Annie. I don't want to hear any of that out of you again. I've seen you with customers. If you think one of them is going to get hurt out on the trail, you don't want them out there, and your methods"—her mother smiled—"are effective."

"This morning at breakfast, Nick did say he's still up for selling our stuff from his Boots Camp. But now that he's doing so well selling supplies on his own, it seems like charity for him to team up with us now. There's nothing he gains from it. But I can probably set it up if you think we should."

"Supplies aren't the only thing Hatherley's brings to the table." Belle took a sip of her wine. "You'd be a huge asset over there, as an instructor, definitely. I know they'd like to have a woman teaching some of their classes. Even though they might not have thought of it yet, they could also use someone to do extractions. It's not like just anybody can do it. It takes time to learn those old logging roads."

"You're saying we should team up with Nick—I mean, the Boots Camp?"

"It's worth considering. But this time, let's think it through. I don't want you to do anything that's not right for you. How are things between you and Nick now? I've seen you two at Flappy's. . . ."

"We're friends. Nick and I are friends."

"Good. I like him. We've had a few conversations about the winter festival he'd like to get going, the Fox Fest. I think it will be great for the town." Belle hesitated. "Speaking of, well, speaking of men, there's something I should tell you."

"O-kay." Annie realized she'd started gripping the edge of the table with both hands and forced herself to let go.

"It's nothing about you. Don't worry."

Don't worry? Annie felt like she could crumble into little bits. The day had taken it out of her. "Just tell me." She'd tried to keep her voice light, tried and failed.

"It's nothing bad. I promise." Her mother took another swallow of wine, a longer one. "Shoo Fly and I are . . . involved. We've been together for just about eleven years."

"What?" Annie yelped. "I don't get it. Why didn't you tell me?"

"We didn't tell anyone. Shoo Fly is very private. You know how he is. He's uncomfortable around most people, especially more than one at a time."

Her mother and Shoo Fly. That was surprising. But not bad. Not bad at all. Nothing to make Annie crumble into bits.

"Although that dog!" Belle continued. "That dog of his has done more for Shoo Fly than I ever have. Once in a while, I'd try to get Shoo Fly to go out someplace with me, but he wouldn't. *Couldn't*, is more like it. But Clarence was in such bad shape when he showed up at Shoo Fly's, and Shoo Fly was determined to get him a home, which meant socializing him, which meant Shoo Fly basically socializing himself in the process."

"I've definitely talked to him more in the last few weeks than I have in the . . . in the ever. He's a good guy, Mom. I'm

happy for you. Any chance that now that he's talked to me a little, the two of you might, I don't know, come over for dinner
sometime?"

"Would Clarence be invited?" Belle asked.

"Of course."

"Then I could see it happening."

"What made you tell me after all this time?"

"Partly because after I told you the truth about me getting
pregnant, I didn't want there to be another lie, even one of
omission, between us. And partly because I realized that your
idea of me as this strong woman who doesn't need anyone—"

"A Hatherley woman."

They both did the *harrh* and arm flex.

"Exactly. A Hatherley woman. When we were talking about
the store, it made me think about what I've raised you to think
a Hatherley woman is. It's not some superhuman creature who
doesn't need anyone for anything. It's a strong woman who
doesn't give up. Which you definitely are. But I've never
thought being with a man makes a woman weak. I love Shoo
Fly, and being with him has made my life hugely better."

"That's great, Mom."

"I was thinking about Chloe, how her idea of her parents'
relationship forms, at least partially, what she thinks her own
relationships with men should be like. I don't want you having
it in your head that having a relationship is somehow not a
Hatherley-woman thing. I'm not saying it's necessary to be
happy," Belle added quickly. "I don't want you to think that.
What I'm saying is, I just want you to figure out what will
make you happy, then go get it."

"Sure, yes, I'll go right out and do that." Belle laughed at the
sarcasm in Annie's tone, and Annie joined in. "I'm really going
to try." And if Annie was honest with herself, she knew where
to start.

* * *

"I'm using this section of wall to set the white balance. That works better than using the auto white," Jordan explained to Nick. He nodded, but he was having trouble paying attention. Annie hadn't been able to make breakfast, but she'd texted to ask if she could stop by Boots that afternoon, and she should be here anytime.

"Now I'm just going to put the phone on the tripod." The tripod she'd convinced him Boots needed to make their vlogs look good. "All you have to do is push the button to start filming." She sat down next to her grandfather. "I'll do some blurry shots later for transitions. And I'm going to go take some B-roll of the trail. He's going to take me." She jerked her chin toward Banana. She was still avoiding calling him by name, but Nick could see them getting closer every day.

"Just one question." Nick hurried over to Jordan, then leaned down to whisper in her ear. "Ask your grandpa to tell you how he got his trail name. I can't convince him to tell me." She smiled and nodded.

"I think I should be informed of whatever she just agreed to," Banana said.

"Just a technical question." Nick walked back to the tripod. "You two ready?"

"How's my head? Is it shiny?" Banana asked.

"You're gorgeous," Nick assured him, then pressed the button, and Jordan gave a little intro, explaining that she was interviewing her grandfather, who was one of the instructors at Boots Camp, and giving a little info about the kinds of classes they offered. Two days ago, she'd actually convinced Shoo Fly to do a vlog with her—her and Clarence. Nick was pretty sure Shoo Fly had only agreed so that more people could see what an amazing dog he had.

"You told me once that one of the reasons you started hiking was because you don't like to be told what to do, and you felt you'd been told black people don't hike." Jordan turned in her seat so she could look at Banana. "Who told you that?"

"No one told me not to hike, not in so many words. Some things are just passed down, and not always intentionally. If your parents aren't interested in outdoorsy things, and they aren't interested because their parents weren't, then you probably grow up without doing a lot of outdoor activities."

"But why weren't they interested?"

"Maybe because movies and TV and ads don't usually show black people hiking or camping or any of that. Maybe because for a long time, parks, including national parks, were segregated." Banana looked back and forth between Jordan and the camera as he talked, the way Jordan had coached him to do. "Maybe because there's not always easy access to a place to hike and camp, and it takes money and leisure time. Like hiking the AT. You want to thru-hike, that's probably close to six months of no work, and it costs on average say five thousand dollars, not including gear."

"Did you ever go hiking or camping with your parents?"

"No. The first time I went hiking was with some friends in high school. One of the guys said—"

Nick heard the barn's door open. He turned and saw Annie step inside. He put his finger to his lips, nodding toward the tripod and phone. In response, she quietly shut the door behind her and came over to stand next to him. He caught the scent of the lavender and clean skin.

"—not the same for me," Jordan was saying when Nick returned his attention to the vlog being filmed. "My mom is so into hiking. She dragged me out onto some trail practically every weekend. One time, it was right when the new Squirrel Girl book just came out." Jordan sounded outraged, just remembering. "So her wanting to hike all the time is your fault, is that right?"

Banana gave his *haw-haw-haw*. "Guilty. Guilty and not at all repentant."

Jordan giggled in response. Nick didn't think he'd heard her giggle since . . . since ever.

"The next vlog we're going to do will be about national parks and how two troops of buffalo soldiers were among the first forest rangers, right, Grandpa?"

Banana's eyes widened in surprise. Nick knew how much it meant to him for Jordan to call him Grandpa. "That's right."

"And for you Clarence fans, Shoo Fly and I are going to do a vlog on how to teach your dog to bring you a soda. If you haven't already seen them, you'll need to watch our vlog on how to teach your dog to open and close the fridge first. See you soon."

Jordan waved, then jumped up and turned off the camera phone, then headed over to Nick and Annie. "I thought you were going to ask your grandfather how he got his trail name," Nick said.

"No time. Grandpa!" Jordan called, completely casual, as if she'd been calling him Grandpa her entire life. "Nick wants to know why you're called Banana."

"I know why," Annie boasted. "I've known for years. He's got the name Banana Split because one day on the trail, his pants split open and he was wearing bright yellow underwear."

"True," Banana told her as he joined the group, smiling at Jordan.

"That's it?" Nick shook his head. "I was expecting some epic adventure."

"What nobody knows, not Annie, not anyone, is *why* I was wearing bright yellow underwear in the first place."

"Well, tell us," Annie said.

"All I'll say is that it involves Bucky, smartest donkey anyone has ever seen or will see."

"Please, please, please tell us," Jordan begged, brown eyes sparkling.

"Maybe. Maybe when you're older," Banana answered. "We should prep for the next vlog if you still want to get it done before my class starts."

"Fine. But I'm going to find out. Let's go rehearse a little." Jordan led her grandfather over to the sofa underneath the windows that ran across the huge room.

"That's something to see. What a change since she got here," Annie commented, looking over at Banana and Jordan and smiling.

"Banana is pretty hard to resist."

"But ten-year-olds know how to dig in. This place, your place, I think it helped them get close, especially now that they're doing vlogs together. Jordan's having conversations with her grandfather that might not have happened any other way. As soon as that vlog goes up, I'm going to email Miranda with an attachment."

"I was happy she decided to let Jordan stay in Fox Crossing until she's back. Happy for her and for Banana. I know the plan was for Jordan to go to her aunt at the end of the summer."

"I think it's going to bring Miranda and Banana closer together. Jordan's going to want to see her grandfather, and that means Miranda will be spending time with her dad." Annie looked over at Nick. "The place looks good. I've seen a little of the renovations on the vlogs, but it's even better in person. This amount of space really allows you to show off the merchandise, like those tents."

"It was Jordan's idea to set each one up on its own area rug, although I think it was partly so she'd have a cozy place to get away from Banana and me when we were driving her crazy." Nick rubbed the back of his neck as he looked around, trying to see the place through Annie's eyes. "The hammocks we have strung up toward the back get a lot of use, too."

He flashed on lying in a hammock almost exactly like one of the ones on display, lying in it with Annie steaming up his glasses. He wanted that with an ache that went all the way to his bones, but he knew the one way to make sure it never happened was to push. Annie didn't like to be pushed.

"Banana told me there's not a farmers market in town," Nick said, the first thing he thought of that wasn't pushing. "I'm toying with the idea of getting one started. There's a great space out back where I could get a roof up, get some tables and stalls."

"The Inn's restaurant uses a lot of local produce. Steve, the manager over there, could probably hook you up with some farmers who'd be interested. And if you're thinking arts-and-crafts kinds of stuff, Honey knows absolutely everyone."

"I was thinking during the Fox Fest I could use the whole barn for an arts-and-crafts show."

"Sounds like a lot of work. If you need some extra help . . ." Annie's face flushed, and she suddenly seemed to have trouble looking directly at him.

"I told you yesterday, you'd be a huge asset here. There are so many possibilities. Like the whole farmers market project. And the Fest. Classes. Instructional vlog posts to show off our products. Kayaking trips for small groups and—"

Annie held up both hands. "Stop for a second. I need to be sure that . . . I don't want you doing this because you feel sorry for me, or because you feel responsible that Hatherley's is—"

"You know I already hired Banana and Shoo Fly. I want the most experienced trail hikers, and that includes you. Are you thinking part-time, like them? Or full? Because I could use you as many hours as you can give."

Annie ran her fingers through her short hair, creating cute little spikes and curls. "I don't know. I feel like I don't know anything anymore."

"Is this about whatever got you hiking the hill so many times yesterday?"

"Not so much, actually. But I had a conversation with my mom last night, and we really talked about the business. I grew up thinking that's what I'd do, that at some point I'd run the Outfitters. I never thought about if it's what I wanted or not. I never thought I might suck at it, or at least big chunks of it." She laughed. "I'm doing a great job selling myself."

"You don't have to sell yourself to me. I know you know your stuff. And if you were training people how to hike safe instead of selling equipment to people you thought were likely to get hurt, you'd be amazing. No question about it."

"Have you thought about offering extractions through Boots? Or offering a tracking service where you, or someone who works for you, would keep watch and be a support person."

"I didn't, and I, out of anyone, should have."

"Well, that would be something I'd be interested in. You might even want to do supply drops for people that don't want to pack in all the food they need."

"Isn't that something you could offer through Hatherley's though? I don't want to take any more—" He stopped himself. "There are lots of things you could do here that wouldn't compete."

"That's a discussion I'll have to have with my mom and my grandparents. It's a family business. But if you want to hire me, I'm here." She threw her arms wide.

"You're hired." He stuck out his hand, and they shook.

Click. Big *click.*

She was going to help the business. He knew that with absolute certainty. But if she never let him out of the friend zone and he had to see her all those hours, day after day, week after week—he might not survive.

CHAPTER 22

Annie sat on her front porch, trying to decide which of her Map & Compass Navigation students would make it here first. Kate had the best skills, but Trevor was the fastest. If he made a wrong turn, Kate would definitely beat him. This was the third time Annie'd led the daylong course, and while she had a few little tweaks she wanted to make next time, she was happy with it, confident that her students would not have to rely on GPS to find their way into or out of the woods.

She heard footsteps heading toward her place, fast. She stood. Nobody should have gotten to her this quick. She caught a flash of sky-blue shirt and blond hair, then Chloe came around the curve in Annie's drive.

"I saw it! I saw it!" Chloe ran the rest of the way to Annie, then had to lean forward and gasp for breath before she could speak again. "Annie, I saw it. I saw The Fox!"

"Chloe! Really? Where? Tell me everything!"

Chloe sucked in a deep breath, then another. "Just now. It was so crazy. I was coming out of Vixen's, and The Fox, she was just sitting on the sidewalk a few feet away. I looked up, and—"

"Why are you stopping? And what?" Annie demanded.

"And Nick was standing there."

"Nick."

"Nick."

Annie had to force a smile onto her lips. It shouldn't have taken so much effort. Chloe was great, and a great friend. Nick was great, and a great friend. Annie had had a great time working with him this past month. Great.

"Great. Great," she repeated, because she didn't think she'd sounded happy enough the first time. "You two will be great together," she added, because she still didn't think she'd sounded happy enough. She wasn't sure that she'd sounded happy at all. But she should be happy. Because it was great when two of your great friends got together.

"You should see your face right now." Chloe did something with her mouth that made her expression a combination snarl and smile.

A *smarle*. Yeah, that's what it should be called. Annie's brain latched on to the combo. Were there other words that should be combined into a new one? Maybe smirk and—

"Annie, you don't think that I'm going to go after Nick, do you?" Chloe sat down on the top step, then tugged on Annie's arm until Annie sat down next to her.

"Why not? You've been waiting all summer to see The Fox so you could find the perfect guy. You're only going to be here a week longer. I know you were afraid it wasn't going to happen. But it did. And Nick. That's great." Annie found herself repeating the word again: "Great."

"It would be great if he wasn't in love with you, and if you weren't in love with him."

"I am not in love with Nick. We're friends. Friends," Annie insisted.

"Annie, it's me. I've seen the two of you together. We were all just at Banana's two nights ago. I've seen how he looks at you, and how you look at him."

Annie made pushing-away motions with her hands. "You're imagining it."

"I'm not. You know what else I'm not imagining? I'm not imagining that Nick has zero interest in me. There's no spark between us. And there's practically danger of an explosion when the two of you are together. Honey saw it that first day, when you two met."

"But The Fox . . ."

"Why are you saying that? You don't even believe in the luck of The Fox." Chloe shut her eyes for a long moment, then opened them and looked at Annie. "I believed in The Fox. I thought I'd see her and get the happily-ever-after fairy tale. But I was wrong. Because there's no possible way I'm going to end up with Nick Ferrone."

"But your parents, and Honey and my grandpa, they—"

"Annie, stop it. You know you don't believe anything you're saying. And it was crazy of me to think seeing The Fox meant anything. It's a lovely legend. But that's all."

"I'm having a hard time keeping up with all this."

"Tell me about it. I just realized if I want the perfect relationship, I'm going to have to figure out why I keep ending up with men who don't want to be with me. Or why I sabotage relationships. Or why I'm so desperate to be in a relationship. Maybe all of those."

"Did you say anything to Nick when you saw him?"

Chloe shook her head. "I don't think he even noticed The Fox. He didn't react. As soon as I saw her, she stood up and darted into that little alley that runs between Vixen's and the bookstore. And I came straight here." Chloe stood up. "I'm going to get water."

Annie stared after her for a moment, then cradled her head in her hands. What was she supposed to do? Wait. This was crazy. She didn't have to do anything. Nothing had changed, except that Chloe had seen The Fox.

Chloe came out of the house and sat back down. She handed Annie a bottle of water, then took a swallow from her own. "So, what are you going to do?"

Annie laughed and realized it sounded a little hysterical. "I'm not going to do anything different than I've been doing. Things are going really well. I never completely realized how stressed I was working at the store, how angry, and how unhappy, so much of the time. But I love all the things I've done at Boots so far, and I'm looking forward to what we're planning for the winter."

"No. Just no. You are going to do something, Annie. As soon as I saw The Fox—The Fox and then Nick—I knew it wasn't right. I didn't even consider that maybe he was for me all along." Chloe wrapped one arm around Annie's shoulder. "You have to give him a shot. If you don't, eventually he's going to start going out with other people. And at some point, there will be no chance left for the two of you. You don't have unlimited time."

"We're so different though," Annie protested. "He's still impulsive and reckless. That hasn't changed just because Boots is working."

"Forget that. Think about this instead. How did you feel when you thought I wanted to try to start something with Nick, because of The Fox?"

"I . . . I think I hated it. I kept trying to sound happy for you, but I couldn't."

"And now that you've finally accepted how you feel, even

though Nick isn't absolutely perfect—what are you going to do about it?"

"Maybe I'll ask him out for a drink," Annie answered slowly. "I don't want to jump into anything too fast. He pretty much started Boots because he freaked about his ex-wife having a baby."

"He told you that?"

"Not exactly. But everything was going great. We were hanging out over here and started talking about trying things long distance, then he got a text and got all weird and wanted to leave right away. Later I found out from Honey that his ex had given birth that night. And that same night he decided to start the business."

"But you're still going to ask him out for a drink, right? You're going to at least consider the possibility that you two might be great together, right?"

"Right."

"You want to go for a drink, Nick?" Annie asked as he was about to lock up the barn for the night.

"Sure. Banana's? But can we not talk about work? That marathon Fox Fest strategy session shut down some key areas of my brain."

"No work talk. But how about we just have the drink here?" She unzipped the backpack she had slung over her shoulder and pulled out a bottle of champagne. "Still decently cold. I used one of our cooler bags. Don't ask me if it's the good kind, 'cause I don't know."

They both laughed, and he was sure they were both thinking about that thank-you dinner, that almost-perfect night.

Annie led the way out to the little patio. Jordan had strung some fairy lights out there, and Nick flicked them on before he followed her, although it wouldn't be dark for at least an hour. He felt like he'd already had a couple glasses of the champagne, a little off-balance, a little fuzzy-headed. What was happening here? Annie'd made it clear she just wanted to be friends, but this was not feeling like a friend thing.

"How are you at cork popping?" She put a couple glasses on the little wrought-iron table.

"Uh . . ." Nick seesawed one hand.

Annie laughed. "Me, too." She turned the tab several times, then aimed the bottle away from them. The cork gently popped with just a little *fffzzz*, and Annie poured them each a glass.

"Is there an occasion I'm forgetting about? Is there something we should be toasting?" She had to be trying to start something up between them. Didn't she?

"We could toast how well my first month at Boots has gone."

Nick could feel himself deflating. He was surprised he wasn't letting out a little *ffffzzz*, too. What had he been thinking? Annie was a straightforward woman, and she'd been absolutely clear that she didn't want to go back to how things had been, to those few days when it felt like something amazing was happening.

"To Boots' new star." He reached out to click his glass to hers, but she pulled hers back.

"I didn't mean the champagne for that though, although I love working here. I thought . . . I wondered . . . Do you think we could—" She seemed to be having trouble finding words, which wasn't like her.

"Yes," he answered, not waiting for her to finish. He hadn't gotten it wrong. "Yes." He was sure he hadn't gotten it wrong, but he felt like he had to make absolutely sure. "You're talking about us getting back together."

"We weren't exactly together. But I want to see if we can get there." She raised her glass in a toast. "To possibilities."

"To possibilities."

They clinked glasses. After he took a sip, he put his glass

down. He had to kiss her. Now. He took her glass and set it next to his, and she closed the short distance between them. Or maybe he did. Or maybe they both did. Somehow her body was flush against his, his arms around her waist, her hands twining in his hair. He lowered his head, and finally—finally, finally, finally—kissed her, losing himself in the sensations, warm, slick, smooth. Annie. Annie.

"There's definitely a spark," she murmured as she pulled away. "Honey said there was that first day we met."

"Honey was right. Although, much as I adore your grandmother, I'd rather not talk about her right now."

Annie lightly nipped his lower lip, then let her tongue explore his mouth. When they pulled apart, they were both a little breathless. Annie reached down and retrieved her champagne, then handed him his glass. "To more than possibilities," Nick suggested, and with a grin, she clicked her glass to his.

"I think you need to go visit your ex-wife and bring a present for the baby."

"What?"

"You didn't even go back home to get your stuff. I thought maybe it would be good to do that. Sorry. My timing sucks. Don't take this as me trying to put conditions on this." She used her glass to gesture from him to her, and a little champagne sloshed over the rim. "I'm not. Whatever you decide, to go or not, I'm open to . . . possibilities."

"Can we go back to talking about Honey?" Nick joked, kind of joked, trying to adjust to the lightning-fast turn in their conversation.

"It's not something we need to talk about now. It wasn't the right time to bring it up." She sat down on the patio's freestanding porch swing, and he sat beside her.

"I've been trying so hard not to think about her. About Lisa, and the baby, and this whole new family she has. I expected it to gut me, even though it's not like I'm in love with her anymore. But, now that I am letting myself think about her, it's actually not so bad." He laughed a little, and Annie took his hand.

"I should make a trip to Bensalem. Lisa and I said we'd stay friends, even though I don't think either of us was ready for that. But it would be worth proving to myself that seeing her, her and the baby and the husband, isn't this huge thing. I have other friends in town, too. It would be good to see them, say an actual goodbye, invite them to come see this place."

"If there's anything you think I should be doing, I'm open to suggestions."

"You? You're perfection."

"We both know that's not true. I have a temper."

"True." He kissed the little hollow between her collarbones. He loved that spot.

"I don't let go of things easily."

"True." He kissed the spot just under her left ear, breathing in the clean lavender scent of her.

"I can be judgmental."

"True." He kissed the corner of one of her pointy eyebrows. "Is that all?" he asked when she didn't continue.

"I'm impatient." She caught his face in her hands and pulled him toward her.

"Impatient? It took you this long to admit that we should—"

She cut him off with a kiss.

Epilogue

"Did everybody remember to put on sunscreen and bring sunglasses?" Annie called to the group gathered in the Boots barn. "That's important when you're snowshoeing. UV rays are stronger when they're bounced off the snow."

"Yes, Annie," they answered in almost perfect unison.

"Does everyone remember what I told you about what to do if you fall?"

"Yes, Annie."

Before they set out, she just wanted to make extra sure. "You should try to fall uphill, and—"

"Annie, we all said yes," her mother interrupted. "And why? Because it's only been five minutes since you explained that."

"She just wants to make sure," Honey said.

Annie smiled at her. Her grandmother looked so cute in her snowsuit with the hood that turned the top of her head into a fox face, complete with two ears sticking up.

"Thank you," she told her grandmother. "That's exactly what I was just thinking. So, you should try to fall—"

Honey cut her off. "And like your mother said, you already told us."

Everybody in the room laughed, including Nick, who slung his arm around her.

Looking at them all got her laughing, too. "Okay, okay. But if you fall down and can't get up"—she shook her head—"yell for me. I'll be leading the group."

"Thanks again to everybody for letting us test our snow-shoeing excursion on you. There will be cookies and hot chocolate when we come back," Nick added.

"Gingerbread people, made by me and my grandpa," Jordan announced. "Although there might not be enough. He"—she gave Banana a gentle nudge in the side with her elbow—"kept breaking them on purpose because I told him he could eat the broken ones."

"We'll have plenty. Nick convinced me to bring some of my cinnamon rolls!" Violet exclaimed. She did a little pirouette. Just Violet being Violet.

"Who are we still waiting—" Nick began, just as Chloe came through the door. She'd decided to stay in town through the winter to keep working on her thesis. She was also helping Nick part-time with the arts-and-crafts part of the Fox Fest.

"Sorry, sorry, sorry," Chloe called to the group. "I just got the most amazing news! Some of you know I used some of what I'm working on for my thesis to write a book proposal. It's all about what's passed down from our families. Anyway, an agent read it and wants to represent me!"

Annie cheered along with everyone else in the room. She was so proud of Chloe. Annie had read the proposal and loved it. It had all kinds of personal anecdotes from people in Chloe's life. She'd done an interview with Annie about how growing-up Annie had just assumed she would take over Hatherley's, even though Belle had never said so. Chloe had also gotten Banana to tell her more about growing up with this unspoken idea that black people don't hike. She'd used her own life, too, writing about how The Fox magically bringing her parents together made her believe that that's how she'd have to find her own husband. Even though her parents would probably have fallen in love if they'd met at Banana's. Probably.

Chloe had been writing like crazy since the day of her Fox sighting, but Annie hadn't pointed out the timing. If she had, Chloe might have started wandering around town throwing pieces of chicken on the ground every time she got writer's block.

"Now who are we missing?" Nick asked.

"Nogan!" Jordan volunteered.

Banana gave a loud sigh. "I bet I know where Logan is. I caught him standing by the back door of Flappy's around lunchtime, just staring out at nothing. I asked what he was doing, and he said Nick over there"—Banana flung out his arm in Nick's direction—"told him he had a beard coming in. Turns out the boy was standing at the door waiting for it to arrive."

Banana had gotten Annie. She hadn't seen the joke coming when Banana said he'd seen Logan at Flappy's. When the laughs, and groans, died down, Banana continued, "I asked him how he knew the beard wasn't going to come in through the front door. He got panicked and started running back and forth from the front door to the back. Probably's still at it."

That got a bigger laugh, and louder groans. Violet's high cackle made it sound like she should be taken to the hospital. "If you liked that one, credit goes to that joke book from ancient Greece, *Philogelos*," Banana let everyone know. "If you didn't like it, same thing."

"Do you think we should head out without Nogan?" Nick asked.

"Roger Gangne hired them to clean out his basement," Honey volunteered.

"They made a deal. He doesn't have to pay them, but they get to keep everything that's not in labeled boxes. They could still be over there," Banana added.

Annie leaned close to Nick. "Of course, Honey and Banana would know," she said, keeping her voice low. Not that either Honey or Banana minded their reputations as town gossips.

"I'll call them." Jordadn pulled out her cell. A few moments later, Annie could hear a cover of "Money (That's What I Want)" playing. Both Logan and Noah used it as their ringtone.

The boys came through the barn's double doors at the same time, announcing in unison, "We are going to Mars! We have the money!"

"We went into Mr. Gangne's basement, and The Fox was in there!" Logan began.

"*The* Fox, not *a* fox!" Honey exclaimed.

"Our Fox. The Fox," Noah answered.

Nick pulled Annie closer against his side. "The Fox is afoot," he said into her ear. "You know what that means."

"I remember." She'd agreed that if they saw The Fox at the same time, she'd seriously consider the two of them getting a place together. Either that or he could move into her place. They'd only been together about three months, and that felt way too fast, even though he had gone back to Bensalem, baby gift in hand, and it had gone fine.

Annie turned her attention back to Noah. "She was clawing at one of the walls. When she saw us, she took off."

"We went over to check out the wall. We thought maybe there were mice living in there or something," Logan continued. He paused for a moment so he and Noah could slap a high five.

"And it turns out the basement was insulated with paper! Including comic books!" Logan cried. "We looked them up, and one had Batman on the cover for the third time."

"Third time ever!" Noah jumped in. "It's worth"—Logan joined him in saying it—"eighteen thousand dollars."

"What kind of condition is it in, though?" Belle asked.

"Not that bad," Noah answered. "It was between some sections of newspaper. But eighteen thousand is the minimum it's worth. Eighteen thousand."

Logan took up the story. "Mr. Gangne said it's ours because when he hired us, he said we could keep whatever he hadn't stowed in labeled boxes, but our parents are making us split it with him. That's six thousand each. Minimum! We have to get it appraised. And we haven't checked all the other walls yet."

"You've got to put this in *Around Town*," Honey told Violet.

"Cover story," Violet agreed. "And second page is what I know will be a rave review for *What the Fox Knows*, starring Nick Ferrone."

"Does Violet write the reviews herself?" Nick asked in Annie's ear.

"No. But no one would dare write a bad one. And who would want to, with you as leading man?" He grinned down at her, and she felt her stomach flip. All he had to do to set off that spark was look at her.

Nick clapped his hands. "All right. Everybody's here. Let's head out."

"But Nogan wasn't here when I explained about what to do if you fall down," Annie protested. "Chloe either."

"We've been snowshoeing before, Annie," Logan said.

"We've even been snowshoeing with you," Noah added.

"And my whole family went snowshoeing last time we spent Christmas here," Chloe reassured Annie. "And anyway, you'll be right there if I do fall, and you'll rescue me."

Nick nodded. "Annie to the rescue. That's what we're going to call her extraction service when we launch in the summer: Annie to the Rescue."

Annie, Nick, her mom, and her grandparents had worked out a deal where certain services and all the supplies would be a joint Boots Camp/Hatherley's Outfitters enterprise. Belle and Annie were starting to interview managers for their place. It gave Annie a little twinge of regret and sadness to turn it over, even though not completely, to someone else, but she was still loving working at Boots and rarely had the urge to yell at anybody.

Once everybody had strapped on their snowshoes, Annie led the way into the woods, noticing Shoo Fly and Clarence joining Belle at the back of the group. Being in the barn with so many people probably still wouldn't feel comfortable for him, but snowshoeing with them must be okay, probably because her mom and his dog were in the mix.

Taking long, slow strides, Annie followed the route she'd checked out the day before. Her heart gave a little skip when she saw the WELCOME TO FOX CROSSING sign. No, not the sign. Who was sitting beneath the sign, tail wrapped around her feet. The Fox.

Nick came to a stop next to Annie. "You know what this means."

"It means we'll talk in the spring." She turned until she could look directly into those warm, chestnut-colored eyes of his. "Even though I love you right now." It was the first time she'd said the words, but they felt true, in a deep, rock-solid way.

"I love you, too."

Then Banana bumped into Nick, almost taking them both down. "Why'd you stop?" Banana complained.

"Over there." Nick nodded toward The Fox. She still sat beneath the sign, unbothered by the sights and sounds of so many people.

"It's The Fox," Jordan breathed, coming up alongside Annie.

It seemed as if The Fox waited for all of them to get a glimpse, then she turned and tiptoe-trotted into the woods.

* * *

As The Fox moved deeper into the woods, her feet protected from the cold by their furry paws, she could feel cords of connection stretching between her and each of the humans gathered nearby. The cords were strongest between her and the two women who were blood of The Woman, but The Fox had connections, some glowing softly, some shining brightly, with all of them. And each tree. And each creature, whether predator or prey. Even the earth itself twined gentle cords around her ankles, twined then released, twined and released as she trotted. Even the stars and the moon weren't so far away that their cords couldn't reach her. Although she was alone, she was connected to everything in her world.

Keep reading for a special excerpt. . . .

Animal lovers, watch out.
This cat will steal your heart.

TALK TO THE PAW
MELINDA METZ

*Inspired by the true story of a Portland, Oregon, cat
who stole from his neighbors—and stole America's heart . . .*

SHE'S PUTTING HER LOVE LIFE ON PAWS

Jamie Snyder is thirty-four and single but *not* ready to mingle. After suffering through The Year of the Non-Committal Man, The Year of the Self-Absorbed Man, and The Year of the Forgot-to-Mention-I'm-Married Man, Jamie's ready to celebrate The Year of Me—and MacGyver, of course. MacGyver is an adorable tabby with a not-so-adorable habit of sneaking out at night and stealing things from the neighbors. That's right, MacGyver is a cat burglar. He's still the only male Jamie trusts—and the only companion she needs. . . .

BUT HER CAT HAS OTHER IDEAS

MacGyver knows his human is lonely. He can smell it. It's the same smell he's noticed on their neighbor David, a handsome young baker who's tired of his friends trying to fix him up. But now MacGyver's on the case. First, he steals something from David and stashes it at Jamie's. Then, he steals something from Jamie and leaves it with David. Before long, the two are swapping stolen goods, trading dating horror stories, and trying not to fall in love. But they're not fooling MacGyver. When humans generate this much heat, *the cat is out of the bag. . . .*

Look for TALK TO THE PAW, *on sale now.*

CHAPTER 1

MacGyver opened his eyes. He lay snuggled with his belly against Jamie's soft, warm hair, his favorite sleeping spot. He purred with contentment. His person's scent, one of the few familiar ones in this new place, comforted him.

Except . . . there was still that tang. It wasn't the smell of illness, but something about it reminded him of that scent. Mac suspected he knew the cause. He hated to think it, but humans were more like dogs than cats, at least in some ways. They needed others of their kind close around them, a pack.

Mac was more than fine being the only cat in his home, surrounded by his food, his water, his litter box, his toys, and his person. Jamie wasn't like that. Mac thought she should just go out and find a human for herself. There were humans everywhere to pick from. But sometimes Jamie missed the obvious. Like she just didn't understand that her tongue was made for washing. There was no need for her to endure submerging her body in water.

His purring faded. Now that he'd noticed the tang, it was bothering him more and more. He stood, abandoning his comfortable spot. It was time for action! He rubbed Jamie's head a few times with his own, so that anyone who smelled her would know she was his, then he jumped to the floor and padded through the living room and out to the screened front porch. Earlier he'd noticed there was a small rip at the bottom of the screen.

He stared out into the darkness. In this new place there had to be someone who could belong to Jamie the way Jamie belonged to him. But she wasn't going to find that person on her own.

Not a problem. MacGyver was on the case.

Mac squeezed through the rip in the screen and paused. It was his first time out in the outside world, at least without a car window or the mesh of his carrier between it and him. There would be dangers out here, but that didn't worry him. He knew he could handle himself in any situation that came up.

Ears forward, tail high, he slipped into the night, taking in the mix of scents—spicy tomato sauce, chocolate frosting, tuna steak, and dozens of other food smells; the waxy odor of the purple flowers that grew up the side of his house; a whiff of something sweet and rancid from the garbage cans along the curb; an intriguing hint of mice droppings; and the overwhelming aroma of dog piss. Mac gave a hiss of disgust. Obviously, there was a dog in the complex who peed on *everything*. The bonehead clearly thought that meant he owned the place. Wrong.

MacGyver trotted over to the tree the dog had doused most recently. He gave it a good clawing, and when he was done his scent was much stronger than the mutt's. Satisfied, he took in another breath, this time opening his mouth and flicking his tongue. It let him almost taste the air.

Jamie wasn't the only human in the area who was emitting that tang of loneliness. Going with his instincts, Mac decided to follow the strongest strain. He stopped a couple times to claw over the disgusting smell of dog, but quickly reached the source of the scent he was tracking, a little house with a rounded roof.

Other than the lonely smell, he liked a lot of the other scents around the house—bacon, butter, a little sweat, freshly mown grass, and nothing sharp, like the stuff Jamie liked to spray in the kitchen, interfering with his complete enjoyment of his food. Now, how to get Jamie to realize that there was a good choice for a packmate here? Mac thought for a moment, then he decided he should bring something from the house to his person. Her nose wasn't nearly as sensitive as his, but he was sure once she had something right in front of her and got a blast of the mix of scents, she'd know what to do.

There wasn't a screened-in porch, like the one at his new house, but he wasn't worried. Mac's upper lip curled back as he continued his surveillance. The bonehead dog had been around, that was for sure. He managed to ignore the reek by reminding himself he was on a mission. His eyes scanned back and forth, searching, searching. Then he saw it, a small circular window standing partway open on the second floor.

Getting up there—no problem. The big tree growing beside the house seemed designed as his personal staircase. He quickly scrambled up, gave the window a head butt to open it wider, then jumped inside. He landed on top of the perfect thing to bring back to Jamie. It was saturated with attractive odors, plus the scent of loneliness that would make Jamie realize the smell came from a person who needed a packmate as much as she did.

Mac snatched the wad of cloth up in his mouth, enjoying the tastes that went with the smells. Filled with triumph, he jumped back to the windowsill, then into the night, his prize flapping behind him.

A high, demanding meow woke Jamie the next morning. "I'm coming, Mac," she mumbled. She climbed out of bed, only about a quarter awake, took two steps, and smacked into the closet door. Well, that got her to at least the halfway-conscious mark.

Okay. Got it. She was in her new place, and in her new place the closet was on the other side of the bed than it had been in her old apartment.

Meooooowwrr.

"I. Am. Coming," Jamie told her cat as she walked the short distance to the kitchen. Mac gave another of his *I-Want-Food* yowls. It was like he had studied her to decide which of the sounds in his repertoire made her eardrums throb the most and now he used them to request meals.

"I keep telling you, if you learned to work the coffeemaker, it would make both our mornings more pleasant," she reminded him. She didn't bother attempting to make her coffee before serving His Majesty. MacGyver had her too well trained for that.

But even jonesing for caffeine, she couldn't help smiling as Mac began weaving around her ankles the moment she took a can of cat food out of the cupboard. She thought her kitty was brilliant, but there were some things he just didn't get. Like that she'd be able to get the food into his bowl a lot faster if he didn't try to tie her feet together with his body.

"Here you go." She managed to get the food into Mac's bowl without dumping any of it on his head. She watched while he took a few sniffs, then a bite, then another bite. It seemed like Alli-Cat was still on his approved foods list. She couldn't believe she was feeding her cat alligator. But the vet had said wild food was good for him, and he liked it—for now. She amused herself by imagining Mac, all eight and a quarter pounds of him, bagging breakfast by twining himself around a gator's big ankles until it went down.

Jamie took a step toward the coffeemaker, one of the few essentials she'd unpacked last night, then sank down in one of the kitchen chairs, suddenly overwhelmed. She'd just trashed her whole life. Quit her job and moved about as far away as she could while still staying in the United States. She wrapped her arms around her knees. What had she been thinking? She was thirty-four. When you were thirty-four, you were supposed to be settling down, not attempting a complete reboot. Her friends had. They were all married now, all as in *all*, and more than half of them had kids—and not just babies. One of Samantha's was an actual teenager.

"Don't do this. Do not do this. This is not how you start." But how *was* she supposed to start? She thought for a moment. First, she had to stand up. She shoved herself to her feet. Now what?

The answer hit her almost immediately. She was going out! And that meant she needed to get dressed. She hurried to the living room and unzipped her biggest suitcase before she could change her mind. She pulled on her favorite jeans and the upcycled top she'd found on Etsy. She'd only worn it once, even though she loved it. It just didn't seem to fit with Avella, PA. It *was* a little crazy, most of it coral with black roses, but with long pieces of colorful fabric in a mishmash of patterns around the hem and green leaves appliqued here and there.

The top was perfect for LA, or at least she thought so. And who cared if it wasn't? Jamie had declared that 2018 would be "The Year of Me." She'd declared it silently, but she'd declared it. She'd gone through The Year of the Self-Absorbed Man, The Year of the Forgot-to-Mention-I-Was-Married Man, The Year of the Cling-Wrap Man, The Year of the Non-Committal Man. And, the worst year of all, The Year of the Sick Mother.

The Year of Me wouldn't involve men of any kind. It would involve wearing clothes she thought were gorgeous, even if no one else did. It would involve following her dream, as soon as she figured out what her dream was. She knew for sure it wasn't teaching high school history.

The Year of Me would involve living in a place where she didn't know anyone and where every place she went was a fresh start. The Year of Me would change her life! She shook her head. Give herself one more second and she'd be bursting into song like Maria leaving the convent in *The Sound of Music*. She grabbed her purse and started for the door, then stopped. Probably she should brush her hair. And her teeth.

That done, she headed out. Her gaze snagged on something crumpled on top of the doormat. She picked it up. It was a plain white terry-cloth hand towel. She was sure it hadn't been there yesterday, and it wasn't hers. She didn't go for plain white anything.

She started to open the screen door so she could toss the hand towel on the porch. She'd only opened it about three inches when suddenly Mac was there—darn those silent little cat feet—and then out.

Jamie bolted out the door after him. Mac had never been outside. Her brain jangled with a dozen horrible things that could happen to him. "MacGyver!" she yelled. He kept going—big surprise. She tried again, knowing it wouldn't work. "MacGyver!"

"The voice of authority," someone said, with a snort. She turned and saw Al Defrancisco weeding the little flower patch that ran beside his porch steps. She'd met him and his wife, Marie, when she'd arrived yesterday. They lived in one of the twenty-three bungalows—bungalows, how glamorous Old Hollywood was that?—making up Storybook Court. It was named for the 1920s storybook-style architecture of the little houses. That architecture, which gave the complex its historical-standing status, was the only reason Storybook Court hadn't been torn down and replaced with a high-rise. She'd so lucked out that one of the adorable houses had become vacant on the very afternoon when Jamie had started searching for a place.

"He comes when he's called . . . sometimes. When I have a can of food in my hand. Or when I'm eating a tuna sandwich," Jamie told Al. At least Mac hadn't gone too far, not yet anyway. Her tan-and-brown tabby was using one of the palm trees near the courtyard fountain as a scratching post.

There were palm trees by her house! How cool was that? This couldn't be her life. But it was. Thanks to the inheritance her mother had left her, she could spend a year here. She didn't even have to get a job. Not for this once-in-a-lifetime year. She had no intention of being a slacker, though. She knew, for sure, she didn't want to teach. But she was going to find out what she did want to do—and then do it!

"Al, I told you to wear a hat." Marie came out of the house next door and threw a straw fedora down to her husband. She was small and frail, both she and Al probably in their eighties, but her voice was strong and commanding.

Al put on the hat. "The voice of authority," he muttered, jerking his chin in Marie's direction.

"Where are you off to?" Marie asked Jamie.

"Once I corral my cat, just out for coffee. I saw that Coffee Bean & Tea Leaf a few blocks away when I was driving in," she answered.

Marie gave a huff of disapproval that seemed to be directed at Jamie and went back inside. Jamie was used to everyone knowing her business in Avella. The town didn't have even a thousand residents. She'd been sure LA would be different, but it was seeming like she was mistaken.

Jamie glanced over at Mac, trying to act like she wasn't checking on him. Knowing her cat, the best way to get him to come home was to act like she didn't care whether he did or not. He was sunning himself beside the palm. "I can't leave him out here. He's an indoor cat. He has zero car sense," she told Al, then added, "He likes it in the courtyard. Maybe I should get him a leash and walk him around."

Al only grunted in response. Jamie debated going inside for a can of food. But Mac had just eaten. She didn't think it would work. Maybe the feathered cat toy . . . Before she could decide, Marie came back out. "Coffee," she said to Jamie, holding a cup over the porch rail. "Twenty-seven cents a cup. It's probably ten times that at your Bean."

"Thanks. That's so sweet of you," Jamie answered. She took a sip. It was perfect.

"Take this over to Helen." Marie handed a second cup to Al. He walked over to the bungalow on the other side of his and Marie's.

"Helen. Coffee," he hollered, not bothering to climb the two steps to the porch.

A few moments later, a woman, maybe ten years younger than Al and Marie, came outside. Helen took the coffee, drank some, then glared over at Marie. "You forgot sugar. Again."

"You don't need sugar," Marie shot back. "You're getting fat." Helen continued glaring. "Nessie still has a lovely figure. You could—"

"I told you not to talk to me about—" Helen stopped. "I'm putting in sugar," she declared, then noticed Jamie. "You! You're Jamie Snyder. I wanted to see you. I have a godson just about your age. You're not exactly his type. He usually goes for exotic, not blond girl-next-door types. But he's a teacher, too. I'm going to give him your number."

Blond girl-next-door type? Was she the blond girl-next-door type? She wasn't exotic. She knew that. But blond girl-next-door type sounded extremely wholesome and extremely boring. Okay, she was wholesome, but not extremely. And she—

"Number?" Helen prompted.

"No. I mean, thanks, but I'm not interested in meeting him. In meeting any guys," Jamie protested, the words coming out too fast and too loudly to be polite. "I mean, I just got here. I want to get settled in." She took another glance at Mac. Still sunning himself. "How'd you know I am—used to be—a teacher?" she asked. She was almost positive she hadn't mentioned it to Al and Marie yesterday, and she hadn't talked to anyone else in the complex yet.

"If it was on the credit check or rental agreement, these two know it," Al said as he returned to his weeding. Jamie was sure it was illegal for a landlord to share that info, but she decided not to make an issue of it.

"Her godson's not right for you anyway," Marie said. "He won't even change a lightbulb for her when she needs it. I have to send little Al, our son, over. He comes every Sunday for dinner." She pointed one bony finger at Helen. "Besides, your godson is too young."

"Only five years younger than she is," Helen retorted.

"My great-nephew is three years older. The man should be older. They mature later." Marie returned her attention to Jamie. "He might be good for you."

Jamie began backing away slowly. As if sensing her discomfort, MacGyver trotted over and gave his *Pick-Me-Up* meow, which was softer and much more pleasant than the *I-Want-Food* one. Gratefully, Jamie scooped him into her arms. She traced the M on his forehead with one finger. The brown marking was one of the reasons she'd named him MacGyver.

"Your godson is allergic to cats, isn't he?" Marie called to Helen, her voice infused with triumph.

"I'm going to get sugar," Helen muttered and retreated inside.

"Just leave the cup on the porch when you're finished," Marie told Jamie and went inside herself.

"I really don't want to be set up with anyone," Jamie said to Al, since neither of the women had paid any attention to her.

Al gave another of his grunts. "You think that matters?"

It definitely mattered to Jamie. She was not letting The Year of Me start with awkward meetings with great-nephews or godsons or any other men.

"You told her about Clarissa, didn't you?" Adam demanded as soon as David sat back down at the table.

David didn't answer, just took a swallow of the sour IPA Brian, owner of the Blue Palm, had recommended. David was usually a Corona guy, but you didn't order Corona at the Blue Palm.

"You don't have to answer," Adam continued. "I know you did. I could see it. I could see the exact second it happened. You walked over to the bar, got a spot next to her and her friend, made some humorous and probably self-deprecating comment. She smiled. It looked good. The friend left for the bathroom, probably to give you two some privacy. She put her hand on your arm. *She put her hand on your arm.* And I'm thinking, this was so much easier than he expected it to be. Then the arm touch turned into an arm pat. A *sympathetic* arm pat. And I knew, I *knew*, you'd brought up the dead wife."

David felt his shoulders stiffen, but he forced himself to smile and lift his glass to his friend. "You nailed it."

"Sorry. I shouldn't have said it like that." Adam popped a pretzel ball into his mouth. "But you can't bring up Clarissa in the first five minutes you meet someone," he said while he chewed. "Not if you want something to happen."

"I don't even know if I want anything to happen. I told you that." His voice had come out with more of an edge than he'd intended, but he'd told Adam—repeatedly—that he wasn't sure he really wanted to "get back out there." Even though it had been three years.

"Well, I'm your friend. I've known you since before you had pubes, so at least five years. And I say that even if you're not sure you want anything to happen, you really do want it to happen."

Adam tried to take another pretzel ball, and David knocked his hand away. "Mine," David said.

His friend went in from another angle, grabbed the pretzel ball, and kept on talking. "Because if you don't do it now, it's just going to get weirder and harder, and then you're not going to be able to make it happen even if you're a hundred percent positive you want it to, and you'll end up a sad, lonely old man."

"I'll end up a sad, lonely old man? You sound like you're writing dialogue for your next episode," David told him.

"I'm serious," Adam said. "It's been long enough. Lucy thinks you should go on counterpart.com."

"This is what you and Lucy talk about when the kids are finally asleep? No wonder you never get sex," David answered.

"Online dating makes sense. You can take it slow. Get to know each other before you meet. And you can think about what kind of impression you want to make. I'm not telling you you can never mention Clarissa. Just not in the first five. You want more of these?" Adam pointed to the empty appetizer plate.

"More?" David protested. "Don't you mean *any*?

"We'll get more." Adam signaled to their waitress, pointed to the plate, and gave her a pleading look, complete with hands clasped to his chest. She laughed and nodded. "We'll also get more drinks. And before we leave here, we're getting you up on Counterpart. I'm a writer. I'm sure I can find a way to make even you sound appealing." He studied David. "People are always saying you look like Ben Affleck, but that's not the vibe we want, what with the cheating and the gambling. And, actually, since you're supposedly writing this, it would probably sound egotistical to describe yourself like a celebrity anyway. So, we'll just go with the basics: thirty-three, brown hair, hazel eyes, six-foot-one, what, about one-eighty?"

David nodded. His friend was on a roll. There was no stopping him now.

"We have to put in that you're a baker. Women will love that. They get you and your hot fudge sundae cupcakes. Maybe your profile pic should have you kneading dough or something. It would be like that scene in *Ghost*, but dough instead of clay," Adam went on.

"I'm not asking why you've seen *Ghost*." Actually, David had seen it himself. Clarissa had watched it for the first time when she was about twelve and it had made an indelible impression. Whenever it came on TV, it was like she'd become hypnotized and had to watch to the end.

The waitress appeared with another plate of appetizers and took their new beer order. "Okay, what else? What else?" Adam muttered. "Get out your cell and set up the account while I think."

David got out his phone, because Adam was Adam and he was relentless. But he just looked at the site without signing up.

"We'll put in that you have a dog. Shows you can at least keep a living thing alive." Adam was scribbling on a napkin now.

"How desperate are we thinking these women are?" David asked.

Adam ignored him. "We'll leave out your silent-movie obsession for now, because that will limit your dating pool. You like long walks on the beach, right?" Adam asked.

David tried to remember the last time he'd gone to the beach. Not since Clarissa. Less than an hour away, a lot less if the traffic was good, and he'd been acting like he lived halfway across the state. "You can't say I like long walks on the beach. That's the biggest cliché ever. I wouldn't want a woman who would want a man who said he liked long walks on the beach."

Adam grinned. "Just wanted to make sure you were paying attention. You're getting into this. Admit it."

Was he? Maybe he was. A little. Maybe Adam was right. Maybe even if he didn't feel like meeting anyone, he needed to try. Try more than that lame attempt he'd made with the woman at the bar, which had been all Adam's idea. "Maybe say I volunteer with Habitat for Humanity," he suggested.

"I like. Makes you seem like a guy with a heart, and also like a guy who might be able to fix things around the house." Adam scribbled away. "We should also say something about what kind of woman you want, what you're looking for."

What he was looking for. Someone who was always up for trying something new. Someone who believed there was always something great out there to discover. Someone who—

He realized what he was looking for was Clarissa.

It felt like one of the salty pretzel balls had formed in David's throat. He couldn't believe this was happening. He struggled to fight down the grief that had had shocked him with its strength. Suddenly it felt like Clarissa's death had taken place yesterday.

"Look, I know you're right. It makes sense for me to try to meet someone new. But I'm not ready," he told Adam. David thought he'd managed to keep his tone casual, but Adam must have seen something of what David was feeling on his face. His friend crumpled up the napkin and jammed it in his pocket.

"I'm not saying forever." David shoved his hands through his hair. "Just not now. I don't know, maybe next year."

CHAPTER 2

Okay, Day Two of the Year of Me, Jamie thought. She wasn't counting the day she moved in. That wasn't a whole day, so how could it count? Besides if she counted it and this was Day Three, then she should have already come up with some kind of plan. But if it was Day Two, it was okay to still be working on one.

She grabbed her bag. It looked like something an old-timey grandma would carry, but in a good way, with flowers embroidered all over it and a wicker handle. It was nice and roomy, too, big enough for the notebook, where Jamie was writing—planning to write—her plan. She had nothing against her laptop, but for lists and plans, she was a pen-and-paper gal.

"I'm heading out, Mac. Don't tell Marie, but I'm going to Coffee Bean." She ticked the tabby under his chin. "I left you surprises." Jamie usually hid a couple treats for Mac when she went out so he'd have something to hunt.

She managed to slither out the door without Mac making a break for it. Then she managed to make it around the corner and out of sight without Marie appearing and asking where she was going. *Good start,* she thought. She decided to walk through the complex and out the other side. She was eager to get a look at the other houses.

The first one along the walkway looked like the house of a Disney witch, with a high-peaked roof that made the cottage look like it was wearing a witch's hat itself. The windows echoed the shape, and the doorknocker was a black iron spider with large eyes of faceted red glass. As Jamie studied the place, a woman came out and hooked a large candy cane over one of the legs of the spider doorknocker. She wore a short green dress that could almost have passed as an elf costume. Her black hair looked elfish, too. It was cut short, with bangs that almost touched her eyebrows. When she spotted Jamie, she waved and called, "I love Christmas, don't you?"

"Um, yes, I do," Jamie answered, though it was kind of a random question for September.

"I'm just getting out my decorations." The woman hooked another large candy cane on the small potted lemon tree on the porch. Jamie tried to guess her age. It was hard to tell. "I've also started baking," the woman added. "Want to come in and have a gingerbread man?"

Jamie tried to remember if she'd fallen into a rabbit hole or been taken up by a tornado recently. She felt like she'd entered another world. "Don't be scared," the woman said, with a smile, clearly sensing Jamie's hesitation. "I know it's September. I just think Christmas is too wonderful to be contained to a month or two. Oh, and I'm Ruby Shaffer. I forgot to say that. Gingerbread? It's good."

"Sure," Jamie joined Ruby on the porch and introduced herself. "I just moved in. My place is right around the corner."

"The one next to Al and Marie," Ruby said, and Jamie nodded. Now that Jamie was closer, she could see threads of gray in Ruby's black hair and decided she was probably fifty-something. "Aren't they a hoot? I love them," Ruby continued. "Marie tries to pretend she's a tough old bird, but she takes care of everyone in her orbit." She opened the door and ushered Jamie inside. She was greeted by an explosion of red and green, silver and gold.

"Like I said, I've started getting out the Christmas decorations," Ruby said as she led the way down a narrow path between piles of lights, ornaments, wreaths, and few dozen stuffed animals in holiday attire.

"Started?" Jamie murmured.

"I'm not a hoarder or anything like that. I keep them in a storage unit from January fifteenth through September fifteenth," Ruby told her. "Have a seat." She gestured to one of the chairs at the kitchen table. The only sign of Christmas in the room was the plate of gingerbread men clad in red and green icing. Ruby took the platter off the counter and set it down in front of Jamie.

"I always kind of hate to eat gingerbread men," Jamie admitted. "It makes me feel like a cannibal."

"Eat the head first, then it won't be staring at you," Ruby advised, then picked up a cookie and decapitated it with one bite. Jamie laughed and bit off the head of her own cookie. She was starting to like this strange woman. It wasn't as if Jamie didn't have a streak of strange herself, she just kept it slightly better hidden, especially when she'd been at the front of a classroom.

"Are you ready for the question?" Ruby asked. "I have this question I ask all new people I meet. It's a shortcut for getting to know them."

"O-kay," Jamie said. Because, really, what else *could* she say?

"What would be the name of the movie of your life?"

"It's hard to say, since I don't know the ending yet," Jamie answered. "I don't know if my movie is inspirational or terrifying or funny."

"Good point," Ruby said. "I've actually never gotten that answer before."

"My right-now movie title would be *The Year of Me*," Jamie blurted out. There was something about Ruby. She made Jamie feel like she could say pretty much anything with no judgments.

"How come?" Ruby bit one of the feet off her gingerbread men.

"I've just had this stretch of time, a long stretch, when my decisions were made based on who I was with. Guys, mostly. Then my mom was sick, and I wanted to make decisions based on her, but now . . ." Jamie pulled in a shaky breath.

"Now *The Year of Me*," Ruby filled in for her. "Nice. My movie would be called *My Amazing Untrue Adventures*. Because I work as a set dresser creating fake worlds. And my imagination is my best friend. I can always find a way to amuse myself. I have lots of mental adventures, some real ones, too."

"So, would you say your job is your passion?" Jamie asked.

"One of them, absolutely," Ruby said without hesitation. "I love the challenge of, say, deciding what a certain character would have in the top drawer of their nightstand. And I love being part of a team, well, mostly. When we're all working together, the director, actors, costumer, everybody, to create something, it's amazing."

That's what I want, Jamie thought. *I want to talk about my job like that.*

"What about you? How do you make your shekels?" Ruby ate the other foot of her gingerbread man. "Is there a word for taking off a foot? Dedepitation?" She shook her head. "Never mind. I want to hear about you."

"I was a history teacher. High school. Loved the history. Loved some of the kids. Hated the discipline and having to teach pretty much only what the kids needed to pass a standardized test. Also, the parents? Most of them were impossible to deal with. Give a kid an A and a parent will be in your office demanding to know why it wasn't an A-plus. And give a kid a C? Forget about it. Parents have gone insane," Jamie answered. "Uh, do you have kids?" she belatedly added.

"Nope. Forgot to ask my now-ex-husband if he wanted them before we got married. I just assumed he did. Stupid. By the time I found out he didn't and we untangled ourselves, it was too late for me. Not him. He now has a toddler and a six-year-old. Men have enough advantages. Do they have to have an unlimited supply of fresh sperm, too?" Ruby had managed to say all that in one breath, and now she sucked in a big one.

She plays fair, Jamie thought. *She doesn't just ask, she tells, too.*

"So, if you're not a history teacher, what are you doing?" Ruby asked.

"My Year of Me is financed by an inheritance," Jamie said. "I'm using it to figure out what I should be doing." She pulled the notebook out of her bag. "I was on my way out to have a brainstorming session."

Ruby stood up. "Then, go! I don't want to get in the way of you and inspiration. We'll talk more, unless you've decided I'm the Storybook Court crazy lady."

"I don't. I'd like that," Jamie answered, shoving the notebook back inside her bag.

"Fabulous purse," Ruby commented.

Yeah, Jamie was definitely liking her strange new neighbor. She promised herself she'd explore her new little neighborhood more thoroughly later, but now she wanted to get to work. She briskly walked through the complex, then made her way to Sunset. She paused to take a picture of the Gower Gulch strip mall.

It wasn't much to look at. Other than an old-style medicine wagon at one end of the parking lot, it could be a strip mall pretty much anywhere, on the shabby side with a Denny's and a Rite-Aid as the highlights. But she'd been reading up on the local history, and she'd found out that back in the day, cowboys looking for work in the motion pictures would gather over there. Just because she didn't want to teach history, didn't mean she didn't still love history, and her new city had some great stories. She'd actually taken a real tour yesterday. She'd decided she needed one day of R&R before she settled down to figuring out the rest of her life.

She walked a few more blocks, then stopped in front of a palm tree with purple morning glories twining around the trunk. She had to get a pic. She hardly ever did this. Some of her friends took pictures of every piece of food they ate, and of course, a bazillion baby pictures, but Jamie usually didn't bother. Maybe it was because back home she saw the same things every day. Here, everything was new.

Just as she photographed the palm, she noticed something moving up there where the fronds were *clack-clacking* together. A rat. Ick.

But not a bad picture. Beautiful flowers, glam palm, gleaming-eyed rat. Nice contrast. She took a couple, checked to make sure she had a keeper, then headed into the Coffee Bean. She ordered herself a large blended Black Forest, because figuring out the rest of her life required sugar—more than just a gingerbread man's worth—and lots of caffeine. She grabbed a table, took out her notebook and opened it to a fresh page, took out two purple Varsity fountain pens, her faves, then . . . sat there.

Sugar and caffeine, she reminded herself. She took a couple big swallows from her Black Forest. Too big and too fast. She now had—*ow, ow, ow, ow*—brain freeze. She rubbed her temples, waiting for it to pass. When it did, she returned her attention to her notebook, to that blank page in her notebook.

She wrote the words "Year of Me" at the top of the page, then scribbled over them. They sounded good in her head, and even as a move title, but they looked silly written down. She thought for a second, then wrote "Things I Like." That's how you were supposed to figure out your passion. Passion equaled what you liked, hopefully something you could make money at.

She underlined the words. Then she sat some more. Stared some more. Then she started writing things down as fast as she could:

Playing with Mac with the laser.
Watching old movies.
Things made out of other things.
Sugar and caffeine.
Smell of rain on hot pavement.
The way sheets feel against my legs right after I've shaved them.
Garage sales.
Old postcards with messages on them.
Old dolls—of varieties both creepy and not creepy.
History—but not teaching it.
Biographies.
Wonder Woman.

Wonder Woman? Where did that come from? Jamie guessed she liked Wonder Woman. She certainly had nothing against Wonder Woman. But she didn't expect Wonder Woman to show up that high on her List of Likes.

Maybe because on her tour yesterday she'd seen someone dressed up as Wonder Woman in front of Grauman's Chinese Theater? She knew it wasn't called Grauman's anymore, but she couldn't help thinking of it as Grauman's. Footprints of celebs equaled Grauman's.

Did that Wonder Woman impersonator make a living at it? Was it her passion? Maybe. If you truly loved and respected Wonder Woman, it could be your passion to be her all day. It made people happy. Everyone taking pictures with her had been smiling. Jamie hadn't taken a picture with her, but she'd taken pictures of people taking pictures with Wonder Woman. Wonder Woman had looked like she was enjoying every second of every encounter.

She'd taken more pictures in the last two days than she had in the last two years. She'd sort of fallen out of the habit, even though back in high school she'd actually taken pictures for the school paper, and she'd taken a couple photography classes in college, just for fun. Maybe she was getting back into it because there were so many new things catching her interest.

She added a few items to her list:

Taking pictures.
Seeing happy people.
Making people happy.

And . . . and nothing else was coming to her. She had to like more than—she did a quick count—fifteen things. But fifteen was a start. She read her list slowly, looking for similarities, connections, inspiration.

Apparently, she liked old stuff. Old movies. Old dolls. Old postcards. History. Garage sales. Even things made of other things, because lots of time the other things were old things. She'd known she absolutely had to live in Storybook Court the second she saw it, because it was straight out of another time. Even when the houses were first built, they wouldn't have looked modern. They looked like they'd been created in a fairy tale and then transported, like Ruby's little witch's house. Al and Marie's was like a miniature castle, complete with towers and turrets, and Helen's place felt like part cozy animal den and part human house.

So her passion had led her to her new home, even though she hadn't thought of it that way. Could it lead her to a new career?

Some people made good money selling old stuff on eBay, but that didn't really appeal to her. She didn't want to look at fabulous old finds and have to calculate how much they were worth.

She wished she could upcycle clothes and make something like her favorite shirt, but she wasn't crafty. When she tried, the results were . . . not good. She'd actually superglued two of her fingers to her hair once. And not when she was in her single digits.

Jamie returned to sitting-and-staring mode. She was starting to feel like she had brain freeze again, even though she hadn't taken another swallow of her drink. "Thinking hard," she muttered, in her Frankenstein voice. Could you make a living in Hollywood with a somewhat-passable Frankenstein impression? Doubtful. She slapped her notebook closed and shoved it in her bag—another old thing she liked. She'd do more brainstorming when the inside of her head had thawed.

As she stepped back outside into the gorgeous day, she decided she really needed to get Mac a leash. He deserved to explore his new neighborhood, too, and not be stuck inside all the time, poor kitty.

Diogee greeted David at the door, leash in mouth, tail—make that his whole rear end—wagging. "Okay, Big D, okay." He took the slobbered-on leash out of his dog's mouth, and clipped it to his collar. As soon as he did, Diogee shoved his way past David and yanked him down the porch stairs.

David knew that he was supposed to be the alpha dog, not Diogee. And as the alpha dog, he was always supposed to go through the door first. But he'd decided that doing battle with a super-size dog multiple times a day went in the category of "life's too short."

First stop, the cedar tree that grew next to the house. Diogee gave it a good dousing of piss, but that didn't mean he was done. D regarded his urine as a precious commodity, and he'd spend the rest of the walk squirting here, squirting there, announcing "this is mine," "this is mine," "and that over there, also mine."

"Not on the fence," David warned him as he opened the gate. He'd built the fence himself when he'd gotten the dog, using twisty tree branches that he thought worked with what he always thought of as his Hobbit-hole house. "Not on the fence," he repeated. He pulled a piece of freeze-dried liver out of his pocket—yes, he bribed his dog routinely—and used it to get Diogee away from the fence before he could mark it.

Diogee galloped down to the wax leaf privet that grew at the side of his neighbor's bungalow and got down to business. He had a technique where he leaned away from whatever he was aiming at, which allowed him to lift his leg farther up and so launch the spray as high as possible. The mutt was almost the size of a pony, but he seemed to want to leave a mark that said a Clydesdale-size beast had been there.

"Excellent work," David told the dog as they continued down the cobblestone sidewalk.

"Diogee, hey!" Zachary Acosta called from across the street.

Diogee lurched toward the boy. David pulled back on the leash until he'd done a car check, then let the dog tow him over to Zachary. Diogee immediately put his paws on the kid's shoulders, and Zachary thumped the dog's sides, their version of a bro hug.

When Diogee finally dropped his paws back to the ground, David got a real look at Zachary's face. There was an angry red circle about the size of a quarter between his eyebrows.

David didn't ask, but he had to force his eyes away. It was so bright and so symmetrical. "What's the up?" he asked. That's the way the kid used to say it when he was little, and it had become part of the language of their friendship.

"School, whatever, nothing," Zach answered.

Sometimes David could hardly believe Zachary was fourteen. How could it have been almost ten years since they started making their trips around the neighborhood? David and Clarissa had only moved in about a week before, and David had made sure to go running at least every few days to work off all the samples he ate when he was developing new recipes. He'd just started down the street when the Acostas' front door had burst open and Zachary had come barreling out wearing an Oakland A's T-shirt, track pants, and tiny Puma sneakers. He'd looked like David's Mini-Me, right down to the color of the Pumas—red and white.

"Wait! Wait! I come!" he yelled.

His mom, Megan, caught up to Zachary before he reached the sidewalk and swooped him up. The boy immediately started trying to free himself. "Sorry, David. He saw you running the other day, and that's all he's been talking about. I thought the gear would be enough."

"Hey, I can use a running buddy," David told her.

"You sure?" Megan asked.

"Definitely. Let's hit it, Zachary." The kid insisted, then and now, on getting the full "Zachary" every time. No "Zach"s. Megan put him down and he hurtled toward David. From that day on, they'd been running together, or the last few years, walking Diogee, at least three or four times a week.

"School, stuff, whatever," David repeated. "Care to elaborate?" Zachary had just started his first year of high school. David was sure there was more to say.

"Squirrel at four o'clock," Zachary announced.

David wrapped the leash around his hand a couple times in preparation. A few seconds later, Diogee spotted the squirrel and gave what David thought of as the Shoulder Popper, a sudden jerk and yank. The squirrel scampered up the trellis of the closest cottage, and Diogee gave an explosion of barks, telling the squirrel exactly what he would have done if he'd been free.

When he finished, Zachary said, "I signed up for the track team. Cross-country. I wanted to do football, but my mom had a freak-out."

Mom might have been right, David thought. Over the summer, Zachary had shot up in height, but he was still all legs and arms and feet. David remembered that stage. He'd hardly been able to walk across a room without banging into something. Not the best time to be on a football field. Not that he'd say that to Zachary. "You've been running since you were five. You're a natural," he said instead, forbidding himself to take another look at that red circle between the kid's eyes. Had it really been a perfect circle? Could he have gotten whammed by a golf ball?

David was pretty sure Zachary's dad played golf, but it didn't seem likely he'd take Zachary along. Zachary and his father had an every-other-weekend thing, which ended up being one night every other weekend way too much of the time. From what Zachary said, they usually went to some trendy restaurant his dad's current girlfriend liked, where there wasn't usually anything Zachary wanted to eat. To be fair, Zachary didn't like a wide variety of food. He seemed to live off of peanut butter and Slim Jims and those red Swedish Fish candies.

They paused while Diogee stopped to sniff repeatedly at a ginkgo tree. "Checking his pee-mail," Zachary called it. After he did his lean and squirt, leaving a message back, they continued on. When they reached the corner—or the closest thing to a corner Storybook Court had, since nothing in the place had a solid right angle—Diogee took a left. The alpha dog always decided which way to go.

They'd only gone a few steps when they heard Addison Brewer yelling. Like Zachary, she hated nicknames. It was the full "Addison" or she'd pretend she didn't hear you. Her voice got louder as they walked. "You said you were going to come over. And you're not in the kitchen eating directly out of the fridge. And you haven't declared yourself King of the Remote. So you're not here. Oh, wait. You could be stinking up the bathroom. No, not there. So, you're not here when you said you'd be. Again. And you didn't look sick in gym. I could see you from Algebra. So, don't even try that."

"The girl is a shrew," Zachary muttered, twisting his head around so only the back of his head would be visible from Addison's house.

"Do you have any classes with her this year?" David asked.

"English." Zachary managed to pack the word with disgust.

"Impressive lungs. She didn't have to take one breath during all that," David said. Zachary didn't comment, just kept walking with his head turned toward the street.

There was a brief pause in the girl's rant. "How much traffic can there be? I'm home, and I take the bus. You said you only had to go home for one minute. Which means you should have been here twenty minutes ago. We're over. We're seriously over. Seriously. Do not ever come over here again. I don't care how close you are. Turn around."

One of the windows of what everyone called the Rose Bungalow—because of the yellow roses painted on the shutters—opened. A second later a purple cell phone with a rhinestone skull on the case came flying out.

Zachary glanced over, then turned his head away again. "Shrew."

"Remember when you gave her flowers for her birthday?" David asked. Zachary glowered at him. Sometimes David forgot how sensitive teenage boys could be. Sometimes he remembered, but he still couldn't resist teasing the kid.

"I was in kindergarten and my mom got to take home flowers from work, because they changed them every couple days."

"Oh, right," David said, deciding to give Zachary a break.

They passed the house with the drawbridge and moat filled with sparking aqua water. Sometimes David felt like he was living inside a miniature golf course. Clarissa's grandmother had given them her place as a wedding present. She'd decided to move to a luxury assisted-living place in Westwood. Storybook Court had felt too cutesy to David at first, but it wasn't like they could afford to turn down a free house when they were barely in their twenties. And it grew on him. Now it was so tied up with memories of Clarissa that he couldn't imagine living anyplace else.

Thinking of miniature golf made him think of that circle on Zachary's face, and this time David shot it a glance before he could stop himself.

Zachary caught him. "I kind of messed up my face."

"What? I didn't—" David stopped. There was no point in bullshitting the kid. "What the hell did you do?"

"You know those things you use to wash your face, with the spin-y brush on the end?"

David nodded.

"My mom has one. When I got home from school, I decided I was going to get rid of these zits. If you use it too long in one place—you get this." Zachary jabbed the bull's-eye between his eyebrows with one finger.

The was the last explanation David had expected to hear. Personal hygiene wasn't a big priority for the kid. Megan had asked David to tell him "real men wear deodorant" a couple years ago when Zachary started getting that ripe sock smell, and David would have thought that was about where his grooming stopped. *Gotta be a girl in the picture,* he thought, but he kept his mouth shut. He'd let Zachary bring that up if and when he wanted to.

"It just happened?" David asked.

"Couple of hours ago," Zachary answered. "I'm not showing up at school like this. The zits were bad enough." He poked the red circle again.

"First, keep your fingers off it," David told him, and Zachary jammed his hands in his pockets. "Maybe try some ice? That might help," he suggested as they continued walking, sometimes half-jogging, following Diogee.

"Did it. It's hopeless," Zachary answered, rubbing the circle.

"No!" David burst out.

"Sorry," Zachary said, jerking his hand away.

"Not you. Diogee. Diogee, no!" Diogee had started turning in those tight little circles that always preceded him taking a dump. And he was on the Defranciscos' lawn. "Marie will have my head. Make that my balls." He started trying to yank Diogee off the grass. Diogee dug in. He'd found the spot he wanted. He started to squat.

David leaned down, wrapped one arm around his dog's middle, and half-dragged him down to the next house. He didn't know who'd moved in there, but they'd have to be more tolerant of dog poop than Marie. It wasn't like he wasn't planning to clean up. Diogee let out a howl that probably reminded the whole neighborhood that he had a good amount of hound dog somewhere in the mix.

"Oh, come on," David said. "As if it matters that much which patch of grass you use." Diogee bayed again, and this time there was an answer, a high, long yowl from a large tan-and-brown-striped cat sitting in the house's screened-in porch. Its golden eyes were locked on Diogee, sending out lasers of hatred. Diogee snapped his jaws in response.

"That's enough, tough guy." David pulled out a liver treat. Diogee's attention immediately snapped over to him. He couldn't believe he'd forgotten to use one when Diogee had been about to bring down the wrath of Marie. He hurled the treat as far as he could, and Diogee ran for it, David and Zachary on his tail.

Diogee snarfed up the treat. He was an addict, and David was his supplier. That meant that, even though Diogee went out the door first, even though he chose which direction they walked, David would always be the alpha dog. Unless Diogee figured out how to obtain cash and get himself to Pet World.

"So, what do you think? Two days?" Zachary asked. He pointed to the red circle, but didn't touch it. "I don't want to miss too much practice. The track coach seemed pretty strict."

David could help with most of the problems that came up for a fourteen-year-old boy. He'd been one himself. But the skin-care malfunction was out of his league. "What I think is that we need an expert." He took out another liver treat. "Turn it around, Big D."

"Where are we going?" Zachary asked as they changed directions.

"Ruby's. She used to do makeup before she became a set dresser. She'll fix you up," David answered.

Zachary stopped dead. He looked as unwilling to move as Diogee had back on the Defranciscos' lawn. "I'm not wearing makeup to school. And anyway, I don't even really know her."

"Think of it as a special effect. And you know her well enough. Besides, I'm friends with her," David told him. Zachary didn't move. "Just let her try. If you don't like it, I'll teach you the best way to fake the flu. All you need is a can of extra-chunky soup."

Zachary didn't say yes, but he started walking toward Ruby's. "Chunky soup doesn't really look like puke."

"It sounds like it, though. You make sure your mom is close enough to the bathroom to hear, then start pouring it in the toilet," David explained.

Zachary snickered. "Sweet."

They followed the curve in the sidewalk, and Ruby's house came into sight. David felt like he'd been gut-punched. How'd he forgotten it was September fifteenth? It was one of Clarissa's favorite days, had been one of her favorite days. She'd never missed helping Ruby decorate the witch's cottage for Christmas.

Seeing something that made her so happy should have been a good thing. But it made him feel like a hole was opening right beneath his rib cage. For the second time in a week, he'd been surprised by how sharp his grief could still feel.

"You okay?" Zachary asked.

"Yeah," David told him. "Yeah," he said again, so he'd believe it himself.

He was okay. But he'd been right the other night with Adam. He wasn't ready to get something started with another woman. No matter what his friend thought, it was still too soon.

MacGyver left Jamie sleeping and made his way to the kitchen. He pawed open the cabinet under the sink and gave a short growl of annoyance. He reminded himself he had to be patient with his person. She was a human, and that meant that her nose was pretty much just a useless blob on her face. He hadn't been expecting this, though. She'd ignored his gift for almost two days. Then, finally, she'd picked up the hand towel. Yeah, she'd picked it up—then sprayed it with something that blocked out almost all the lonely smell he'd been trying to get her to notice, and rubbed it all over the table. He couldn't stop himself from letting out another little growl as he flicked the cabinet door shut.

Patience, he told himself again. He couldn't expect Jamie to understand with only one try. It had taken her a few times to find his favorite spot to be scratched. Right behind the whiskers. Pure bliss. It had also taken her a few times to realize she should never give his belly more than three rubs at a time. He'd had to give her a light bite to get that through her head. He hadn't liked to do it, but she'd had to be trained.

MacGyver just needed to put more effort into making his person see that what she needed to be happy was the right packmate. He was up for the challenge. Anything for Jamie. She was flawed, true, but she was his. He trotted to the porch and slipped through the hole in the screen. Before he could do anything else, he had to deal with the stench. He went straight to the palm closest to the fountain and gave it a good scratching, obliterating the odor of dog piss with his own musky smell. There. Now he could focus on his mission.

He tilted his head back and flicked air into his mouth with his tongue, smelling and tasting at the same time. The loneliness was strongest in the same place it had been two nights ago. He wondered if he could train Jamie to use her tongue to get information about her surroundings, including his gifts. Doubtful. If her sense of taste was working correctly, she'd never eat grapefruit. He could hardly stand to watch her jab her spoon into the disgusting thing.

It didn't matter. Mac's nose and tongue were good enough for both of them. He started toward the lonely smell. Unfortunately, the reek of dog pee got stronger and stronger the closer he got to his goal, so strong he almost wished he had a human nose. Almost. He could never actually make the sacrifice. He slowed his trot and dropped into a stalk as the house with The Smell came into sight.

That dog Mac had seen earlier stood in the yard, a grotesque mishmash mutt with long, floppy ears, a long, wide body, long legs, an oversized head, and a mouth that excelled at slobber production. Mac knew he wouldn't have a problem eluding the bonehead, but he knew the mutt could bark as well as he drooled, and Mac didn't need a commotion when he was in stealth mode.

He decided he'd come back a little later. For now, he'd do some exploring. He caught a whiff of a different strain of loneliness, and decided to track it. It led to a house with a window in front open so wide it was like an invitation. Mac accepted by leaping inside. He landed softly, quickly assessing the room.

Even if he'd landed with the bang of a firecracker, he probably wouldn't have woken up the person sleeping on the sofa. Her scent was potent, an odor Mac had learned to associate with a human female who wasn't a little girl or an adult. Their sweat was especially strong, although they almost always tried to disguise it. This one's true scent was masked by something that smelled sort of like apples and melons and flowers, but sweeter and sharper at the same time. Mac could still make out the odor of anger coming off her, anger mixed with a little loneliness.

She wasn't the one producing the scent he was tracking. He followed that scent out of the room and down the hall. The girl inside was young. A young one shouldn't have such a powerful lonely smell. She still needed a pack leader to survive, and it didn't smell like she had one, at least not one who was nearby. Mac decided to find her one. He was a cat with skills to spare. They shouldn't be wasted. He leapt up on the bed and brushed his cheek against the girl's, a silent promise that he'd be back.

But now it was time to return to his primary mission. On his way out of the house, Mac paused to take a few licks of the potato chips lying on the table near the older girl. He didn't especially like chips, but he loved the salt.

When Mac got back to the house with The Smell, the bonehead was still in the front yard, sniffing around under the tree that Mac needed to climb to get into the house. The dog dropped into a squat, and Mac took the opportunity to race toward the tree. He scrambled straight up the otherwise-occupied dog's back and shimmied through the window.

The dog started yammering, but Mac didn't care. The opportunity to use the bonehead as an on-ramp had been too perfect to pass by. And anyway, dogs were always barking about something. They didn't have the brain power to decide what was important and what wasn't. "Diogee, shut it!" he heard a man call from downstairs. His voice didn't have any anxiety or fear in it. Clearly, he didn't rely on the dog for warnings. A sensible human, then. Except that he'd chosen to live with a bonehead.

It didn't take Mac long to find the perfect thing, ripe and rich with scent. Jamie would have to understand his message this time!

Connect with U s

Visit us online at
KensingtonBooks.com
to read more from your favorite authors, see books
by series, view reading group guides, and more.

for sneak peeks, chances to win books and prize packs,
and to share your thoughts with other readers.

facebook.com/kensingtonpublishing
twitter.com/kensingtonbooks

Tell us what you think!

To share your thoughts, submit a review,
or sign up for our eNewsletters, please visit:
KensingtonBooks.com/TellUs.